Praise for *Big Sky Fallen*

"*Big Sky Fallen* could be a story written in the future as historians look back at where it all went wrong. Each character reminds me of someone I've met along the way, and the plot twists and action kept me turning the pages. I blew through this book because I kept picking it back up. If you want to experience what a survival group would likely face when the rule of law is up for grabs, read this book!"

—Charley Hogwood, author and survival consultant

"It's a fantastic read! It has an amazing, action-packed, well-thought-out plot, with believable, easy-to-love characters."

—Sandra Richardson, Jeanz BookReadNReview

BIG SKY FALLEN

THE UNRAVELING: BOOK ONE

Kevin Craver

ISBN e-Book: 979-8-9882166-2-9

ISBN Paperback: 979-8-9882166-0-5

Library of Congress Control Number: 2023907441

First Edition, 2024

Printed in the United States of America

Cover design by Christian Bentulan

Created with Atticus

For the record, this book was proudly written by a human being. No AI software was used at any time to develop, write, or edit this work. By buying this book, you support actual *homo sapiens* authors who do honest work. Buy human—don't give your money to douchebags who ask an AI to write a book for them and get paid because they're too lazy or stupid, or both, to do it themselves.

CONTENTS

Disclaimer

This novel is a work of fiction. Fiction, according to the dictionary, is literature that describes imaginary events and imaginary people.

Let's start with imaginary people. All the characters in this book, with the exception of the mention of certain celebrities, leaders, and historical figures, are figments of my imagination. Any resemblance to real people, either living or dead, is purely coincidental. That's right, boys I knew and girls I dated—you're not in here. You're not all that exciting, and neither am I.

This brings us to imaginary events. This novel deals with, among other things, a breakup of the United States. Despite my profound disgust with how the federal government has been outright weaponized against us—including the possibility that I'm now on some FBI shit list for writing this book, and you're on another FBI shit list for having bought it—let it be known that I wholeheartedly oppose armed insurrection against lawful authority. I'm a lover, not a fighter.

In the one-in-a-million chance that you happen to be a woke social justice warrior who enjoys the guilty pleasure of reading prepper fiction, I absolutely abhor racism, sexism, or any other -ism. Spoiler alert: of the novel's four main protagonists, one is Hispanic, one is black, and one is a woman, so good luck finding any of the aforementioned societal ills in these pages.

It's disturbing to see a growing number of Americans clamoring for "trigger warnings" at the start of books to mollycoddle people who are scared spitless of being exposed to new ideas and new thinking. However, in my desire to be as accommodating as possible to my fellow human beings, I will include a trigger warning for this book.

Trigger warning: this book contains triggers. On guns. And when these triggers are pulled with a round chambered and the safety off, the guns fire bullets. I understand that firearms aren't everybody's cup of tea, but if you're offended by the fact that struggles for freedom and liberty are won more often than not by force of arms rather than by flowers and Hallmark cards, you might want to set this book down and slowly walk away from it.

Still with me? Great. We're almost done.

Some of the firearms in this novel, and other equipment such as high-capacity magazines and body armor, might not be legal to possess where you live. Please consult your applicable laws.

While this novel is set in a world without rule of law, the rule of law very much exists at the time of its publishing. A number of the activities described in this story, including but not limited to owning an unlicensed machine gun and wiping your rear end with the National Firearms Act, broadcasting pirate radio transmissions on amateur radio bands, practicing medicine without a license, booby-trapping your property with punji sticks, etc., will get you in very deep trouble with local, state, and federal law enforcement, to say nothing of those humorless busybodies on the board of your homeowner association. You, dear reader, are solely responsible for your own actions, and the consequences of your own carelessness or stupidity. Come to think of it, if you do in fact happen to be stupid, you may want to set this book down and slowly walk away from it.

In short, you are officially on notice that the author is neither liable nor responsible for any damage or injury caused, directly or indirectly, by the information contained in this work. And if you do happen to get busted, don't bother calling me and asking for bail money.

Now all you kids get off my lawn.

For Dad

The average age of the world's greatest civilizations has been 200 years. These nations have progressed through this sequence: From bondage to spiritual faith; From spiritual faith to great courage; From courage to liberty; From liberty to abundance; From abundance to selfishness; From selfishness to apathy; From apathy to dependence; From dependence back into bondage.

—Alexander Fraser Tytler

PART ONE

Always predict the worst, and you'll be hailed as a prophet.
—Tom Lehrer

CHAPTER 1

I should be dead tired right now, Eric Jaeger said to himself as he nervously stared over his rifle scope into Montana pine forest rendered black as pitch by a new moon. *Nothing like going out and killing people to get the blood flowing.*

He pushed the thought away and silently ordered himself to focus on the job at hand as he and his friends lay shrouded in the thick darkness of Helena National Forest. While Eric and his comrades in arms guarded their temporary perimeter, his friends Manny Landeros and Travis Slocomb were sneaking one last look at the bandits they came to slaughter to the last man.

A silhouette materialized from the darkness with a rustle of dry brush. "Halt! Identify yourself," Eric said just loud enough to be heard. He knew it was his best friend, but this was a night to do everything by the book.

"Manny Landeros, leader's recon," the visitor whispered back in Mexican-accented English.

Eric fought a flash of panic as he struggled against the worries swirling through his head to remember the verbal challenge and password combination to identify friend from foe. "Dictionary," he blurted after a moment's hesitation.

"Hedgehog," Manny replied before making an angry beeline for the man lying prone to Eric's left and smacking his military surplus Kevlar helmet with a dull *thunk*.

"What the hell you looking at the sky for, *pendejo*?" Manny hissed in the young man's ear. "You think the bad guys are gonna beam down from outer space?"

"Uh, no. No, Manny," Allan Schmidt meekly stammered.

"You can admire the Big Freakin' Dipper when we're safe at home," Manny seethed between clenched teeth. "Keep your eyes on your sector of fire. I'm not dying tonight because you're busy wishing upon a star."

"Yes, Manny—sorry."

"Ssssh! *¡Cállate!* Just do your job!"

We'll have to straighten Allan out later, Eric thought. Allan was a communications wizard who could figure out how to talk with someone on the other side of the globe with two paper cups and a very long string; it was a vital skill in this new world where smart phones, email, and twenty-four-hour news joined the dodo bird in the dustbin of history. But in the grim aftermath of economic collapse and pandemic flu that Eric had come to call the Unraveling, everyone was a soldier first, and anyone who couldn't fight was worthless. Part of Eric couldn't blame Allan for admiring the night sky, which blazed with thousands of glittering stellar jewels and the splendor of the Milky Way—a spectacular view made possible by the lights all over the former United States going out and staying out.

Eric gulped down the lump that had risen in his throat. *It's hard to believe that the COVID-19 pandemic—and all the misery and bullshit that came with it—turned out to be an exhibition game. It's opening day now.*

Manny crept to Eric, twigs and pine needles crunching under his boots. "I need to pick your brain, amigo—always good to get a second opinion."

Eric took a knee at the center of their small perimeter of ten men and women, which was the maximum that Manny was comfortable taking without leaving his home turned survival retreat defenseless. He shivered as he waited for his friend, more from fear than from the end-of-summer September chill that had begun to set into Rocky Mountain evenings. He and Manny had made it through their entire stints in the Army without having to shoot anyone, and here they were—*in Montana, for Christ's sake*, Eric thought with a disbelieving shake of his head—about to ambush and kill fellow Americans.

The bandits had taken full advantage of the collapse of law and order to plunder the countryside; they avoided the nearby state capital of Helena, but terrorized rural homeowners for what little food and gas they had left in exchange for their lives. However, they spent every night at the same abandoned campground off of US Route 12, five miles west of town. Manny's neighbor, whose friends had fallen victim to the miscreants, had relayed the tip several days prior before fleeing with his wife to take refuge with relatives in Utah, and leaving Manny their house and everything they were forced to leave behind.

Manny and his ragtag strike force had set out for the ambush site at sunset after one last review of the sand table model that Eric had dug in the backyard to help visualize their route and their objective. They snaked single-file through the fragrant conifer forest, sacrificing safer tactical movement for speed while trying their best not to sound like a herd of elephants crashing through the woods. The group had reached their objective rally point several hours later, fanning out into a circle behind whatever cover they could find while Manny and Travis left to recon the target.

Eric popped the button of his helmet strap and scratched his head, his brown hair shorn to a high and tight. His mind drifted to his past life, which had abruptly ended six weeks prior, as a Wisconsin high school history teacher and closeted survivalist—memories now tainted by the realization that his students were likely dead. *Did the H7N9 flu get them, or were they murdered by monsters like the ones we're about to kill? Are they alive, but starving?* He banished the horrible images parading through his imagination as Manny knelt beside him.

"We're facin' a bunch of amateurs, just like we hoped," Manny whispered, peeling his helmet from sweat-matted, jet-black hair. "Still ten of 'em, so a one-to-one match. These guys are dumber than a bag of hammers—just sitting right out in the open with no cover. Idiots got a campfire going, and they're lit up like neon signs. Makes our job easier, but I'm still kicking myself that I never got around to splurging on a decent set of night vision goggles. They're passing around a bottle, and get this—they got a jam box set up and they're playin' music."

"They taking requests?" Eric joked.

Manny flashed the briefest of grins for his friend's irreverent sense of humor. "I wish—these guys listen to *mierda*. But seriously, we got a perfect setup—an undisciplined and sloppy enemy distracted by music and a fire, and numbed by booze. We can take 'em."

"They got any security posted? Anyone who looks like they have half a brain?"

Manny nodded. "Just one guy with a pump-action shotgun, but he's only watching the road, not the woods—bad for them, good for us. Everyone else is armed with a mix of shotguns and rifles—most don't even have 'em in arm's reach—but two of them have military rifles. Those guys are top priority to be taken down. Whaddya think, brother?"

Eric swallowed hard. He preferred numerical superiority, but they had the next best thing—the element of surprise against a bunch of good ole' boys half in the bag and not expecting trouble. "I say we go. If we don't take out this trash, sooner or later they'll find their way to our front door. Fortune favors the bold."

Manny slapped Eric's shoulder and rose to his feet. "Great minds think alike," he said before ordering the perimeter in a loud whisper to meet in the center. He keyed a small black radio strapped to his tactical vest to check in with Travis, who was still watching the objective from their planned ambush site; Manny had broken a cardinal rule of night fighting by leaving a man by himself, but his limited numbers left him little choice. "Shaft, this is Culebra, any change in target, over?"

"Negative—they're still sitting around begging to be killed," Travis's deep voice crackled back as team members made their way to Manny and Eric, the older-generation Kevlar helmets on their heads making them practically indistinguishable from one another in the dim starlight. They all were armed with semiautomatic civilian versions of military rifles, and wore tactical vests bulging with magazines, canteens, and first-aid kits. Manny was taking a risk by collapsing the perimeter to address everyone at once, Eric thought, but they weren't dealing with a professional opponent that would be sending out patrols that might stumble upon them.

Anxious faces smeared green, black, and brown with camouflage paint stared back at Manny as he rehashed the plan for the hundredth time. Eric glanced at Susan Walker, the paramedic who rode shotgun with him during their harrowing cross-country trek to Manny's house, as she shifted the weight of the large medic bag on her back.

Manny exhaled loudly over the chorus of insects chattering in the night. "I know you're conflicted over what we're about to do, but we're stopping some despicable excuses for human beings from hurting anyone else, or finding our home and hurting us. When you got your man in your sights, think about the victims who begged him for mercy before they were robbed, beaten, or raped. Think about the lives we'll save down the road. Only God can judge these animals, but we're gonna arrange the meeting. Let's get it done. Follow me, five meters between each person—don't bunch up."

Eric brought up the rear behind Benny Rodriguez, Manny's cousin; Benny was a natural outdoorsman with an innate aptitude for small-unit tactics, despite never having served in the military. Out of habit, Eric turned around every few meters to ensure they weren't being followed—the stories his old drill sergeants had told about the tail man getting his throat cut by a stealthy enemy had always given him the creeps.

What's God gonna say about this when I meet Him? This won't be the last time that I have to kill before all of this is over. If it ever will *be over,* Eric thought. Pastor Kris Reynolds didn't address the issue when she saw them off with a prayer for safety and success; Eric knew he wouldn't be the only person seeking her counsel when they got back. The faint sound of rap-metal music from the camp brought Eric's attention back to the mission. *Manny was right—these losers listen to garbage,* he said to himself, again turning to check his six.

Their path to the ambush site—a hill overlooking the campground on the other side of Route 12—meandered in such a way that the group could climb into position without cresting the hilltop and silhouetting themselves against the night sky. Eric nervously reassured himself about the odds; they were the professionals, unlike the filth across the road who had no idea they had minutes left to live.

The uphill climb burned Eric's calves and quickened his pulse. He became aware of every detail around him—the smell of his insect repellent and the pine trees, the sounds of the forest, the mosquitoes buzzing in his ears, and the large serrated hunting knife that Benny carried in a sheath on his hip. Fear was sharpening Eric's senses to a fine edge. Fear is an ally and a gift if subdued and mastered, one of his sergeants had once told him—those who conquer their fear stay alert and stay alive, while those who let their fear overwhelm them run in circles, wave their arms and scream, and end up as statistics.

Travis, his rifle pointed downhill at the campground across the four-lane highway, was the first man Eric passed on the ambush line just inside the woods before the trees gave way to the brush and rock of the downhill slope to Route 12's shoulder. He was ex-military, like Eric and Manny, although he had served in the Marines rather than the Army; the group's sole black member was a police officer before the Unraveling, hence the radio call sign the group had bestowed upon him.

Manny set Eric behind a large pine tree at the center of their linear ambush, and signaled Benny to follow him at a crawl to the far end of the line. Eric blinked and peered through his rifle scope at their targets—thanks to the campfire and the relaxed atmosphere it encouraged, the bandits could be seen and heard a mile away. Their opponent was contemptible, both in spirit and in discipline.

Travis and Benny had scouted the campground the previous night to determine the bandits' guilt; Manny couldn't in good conscience condemn men to death based solely on his neighbors' word. The haunted looks on their faces when they returned at sunrise had said everything. "They're guilty, all right," Benny had told Eric in his Tejano drawl while he wiped the paint from his face with a rag in the early morning twilight. "They were sittin' around bragging about the house they just plundered. *Jesucristo*, they were laughing about havin' their way with the family's daughters. These guys are scum, every last one."

Manny quietly slid down next to Eric. "I'd tell you to kill the fat white redneck, but that wouldn't narrow things down. Look to the back left for the guy with the red hat and the Kalashnikov." Eric quickly found his mark—a pudgy man with stringy hair sitting in a cheap gray folding easy chair, cradling a weathered AK-47 clone and reaching for the whiskey bottle that again made its way to him.

"The peckerwood taking a swig of Jack?"

"He's yours. I've got the guy with the AR-15 off to the far right. You and I are taking the first shots. On three, cry havoc and let slip the dogs of war."

"*Julius Caesar*," Eric nervously muttered, nestling into a stable firing position on his bed of pine needles and weeds. "Act three, scene one."

"*Sabelotodo*. Stay safe, old friend."

"You, too," Eric whispered before slowly thumbing the safety on his dull black military-style rifle to "fire." While every member of their survival group owned the ubiquitous AR-15 platform that fired a 5.56-millimeter or .223 Remington round, their rifle of choice was the AR-10, which was chambered in the larger and deadlier .308 Winchester. Eric slowed his breathing and took aim at the man's center of mass, just like he had practiced on innumerable Army firing ranges—his crosshairs bobbed up and down as he struggled against the adrenaline surging through his body. *It's a paper target*, he reassured himself. *It's not a human being, but an animal to be put down before it hurts anyone else.*

"Got your shot, Eric?"

"Roger."

"On three. One. Two . . ."

Eric stopped breathing and slowly squeezed the trigger.

"Three!"

The thunderclap of the shot startled Eric as his rifle bucked, the dull pain of the recoil burning into his right shoulder. The fat man flew back in his easy chair, his whiskey bottle spraying its glistening amber contents as it tumbled through the air. Training and instinct took over as Eric shot the man twice more, adding to the deafening roar torturing his eardrums from the fusillade to his left and right. He found the two men nearest his target, who were already down, and fired two rounds each into their splayed bodies.

The slaughter ended seconds after it started; the bandits, who a minute earlier thought themselves unstoppable and accountable to no one, were dead or writhing and screaming in agony. Their trashy music added a surreal feel to the gory scene until Manny put a round through their cheap jam box.

"Listen up!" Manny hollered, the need for noise discipline out the window. "Benny, Travis, watch the road and our flanks! Everyone else, watch your targets! If they're still moving, put 'em out of their misery! If not, let 'em bleed out!"

It was obvious to Eric that his target's pillaging days were over. He laid flat on his back, his chair crumpled next to his fat behind, and his white t-shirt crimson with blood. Eric caught movement from a neighboring body and pivoted to engage, but a rifle cracked to his right before he could take the shot and the top of the man's head exploded, spraying more colors onto the fat man's shirt.

With the shrill blast of a whistle tied to Manny's tactical vest, the entire group minus Travis and Benny leaped forward and ran down the hill on line toward the campground, the rustle of small rocks and loose dirt underfoot giving way to the thudding of their boots across Route 12. They charged straight through the kill zone, shooting into bodies as they ran. Adrenaline and military training sang in Eric's veins, and he realized that he was screaming at the top of his lungs. A dying man at Eric's ten o'clock struggled to sit up with his shotgun in a vain effort to evade his fate, but was knocked back down for good by three rounds from Susan's rifle.

"You owe me one!" she screamed to Eric without looking at him.

The attackers dove to the ground once they mowed through the bloodbath they created, aiming into the woods in case any escaped bandits attempted to mount a counterattack. "We got five minutes!" Manny yelled. "Alpha Team, check those trucks for anything valuable! Bravo Team, check the dead for weapons and ammo! Just like we rehearsed! Go, go, *go!*"

Susan and Jay Kowalsky, a middle-aged man and the oldest on the mission, sprang to their feet and dashed for the bandits' pickup trucks. A horrid gurgling sound from one of the dying bandits and the stink of freshly evacuated bowels competed for Eric's attention as he watched the woods in front of him. *Hollywood always made killing look so tidy and immediate,* he said to himself—the dying never twitched in the movies, or shit themselves, or choked on their own blood until their heart and lungs finally got the memo that the brain was permanently closed for business.

A loud hiss and a pillar of smoke and steam displaced the sounds and smells of death as Manny dumped the bandits' cooler over the fire, wrapping the attackers once again in the protective shroud of darkness. Out of the corner of his eye, Eric caught the flashes of Susan's and Jay's red-lens flashlights as they tore apart the insides of the trucks. Another sickening gurgle rose over the crackling of the embers as Allan rose to his knees and vomited, his rifle still pointed into the woods. "Not now, soldier," Manny said, tossing the empty cooler to the ground. "We need you watching the line. Puke later."

Matt Baus and Pete Mick almost tripped over Eric's boots as they dashed to the man Susan had shot. Eric heard the metallic clatter as Matt kicked away the bandit's shotgun, followed by a sickening *thump* as he kicked the corpse in the groin to ensure that he was dead before rolling him on his side to check for weapons underneath. "Clear!" Pete yelled in a young and agitated voice.

Dual footfalls announced Susan's and Jay's return from their scavenging mission—Eric mouthed a silent prayer of thanks that Susan had made it through the fight unscathed.

"Nothing useful in the trucks except for a few boxes of ammo and some canned food," she told Manny as Jay held up an almost empty olive-drab military duffel bag. "Other than that, a can of gas, a baggie of weed, and a hot-rod magazine with a half-naked lady on the cover. Real classy guys."

Jay struggled to catch his breath. "Too bad we walked here and don't got time to strip the trucks," he gasped. "Tires an' batteries are gonna become scarcer 'n hen's teeth."

"Did you look for maps?" Eric interjected without taking his eyes off the woods. "Go back and grab every map, every piece of paper, and every CB or handheld radio you find! We could learn something about these guys."

Susan darted back for the trucks, Jay biting off a curse before jogging after her. "You got two minutes!" Manny called to their backs before Matt and Pete breathlessly ran up to him, Pete struggling under the weight of a duffel bag swollen with firearms and ammunition the bandits no longer needed.

The clanking of handheld and truck-mounted radios heralded Jay's and Susan's return to the hasty perimeter several minutes later. Jay uttered another winded curse as Manny sprinted to a large pine tree at the entrance to the campground turned graveyard and again blew his whistle—it was time to get the hell out of Dodge. The team, with Susan in the lead, ran to line up behind him, taking cover behind the tall pine trees lining Route 12.

"Scroll to the road. Go!" Manny told Susan and tapped her arm. Susan ran to the shoulder of the road and dropped to one knee facing right, aiming her rifle down the lanes. Jay ran up and took her place, and she bolted across the road and knelt again, facing the other direction. Matt then ran up to replace Jay, who replaced Susan, who began scrambling back up the hill under the watchful eyes of Travis and Benny. The maneuver, created by Army Rangers and named for the distinctive scroll patches they wore on their left shoulders, balanced speed with security when crossing a road by exposing only a handful of soldiers at any time to enemy fire.

Manny tallied his people as they crossed, and brought up the rear to find his troops in their original hilltop positions, tired but uninjured. He allowed himself a moment to catch his breath and savor the mountain pine air as he gazed at the star-filled sky that had earned Allan his earlier scolding. Manny glanced east toward Helena, hidden from view in the valley—he didn't want to think about what was going on down there, or in any other city in the wake of the collapse.

Eric slapped Manny on the back. "You did good, brother. Real good," he whispered.

"Don't dump Gatorade on me 'til we get everyone back," Manny replied before ordering Travis to lead the group home by way of their alternate route. Travis nodded and swung his left arm overhead and forward to signal everyone to move out, glancing behind him to ensure that Julie Eddington, Allan's girlfriend, saw him and relayed the nonverbal command. Manny warned people one at a time as they passed by to stay alert until they were safe at his home.

If life as I knew it didn't end when Susan and I made it to Manny's house by the skins of our teeth six weeks ago, it sure as hell ended just now, Eric thought as Manny trotted past him through the dry weeds. *I'm gonna have a long talk with Pastor Kris about what we just did. And you know, Allan had a good idea. I think I'll throw up, too.*

CHAPTER 2

"If you're just joining us on Newsradio 950, riots are raging out of control in every major city following the federal government's closing of all banks nationwide in response to the worsening economic crisis. Hospitals are overflowing with victims of the H7N9 flu . . ."

Eric drove, white-knuckled, as he and Susan approached the final miles of their cross-country drive to the Montana home of his best friend—a safe haven that meant the difference between life and death in a world gone mad. He had picked her up thirty-six hours earlier at her Lake Geneva, Wisconsin condo, hastily cramming the bed of his Ford F-150 pickup truck with her last-minute supplies in the blistering August heat before heading west, listening to news radio as the United States of America died.

Susan fidgeted in the passenger seat, watching ahead as Route 12 took them into Townsend, a town of nineteen hundred people at the southern tip of Canyon Ferry Lake Reservoir, a beautiful lake east of Helena where Eric loved to fish whenever he came to pre-position supplies in Manny's basement. Eric ran a free hand across the stubble of his unshaven face and nervously pondered the remaining miles ahead. Traffic had been surprisingly light, but the Big Belt Mountains they had just crossed, and the Elkhorn and Boulder ranges ahead of them, created more potential choke points than Eric cared to think about. Montana's unmatched beauty on the sunny and cloudless afternoon made their dire situation that much more surreal.

"Almost there," said Susan. "I'll never be so happy to reach a destination in my life—I can't believe this is happening."

"You and me both," Eric said. "I hate to take a set of eyes off our surroundings, but try finding any news you can of the road conditions ahead on your phone—Twitter, government Facebook pages, local media, anything." He snuck a glance at Susan as she reached into her pocket for her iPhone, her light green polo shirt lifting up to reveal a hint of toned midriff, before silently chastising himself to focus on the road.

"*. . . and CDC officials believe the H7N9 virus entered the US simultaneously through Seattle, Los Angeles, and San Diego within days of the first reported outbreak in China. You're listening to 950 AM KLGK, your news and information station, and we're interrupting our lineup of syndicated talk shows to provide nonstop coverage of the ongoing crisis. I'm running a one-man show, so bear with me, folks—the rest of the staff either took off or never showed up . . .*"

Townsend was the latest of the many small towns that Susan and Eric had passed through as they crossed Big Sky Country. It was *Götterdämmerung* in the big cities and densely populated states, but in Montana, where people were much fewer and a lot farther between, the full effects of the economic crisis and the pandemic had yet to fully manifest.

Susan set her pink-cased phone on her thigh and tied her shoulder-length blonde hair into a ponytail. "So far, it looks like everyone's just parroting the usual feel-good nonsense—stay calm, stay indoors, et cetera. Nothing so far on traffic or the situation in Helena." Their route to safe haven would take them uncomfortably close to, but not through, the state capital; even though only about thirty-two thousand people lived there, Eric wouldn't breathe easy until they skirted the city's southern limits and reached the woods where Manny and his family lived.

"The whereabouts of the president and senior members of Congress are still unknown," the newsman continued. *"Reports state that much of Washington, D.C. outside of the capital area is burning . . ."*

Eric silently worried about the bridge over the Missouri River just past Townsend. If it was blocked, they would have to double back and circle around the reservoir—one of Montana's largest bodies of water—and cross over the ribbon-thin road on top of the dam at the north end. That would add at least another twenty miles and God knows how much more time—unless that crossing was closed as well.

"There's a huge pile-up on I-15 south of Helena, between Clancy and Montana City," Susan reported, her finger scrolling her screen.

Eric glanced at his rear-view mirror at a sheriff's patrol cruiser crossing the intersection they had just passed through. "Good thing we're not taking I-15—if we had tried taking I-90 to get out here, we wouldn't have made it ten miles before getting stuck in a permanent traffic jam. All it takes is one crash or one idiot running outta gas to gunk up the works." Their route from Wisconsin avoided interstate highways, and state routes wherever possible, because they quickly become parking lots in emergencies—Eric had watched too many news stories of bumper-to-bumper traffic fleeing incoming hurricanes with the speed of an old woman with corns.

Pleasant single-family homes gave way to Townsend's business district just past the red brick Broadwater County Courthouse. The idyllic rural town was a stark contrast to the horrors described on the radio, but Eric realized it was only a matter of time before small towns also ran out of food and started getting sick. The eighteen-wheel trucks that resupplied America's grocery stores started grinding to a halt when Uncle Sam officially defaulted on the national debt and the economy went into free-fall—Eric couldn't imagine what it was now like with a deadly flu thrown into the mix.

Eric turned right at the intersection where Route 12 and US Route 287 merged for the next leg of their trip, skirting the Elkhorn Mountains dominating the western horizon. He deftly swerved around the end of a long line of cars stretching onto the road as they waited to fill up at a nearby Exxon station—the crisis had blasted the cost of gasoline, already at historic highs because of inflation and Washington's long war on domestic fossil fuel production, into the stratosphere.

"Now *that's* gonna get ugly once the pumps run dry. Good thing we brought spare gas cans in the back."

Susan pointed to a full parking lot at a pharmacy across the street. "No, ugly is gonna be when the tens of millions of Americans who are dependent on psychiatric drugs run out of their meds. Everyone's gonna snap. All at once. In a nation that's up to its eyeballs in guns."

The duo sped out of town, the desperate line of motorists receding behind them. Even though Eric carried his concealed .45-caliber Ruger handgun on his hip, he felt naked without their rifles, which at Susan's insistence remained buried under the supplies in the truck bed instead of within arm's reach. With the news getting uglier with each passing minute, Eric had tried to pull over outside of White Sulphur Springs to retrieve them, but Susan flatly and angrily refused. He couldn't blame her—weeks after he helped her buy her AR-10 rifle, she was called to respond to a mass shooting at a strip mall in a neighboring county. Susan cultivated a dislike for firearms after that, and had almost left the group as a result, until Eric and Manny convinced her that the bad people who would take advantage of a collapse would not share her aversion. She grudgingly spent her free Saturdays with Eric at the McMiller Sports

Center, in Eagle, learning the ins and outs of the rifle, and ironically blossomed into a very good shot.

Susan's right—we'd have some explaining to do if we got pulled over by a nervous cop with two loaded freedom sticks in plain sight. We're not gonna survive the end of the world in the pokey.

Eric breathed a sigh of relief as they crossed the Missouri River without incident—the last water obstacle between them and what almost certainly would be their home for the foreseeable future. *Provided we can get past Helena*, he said to himself before realizing the radio had fallen silent. He reached over to scan the rest of the AM band.

"We're back, ladies and gentlemen!" the newsreader blurted as Eric withdrew his hand with a start. *"That's the third time today we lost power. I don't know when we'll be off the air for good, but I'll stay on as long as I can."*

"Any trouble ahead?" Eric asked Susan for the hundredth time.

"No—uh, no, I don't know," Susan sheepishly answered, her face etched with worry. "I was, um, trying to text Mom and Dad in Waukesha. Can't call because the cell network's overloaded."

Eric flashed an understanding smile. "That's OK. At this point, I think I'd rather have you watching our flanks than looking for news. We're all friends here—if you were on a dating app, I won't tell anyone."

Susan forced a smile back. "I just updated my profile to add 'Armageddon' to my interests, right after long walks on the beach and good times with friends."

Eric allowed himself to relax a bit as mile after mile of scenic, semi-arid Montana valley raced by in flashes of green, amber, and brown. After almost two days of driving on back roads as the nation he once pledged his life to defend crumbled from the one-two punch of economic collapse and plague, safe harbor was close enough to taste, and Eric constantly fought the urge to floor the accelerator. *Slow and steady wins the race*, he admonished himself. *Don't die in a crash so close to the finish line.*

The newsreader's increasingly agitated and trembling voice reclaimed Eric's attention. *"We have no updates on what we reported earlier regarding Governor Claire Kellerman countermanding the president's order federalizing all Montana National Guard troops who haven't already been deployed. Kellerman insisted that the Pentagon's deployment of the state's military helicopters to Joint Base Lewis-McChord outside of Seattle, and the redeployment of most of its armor from annual training in California to cities along the West Coast, was plenty enough. She said the state's remaining guardsmen 'are needed right here in Montana, not patrolling big cities a thousand miles away.'"*

Susan shook her head. "I don't think the governor will get any more use out of the National Guard than the president. Reservists aren't gonna abandon their families. I'd be amazed if one soldier in ten reports for duty."

"After weeks of silence following allegations of improper campaign contributions to Kellerman's political rivals—including her very own lieutenant governor, Jeremy Matthews—local tech magnate Stuart Magnuson took to Facebook to call the unfolding financial and public health catastrophe 'the chickens coming home to roost.' Magnuson, of course, made his fortune in the wake of the COVID-19 pandemic pioneering the software allowing governments and health officials to track people's movements to enforce social distancing measures and to monitor 'disinformation' on social media . . ."

Eric and Susan passed without incident through a handful of minuscule towns that were barely more than clumps of houses before approaching the suburb of East Helena, and the plumes of thick black smoke rising from it.

"We have to drive through that?" Susan gasped.

"No. Route 12 only skirts the town. State Highway 282 is right up ahead to take us from the Helena area altogether, which is fine by me, because the natives are getting restless." Eric pointed to a crowd mobbing a supermarket on the frontage road. "Those store shelves got emptied by panic buying a long time ago. You'd think people would've learned their lesson after COVID and the years of supply chain problems that followed—those idiots probably thought they'd be able to sit at home ordering Chinese take-out and streaming porn until Uncle Sugar borrowed our way out of yet another mess. The only thing those people are gonna bring home to their families is the flu."

"While the H7N9 pandemic is ravaging Seattle, Portland, and southern California, the Montana Department of Public Health said in a statement that widespread cases have not as of yet been reported here. Of course, that statement is almost two days old, and I'm not in a position to . . . oh, sweet Jesus—"

"We interrupt our programming," a familiar and creepy computer-generated voice intoned seconds later. *"This is a national emergency."*

The hair on Eric's arms stood with the Emergency Alert System's grating interrupt signal. He stared in mute shock at the radio before Susan's piercing scream brought his attention back to the road, and the windowless white van that had blown the stoplight ahead of them to race directly into their path. Susan's scream created a demonic harmony with the emergency alert tone as Eric hooked hard right behind the van, the truck's squealing tires adding to the unholy chorus like fingernails on a chalkboard. The other driver's attention was riveted straight forward, either in desperation to get to where he was going, or to flee from wherever he had been.

Eric cleared the van, but barreled toward the corner Conoco gas station, which like Townsend was packed with cars and desperate drivers. The thought of the two of them being savagely cremated in a gigantic explosion flashed through his mind as he spun the wheel to swerve back into their lane, his front tire catching the curb before Eric straightened out and continued west.

"Asshole!" Eric hollered out the driver's side window before laying on his horn in sheer terror, drowning out the automated voice informing listeners that it was interrupting the hapless newscaster at the request of the White House. Susan lunged forward and stabbed the radio off.

"You OK?!" Eric asked breathlessly.

"No!" Susan shrieked, her face white as the van that almost killed them. "This is the least OK I've ever been!"

Eric pondered turning the radio back on to hear the emergency message, but decided against it until Susan settled down. He guessed that it wasn't an incoming attack—the Russians, North Koreans, or whomever, wouldn't waste perfectly good nuclear warheads destroying a nation that was doing a spectacular job of destroying itself.

The truck's tires squealed as Eric peeled left without slowing down onto Highway 282 to begin the final leg of their trek. The road meandered southwest into the forest-carpeted Boulder Mountains, which Eric, Susan, and the rest of their group of prudent survivalists would wrap around them like a security blanket.

"We need to get a hold of Manny and let him know we're close—I don't wanna get shot by any itchy trigger fingers," said Susan, her composure returned. She picked up her iPhone, its screen filled with the presidential emergency alert, then tossed it between her feet with a curse. "Well, if the network wasn't already overloaded, it surely went to hell the moment the president took over the airwaves."

"'Do not use your telephone. The telephone lines should be kept open for emergency use,'" Eric recited from the emergency alert script in a mock officious voice. "People don't follow instructions in emergencies, which is precisely why we're bugging out to a place with no people."

Susan gestured at the truck radio. "Should we listen to the message?"

"Why bother? What's the president gonna say—please don't loot and riot, and cover your mouth when you sneeze? We need to focus on contacting Manny—they've gotta be monitoring the radios at the CQ desk if the phones are out."

Susan leaned back and grasped the handle of the olive drab metal ammunition can behind her seat. The weathered and rust-mottled box, the yellow stenciling describing the caliber it once held long since faded, rattled as Susan popped open the lid and pulled out a green marine radio and its antenna. Allan, the group's communications guru, had instructed every member to buy a marine radio for emergency communications during the critical first days of a major disaster; in a place like Montana, far removed from the ocean and waterway shipping, marine radios would provide an almost personal network while the hysterical public jammed other frequencies and overloaded cell phone towers. While federal law set steep fines for broadcasting on a marine radio for anything other than maritime purposes, Susan wagered that the FCC was dealing with far bigger problems at the moment.

She lowered the passenger window to give the antenna open air—Susan wasn't about to ask Eric to pull over so she could step out. "Base, Base, anybody there with their ears on, over?" Susan broadcast as their truck raced toward the I-15 overpass, the last location in Eric's mind where something could go wrong. A column of oily smoke rose to the south from the major pile-up they had heard about in Townsend.

A jubilant woman's Mexican-accented contralto voice leaped from the marine radio's speaker. "Susan, is that you? *¡Gloria a Dios!* Is Eric with you?"

"Yes, and yes! Carmen, I can't tell you how wonderful it is to hear your voice! Is there room at the inn?"

"Beds are made, mini-fridge is stocked. Wha . . . honey, wait your turn!" Carmen protested as her husband grabbed the radio out of her hands.

"Eric, my brother, you close?"

Susan held the radio to Eric's cheek. "Very close—it's been far too long!" Eric exclaimed over the howling of the wind through the windows as they sped across the overpass—I-15 below was inexplicably almost clear of traffic. "Could you make sure you let the, uh, hotel doorman know we're coming?"

"Carmen's on it—you won't get shot coming in," Manny answered. Eric was relieved that Manny decided to have an armed member in the retreat's outdoor LP/OP, or listening and observation post. It also answered a question that Eric didn't want to ask on the air—other members had made it.

"You hearing anything on your end?" Eric asked.

"From the government, nothing but that stupid emergency alert. Up until that, the media were pumping out their usual nonsense—every network but Fox News trying to blame this on the Republicans, Fox News trying to blame it on the Democrats, and none of them telling anybody anything useful, like how not to be dead by this time next week. Get over here fast, buddy."

Eric's grin stretched from ear to ear until they reached Manny's house.

CHAPTER 3

Privates Eric Jaeger and Manny Landeros first met as roommates at Fort Polk, Louisiana, after graduating the Infantry Basic Training and Airborne schools at Fort Benning, Georgia—just as both posts were poised to be stripped of their names honoring Confederate generals.

Their backgrounds couldn't have been more different. Eric grew up in Chicago's far west suburbs, while Manny was raised in the Texas Hill Country. Eric, the son of teachers, grew up wanting for little, while Manny, the son of a day laborer and a cashier, grew up not having much of anything. Eric joined the Army out of patriotism and tradition—he wanted to serve like his father and grandmother before him—while Manny, whose family came over the border illegally from Mexico for a better life, wanted a fast track to citizenship. They couldn't explain why, and never wasted time trying to figure it out, but they became inseparable best friends who did everything together—that is, what few activities a backwater post surrounded by woods and swamp had to offer. The rest of their platoon in the First Battalion, 509th Infantry Regiment, "The Geronimos," jokingly called them the Landeros brothers.

Eric and Manny liked the mission the Geronimos had at Fort Polk's Joint Readiness Training Center—First Battalion was OPFOR, or opposing forces, whose members portrayed the enemy in war games to train units bound for the Middle East and other hotspots. The OPFOR units were the most hated in the Army, and maintained fearsome reputations for handing humiliating defeats to elite units. Playing the bad guys gave Eric and Manny a rush, and they liked the added bonus of getting to grow beards to blend in with the locals who made extra money portraying civilians on the battlefield. During the day, they waved and flashed the thumbs-up sign to American soldiers—who didn't know that the raised thumb was the Middle Eastern equivalent of the middle finger—and then proceeded to keep them up all night with roadside bombs and ambushes.

One fateful June evening, Manny and Eric knocked back cold beers outside the barracks in the black of a widespread power outage while they watched the sky erupt with flares and pyrotechnics that their fellow enlisted soldiers had illegally hoarded from past range trips and field maneuvers.

"Wonder if this is what things'll look like when the shit hits the fan," Eric said, pleasantly squiffed.

Manny crushed his empty can of Shiner Bock and fished through the cooler's icy water for a reload. "Say again?"

"When civilization ends. The day the lights go off and never come back on. I read this book in junior high—*One Second After*—about the power grid and everything electronic getting knocked out by an electromagnetic pulse attack. Real sad book—nine out of ten people end up dying."

Manny cracked open a fresh can of suds as a green star flare arced up the sky with a *whoosh* from the barracks across the street. "Could that happen?"

"Yeah, actually—had to write a book report on it. A Congressional study concluded that 90 percent of the population could be dead in a year if an EMP fried the east, west, and Texas power grids. Things would get medieval fast."

Manny held up the glowing screen of his smart phone. "Well, Carmen just texted me, so it wasn't an EMP that killed our lights," he said, staring forlornly into a cooler filled with more floating ice than beer. "Hope they get the juice back on by tomorrow—at least to the walk-in fridge and the cash register at the Class Six store."

They laughed as a parachute flare popped to life overhead and bathed the picnic area the boozing soldiers had commandeered in chalky white light. Eric polished off his Abita Purple Haze while the shadows of the trees eerily shifted with the drifting of the flare on a light summer breeze that did little to ameliorate Louisiana's soul-crushing humidity. "If you think about it, that's only one way the system could come undone. Maybe America will go bankrupt; Uncle Sam spends about double what he makes in taxes. Or maybe it'll be a flu pandemic like *The Stand,* or climate change, or World War Three."

"We got a word where I come from for people like you—*aguafiesta,*" Manny said.

"What's that mean?"

"Means you're a buzzkill."

Eric belched and waved his non-drinking hand at the non-regulation fireworks display around them. "If this ever becomes real, a lotta people won't make it. They're too busy following their favorite reality TV shows and sports to make any preparations; heck, most folks aren't even ready for a tornado or snowstorm. When the system comes crashing down—and after the whole 'rona shitshow, I think it's more a 'when' than an 'if'—people are gonna get very mean very fast. And then they'll die."

Manny took a long pull from his Shiner to fight off the hot and sticky Louisiana night. "You implyin' that our all-knowin' government can't be trusted to take care of us? That it's up to us to watch out for ourselves? That's treason," he slurred with a crooked smile.

"Isn't treason if it's true," Eric shot back as a military police cruiser peeled down the darkened street, its mounted spotlight hunting for the culprits shooting off pyrotechnics.

The lights came back on thirty minutes later, but their discussion kept them up to the early hours of the morning, which made for a very long and hung over duty day. That weekend, they drove to the post library and walked out with a small stack of survival books.

***

A year later, the Army transferred Eric and Manny to another OPFOR unit. While they agreed that an act of God had kept them together, they also concluded that it was His opposite number who typed up their transfer orders to Fort Irwin, California.

Smack in the middle of the Mojave Desert, Fort Irwin was home to the Eleventh Armored Cavalry Regiment, "The Blackhorse Cav"— and like Louisiana, also was home to snakes, scorpions, and other poisonous creatures with a taste for soldiers' flesh. Barstow, the nearest town, was an hour south; every night, just to tease soldiers, the lights of the Las Vegas Strip and the Luxor Sky Beam more than a hundred miles over the Calico Mountains lit up the northeast sky.

Eric and Manny spent another two years playing the enemy, and both earned their sergeant's stripes, but mutually decided that they had had enough and wouldn't reenlist. It wasn't a hard decision for them to make. Besides the COVID-19 nonsense that had made shitty military life even more so, they felt the Army was beginning to look at people like them as an actual enemy rather than a fictional one. The Army just didn't *feel right* anymore—leadership and training became increasingly obsessed with "domestic extremists," and prioritized identity politics over training to fight and win wars. It became obvious to Eric and Manny that true patriots were increasingly unwelcome in this new military, and the duo were happy to oblige.

It was at Fort Irwin that Manny married his high school sweetheart, Carmen de la Vega, and Eric served as his best man. The newlyweds moved into a house on post while Eric was forced to continue enduring barracks life, at least in theory; he became a fixture at the Landeros's dinner table, and considered Carmen's cooking to be the best Mexican food to be found anywhere.

Their survival circle increased as well. They met Matt Baus, a combat engineer they stumbled upon in a lounge reading a survivalist book. Matt introduced them to Travis Slocomb, his friend from his Tennessee hometown, who was stationed at Marine Corps Logistics Base Barstow, and who like them was counting down the days until returning to civilian life. Unlike Eric and Manny, who had never been deployed, Travis had two tours in Afghanistan under his belt, including being one of the last Marines out during the United States' haphazard and incompetent withdrawal.

Having an actual house to serve as a base of operations gave the fledgling group the opportunity to practice canning, food storage, and other self-reliance skills that couldn't be done in the barracks, and gave them a place, albeit a small one, to store whatever supplies they could gather on enlisted soldiers' salaries. The five of them knew they would be dead meat if the shit hit the fan while they were stuck in the middle of the desert, but they valued the practice. They decided that the best thing they could do was continue to train hard in the military and master weapons, marksmanship, and small-unit tactics.

While Eric, Matt, and Travis enrolled in college with their GI Bill benefits upon their discharges, Manny went back to Texas to work for a local manufacturer to provide for his wife and their newborn daughter; the pregnancy and delivery had almost killed Carmen, and their daughter, Luisa, ended up being an only child as a result. Manny shot up the ladder quickly thanks to his work ethic and brains, and ended up owning the company after the retiring owner decided to sell it to him rather than leave it to his business partner, who was little more than a skirt-chasing alcoholic. Manny doubled the company's sales in a couple of years with a series of forward-thinking changes, and in turn sold the business to a group of local investors, with the promise that no workers would be let go.

While Manny loved the Texas Hill Country, he knew it was too densely populated to safely ride out the rough times he'd been wargaming with Eric since they were young privates picking off leeches in the Louisiana bayou; he figured the inland Northwest would be the next best thing, with a sparse population and abundant resources to boot. His newfound riches came in handy—years of interstate migration, led by COVID-19 refugees who could work remotely, had sent Western real-estate prices soaring. He found a nice home on twenty forested acres near Helena, and made an offer on the spot—if you wanted to beat out all the rich carpetbaggers, you brought cash to the table.

The ink was barely dry on the papers when he called Eric, Travis, and Matt and proudly told them that they had the perfect port to ride out the storm they knew would one day come.

CHAPTER 4

"Lord, are you a sight for sore eyes!" Eric whooped as he hugged Carmen off her feet in the Landeros's living room, the turmoil engulfing the world temporarily forgotten.

"Right back at you!" Carmen gasped, half struggling for breath. "But you better put me down before my extremely jealous husband gets the wrong idea!"

"Got any candy, Uncle Eric?" Luisa jokingly asked. The thirteen-year-old girl was a spitting image of her mother; she had grown like a weed since Eric saw her last, her black hair and dark eyes a harbinger of an adolescence of breaking boys' hearts.

"I'll make you a deal—your mom hooks me up with her legendary tamales, and I'll hook you up with some sweets." Eric had brought some candy as a pick-me-up for the group, but it was buried somewhere in the truckload of supplies they had hauled from Wisconsin.

The wall-mounted TV shut off, silencing the droning emergency alert message that had been playing in the background since Eric and Susan stepped through the front door. "Hey, strangers!" Manny exclaimed, tossing the remote on the couch and wrapping Susan in a bear hug. He stuck out his tongue at Eric behind her back, eliciting a glare of disapproval from Carmen and a giggle from Luisa; even though Eric never advertised his feelings for Susan, Manny could read his old friend like a book.

"How many of us are here?" Susan asked the moment Manny set her down.

"Almost everyone. Allan's zonked out after almost two straight days glued to the ham radio, Julie's charging batteries, Jay's on LP/OP duty, Pete's on the CQ desk, and Matt, Angel, and Travis are in quarantine in The Cooler . . ."

"Oh God, they're not sick, are they?" Susan interrupted. Manny had moved his modest recreational vehicle behind and downwind from the house to serve as a makeshift quarantine room when the flu pandemic first hit the news; Manny had nicknamed it "The Cooler," in tribute to one of his favorite movies, *The Great Escape.*

"They're fine—unlike you and Eric, they couldn't haul enough fuel to get here without stopping to gas up and deal with other human beings." Their old buddies from Fort Irwin, plus Matt's new bride, Angel, lived in central Tennessee, and had the farthest to travel of all the group. "We just wanna make sure they didn't pick up H7N9 along with diesel and beef jerky."

"I'll bet there are survival groups out there who are sick as hell because they didn't have a plan to quarantine stragglers," Eric interjected, scratching his head and chest; he was dying for a shower.

"Pastor Kris and Roger will be here soon from Butte—they'll replace the other three in The Cooler until we're sure they didn't catch something," Manny said matter-of-factly. As Carmen and Susan continued the conversation, Manny clandestinely jerked his head for Eric to meet him in the kitchen.

A *ding* from Luisa's iPad on the granite kitchen island greeted Eric—curiosity immediately overcame common courtesy, and he found himself snooping through her Facebook Messenger chat for the students in her homeschooling group.

> we keep losing wifi and power

> Dad didn't come home from store. So scared!

> MOM'S IN NYC AND CNN SAYS CITY'S BURNING

> News says people r dying everywhere oh God

> What r we gonna do?

> LUISA, WHERE R U? U OK?

>> I'm OK—we're all OK.

>> OMG can you believe this?

Eric took a ragged breath and fought the urge to cry, his heart sinking. *Is this what my students are doing right now? Huddling in their homes and texting each other as they wait to fucking die?*

"And that's gonna be Luisa's final message for a long time," Manny said from behind, startling Eric into almost dropping the iPad.

"Dude, I'm sorry—didn't mean to look through her stuff."

"No worries, brother," Manny said, his expression pained. "We got into it right before you radioed in. She lets anything slip about our preps, and their families'll be beating a path to our door—and then I gotta be the heartless monster who shoves a shotgun in their faces and tells 'em to leave. But my daughter thinking I'm the biggest jerk who ever lived is the least of my problems right now." He pulled Eric to the corner and nervously glanced around. "Ed and Mina are trapped at home," Manny whispered. "They're sick."

"Jesus, Mary, and Joseph," Eric said, mouth agape. Ed Houston, an accountant, supervised the group's logistics and supply—his meticulous nature made him a natural for the job. Mina Houston, a nurse and the group medic, was six months pregnant.

"Ed called last night, just before the cell towers started goin' down," Manny croaked. "They can't go to the hospital—wouldn't do any good, 'cause hospitals are all deathtraps by now, anyway. He all but—" Manny's voice caught in his throat. "He all but told me goodbye. He sounded so delirious . . ."

Eric pulled Manny into a hug; he didn't need to be told the odds. The Houstons lived in Boulder, Colorado, a city of more than one hundred thousand people, north of the almost three million who lived in the Denver metropolitan area. If the flu didn't kill them, other people would.

"Who else knows?" Eric asked.

"Benny does, and I swore him to secrecy—that's why I got him downstairs tallying our supplies, in case he has to become the logistics guy if the Houstons don't make it." Manny swallowed hard and looked down at the tile floor. "Everyone's already on edge watching the world fall apart. Now isn't the time. I'll do it when we all sit down to go over everything."

"Can I grab Benny to help bring in our stuff?" Eric asked after a respectful pause.

"Sure. Shake Allan awake, too. He could use the workout," Manny said—Allan weighed 120 pounds soaking wet. "When you're done, park your truck out back with the others, and you and Susan grab some carne asada out of the fridge. Enjoy the homemade guacamole—I don't wanna place bets on the next time we'll see an avocado. Then head downstairs and get some sleep—I wanna put you on the LP/OP tomorrow morning."

Eric and Susan were amazed by the mountains of supplies the group had squirreled away as they hauled their cargo down creaky wooden stairs, one armload at a time, to the basement. Buckets of food, containers of medical supplies, and ammunition cans—"beans, bullets, and Band-Aids" in survival parlance—stretched floor to ceiling. Benny, who looked like an older, slightly heavier version of Manny, inventoried the new goods on a laptop computer and printed out hard-copy backups on the upstairs wireless printer.

A loud *snap* and a shooting pain in Eric's left foot instantly cured him of the fatigue that had been threatening to overwhelm him after days of running on caffeine and adrenaline. He barked a loud curse and looked down to find the big toe of his gym shoe clamped tight by a mousetrap.

"I thought you woulda seen that," Benny said in response to Eric's dirty look over Susan's howls of laughter. "The Orkin man's out of business right along with Costco, compadre. If critters eat our food, we starve."

Susan and Eric grabbed Carmen's leftovers from the fridge and wolfed them down in silence. He barely grunted goodnight to Susan as the kitchen clock chimed midnight, and headed back downstairs to the empty half of the basement that Manny called "Bachelor Country," where he and the other single men would lay their weary heads on military-surplus bunk beds.

He plopped onto his bottom bunk, exhausted and emotionally drained, and absentmindedly gazed around the dark and empty room, barely illuminated by a small outlet night light. Benny snored soundly in the bunk next to him. Allan's rack was empty, as he was on CQ duty, and his girlfriend, Julie, was bunked with Susan in the bachelorette room upstairs—Manny and Carmen had made clear that there would be no premarital bed sharing in their house. The two married couples—Matt and Angel, and Roger and Pastor Kris—would share the spare bedroom.

Eric slid to his knees and thanked God for shepherding Susan and him to safety, prayed for the Houstons and their unborn child, and asked for strength in the days ahead. He had barely managed to ask for mercy for his former students before he broke down, their faces flashing before him as he covered his face and sobbed. Eric wiped his nose on the back of his hand and crawled into his bunk, the outpouring of grief sapping what little energy he had left.

Oh, God, did I abandon them? Eric asked the Almighty before sleep claimed him.

The group never heard from Ed and Mina Houston again.

CHAPTER 5

S usan slapped her cheek a second too late to stop the mosquito that had dropped by the LP/OP for a late-night snack.

On the bright side, I'm awake now, she said to herself as she peeled off her black leather work glove and scratched the itch, scraping off a strip of the green paint she had slathered on her face for her six-hour shift watching the woods around the retreat. Susan made out the silhouette of Manny's house—coal black save for the faint starlight dancing on its array of rooftop solar panels—two hundred meters downhill from the LP/OP dug just inside the woods.

It was her first guard stint since she and Eric had arrived three days prior, and she realized an hour into her shift that sweltering in an earthen-roofed foxhole in full combat uniform in the dog days of August was not her idea of a good time. Susan briefly pondered what she hated more—the sticky heat, the bugs, or the face paint—before realizing she would miss all three when she was standing watch in January.

With two hours to go before her midnight end of shift, she reached for the green military surplus TA-1 landline radiophone connecting the LP/OP with the CQ desk in anticipation of the hourly radio check—the current CQ always called her several minutes early. *And I have a pretty good suspicion as to why*, she thought with a wry smile as the phone's dim glow-in-the-dark disc flashed with a *click-clack* sound to stealthily announce the incoming call. She cranked up some current with the thumb switch and squeezed the rubber push-to-talk button.

"Base, this is Eyes, send your traffic, over," she told Eric.

"How you doing out there?"

"Hot and tired, but it beats being an unburied corpse back in Wisconsin. You?"

"Lousy—I've been trying to write in my journal while you're watching the line for uninvited guests, but I have writer's block."

"You wanna switch? I'll stare at a blank page while you get assaulted by mosquitoes."

"No chance. You got a radiation reading?"

Susan knelt in the foxhole and briefly flashed the LCD readout screen of the handheld dosimeter Eric had panic-bought following Russia's ill-conceived invasion of Ukraine. Rumors had swirled on ham radio and local CB frequencies that Seattle had been nuked, and that the Columbia Generating Station in eastern Washington had melted down. While Manny thought the rumors were hogwash, he had the dosimeter placed in the LP/OP just in case.

"Zero, thank goodness," Susan reported. "Then again, if I start glowing in the dark, I won't have to stand watch at night anymore, will I?"

Eric laughed. "Nice try—I'm not gonna pick up your slack on the schedule just because you become a post-atomic mutant. Out." He set the bulky phone on the oaken CQ desk and glared at the blank page mocking him. Eric had stashed a small box of blank books during one of his summer supply runs from Wisconsin; chronicling this unprecedented historical event would be how he kept sane. A brisk walk—Eric's traditional cure for writer's block—wasn't an option; his camouflage uniform, and his helmet, tactical vest, and rifle leaning against the wall, reminded him that he had a post and couldn't abandon it.

The burgundy walls of Manny's home office, which only weeks prior had held family pictures and some of his work and military awards, were now plastered with local, state, and national maps, as well as dry-erase boards listing the radio frequencies and passwords in use, and who was on duty doing what, and where.

A collection of radios lined the front of the desk. Next to the TA-1 sat a single-sideband CB base radio, a police scanner, a marine band radio, and one of the handheld MURS radios that each group member carried to talk to one another. Multi-Use Radio Service radios were affordable, had decent range for their size, and most importantly, were relatively unknown by the general public, which meant more privacy. A yellow handheld radio that scanned the popular Family Radio Service and General Mobile Radio Service frequencies sat at the desk's far end. It was useless for gathering intelligence—contrary to misleading advertising, their range was limited to a few hundred feet in Montana's forests and mountains. However, because the cheap and ubiquitous radios likely would be standard issue for criminal gangs, it would pick up their chatter and serve as an early warning system. A corner desk held the ham radio that served as the group's window to what was left of the world.

A notebook sat on the desk for the CQ to log every transmission overheard; it was an almost impossible task during the first few days of the collapse, when the airwaves were a jumbled mess of overlapping and frantic transmissions, but traffic had thinned out as people lost power or died. Eric flipped to a random entry.

0314 HOURS, 17 AUGUST (CB CHANNEL 9): WOMAN AND DAUGHTER OUT OF GAS ON I-15 NORTH NEAR GATES OF THE MOUNTAINS EXIT, MILE MARKER 209, CALLING FOR HELP FROM ANYONE LISTENING.

0345 HOURS, 17 AUGUST: WOMAN FROM 0314 CALL ASKS TRUCK PULLING UP BEHIND HER IF HE'S RESPONDING TO HER DISTRESS CALL. SCREAMING, THEN SILENCE. NOTHING FURTHER.

Eric snapped the notebook shut with a shiver and returned to work on his journal.

Pastor Kris and Roger got sprung from The Cooler once it was clear they weren't sick. It creeped me out to deliver their food to them in Tyvek overalls and a respirator like in those old pandemic movies, but they were such good sports about the inconvenience. They don't live far—Butte is only about an hour away—but they were the last to arrive. Kris probably wanted to do what she could for her flock before leaving them, which couldn't have been easy for her, even though she spent years weaving self-reliance and preparedness into her sermons.

At least they made it. I'm trying not to think about the Houstons.

Manny broke the bad news when we met for the first time since we all arrived. The joy of having everyone together was shattered after learning that two of our own—and their baby—are probably dead. I'll remember Carmen's screams for the rest of my life.

CHAPTER 6

"We gotta do something!" an exasperated Matt insisted, standing in Manny's living room in his uniform and tactical gear, his jet black rifle slung across his chest and his face paint masking the flush of his cheeks. He was set to replace Pete on the LP/OP, meaning Manny would have to take Pete aside and bear the horrible news about the Houstons a second time.

Eric understood the desire to "do something." Combat soldiers lived by a credo to never abandon a fallen comrade, and losing a bunch of soldiers to bring home one was the price of brotherhood—you risked everything for your buddy because he would risk everything for you. But in this case, it was an oath that could not be honored.

"Do what, Matt? Mount a rescue mission?" Eric said with as measured a tone as he could muster. "You're talking about crossing a whole lot of Montana and all of Wyoming to get to them. Right now, we can't get reliable news about what's going on in Helena, and that's ten miles away. The phones are down, Ed and Mina don't have a ham radio, and the internet's on its last legs. Boulder's a round trip of sixteen hundred miles, and we have no idea which towns have burned to the ground, which ones are crawling with H7N9 flu, and which ones are stopping travelers and confiscating everything they have." Eric left unsaid that he knew the distance because he, too, had pondered a possible rescue.

Manny sighed. "Eric's right. It's a lousy thing to do, and it goes against everything we believe in, but if I let you or anyone else go gallivanting off on some kind of recovery operation, I'll be signing your death warrants." Carmen started to cry again as Matt slumped, defeated, on the couch next to his wife. Sniffles from group members punctured the long silence.

"I've asked Benny to take over as logistics boss—you don't take a single grain of rice without asking him first," Manny continued, trying to keep his voice steady. "I don't know if any of you have noticed, but Walmart is closed, and paper money's good for nothing but starting the fireplace or wiping our asses when our supply of Charmin runs out." He looked to Susan, who was consoling Carmen with Pastor Kris. "With Mina absent, you're promoted to chief medic. Congratulations—you just received the first battlefield commission of whatever the egghead historians like Eric over there end up callin' this." Eric wordlessly gave Manny the finger, which gave everyone but Pastor Kris a needed chuckle.

"I'll patch up everyone's boo-boos," Susan said. "I don't need to be saluted."

"This brings us to the business of staying alive," Manny said, wanting to change the subject from the Houstons. "Seeing as how law enforcement is on indefinite leave, I've drawn up a schedule of six-hour LP/OP and CQ shifts. Report at least fifteen minutes before your shift starts, in case the person you're relieving has information to relay. I want radio checks on the landline at least hourly, and any suspicious activity is to be reported immediately. And I'll say this once—no sleeping on guard duty. All it takes is one person napping on the job for all of us to wake up with our throats cut."

Manny held up a well-worn copy of *Infantry Rifle Platoon and Squad*, the Army's bible for small-unit tactics, and informed everyone that, starting the next day, they would begin training until they knew its tasks forward and backward, with a number of changes tailored to their situation. He also mandated that anyone going outside for any reason, as well as the CQ, had to wear camouflage and carry their rifle, without exception. Manny looked to Allan, who stooped to lift a large olive drab ammo can at his feet. "They're gonna love you, *jefe*," Manny muttered and slapped his back.

A chorus of groans rose from the group when Allan instructed them to pass the box around and surrender their smart phones, FitBits, and other handheld electronic devices with internet or GPS. "Our high-tech doodads aren't even working right now, but we have to play it safe in case service returns. No communications can go out without us knowing."

Jay, the group's mechanic, cleared his throat. "I modified this ammo can into a Faraday box, same as the ones we use to keep our spare radios safe from EMP—it's got a complete, nonconductin' metal seal that won't let any signals in or out."

"Is this necessary?" Angel groused as she gingerly laid her Apple Watch in the box.

"Absolutely necessary," Allan said, pushing his wire-rimmed glasses up to the bridge of his nose and sweeping a mop of sandy brown hair from his eyes. "The military discovered shortly after the fitness tracker craze started that their own soldiers' movements had inadvertently created detailed maps of secret bases through their tracking apps. And don't even get me started on Big Tech getting into bed with the government security state to illegally monitor our speech and thoughts. We're not taking any chances—or making any assumptions that whatever adversaries we end up facing will be technologically illiterate."

Manny raised a finger. "For the record, Luisa gave up her phone in the name of security, and if my teenager can pry hers out of her hands, so can you grown-ups."

"Um, Allan? Our sons . . ." Pastor Kris fretted in a quivering voice as she and Roger laid their iPhones into the box—they had been trying to reach their two grown children, who lived in Atlanta and Miami.

"I know, Reverend," Allan responded sympathetically. "Like I said, this hopefully is temporary. But we have no idea who could be listening, and if state and federal government are still around, how faithful they're gonna be to the Bill of Rights and the rule of law—since 9/11 and the Twitter Files, you can color me skeptical. You can keep your iPads, e-readers, and laptops, but you need to turn off their wireless capability and keep it off. Right after this meeting—not that it's been working—I'll be unplugging the house's router. We can't have anything on that could act as a beacon for any bad guys with a device that seeks out Wi-Fi."

The box came back around to Allan, who set it down with thin, trembling arms. "One last thing, and this is vital," Manny said, stepping forward. "Under no circumstance is the CQ, or anyone at any time, to respond to any unknown radio caller without my permission. One of the main factors that will determine whether we live or die is our ability to remain undetected, and one wrong move on the radio could lead the world to our door. We're sittin' on mountains of guns and ammo, and we're trained to use 'em, but if the fifteen of us end up facing fifteen hundred starving and desperate people, we're gonna lose."

Travis raised his hand. "We got any news from outside the wire?"

Manny frowned. "If by news you mean a bunch of contradictory *basura*, we got plenty—reliable information, not so much. News stations and websites are down. Our police scanner at first gave us real-time intelligence of where trouble was brewing, but it became useless once first responders and dispatchers realized the situation was hopeless and stopped reporting for duty."

"A lot of cops probably saw the writin' on the wall and bolted the moment they called for backup and none came—looks like the old 'defund the police' crowd finally got their wish," Travis said. "I didn't even wait *that* long to pop smoke with Matt and Angel here."

Matt slapped Travis on the back. "We're glad you did, dude."

Allan saw a hunger for information in the faces of friends who suddenly found themselves in a cold-turkey detox from twenty-four-hour news and social media feeds; their smart phones—which for many Americans had been all but glued to their hands and eyes—were locked away in a box at his feet. "It looks like we're back to the old days when radio reigned supreme. There are ham radio operators who still have power, as well as a handful of shortwave stations, here and abroad, that are still on the air. Our most reliable information source right now is Redoubt Radio—it's an emergency ham radio network based in Idaho that's run by preppers and survivalists like us. We don't know much right now, but what we've heard is . . . um, sobering."

The group listened aghast, sitting on the edges of their seats, as Allan upended what was left of their world. The president, or whoever was acting as president, had declared martial law nationwide. Rioters were ripping major cities to shreds, with no law enforcement or National Guard in sight, and surviving governments had lost count of the pandemic's casualties. Multiple sources had reported that all of Washington, D.C. had burned to the ground, and that the governors of several states were openly threatening secession over the federal government's mishandling of the crisis. The governor of Texas had one-upped the president—she not only issued shoot-on-sight orders to deal with criminals, but also granted blanket amnesty to any civilian or neighborhood watch group that stopped violent crime or looting with deadly force. The rest of the world wasn't faring any better—it seemed as if no corner of the globe was spared from the H7N9 virus, and world economies had promptly followed America's down the drain.

Allan wiped his brow and promised to compose a one-page newsletter whenever he could and tack it to the bulletin board that Manny had bolted to the living room wall. He also pledged his free time to help members reach their loved ones—Pastor Kris and Roger held back tears when he told them that they were at the front of the line.

"That's a great place to end this," Manny said, not wanting the discussion to devolve into the spreading of anxiety and rumors. "Listen up, everyone—we're gonna be OK. This is what we've prepared for. We're not some group of frightened survivors huddled around a candle in the dark with a hand-crank radio and a can of cold refried beans. We knew what was coming, we knew we couldn't rely on the government to take care of us, and we got ready."

"Proverbs 22:3," Pastor Kris said. "A prudent person foresees the danger ahead and takes precautions; the simpleton goes blindly on and suffers the consequences."

"Amen, Reverend," Travis said, looking around the group. "Keep all this in mind when we start our tactical training tomorrow. Our survival depends on each other. From this point forward, mistakes are gonna be measured in blood."

A hush fell across the room.

"No pressure," Angel muttered.

CHAPTER 7

The clock on the CQ wall told Eric he had forty-five minutes until Julie relieved him at midnight. He grabbed the TA-1 for a quick radio check with Susan, and sipped his cold coffee from a mug positioned well away from the electronics. The military and teaching—and his late German mother who started him on coffee when he was six—had turned him into a java addict. Eric tried not to think about the day that his supply would run out.

His muse had returned from wherever she had been hiding; Eric took pen to paper, his hand struggling to keep up with his mind as the words flowed freely.

I have an hour left and the radios are silent, so maybe I'll take a stab after all at why America crumbled to pieces in such short order.

The simple answer is that we suffered the double whammy—talk about lousy timing—of a long-overdue economic collapse and a deadly pandemic. But America endured all sorts of catastrophes prior to this: the Great Depression and the Great Recession (not to mention all the depressions and panics that came before them), a brutal civil war, two world wars, the September 11 attacks, and so forth. Why did we persevere through all those, only to collapse like a house of cards now? The answer, in my arrogant opinion, is that America has been a house of cards for a long time, just waiting for the right huff and puff to blow it down.

A case of the flu is a timely analogy. When healthy people catch it, they're miserable for a while, but they make a full recovery. When sick or weak people catch it, they die. Our nation, from the White House down to Main Street, was sick and weak, and as a result, we couldn't fight this one off.

I'm amazed it took this long for our financial day of reckoning to come; Uncle Sam had one hell of a big bag of tricks to stave it off for as long as he did. We had two back-to-back emergencies—the Great Recession and the COVID-19 pandemic—that Congress essentially "solved" by drowning them in trillions of dollars in fake money on top of more than half a century of unchecked deficit spending. But in the end, the bill always comes due. Anyone with a third-grade education understands that if you keep spending more than you make, ratcheting the national debt higher and higher and faster and faster, there will come a mathematically inevitable default. But Americans foolishly thought that the Greatest Nation Ever in the History of the Universe was somehow immune from the laws of mathematics. Funny thing about the universe—it runs on math, which is why Albert Einstein figured out how the whole shebang works with a blackboard and chalk.

Americans wanted the huge social safety net the Democrats promised and the low taxes the Republicans promised, and kept electing politicians who were more than willing to drive us off the cliff if it meant reelection. Our money was backed by nothing but hot air and empty words, and the day finally came when our creditors no longer trusted our ability to pay them back. Things went from bad to worse when the damn fool public ran on the banks and demanded their savings in cash, prompting the government to start printing it like mad and running inflation even more white hot. Right when the economy started to tank, H7N9 struck—ten times as contagious as COVID-19 was, and a hundred times deadlier. While coronavirus preyed on the elderly and the weak, H7N9 went after everyone with the same lethal ferocity.

But like I wrote earlier, this disaster isn't America's first rodeo. So what changed? I guess we did. We became so divided that uniting against this latest threat became impossible.

America became two nations long ago: a blue, liberal one, and a red, conservative one, both of which in the end absolutely loathed one another. The divide ran so deep that we had nothing left in common at all—ironically, I think Northerners and Southerners during the Civil War had much more in common than Red and Blue America did. Both sides ended up with their own news, their own entertainment, and thanks to social media, associated only with their own kind; Facebook killed our sense of national identity right along with high school reunions. The divide crept into everything—movies, TV, sports, late-night comedy, you name it. There was no escaping it. Things got so bad that people stopped recognizing the legitimacy of elections; the losing side always reflexively accused the winning side of fraud. Democracy is in deep trouble when people stop believing that it works. Well, these people got their wish—it's gonna be a long time before anyone gets elected to anything.

In the past, we were divided on the issues, but at the end of the day, we were all Americans. That mutual respect evaporated long ago. We devolved to mutual disrespect, and then mutual hatred. The other side stopped being merely wrong, and became stupid and worthless as well. Abraham Lincoln said that a house divided cannot stand, and when this catastrophe struck, we couldn't band together because we had become a collection of ideological tribes instead of one nation, indivisible. Notice I didn't write "under God"—America told Him to buzz off a long time ago, and it seems He's more than happy to grant our wish. In the end, I think

America just gave up on itself. Rather than unite to face the crisis, we chose a great unraveling. Maybe that's what the "egghead historians" Manny joked about will end up calling this. It does have a nice ring to it.

Just like the Soviet Union before us, which could put on a great May Day parade of military might to cover up its systemic and terminal rot, the United States of America was a mighty tree that looked tall and strong on the outside, but was rotted out and infested with termites. All it took was one good shove, and down it came.

This would've been one hell of a lecture for my students. The ones who aren't dead, anyway. Damn.

Eric closed his journal and massaged the crick in his neck as Julie walked in to relieve him. The group's tech-head, her fiery red hair in a braid, leaned her rifle against the wall and opened up her paper-thin Apple laptop with a welcoming chime.

"Allan agreed to turn the Wi-Fi back on for a bit so I can poke around if the internet is still up. We figure it's safer at zero dark thirty." Julie slid into the black leather office chair and pulled a can of Coke from the cargo pocket of her camouflage trousers, which hung loose on her thin frame. "Don't you dare say enjoy them while they last," she admonished Eric. "I hear that one more time, and I'll have no problem pouring this precious commodity on your head."

"I won't," he assured with a laugh as he grabbed his rifle and gear to head downstairs. *I hope I enjoyed America while it lasted,* Eric thought over the creak of stairs to his bunk. He desperately wanted to sit in the kitchen and wait for Susan, but sleep was calling to him. *America had its problems, but I will miss it so.*

CHAPTER 8

Lieutenant Governor Jeremy Matthews paced the worn nylon carpeting of the spartan nondescript office, his flask in one hand and a Smith & Wesson handgun in the other.

He nervously set the gun on the dusty desk next to pictures of the unknown office worker's husband and kids, and unscrewed the flask with an unsteady hand to belt back a gulp of vodka. "This is it," he said to himself. *We're—I'm—really gonna go through with this.*

Matthews had no idea where he was, or how the mercenaries who had brought him to the abandoned agricultural supply business outside of Helena had managed to get the power on. All he knew was that it was time to seize his destiny. But the rough men in the employ of his benefactor wouldn't be doing Jeremy's dirty work for him—he would have to do that.

It was far too late to turn back, Matthews realized as he grabbed the gun with both hands and stared at it, the faint scent of gunpowder and cordite reminding him that he had already become a murderer. He began pacing again, loosening his tie from the collar of his wrinkled dress shirt before anxiously running his hand through jet black hair dyed to cover up the full gray that had set in upon turning fifty. The lieutenant governor briefly considering having another snort of liquor before forcing himself to temporarily abstain until the deed was done.

The sound of boots on metal grating announced the entrance of the deadly-looking mercenary whose men had snuck Matthews there under cover of darkness from the State Emergency Coordination Center, where he had been holed up since the collapse. The mercenary's mottle-painted military rifle dangled from a triple-point harness over a brown tactical vest; between his gear and his utility khaki trousers and tan ball cap, he matched a Hollywood screenwriter's stereotype of a soldier of fortune.

Red Beard pulled off his hat and scratched the red hair and matching goatee that had earned him his nickname from men who feared him and what he was capable of doing. "Let's go, Mister Governor. It's time."

Matthews nervously blew out a ragged breath. "Don't call me that yet."

"Well, it's gonna be official in about three minutes," he shot back unsympathetically, jerking his head toward the doorway.

"Could you just give me a fucking moment? I'm freaking the fuck out here!" Matthews barked, rubbing his head and waving his gun.

In a flash, Red Beard closed the distance, grabbing Matthews with iron talons and painfully locking his arm upright so that his handgun pointed at the ceiling. "You ever—*ever*—flag me again with a loaded fucking weapon," he growled in his face, lower lip bulging with a wad of dip, "and it's your ass—I don't give a shit how important you are to the boss. Understand?"

Matthews meekly nodded. Red Beard grabbed the pistol from his hands to ensure that the safety was on before shoving it back into the politician's chest with barely concealed contempt. "This is what you wanted. Let's go," he said, his angry enunciation of each word carrying an implicit threat that he was done dealing with cowardice or second thoughts.

Red Beard ushered Matthews out to a metal walkway that granted access to the second-floor offices overlooking the warehouse floor, which was empty aside from several scattered wooden pallets and abandoned forklifts—once it was obvious that the US dollar would go the way of the Weimar mark, farmers, like every other consumer, had bought up anything and everything tangible while their money still had value. The rising sun peeked through a line of top-floor windows on the warehouse's far side, illuminating a path to a set of metal stairs leading down to a small general purpose room, its fluorescent strip lights shining like a beacon through a lone interior pane. Matthews stepped through the door to find two of Red Beard's equally intimidating henchmen standing over a hooded woman lying motionless on the yellowed tile floor in her pajamas, her wrists flex-cuffed behind her back and ankles bound. With a nod from their boss, the duo hoisted the woman to her knees and ripped the burlap bag from her head.

Claire Kellerman's eyes jammed shut as her world exploded from stifling darkness to blinding light. She squinted as her vision adjusted to see two men standing over her . . .

Jeremy?!

Her eyes went wide as saucers in anger as much as fear, the pain from the sudden input of light jamming into her brain like an ice pick. She screamed into the thick gag silencing her and flexed her arms against their bonds in a show of defiance, until a menacing step forward from Jeremy's bearded friend cowed her.

Red Beard held up a small bottle of water, Claire silently nodding her consent to the unspoken deal of a drink for cooperation. A gloved hand yanked the gag out of her mouth and thrust the bottle in, which Claire greedily gulped, lukewarm water running down the front of her pajama top.

"Jeremy," she gasped, "where's Ben? What did you do with him?"

"Nothing—my business is with you," Matthews lied; he had shot her holier-than-thou husband as a warm-up to steel himself for what he had to do next—what he wanted to do. He had spent his life rising through the ranks of Montana politics, paying his dues and putting in his time. He had been elected to the House and then the Senate, spending years fixing the support and forging the alliances he would need to run for governor. When his chance came, he seized it, and his momentum seemed unstoppable—until he was utterly blindsided by Claire, a rancher twenty years his junior whose dark-horse, grass-roots campaign came out of nowhere to sweep him aside in the Republican primary and propel her to victory. When the elected lieutenant governor abruptly died four months into his term, Matthews exerted his still significant pull, and the Republican establishment and legislative leaders strong-armed Claire into appointing Matthews to fill the remainder of the term as a condition of their continued support. Facing the reality of her legislative agenda being dead on arrival, Claire very reluctantly agreed.

Matthews struggled to recall the verbal comeuppance he had rehearsed endlessly since the plot was hatched, but the words were nowhere to be found. "There's gonna be a change in management," he blurted.

"Is that what this is about, Jeremy? Politics?" she cautiously lectured as the older man started to nervously fidget with the pistol. "Jeremy, there's no more politics. No more elections, no more campaigns. There's no throne. It's all gone. The world's ended." She struggled to keep her balance as she fought the panic coursing through her, speaking to Jeremy like a mother trying to explain a complicated issue to a child. "A lot of people out there need our help, and they'll die if they don't get it." *And you're barely capable of tying your own shoes, much less rising to this challenge.* "That's what we—you and me and everyone else—have to focus on. Helping people make it through this."

Matthews shot a nervous glance at Red Beard. "Oh, Jeremy, who put you up to this?" Claire sadly asked, already knowing the answer.

The hulking mercenary didn't acknowledge Matthews at all; the lieutenant governor looked back at Claire, and realized in a moment of clarity from the anxiety and alcohol fogging his brain that the situation had become a matter of his survival as well. If he didn't finish what his new friends were expecting of him, Claire Kellerman likely would be the last thing he ever saw.

Matthews raised the handgun, which shook in his hands like a leaf as the mercenaries on both sides of the governor stepped clear.

"You have to make me a promise, Jeremy. My children," Claire rapidly pleaded, eyes watering and lip quivering as she rose on her knees; her two youngest sons were attending Montana State University, and hadn't been heard from since the collapse. "If they turn up, leave them be. They can't hurt you. Please. You won. Spare them. *Please.*"

Matthews stopped himself just in time from looking to Red Beard for guidance. *You're in charge now, dammit,* he castigated himself—*not him, not the little shit holding his leash. This should've been your job in the first place. So take it. Now.*

The handgun steadied in Matthews's grip. "You have my word," he said—truthfully, this time—before unloading the magazine into the governor.

CHAPTER 9

Rayford Schneider spun at the sound of his eldest daughter screaming for him over the sounds of the dying battle that had engulfed their town.

Amy dashed toward her father down the small main drag of the tiny village of Drummond, her shoes crunching on the broken glass scattered in front of what was left of its businesses. She collapsed into her father's arms as a nine-man squad of National Guard soldiers darted past them to help finish routing the marauders that had barreled down I-90 at sunrise to overrun the ranching town. A menacing eight-wheeled Stryker armored personnel carrier rolled down the road, keeping pace alongside the dismounted troops.

"I was so scared," Amy cried, shaking with fear as her father frantically patted her down for injuries, not believing his eyes that she was all right. "Are Mom and Kendra and . . ."

Rayford hugged her tight, stroking her matted hair. "They're fine," he said, voice trembling. "Everyone's fine—"

Amy screamed and dropped to her knees with the deafening *pum-pum-pum* of the olive drab Stryker's unmanned roof-mounted .50-caliber machine gun spitting out its huge rounds at the State Route 1 overpass a quarter mile away, where the surviving marauders were fleeing south over the railroad line that had long served the area's ranchers. The driver floored it and the Stryker tore down the road to press the attack.

"Rafe!" An old man cradling a double-barreled shotgun flagged down Rayford from down the side street and turned to the trio of soldiers following him. "Right there, boys—you want someone on the Town Council, he's your guy!"

Rayford looked his daughter in the eyes, turning her away from the storefront of Drummond's lone market, its shattered front door propped open by the bloody body of the owner who had died trying to protect what little he had left. "Go straight home, hon—I'll be along soon." She tearfully nodded and ran off as the soldiers approached.

A handsome, chiseled officer stepped forward. "Pleased to meet you, Mister Schneider, although I hate the circumstances—Captain Jeff Antonelli, Charlie Company, 163rd Cavalry Regiment."

"Call me Rafe. Thank you—you guys showin' up when you did is nothin' short of divine intervention. Are they gone?"

"Roger—killed a bunch of 'em and got the rest on the run," Antonelli answered, a burst of fire from the Stryker lending credence to his claim. "Sir, I know you've been through a lot, but we gotta talk."

"I'm on the Town Council, like you heard, but you need to be havin' this conversation with the mayor—"

"She's dead," Antonelli cut him off in an emotionless monotone after months of being the bearer of horrible news to far too many people. "You're all that's left."

Rayford took a staggered step back and pulled off his ball cap to run a hand through his hair. "Aw, Jesus Christ, God Almighty."

"We've set up an aid station at City Hall to treat the injured the best we can with what we've got, but it's not much, so any help you folks can spare would be appreciated."

"Spare?!" Rayford asked incredulously. "Listen, I don't mean to sound ungrateful after you folks saved us from bein' pillaged and murdered, but we barely had anything left *before* the damn Mongol horde came ridin' into town! We're runnin' low on medicine *and* food—we asked the ranchers and farmers around us if they could give us a hand, and they told us, to a man, to play hide and go screw ourselves! Can you get us anything? Anything at all?"

Antonelli nodded. "Yes, if you work with us. The governor's trying to restore order, and keeping I-90 open between what's left of Helena and what's left of Missoula is a big part of that—Drummond's smack in the middle, which makes it prime real estate. We'd like to keep a follow-on platoon here as a permanent garrison, augmented by as many able-bodied adults as you can spare, which would mean security for you, and some food resupply—not much, 'cause there isn't much to go around right now, but better than nothing."

Rayford blew noisily. A distant pair of gunshots announced the summary executions of two marauders who couldn't escape town. "Well, it's this or starve to death or get slaughtered by some other group of bandits, so it looks like you got yourself a deal, captain. Lord, ain't this some mess."

"We won't let you down," Antonelli said as they shook hands. "Let's get to work."

***

The man watching the new mayor seal the deal from the small mountain across the interstate from Drummond set down his binoculars with disgust and shifted his elbows on his uncomfortable bed of loose stone.

"And with a handshake, another town unwittingly makes a deal with the devil thinking it'll keep 'em safe."

An older man with steely gray eyes lowered his own binoculars and sat back against the rocky outcropping that provided cover and concealment from the people below. "Well, Raider, it's worked everywhere else that whoever's in charge has tried it—pay off a bunch of bandits to sack a town, then backstab 'em by sendin' in the National Guard or local militia to save the day, and win over hearts and minds. No honor among thieves," he explained in a Southern drawl. "If it's stupid but it works, it ain't stupid."

"Lotta cattle around here, and Drummond is where I-90 meets the railroad—whoever's sitting in Helena playing Napoleon is getting smart about controlling food, which is gonna be all that matters when winter comes," Raider said, scratching his beard. "So, what's the plan, boss?"

The older man nodded back the way they came, over the small mountain at the foot of the Garnet Range. "Get outta here before they spot us."

Raider stowed his binoculars and rose to a crouch, swinging his SCAR-H military rifle around to his chest. "After that, smart ass."

"Bide our time," the man said, scanning the rocky gully that would conceal their withdrawal to the rest of their survival group on the mountain's far side. "Wait for this little wannabe tyrant, whoever he is, to fuck up, and be ready to exploit it. And in the meantime, we find friends. Lots of them."

"Provided any friends are left alive come spring."

"Boy, you're Mister Jolly Happy Fucking Sunshine," the man shot back. "Let's move—you lead."

CHAPTER 10

Manny cautiously crept through the woods near his home, silently praying that his wife wouldn't shoot him dead.

He struggled to stay alert as he scanned the pitch dark for the LP/OP where his Carmencita was standing vigil; the adrenaline that had surged through Manny and his teammates two hours earlier when they killed the bandits at the Route 12 campground had long since worn off. Fatigue weighed on the team like hundred-pound rucksacks, and Manny wanted to get everyone cleaned up, fed, and bedded down. He had radioed Angel on the CQ desk to let Carmen know they were coming, but that didn't stop him from worrying that she would mistake him for a post-apocalyptic marauder and blow him away.

"Halt! Identify yourself!" Carmen hissed from the black.

Manny sighed with relief—no friendly fire today. "Manny Landeros, leading a ten-person raiding party."

"Advance and be recognized."

Manny walked, slowly and deliberately, toward his wife's voice. One of the group's standard operating procedures was for every patrol to enter and leave the property at the LP/OP, which reduced the odds of a surprise attack on the retreat, because a party approaching from any other direction would immediately be known as foreign. He answered Carmen's verbal challenge with the password—having one person give the password for the group prevented a concealed enemy from learning it as soldier after soldier repeated it—then trudged toward the earthen covering of the LP/OP and knelt by the port through which Carmen was watching.

"Hey, baby, come here often?"

"Sorry, *señor*, but I'm married. You didn't even buy me a drink." Carmen sniffed the air loudly. "Besides, I smelled you before I heard you. You reek."

"I like a woman who plays hard to get," Manny said, beckoning his team forward in a single-file line and ordering Travis to assemble everyone in the barn adjacent to the house to clean their weapons and conduct an after-action review of their mission. Manny counted everyone off as they passed, reminding each of them to clear their weapons at the door. He leaned into the LP/OP to grab a quick kiss after Benny, the last man in line, shambled toward the barn.

"You do owe me a drink—I was worried sick," Carmen scolded her husband.

"I need one after tonight," Manny retorted in Spanish and followed his friends down the hill. The rust-red barn stood to the left of the Landeros home as one would see driving up the winding gravel driveway to the three-car garage. Built as a vanity project by the previous owner, Manny had converted it into a combination workshop, raw materials storage area, and multipurpose building. The side door, lined with white wood, blinked with light as each team member entered, but the barn's windows, like those of his home, were dark. The group practiced strict light discipline—no light was allowed to be on in any room at night without a blackout curtain drawn; in a world without grid power, artificial light would attract predators and desperate survivors like raw meat attracts wolves. Manny made a mental note to issue a standing order to keep the barn lights off until everyone was inside, so outside observers couldn't count the flashes to learn the group's size or their comings and goings.

He glanced over at his darkened home as he strolled up the gentle incline to the barn. The spacious house wasn't the most practical structure from which to ride out the collapse, but Carmen had made clear to him that she had no intention of living in a concrete bunker when they could afford their dream home—and that if he insisted on doing so, he had better hire a good attorney to make it through the annulment with anything more than the shirt on his back.

Manny chuckled at the memory as he opened the barn's side door, his eyes adjusting to the light just in time to catch Luisa leaping into his arms at full speed.

"Wow, Dad, you stink!" she said after kissing his cheek.

"So I've heard," Manny laughed. "Enough about me—shouldn't you be in bed?"

"Like we could sleep with everything going on," Pastor Kris said as she and Roger distributed mugs of hot chocolate to members of the assault team, who had carefully disassembled their rifles on plastic mats laid atop folding tables. While everyone made sure to order spare parts when they bought their firearms, they took no chances—one lost component would turn a weapon into an expensive paperweight.

Manny turned to his daughter, a smear of his camouflage paint across her face. "Do us a favor, *chiquita*—would you, Roger, and Pastor Kris be so kind as to break out some pancake mix and syrup and whip us up some breakfast?"

Luisa nodded and bounded out the door, her flip-flops smacking on the barn's epoxied concrete floor. Roger strolled up to Manny and handed him a mug of peppermint hot chocolate; the peppermint, Manny was pleased to discover as he took a long pull, was one-hundred-proof schnapps.

"Have one on the house. Figured you'd need a splash of secret ingredient after the night you guys had," Roger said as Manny downed the drink with impressive speed. "Part of me wishes I woulda gone with you."

"No, you don't—at least, not with that ticker of yours," Manny said. Roger had been diagnosed with heart arrhythmia a year prior; when the stock market showed early signs of a crash, he had the foresight to convince his preparedness-minded doctor into writing him several large prescriptions of his beta blocker to see him through as long as possible. Manny handed the mug back to Roger to the muted chorus of metal bristles scrubbing carbon from rifle bolts. "I can't wait to work with you on our side project once we get into more of a routine."

"You and me both—my liver, not so much," Roger said and left the barn with Kris.

Manny got the group's attention as he started breaking down his rifle so they could review the mission while it was still fresh in their minds—what went right, what went wrong, and what they could do better next time. His skin turned to gooseflesh at the thought of a "next time" as he turned the floor over to Eric.

"I don't think we need to rehash what was supposed to happen and what did happen; I think we rather decisively took care of the vermin problem we were presented," Eric said, running a cleaning rod down his rifle's barrel. "So, what did we do right?"

"I think we knocked this out of the park—I'll give this operation the Marine Corps seal of approval," Travis volunteered. "No offense to anyone, but I was worried a lot of you wouldn't pull the trigger."

Pete, the newest member of the group, and at twenty-two the youngest, shyly cleared his parched throat. "Eric, that was a great idea you had to grab the radios and maps out of the trucks. You think on your toes," he said to a number of "hear, hears." Eric felt a brief swell of pride when he heard Susan's voice among them.

"That reminds me—we need to see if that stuff has any intelligence value," Manny interjected. "Eric, Allan, Julie, congratulations—you just volunteered to become our intelligence section. After you three get some food and some sleep, go through that post-apocalyptic swag bag Susan and Jay collected."

Benny raised his hand and scratched his mussed black hair. "I wanna thank everyone for stayin' in your lanes—not runnin' in front of or behind one another—when you all rushed the objective. You eff that up, you either shoot your buddy, or your buddy shoots you. Thank God we didn't need the aid and litter team tonight."

"Amen," Eric said—he and Manny would have been responsible for carrying any wounded team members back to the rally point for Susan to stabilize.

"Oh, snap!" Susan blurted as she reassembled her bolt. "Pete, Matt, you guys wore gloves while you were searching bodies, right?" Both men nodded; team members wore military-surplus leather gloves to protect them from all of the items in the Montana woods that could cut, puncture, and irritate skin. "Make sure you scrub 'em down with bleach and water—same goes for those boots you used to send the dearly departed off to hell singing high soprano. Wash your uniforms too, and provided Manny says it's OK, take a long shower until you come out shinier than a new dime."

A hint of worry crossed Matt's face. "Hasn't the pandemic burned out by now, Doc?"

"Yes, and that's not what concerns me. Basic sanitation collapsed along with everything else, which means people are drinking untreated water, pooping everywhere, piling trash that attracts rats and fleas—you get the idea. Those good ole' boys you were manhandling could've had dysentery, cholera, typhoid, all sorts of bad stuff. And with the crude tattoos some of those jokers were sporting, you can add hepatitis to the list too."

Matt grimaced. "Manny, request permission to fill the shower stall with hand sanitizer and float in it like Luke Skywalker after the wampa kicked his ass in *The Empire Strikes Back*." Chuckles rippled across the barn.

"Denied, but the long shower is authorized, and make sure to clean your gear like Doc ordered," Manny said—hot water was rationed because the house's solar water heaters couldn't keep up with fifteen people bathing whenever they wanted.

Eric opened the floor to discussion of what went wrong and what they could improve while they reassembled their rifles and wiped down sidearms that weren't fired. "We left behind some good stuff," Jay said, wiping his hand on his slight middle-age paunch. "I understand the short notice we had, but we shoulda had a plan to strip the trucks of their tires, batteries, and spare parts. If this collapse lasts a long time, the lack of parts'll sideline a lot of vehicles that'd otherwise run. If it's all the same, Manny, I'd like to talk to you about sneakin' back there and seein' what we can make off with."

"No offense, but you up to it? You were draggin' your tail running around out there."

"Don't let the gut and the salt-and-pepper hair fool ya—I can hang with you kids, provided you don't pair me again with Flo-Jo over there," Jay said, nodding his head at Susan, who impishly stuck her tongue at him in return.

Manny wiped his nose on the back of his solvent- and carbon-soiled hand. "I think we covered all the important bases—we're struggling to stay awake. I wanna say that I'm proud of all of you—your bravery rivaled any unit I was ever with. This had to be done, and you did it. One last thing, however, and this is crucial." His expression turned deadly serious. "Never, ever discuss this with any outsiders. We don't live in Texas, where the governor granted everyone a scumbag hunting permit with no limit. If law and order is ever restored, the authorities might consider what we just did mass murder rather than a community service. We can talk about it amongst ourselves, just not outside the wire—and Pastor Kris wants you all to know her door is always open."

Manny let his warning soak in before ordering everyone to grab some breakfast and some sleep. He motioned Jay over to discuss a mission to cannibalize the bandits' trucks as everyone else shuffled out of the barn, rifles slung on their backs and food on their minds as the rising sun began coloring the eastern horizon.

CHAPTER 11

Eric shoved a forkful of pancakes dripping with syrup and canned butter into his mouth, absentmindedly gazing at the rest of the assault team packing the kitchen to standing room only and wolfing down flapjacks as fast as Roger and Pastor Kris could fry them.

Luisa spooned a dollop of home-canned strawberry preserves onto Cousin Benny's plate and gave him a kiss on the cheek. Benny was the first person brought into the group after Manny, Eric, Travis, and Matt left the military. He had lived an outdoorsman's life when he wasn't on the road as a long-haul trucker, but his wife had grown tired of him always being away and left him for another man. Doomsday prepping gave him a desperately needed sense of purpose, and he took to it like peas take to carrots.

Benny followed his cousin to Helena and took a job with the Montana Department of Transportation, where he met and brought in Jay, a talented mechanic who, like Benny, was divorced. The retreat owed many of its upgrades, such as the security fence and its iron front gate, to their hard work and strong backs. They also built the retreat's wooden outhouse so all fifteen of them wouldn't overload the septic tank; with autumn only days away, group members began worrying about trudging through snow and whipping winds to answer nature's call.

Eric snuck a glance at Susan, who thumbed a dribble of syrup from the corner of her mouth, and smirked as he recalled the fateful day he met the Lake Geneva Fire Department paramedic at a career expo at his high school. He had overheard her talking with the firefighter at their booth about the fragility of the economy and the deep financial trouble that neighboring Illinois was in; he inserted himself into the discussion and quickly got the feeling that she shared the group's mindset. However, Susan proved to be a hard fish to reel in, likely interpreting his sincere efforts to recruit a medical professional as an insincere effort to get into her pants. He eventually won her trust, and her friendship.

Matt walked into the kitchen with Angel, who had just wrapped up her CQ shift. Matt had returned to Tennessee after his discharge, where he earned an engineering degree and got a job with an urban planning firm. He married Angel, a first-grade teacher, which meant she also married into their eclectic post-apocalyptic family, but she was a city girl who tolerated, but never embraced, Matt's survivalism; Eric once joked to Manny that he was saving one of his blank journals so he could write a book about the struggle to get Angel to even hold a gun, much less learn to shoot one. Eric sensed that she, too, was struggling with leaving her students when the Unraveling began, but she always changed the subject the few times he attempted to discuss it with her.

Shortly after Eric earned his ham radio license, he happened across Allan on the airwaves and struck up a rag-chew that led to his membership. The Spokane native brought in Julie, who thought what they were doing was cool and, unlike Angel, needed no prodding. Allan, who had made a full recovery from his queasiness on the mission, held out his plate so Pastor Kris could serve him seconds. Manny and Carmen had brought in Kris and Roger after meeting them at an interfaith prayer breakfast hosted by the Cathedral of St. Helena; the middle-aged couple's passion for organic gardening made them a vital acquisition for a post-collapse world bereft of artificial fertilizers and pesticides.

Pete handed his empty plate to Luisa and hugged Pastor Kris before heading to Bachelor Country to bed down. The young and talented electrician was one of her parishioners, who she recommended to Manny when he wanted to add the solar water heater. Pete jumped on the offer to join up before Manny even finished his sentence; he had jokingly told Pete that his membership was contingent upon shaving off his mullet haircut, and the eager young man went straight to the nearest barber. The memory always made Eric smile; shortly after they arrived, he told Pete that he didn't care if he grew his hair to his ass like Crystal Gayle, as long as he kept the lights on.

Eric's smile withered as he remembered Ed and Mina Houston. The newlywed couple jumped out at Manny on a preparedness website he had stumbled upon one day—unlike the tinfoil hatters on the forum with them, they had useful skills and their heads were screwed on straight. They spent a three-day weekend as Manny's and Carmen's guests, and accepted the subsequent invitation to join.

I hope you two and the baby are OK. If not, I hope you're safe in God's hands, Eric silently prayed before rising with a groan to hand off his dish and silverware and plod to his bunk, realizing with a clandestine whiff under his arm that he would eventually have to clean up and do his laundry. Shortly after their arrival, the group lugged the washer and dryer to the garage to convert the laundry room into a makeshift doctor's office for Susan—they couldn't justify wasting power and their limited supply of natural gas to do something they could do by hand. Roger had artfully turned scrap wood, dowels, and lacquer into two scrubbing boards, and had strung up clotheslines in the barn.

Eric lumbered by Susan, who was reading Allan's latest news report tacked to the living room bulletin board.

"Good job out there," she said.

"Right back at you," he grunted—his bunk was calling to him like a siren from Greek mythology.

"We just killed people, Eric."

He stopped and turned to face her. "Yeah, we did."

She looked down at the unloaded black rifle slung across her chest, raising her hands away from it as if it was cursed. "I was hoping to never have to fire this thing in anger," she resignedly said. "I saw what these weapons can do firsthand when I responded to that shooting. My patient died in my arms in that parking lot. And now I went and did this to someone myself."

Eric sighed. "Susan, do you remember the time we ran into one another at Woodstock Groundhog Days, just before the shit hit the fan?" Susan nodded with the faintest of smiles as she recalled her annual pilgrimage to the celebration held in the small northern Illinois town where the cult classic movie *Groundhog Day* was filmed. "There was this guy on the square sculpting this beautiful angel, wings outstretched, out of an ice block. Must've had fifty people around him watching him work. That man used his chainsaw to create an object of beauty. Had he been a maniac, he could've used it to slaughter his audience. His chainsaw had no mind of its own, and it wasn't inherently good or evil—just like your rifle. You wielded it tonight to end the reign of terror of some very bad men—and you shot one of them before he could shoot me. Thank you."

"You're welcome. And thank you for telling me what I needed to hear," Susan said. "But for the record, when all this is over, I'm having this fucking rifle melted down into gardening tools. I became a paramedic to save lives."

"I know. You saved mine tonight. You're a damned good paramedic. You're also a damned good soldier." *And the only reason I went to that stupid festival was because I knew you'd be there. Because I'm madly in love with you.* "Tell you what—how about we grab a cup of coffee tonight in the sunroom and talk about it? Nineteen hundred sound good?"

"I just might be awake by then. You're on."

"I'll put a reminder in my phone, provided I can find where Allan hid it. And, uh, since the fiat currency in my wallet has become worthless, can you pay?"

Susan's brief laugh was stifled by a loud yawn. "Good night, Eric."

Now I'll definitely have to get cleaned up, he thought as he resumed course for his bunk. *Can't smell like I went ten rounds with a skunk.*

Travis's loud snores reverberated through the door to Bachelor Country. Eric was too tired to care, and also had no desire to roust a six-foot-two Marine cop and ask him to roll onto his side—he had risked death enough for one day.

A minute later, Eric's snores joined a growing chorus that echoed through the house.

***

Pastor Kris stomped her feet on the LP/OP's plywood floor to fight off the slight chill that she knew with dread would become chillier with each passing day. The final two hours before her 6 a.m. end of shift would be uncomfortable.

Her duties as counselor had kept her busy in the day since the ambush. Many of the participants sought her counsel and her prayers—more than a few tears were shed, and worries about what God would say on Judgment Day often turned into worries about loved ones, and exasperation over the collapse. She briefly closed her eyes and prayed for the thousandth time that her sons were alive and well, and was about to ask God yet again for their father's safe return from his current mission when the *click-clack* of the TA-1 field phone rose over the cold breeze on the gloomy, overcast night.

"How goes it, Eyes?" Julie asked.

Kris grinned—she liked working with CQs who weren't sticklers about radio procedure. "No complaints—the face paint covers up my age lines. What's up?"

"Just letting you know that the, uh, delivery boys are almost home," Julie said, being vague despite the fact that the only way for an eavesdropper to listen in on the TA-1 was to dig up the wire and splice in a line. "They left in one truck, but are coming back in two. Two trucks. You get that, over?"

Thank you, Heavenly Father. Thank you, thank you, thank you. "Two trucks—got it!"

Pastor Kris peered through her rifle scope at the dim and distant front gate. Two sets of headlights taped to thin slivers like cats' eyes crept up to the gate, where a figure jumped out to unlock it and wave the trucks through. As they approached, Kris could make out Jay and Benny leading the small convoy in Benny's four-by-four, while Travis, Pete, and Roger brought up the rear in a pickup absconded from the campground. From her uphill vantage point, Kris could see and hear spare tires, truck batteries, parts, and tools rattling in the stolen truck's bed.

She slewed her rifle to follow them, the sounds of tires rolling on gravel and the clanking spoils of war fading as the trucks crawled up the winding driveway to the barn. They pulled inside and shut the large doors behind them. The remainder of Kris's LP/OP shift passed quickly.

CHAPTER 12

The sun had just dipped below the horizon as Manny tiredly hung up Roger's scythe in the garage, his sore arms and back protesting even that simple move after a day of cutting the grass of his spacious yard the old-fashioned way.

The very *old-fashioned way*, he groused, staring forlornly at his John Deere riding mower in the corner. He couldn't justify burning one drop of gas from his underground storage tank to mow the lawn—to say nothing of risking the sound of a mower advertising to a starving and desperate world that he had fuel to spare—even though trimming his overgrown grass had more to do with denying any potential intruder concealment than it did with aesthetics.

Manny glanced at his watch—he was two minutes late for his meeting. He peeled off his clipping-covered boots in the garage and made a beeline for the CQ, its drawn blackout curtains shielding its occupants' important work from shining through the growing darkness outside. He could tell with one glance at Eric's face that his fledgling intelligence section wasn't going to be the bearer of good news.

"You look uglier than usual, which tells me I'm not gonna like what I'm about to hear, so let's hear it."

"The three of us analyzed the maps and radios from the campground, just like you asked," Julie said, gesturing to more than a dozen red dot stickers plastered south and west of Helena on the wall map. "A few of their maps marked these spots outside city limits—our best guess is that these are the locations of homes and businesses the bandits had previously hit."

Eric grabbed one of the folded maps from the CQ desk and handed it to Manny. "But while these jokers were dumb enough to mark where they'd been, they offered few clues as to where they may be from. One or two of them were folded in such a way that exposed Fort Harrison; a handful of pencil and pen marks on the fort, and in the wooded mountains to the northwest, hint that the area holds some kind of importance to them."

Manny studied the beaten up, oil-stained gas station road map in his hand. Fort Harrison, on the northwest edge of Helena, was Montana Army National Guard headquarters, and home to several units and a VA hospital; he didn't want to think about the conditions at the latter. "These losers definitely weren't National Guard. And where the hell were these guys finding the gas to get around like this?"

"That brings us to their radios—they tell us that these guys have some sort of logistical support, which means they're part of something bigger," Allan said, turning in the swivel chair by the ham setup. "All four trucks in their convoy had CB radios we assume were used for truck-to-truck communications, but one of them also had a ham rig set to 147.1 megahertz on the two-meter band. That hits an open repeater that's being powered somehow, and traffic's been yielding some interesting nuggets." He flipped the ham radio logbook open and nestled his glasses in his hair. "At 2200 hours the day after our raid, a station named 'Alpha' made two attempts to reach a station named 'Cobra.' The FCC forbids using code names on ham radio frequencies—not that it matters much because there's no more FCC—but this tells us that we're listening to people who don't wanna be identified."

Allan turned the page and continued reading. "At 1000 hours this morning, and again about thirty minutes ago, Alpha tried again to reach Cobra, and added, I quote, 'Guys, the boss has more jobs. Quit fucking around and respond.'"

"All we have right now is a theory that happens to fit the facts," Julie said. "But we suspect 'Cobra' is back at the Route 12 campground being nibbled on by foraging animals, thanks to us."

"Which means," Eric said, sipping from a black Yeti mug of coffee, "We may have just turned their friends into our enemies."

Manny stepped up to the Helena wall map and stroked his chin. "Allan, did you bring your direction-finding toys with you from Spokane?" Allan nodded—before the collapse, he and Julie enjoyed the ham radio pastime of searching for hidden transmitters with handheld antennas. "Good—we may need 'em. Excellent work, everyone—even you, shitheap," he said to Eric. "Keep me informed, but I don't want any of this information leaving this room. We don't need rumors spreading that Lord Humungus and The Marauders are roaming the countryside. And on that happy note, I'm goin' to bed to enjoy the nightmares you nerds just fueled."

"Does Eric always drink this much coffee?" Julie said to Manny's back as he left.

"One time at Fort Irwin he got wasted and snorted an entire packet of freeze-dried Taster's Choice from an MRE," he answered without turning around.

Allan shot Eric a puzzled look. "Who's Lord Humungus?"

"It's from *Mad Max*."

"Who's Max?" Julie asked.

"Jesus wept," Eric groaned, burying his face in his palm. "We gotta get a movie night up in here."

***

Red Beard stared with contempt at the corpulent, putrefying body sprawled at his feet.

The eight-man team he had led to find their missing band of local hired guns milled about with their search at an end, ignoring the overwhelming stench and the clouds of flies buzzing about the bodies scattered around the long-cold campfire off of Route 12. "This is ev'ry-one—they smoked 'em all, no survivors," one of Red Beard's henchmen reported; he glanced down at the fat man's corpse, which was missing its face, courtesy of some hungry forest dweller. "Whoever did this was really good or really lucky."

"Luck had nothing to do with it," Red Beard curtly replied. "This was a textbook point ambush—amateurs don't leave the alcohol and take the radios. But that's not to say these assholes didn't make it easy for 'em." He reached down to pick up an empty bottle of Jack Daniel's. "Sittin' around a campfire, braggin' about shit they never did and women they never had—probably didn't even have a guard posted."

"God always takes care of the dumb ones," the henchman sneered. "Orders?"

Red Beard looked around one last time, the grisly scene similar to so many other bloodbaths he had seen during his years in the military, and as a soldier of fortune willing to do other people's dirty work for a paycheck. He wasn't ready to chalk up the setback to organized resistance, or National Guard soldiers who didn't want to go along with the boss's plan; but regardless, it was obvious to him that whoever did this knew exactly what the fuck they were doing. Whether they were just protecting their turf or wanting to pick a fight remained to be seen.

"Let's go tell the boss—nothing left for us here. Mount up!" Red Beard yelled to his team, spinning his finger in the air. As the men eagerly piled into their two armored Humvees to leave, Red Beard hurled the whiskey bottle at a nearby boulder, where it shattered with a satisfying crash.

"It sure is hard to find good help these days," he said to the corpse.

CHAPTER 13

Allan warily set down his Grundig G5 portable radio the moment Manny and Travis strode into the sunroom on the gorgeous early October morning.

"What'cha doin', buddy?" Travis asked with a saccharine smile.

"Nothing—but I have the feeling that's about to change," Allan said, carefully pulling the radio's listening bud out of his ear.

"Right you are," Manny said, offering Allan a hand to pull him off the couch. "Grab a canteen and an FRS radio and meet us out front. You can wear civvies—in fact, wear the brightest shirt you have."

"You trying to use me as bait or something?" Allan groused as he grabbed his rifle and headed to Bachelor Country to change.

"Nope!" Travis laughed. "All you're gonna do is walk—a lot. It's a beautiful day, and quite frankly, white boy, you could use the exercise—and some sun, as long as we're being honest."

Wearing a tacky red shirt he got for working a ham radio Field Day exercise two years prior, Allan slowly walked a meticulous line pattern up and down the uphill-sloping front yard of the three-acre clearing around the Landeros home; Manny watched from the front of the house, Travis and Matt from the top floor, and Eric from the LP/OP. Two hours later, Allan gulped water on the front porch after walking the entire length of the drainage ditch that ran parallel to the iron fence and trees lining the gravel county road. His pale arms and neck had started to redden with autumn sunburn.

"So, Allan, ya figured out what you're doing?" Manny asked.

Allan ripped off his camouflage boonie hat and dabbed water on his forehead. "If I had to guess, the veterans in the group are either hazing me or trying to figure out where attackers could take cover from our fire."

Manny nodded. "We've been watching you from the places we'd be shooting back, and any place we couldn't see you is dead space that we have to figure out how to cover. If this was an Army or Marine combat unit, we'd take care of them with antipersonnel mines, grenade launchers, all kinds of fun stuff—but seeing as how we couldn't just hop on down to the sporting goods store and buy stuff like that, we gotta figure out alternatives to deny attackers any places to hide."

Allan glanced around for prying ears. "Manny, does all this have anything to do with those messages we intercepted a few days ago?"

"*Un poquito.* Truth is, as much as we've been hopin' for the best, we're in the middle of a full-blown collapse of law and order, and we need to be a hard target," Manny said, pointing at the unpaved rural road past his house. "No matter how careful we are, no matter how low a profile we keep, as long as there's a road leading to our front door, we'll be found one day. That, as Eric would say, is mathematical certainty."

Allan plopped his sweat-rimmed hat back on his head. "So what now?"

"More strolling!" Manny said, slapping Allan on the back. "Back yard, this time."

***

Matt peeled off his metal-studded leather gloves and wiped his brow with his forearm the moment he dropped his coils of barbed wire into the growing pile in the front yard. Under his supervision as a former combat engineer, the group had spent three straight days converting the Landeros home into a fortress.

Members were hard at work digging long triangular ditches on both sides of the property's winding gravel driveway, from the front gate to the fork that split to the garage and the barn, to keep any attacking vehicles on the driveway and therefore easier to engage. Three meters wide, and one meter deep at the farthest end, each ditch sloped down to end in a vertical wall that nothing short of a tank would be able to scale.

The woods surrounding Manny's home, the deciduous trees sprinkled amongst the conifers providing gorgeous autumn splashes of red, yellow, and orange, now bristled with early-warning devices to alert them to any interlopers. Members had rigged the most likely avenues of approach with trip flares and noisemakers, both purchased and improvised—Jay had whipped up a particularly ingenious device that set off a blank shotgun shell with a mousetrap if a tripwire was pulled.

Matt grimaced and rubbed his lower back as Travis approached from the barn with an armload of dull green metal fenceposts to string the wire across the front lawn. Unlike the other group veterans, who had maintained their exercise regimens after leaving the military, Matt eventually surrendered to marriage and a cushy desk job—which his sore muscles reminded him with each move.

"How ya holdin' up, brokedick?" Travis asked, dropping the posts with a loud clatter. "Told ya all those twelve-ounce curls would come back to haunt ya."

"Don't remind me of beer, jarhead—I'm dying for a cold one."

"You and me both. Tell you what, picket pounder—we ever get back to Tennessee, first pint at Hutton & Smith's on me," Travis said and headed back to the barn for more posts.

Matt's mood soured with the remark about returning to their home state—a fantasy that Angel consistently clung to as if the collapse was just a momentary setback. He stared at his wife, who was half-heartedly shoveling dirt on the driveway work detail, as Pastor Kris walked up to him and handed him a glass of orange Gatorade from a tray.

"How'd you luck out with waitress duty, Reverend?" Matt asked with mock envy before taking a long pull.

"Well, in the alternate universe where I'm the combat engineer and you're the preacher, you're handing out the drinks and I'm the one playing with barbed wire." Kris cocked her head toward the heap of coils. "You about to string it up?"

"Yup," Matt said, kicking the pile with a metallic rattle. "This'll stop anything or anyone that manages to get over the trench and onto the front lawn."

"Won't a truck just cut right through it?"

"If it's strung up right, a barbed-wire fence will stop a truck cold, or wrap around the axles and bring it to a halt. I'm glad Manny had the forethought to stock up on barbed wire and stakes. Stuff was relatively cheap and plentiful, even with all the never-ending pre-collapse shortages."

Matt's gaze returned to his wife. "How's Angel holding up?" Kris asked after a long pause.

"Better," Matt sighed. "At least she finally understands we'd be dead if we hadn't come out here. But she doesn't like the hardship, or sharing a room with another couple—no offense, Reverend."

"None taken—before the collapse, the only person Roger woke up with his snoring was me."

Matt finished his drink. "Angel's still clinging to this delusion that everything will be back to normal in a few months and we can head back home like nothing happened. It's taken a lot of effort on my part to keep from shaking her by the shoulders and telling her that the world she knew isn't ever coming back. She lost her grandparents to COVID-19—she of all people should understand."

"She'll come around, Matt," Kris reassured. "Normalcy bias can be hard to kick. Give her some time."

Susan marched up the lawn, holding the Dakota alert cable and probe she had just dug up from the end of the driveway. The alert system, which used MURS frequencies to sound an alarm in Manny's house if it detected a vehicle, would be relocated to the road at the eastern edge of the property to give them early warning of any traffic approaching from the direction of Helena. She made a beeline for Pastor Kris and snatched a glass of Gatorade that she knocked back in a matter of seconds, a trickle running down the corner of her mouth.

"Everything all right, dear?" Pastor Kris asked.

"I'm up to my ass in alligators pulling double duty! Besides *this* nonsense," she groused, shaking the dirty coil of black cable, "I'm treating a never-ending parade of scrapes, bruises, and blisters." She gestured to the wire at Matt's feet with a scowl. "You're not handling that crap bare-handed, are you?" Matt pulled the wire gloves out of his cargo pocket and dangled them in front of her. "Good. I read Manny the riot act earlier for standing near Jay's chainsaw without wearing goggles.

Seeing as how we don't have a stash of seeing-eye dogs in the basement, he'd be screwed." Susan wiped her forehead with the condensation on the glass and set it back on the tray. "Thanks for the drink," she muttered before heading toward the barn.

Matt glanced at Eric, who had taken a break from shoveling detail that had just happened to time perfectly with Susan's pit stop. He got back to work the moment he caught Matt's stare.

"Eric thinks he has a good poker face, but he's got it bad," Matt said, looking over his shoulder to ensure Susan was out of earshot. "You think she knows?"

"Matt, my dear," Kris said with a smile as she took his empty glass, "women always know."

***

Eric plopped down at the wooden table on the backyard deck and shoveled lunch into his mouth, the stenches of body odor and the fire pit he had been tending for the past hour doing nothing to diminish his appetite.

A pile of fire-hardened wooden stakes cooled in the autumn air near the rock-lined pit; after chow, he would lead a detail to pound them into the dead space in the front-yard drainage ditch and a side-yard culvert by the woodline to impale any careless attackers. A faint wisp of smoke rose from the dying embers, prompting Pete to jump up from his lunch and douse it with water from one of several metal buckets they had had on standby. The group lived in constant fear of forest fires burning down the retreat; Pastor Kris and Roger, who had lived in Montana their entire lives, had shared harrowing stories about wildfires that had scorched huge swaths of the state and blanketed it with an acrid, choking pall. Decades of federal mismanagement, and lawsuits filed by environ-mentalists to block the harvesting of dead trees, resulted in millions of acres of forests packed with billions of tons of dead wood. The beautiful green vistas of Montana and the Pacific Northwest had become giant tinderboxes waiting for a careless camper or a lightning strike to set them aflame.

No sooner had the brief commotion ended than Angel resumed her nonstop bitching. She had done her best since the work started to make sure everyone knew she was having a hard time; no one said anything whenever her rants began, because she didn't gripe for long, and because they didn't want to upset Matt. But during lunch, with Matt away, Angel wouldn't stop; she complained about her blistered hands, her sore back, and life in general.

Shut—the fuck—up, Eric growled to himself, grinding his teeth. *We're way too fucking tired for this shit. This nice weather's gonna be replaced with snow before we know it—and in the Rockies it's measured in fucking feet. Can we just fucking* have *this?*

Angel's kvetching continued unabated. Eric slammed his fork down, startling Susan next to him, and opened his mouth to tell Angel to stuff it, her feelings and her husband's anger be damned.

"Angel, honey, we understand," Pastor Kris interjected, shooting a glance at Eric, who pursed his lips and fell silent. "But don't you think there are millions of people right now who would give anything to switch places with you for just one day?"

Angel stared back as if she had been slapped.

Pastor Kris's eyes bored into Angel's as her mind took her to places and times she had tried very hard to forget. "Roger and I have seen squalor on our mission trips that's impossible to fathom unless you've witnessed it yourself. We've visited Third World nightmares torn apart by civil wars that had gone on for so long that nobody could remember why they started. We've seen mothers cradling children dying from starvation and disease. If you controlled the food, you controlled everything—and all too often, the men in control were the most reprehensible people you could imagine. Young mothers often faced a choice of putting their starving children to bed hungry, or . . . submitting to these men's desires so their kids could have a meal and make it another day. You never heard about that on the news, but it happened all the time."

Angel cried with her hands to her mouth, the rest of the pastor's audience riveted to her every word. "I guess we're the Third World now, too. Mothers here in America, the greatest nation on Earth, are losing children to diseases that a few months ago would've been cured with a prescription—children like your former students. And how many mothers are facing that same unthinkable moral dilemma of either surrendering their virtue or watching their children starve? Too many people before the collapse behaved themselves only because they didn't want to go to prison; God was nowhere in their hearts, and His laws meant nothing to them. With the threat of arrest and punishment gone, they're running wild, and heaven help anyone in their way." Pastor Kris struggled to keep her voice from cracking. "Angel, the problems you're facing right now are a luxury. Believe it or not, you're the luckiest woman in the world."

The rest of the group sat in silence, absorbing Pastor Kris's words as she rose to console Angel, who sobbed uncontrollably. *Not even a month ago, I wrote that people in the old America stopped caring and stopped listening, and here I was about to tell Angel to shut her yap,* Eric berated himself. *Some philosopher you turned out to be.*

CHAPTER 14

T he pleasant synthetic melody of the Dakota Alert test chimed through the CQ office.

"Well, it works," Susan told Pete as he adjusted the base unit's antenna on the desk. The duo and Manny, under cover of darkness, had buried the vehicle early-warning sensor down the road, and emplaced the three Dakota pedestrian monitors along the shoulder, a deer trail that opened up into the retreat, and a sliver of woods obscured from the LP/OP by the barn.

"Sure does," said Benny, who was on CQ duty. "But could we change the alarm to somethin' a little more unpleasant? Kinda surreal to be alerted to the zombie mutant cannibals with a Mozart lullaby."

"That's Beethoven, actually—*Für Elise*," Susan corrected him. "My mom made me take piano lessons, and I had to play that at my recital, so that alarm scares me just fine—you have a good point just the same, though."

Pete pushed a button on the Dakota, and Beethoven was replaced by the loud wail of a police siren. "*Jesucristo*, turn that off before you wake everybody up!" Benny hissed, darting from the leather office chair to shut the door as Pete fumbled with the base unit to silence the alarm.

"Sorry!" he whispered. Twenty seconds went by without any rudely awakened people storming into the CQ to give them what for. "Thank the Lord—rousing everybody after all that hard labor would've been cruel and unusual punishment!"

Susan glanced at the digital wall clock—0230 hours—and tried unsuccessfully to stifle a long yawn. She excused herself to take a shower and get some sleep; after almost a week of hard and filthy work, Manny had temporarily relaxed the limitations on bathing, as long as people were smart about water usage. She crept up the master stairs and gingerly opened the door to the guest bedroom that she and Julie shared as the group's single females. Susan quietly set down her rifle and tactical vest, and had started to peel off her camouflage top when the sound of a man's snoring stopped her cold. She looked over at Julie's bunk in the far corner, her eyes adjusting to the dark to reveal her roommate passed out on top of Allan, their clothes on but very much disheveled.

Allan snored again and Susan bit off a laugh—the couple had tried to take advantage of everyone being dead tired to sneak in some sexy time, but themselves fell asleep. *This is gonna be awkward*, she thought as she tiptoed to wake Allan before Manny caught them *in flagrante delicto*—but her foot struck something hard that glided across the carpet. She flinched as it struck the baseboard with a dull *thud* just under the room's night light, its dim soft white glow revealing Allan's logbook for recording whatever news he could glean from the outside world.

The voice in Susan's head telling her the book wasn't hers to peek through was drowned out by Ludwig von Beethoven and the memory of her proud parents at that recital from so long ago—parents she was desperate to find. A minute later, she was sitting in the hallway thumbing through Allan's notes with a pen light for any news from Wisconsin and the Milwaukee area, each turn of the page exploding the world Susan once knew.

State government was broadcasting that it still existed, that order was being restored, and that it was working nonstop to get the power back on. However, ham radio and CB frequencies were filled with stories of desperate and starving people all over Montana, as well as reports accusing authorities of seizing food, firearms, and fuel—Susan briefly pondered a note about the Route 12 campground raid, and multiple references to an unnamed acting governor and some man named "Red." Kalispell, Butte, and Great Falls were among the handful of Montana cities along the Rocky Mountains that had independently restored order, but most of Billings, the only Montana city with more than one hundred thousand residents, had burned down, as had Bozeman to the west on I-90.

Texas had officially seceded from the Union, and subsequently invited all surviving military on its soil from "the former United States" to join a new Texas Defense Force; Arkansas and Oklahoma were considering following suit and joining Texas in a loose federation. The federal government, operating from an unknown "secure location" because the District of Columbia had burned to ash, maintained that it was still in control, that help would be coming, and that secessionist activity would be crushed by force. However, rumors abounded that the president and much of the chain of succession were dead, and that multiple people were claiming to be next in line. As evidence of a shattered chain of command, Allan had drawn a big red circle around an entry regarding the commander of Malmstrom Air Force Base in Great Falls removing the missileers of the 341st Missile Wing from their underground launch capsules, thus grounding its entire flight of 150 Minuteman III ICBMs.

Allan, who was from Spokane, had compiled multiple entries for news regarding the partition of Washington State—as well as his futile attempts to get a hold of his older brother and his family. A movement had gained momentum before the Unraveling for the conservative eastern half of Washington to split off, and several groups were rising up against the post-collapse tyranny of the surviving state government to create the new state of Cascadia. Similar partition movements were sprouting up in eastern Oregon and northern California, where the collapse had galvanized the century-old fringe movement to create the State of Jefferson.

The situation nationwide was bleak as well, with radio operators relaying harrowing tales of hordes of fear-crazed survivors fleeing the big cities and ravaging everything in their path. New England, Florida, and southern California were silent. Susan's heart sank with an entry regarding the utter devastation of the Denver and Boulder metro areas—which shattered what little hope remained that Ed and Mina Houston, and their baby, were still alive.

She soon noticed that entries germane to group members and their loved ones were highlighted in yellow. She jumped with Allan's loud snort behind the door, and picked up the pace of her snooping, flipping past pages detailing much of Europe laid to waste, and the remnants of China and India plunging into civil war after the flu had mercilessly slashed through their dense populations.

True to his word when they first arrived, Allan had put a top priority on trying to find Pastor Kris's and Roger's sons in Atlanta and Miami, but the news was nothing but false hopes and dead ends. Atlanta had burned for the second—most likely final—time in its history. Miami had been thoroughly devastated along with the rest of Florida outside the Panhandle—what's more, it looked like a hurricane, and a powerful one at that, had recently torn through.

Her heart pounding in her chest, Susan finally came across an entry for Wisconsin, dated a week prior.

Milwaukee and Madison gone.

Suburbs overrun by Milwaukee/Chicago refugees. Big Illinois reactor meltdown over the border drifting northeast (radiation?).

All of SE Wisconsin and northern IL silent—nothing from Waukesha. Tell Susan?

Susan dejectedly closed the notebook and struggled to her feet, her sore calves burning with the effort. *If this doesn't teach me to mind my own business, nothing will*, she said to herself, opening the door to shoo Allan out of their room.

CHAPTER 15

Pete's trembling hand gingerly slid a small wooden plank from the middle of the Jenga tower rising from the living room coffee table.

"There you go," he sighed with relief the moment it came free. "Too easy . . . no, no, *no*!"

Luisa cheered triumphantly as the tower toppled to the laughs of their small audience. "We have a winner, and at 6-0, still undefeated champion!" Angel proclaimed, grabbing the teenager's hand and thrusting it into the air to the applause of other group members in formal attire.

"And now, the champion can come back and give Mom a hand!" Carmen yelled from the kitchen, which had filled the house with the intoxicating scents of the Christmas feast the group had spent the entire day cooking; the main courses consisted of a wild turkey, and a rib roast from an elk that had had the misfortune of strolling onto the property when Benny was on LP/OP duty. Luisa trotted away in her red holiday dress, leaving Angel and Pete to pick up the pieces.

Pastor Kris's suggestion to Manny that the group needed a morale officer, and that giving Angel the job would help her fit in and deal with the collapse, turned out to be a godsend. At first, Manny cringed at memories of the military's Morale, Welfare, and Recreation program—which all too often became "mandatory fun" that soldiers wanted no part of—but the former teacher took to the job with gusto, organizing card games, board games, movie nights, and other events.

Susan gazed across the living room, smiling in spite of herself. She and Eric had spent the morning decorating the Christmas tree and stringing up the Landeros's outdoor Christmas lights throughout the living room and the CQ, both of which were now ablaze with color. The duo had gotten silly and, to Manny's amusement, had draped the surplus lights around the layer of vinyl sandbags reinforcing the wall underneath the bay window. Carmen had not at all been amused by Manny's decision to stack sandbags along the walls under every window that would serve as positions to return fire in the event of an attack—she had sternly told her husband that he would be the one cleaning up the heavy mess if things ever returned to normal.

Susan's smile waned with a glance at the large blackout curtain covering the living room window. Not that there was much of a view to begin with; winter winds had piled snow halfway up, and the remaining top half was iced over. Mother Nature had decided that Montana's survivors of the Unraveling hadn't suffered enough—more than a foot of snow had fallen by Halloween, and it just kept coming, with temperatures plunging well below freezing for long periods. Members dreaded the frigid LP/OP shifts but considered themselves fortunate, as the radio waves were filled with stories of the first post-collapse winter cutting down the young, the old, and the unprepared like a scythe. While members were rotating CQ duty every fifteen minutes so that everyone could enjoy the Christmas festivities, Eric had volunteered to stand watch at the LP/OP that evening as his present to everyone—he joked as he bundled up that he was "playing the lead in the worst Hallmark Channel Christmas movie ever."

The surprise giving of good-intentioned gag gifts lifted everyone's spirits and gave everyone some sorely needed laughs once they sat at the Landeros's dining room table. Allan received a paper bag for throwing up during the campground ambush, and Travis, a former police officer, received an expired gift card from Dunkin' Donuts. "The way things stand, I could probably buy the entire corporation for a one-ounce silver coin and a box of .22 rimfire," he joked.

Allan, who was practically swimming in a holiday sweater he had borrowed from Manny's wardrobe, pulled a small box from his pocket and handed it to Angel. "Merry Christmas—Julie and I really wish we could've gotten one of these for everyone." Matt peered over Angel's shoulder as she lifted the lid to find a slip of paper with a frequency and a time scrawled on it. "Your sister, Melissa. She's alive—her family, too," Allan explained as Angel's face melted from bewilderment to joy. "Ten a.m. tomorrow, they'll be waiting by her community's ham radio for your call," he explained over the group's deafening applause as Angel bolted out of her seat and rounded the table to give Allan and Julie a hug.

Roger and Benny rose with the dying applause. "Is that our first successful family contact?" Roger asked. Allan nodded.

"That calls for a drink!" Benny said—the duo disappeared for a moment before waltzing back into the dining room and setting four large growler bottles on the sturdy wooden table with a *thump*. "Is that what I think it is?" Matt exclaimed as eyes went wide and mouths dropped open.

"Yup! Beer!" Roger said to another wave of applause. "Started brewing it shortly after we all got here. It took some stealth and some crafty scheduling, but you folks were always so busy that you never noticed me."

Benny loudly popped the cap of the nearest growler. "Roger planted the hops trellises last summer. Eric, of course, figured out right away what they were, but me an' Manny swore the freakin' brainiac to secrecy on pain of death."

Manny held out his pint glass for his cousin to fill, admonishing everyone to drink responsibly and not get hammered, especially if they were in line for watch duty. Pete passed a growler to Jay, who handed it off to Angel. "You're not partaking?" she asked.

"Nope. Been sober fifteen years," Jay said matter-of-factly. "I'm not 'bout to burden you all with havin' to deal with a drunkard."

"Oh, goodness, I'm sorry."

"For what? If you wanna feel sorry for somebody, feel sorry for my ex-wife. Laura. She was a helluva woman, but she couldn't handle my drinkin' and moved back to her parents in Wichita. And every day, I wonder . . ." Jay stopped, jaw quivering.

Pastor Kris reached for his hand. "Jay, you don't have to do this."

He smiled as a tear ran down his leathery face. "Confession's good for the soul, Rev'rend," Jay raggedly sighed. "And every day, I wonder if I killed her. If I'd been a good husband, she'd be safe with us, not dead or dyin' somewhere." He grabbed his napkin and sniffled loudly. "Sorry, folks. Didn't mean to ruin Christmas."

Angel shook her head and wiped her eyes with her forefinger and thumb. "You did nothing of the sort."

"I'd like to make the first toast, if our gracious hosts would allow me the honor," Jay said, raising a glass of water with Manny's and Carmen's approving nod. "To us."

"To us," everyone echoed to the clinking of glasses that, at least for that moment, drowned out the world around them.

***

The blast of warm air that still carried the aromas of Christmas dinner was a present in and of itself for Eric after six hours of LP/OP duty in the freezing cold; his stomach growled at the thought of diving into leftovers that had just gotten to know one another. The feeling had started returning to his numb and reddened face as he shuffled into the kitchen—and found two plates already made up and a candle burning on the table.

"Just in time," Susan said, setting down a growler of beer and two empty glasses, still dressed in her red Christmas sweater. "Any longer and I would've thought you'd volunteered for a double shift."

Eric pulled off his itchy wool-knit cap and unbuckled his tactical vest, unsure of what to make of Susan's gesture. "Did you really wait for me, or is this an excuse to grab seconds?" he cautiously joked as he leaned his rifle against the wall and unzipped his parka.

"I didn't want you eating Christmas dinner alone after you took LP/OP duty for everyone. I only nibbled—gotta watch my girlish figure, you know."

You have nothing to worry about, Eric responded in his head. "Your invite didn't say anything about attire, so I went with stinking, dirty fatigues. My ugly Christmas sweater with Santa riding a tyrannosaurus rex is at the laundromat."

"Sit down and eat, Eric. I'm starving."

CHAPTER 16

Governor Jeremy Matthews struggled to fake a normal gait as he marched into the ornate office of the powerful man who mistakenly believed he owned him. The three Grey Goose martinis Matthews had imbibed in quick succession to help steel himself to set the little weasel straight had had the opposite effect on his gross motor skills.

"What brings you back to my beautiful mountain abode, Mister Governor? Must be important for you and your escort to brave this horrible snow," Stu Magnuson condescendingly said from behind his desk. The trim, athletic man wrinkled his nose. "Smells like you've gotten a head start on New Year's Eve—hope your driver didn't partake."

Matthews, his face ruddied by anger and alcohol, slammed a sheet of paper on the maple-finish, gold-trimmed desk. "My resignation, Stu. I'm done."

"Ah—so liquid courage then," the former Silicon Valley CEO turned political fixer wryly observed before nonchalantly skimming the letter. "Hmm—no mention of you getting your promotion by shooting Governor Kellerman and her husband dead. Did you start drinking before or after you wrote this?"

"You put me up to it!" Matthews shouted with a slur. "Killing that bitch was one thing, but . . . ordering the deaths of the house speaker, the senate president . . . the city council! They never did me a bad turn!"

Matthews stifled a sob as Stu shook his head with a *tsk-tsk-tsk*. "It's a touch too late for you to be growing a conscience, Mister Governor. Take the king's shilling, dance the king's tune—and you never had a problem before the collapse accepting all the shillings I threw your way. You sure I can't change your mind to see this through? After all, we have such a long history together."

"I said, I'm *done*!" Matthews thundered. "Power's not worth all this blood on my hands!"

Matthews was taken aback by Stu's genuine look of disappointment as he rose from his plush chair. "I'm sorry to hear that. Well, if I can't dissuade you, I may as well wish you good luck in your future endeavors," he said before shifting his eyes to Matthews' left and giving the slightest of nods.

"Wha—" Matthews managed to utter before Red Beard viciously grabbed his head and broke his neck with a wet snap. The governor crumpled to the wooden floor and stared up in horror as his last breath, reeking of vodka and vermouth, rattled in his throat.

Stu suppressed a brief flash of anger over Matthews forcing his hand before his usefulness had ended—so much of the master plan of which Stu had been a part had already been shot to hell by the unforeseen circumstances of the collapse. "You can tell the former governor's security detail they'll be staying here tonight until the storm passes," he told Red Beard. "Tomorrow, be sure to have them stumble upon Mr. Matthews hanging from the rafter in the guest room—it's sad he never reached out to anyone for help."

Red Beard grabbed Matthews's legs and dragged him toward the office door. "We're better off without him, boss—man was a bona fide pain in the ass. On the other hand, it looks like we're fresh outta governors."

"Maybe," Stu said as he watched his henchman and their dearly departed puppet disappear from sight. "Then again, maybe not."

CHAPTER 17

The freezing night air slapped Private First Class Tim McCormick in the face as he pushed a rusty red dolly piled high with boxes of stolen MREs onto the rear loading dock of Fort Harrison's main building.

Winter's howl drowned out the dolly's rhythmic squeak with the young man's trot down the length of the dock toward Sergeant Steve James, who waited at the back of a canvas-covered Light Medium Tactical Vehicle crammed with stolen military property. Their three partners in crime—some would say treason—darted past Tim on the blustery New Year's Eve night with empty dollies of their own to swipe one final load of supplies before all five of them deserted.

Tim anxiously tossed the cardboard boxes to Steve in quick succession as the biting Montana wind whipped snow off the building's roof into beautiful shifting patterns overhead. "Easy there, private!" Steve grunted after the last box caught him in the chest. "A few more minutes, and we're outta here to find a place to hide."

The nineteen-year-old nodded, dashing back with the squeaking dolly to rejoin his co-conspirators on a clandestine mission that, if discovered, would land them on the receiving end of a firing squad. Steve for the hundredth time scanned the vast and dark vehicle lot behind him and their soon-to-be-purloined LMTV, a boxy armored truck that had replaced the Army's venerable deuce-and-a-half. Their fellow soldiers had managed to keep the main building powered, but not the lot lights—which Steve didn't mind, given the circumstances.

The fort on the northwest edge of Helena was home to the support element of the First Battalion, 163rd Cavalry Regiment, which had units throughout the state—at least on paper. A number of soldiers outright ignored their mobilization orders when the collapse started, choosing instead to stay home with their families or flee as the news filled with images of rioting, looting, and doctors and nurses in hazmat suits milling among flu victims packed like battery hens into overflowing hospitals. The soldiers at Fort Harrison, almost all of them single, were a hodgepodge of men and women cobbled together from various units as former deserters were rounded up and given the choice of returning to duty or being summarily executed.

Steve, who had been home with his parents after graduating with a business degree from the University of Montana, had decided to drive to Fort Harrison in the absence of orders and volunteer for duty. He had kicked himself for his stupidity every day since—it didn't take long for him to realize he had made a big mistake.

His unit at first conducted harmless "presence patrols" to help remaining police, sheriff's deputies, and state troopers maintain order in Helena and surrounding counties, but their orders grew more heavy-handed with each mission. Presence patrols soon became detaining people without probable cause and executing warrantless searches for "contraband," which became the seizing of spare food, supplies, and legally owned firearms and ammunition.

And then there were the posses and civilian "contractors" brought in to help enforce order by whoever was calling the shots—and there were more than a few rumors of what they did to people with no police or soldiers around. Steve despised them; most were nothing more than local boys who stumbled onto a good thing, or wannabes who were too fat or too dumb to get into the military or law enforcement. Some were honest-to-God mercenaries—one in particular, a hulking man with a red beard who seemed to be in charge of the rabble, was particularly fearsome. Steve had no idea how the government was paying them, given that money was worthless, but he suspected their "salaries" consisted of a cut of whatever they seized. Tonight, however, the booze these lowlifes had liberated was helping everyone on post ring in the new year by getting them three sheets to the wind, and therefore improving the odds of Steve and his friends making their escape.

Steve at first had no idea who to turn to in a slapdash unit full of strange faces, but one by one, he met others disgusted by what they saw, and who knew that their orders violated their oaths to uphold and defend the Constitution. There was Sergeant Andy Reese, who grew up on the Flathead Indian Reservation and lived in Deer Lodge; Specialist Liam Littlejohn, born and raised in Billings; and Private McCormick, who grew up in Townsend. The last member of what they came to call their "conspiracy" was Cadet Katie Gutowski, a Boise native who was a senior in the ROTC program at Carroll College, the small private Catholic university in town.

The conspiracy kept itself to five members—any more, Steve concluded, would increase their chances of being compromised. They quickly decided that open or passive resistance would get them killed without making any kind of a difference, which left them one option—go AWOL with whatever supplies they could steal, and find a safe place to hole up and figure out their next move.

The double doors to the dock slammed open as Steve's compatriots wheeled out one last load and hastily packed their stolen supplies into the truck. He huddled them in, the winter chill blowing down the back of his neck as he took one last look around for unannounced visitors through the fog of their heavy breathing. "Get your snivel gear on and get on board, kids—it's time to tear ass outta here." He looked over at Andy. "You type up our bullshit orders?"

"Roger that. Says we're resupplyin' the troops guardin' the TV tower and repeater on Hogback Mountain—except, of course, we're goin' the other direction."

"Should we grab any more stuff?" Tim asked excitedly.

"Negative," Steve replied. "We've been insanely lucky tonight. If we get greedy, we get caught, and then we get dead. We need to pop smoke. Right now."

Katie shrugged. "So much for our Good Conduct Medals."

"We're doing the right thing. The orders we've been receiving are unconstitutional, and we're just as guilty if we obey them," Steve said as he looked into his soldiers' faces. Liam, a large, muscular man of few words, nodded back. Steve asked Katie to lead them in a prayer for safety—the conspirators bowed their heads as Katie asked God for travel mercies, and asked forgiveness for stealing the truck and the supplies, even though they were keeping them out of the hands of people who would do bad things with them.

Steve stepped back and clapped his gloved hands, trying to show more courage than he felt. "Saddle up! And once we get rolling, lock and load. Safe your weapons, and no fingers on triggers. Andy, you're up front with me."

"Did you pack your stupid drone?" Katie ribbed Tim as she wiggled her way in the dark around the boxes of supplies under the LMTV's cover to find a seat.

"Don't leave home without it!" he quipped, patting the hardshell case on his back.

Steve knelt beside the LMTV to turn on its power supply with a twist of a hidden undercarriage switch. He popped open the door and climbed into the driver's seat, grinning as the truck's engine roared to life with the push of a button; Steve released the airbrakes, turned on the headlights, and drove into the snowy night with a belch of diesel exhaust as their former comrades were drunkenly counting down the final seconds of an awful year.

CHAPTER 18

"Are you up for it?" Manny asked as Eric contemplated his next move on the ornate wooden chessboard.

"Winning this game? Absolutely," Eric replied, moving his black queen's rook and glancing out the sunroom's tall glass panes at the gray and rainy spring morning—March was coming to an end. "As for leading the first patrol when the snow melts, yeah, I'm up for that, too. I'll let you know who I wanna take with me, and then we'll start rehearsing."

Manny examined his dwindling options for moves with a grimace. "After a long and cold winter trapped indoors, you'll be fightin' off volunteers with a whip and a chair—that is, 'til they learn the catch is that they'll be led by your stupid ass." He moved a tan pawn one space forward. "We'll start simple and make contact with our immediate neighbors to see if they're still alive. Sorry to say you'll probably be talkin' to corpses, *hermano.*"

Eric sipped his increasingly precious coffee. "Don't care—we've been cooped up for seven months, and I'm going stir crazy. And you have a big house! I can't imagine how other people are dealing with this." He jumped his remaining knight. "If they didn't have games, books, and other non-electronic diversions, it'd be like living in the waiting room of a doctor's office and its thirty-year-old magazines, multiplied by a million."

"I don't wanna imagine that," Manny said. "You don't truly appreciate freedom of movement—the right to hop in your car for no reason and take a drive or grab a burger—until you're deprived of it. Got a taste of that shit under COVID, and that was murder."

Julie walked in and handed Manny the draft copy of Allan's next news dispatch. "So, how exquisitely screwed is the world today?" Eric asked her.

"Well, for starters, the reconstituted legislatures of Oklahoma, Arkansas, Missouri, Mississippi, Kentucky, and Tennessee are following Texas out the door. The northern counties of Louisiana—"

"Parishes," Eric interrupted. "In Louisiana, they're called parishes."

"The northern *parishes*, Mr. Know-It-All, wanna join up with Texas, given that New Orleans, Baton Rouge, and the rest of the I-10 corridor are one big graveyard. If Louisiana and Texas join together, that gives them control of the Strategic Petroleum Reserve. Hundreds of millions of barrels of crude would go a long way toward recovery."

"The federal government's screamin' that the states don't have the right to secede and ordered them to stand down," Manny read to Eric. "The governor of Texas replied, and I quote, 'Well, why don't you draft some hundred-pound soyboys from what's left of New England and send 'em on over to stop us?'"

"She's got a point. Feds are spread pretty thin—heck, how much of their remaining military beef is tied up in my home state alone?" Julie asked as Manny resumed reading. Washington's counties east of the Cascades had split to form Cascadia the previous fall, and were now locked in a guerrilla war against the old state government in Olympia, and the 2nd Infantry Division and the 16th Combat Aviation Brigade at Joint Base Lewis-McChord.

Manny handed the paper back to Julie and, after a second of thought, edged his king's bishop forward. "Idaho's pledging to support Cascadia. That's smart on their part, seeing as how Idaho seceded as well—Cascadia's essentially a buffer zone tying up those federal troops."

Julie glanced at the chessboard. "Speaking of good strategy, Eric has you checkmated in one move."

Eric tapped his queen against Manny's king's knight with a wooden *clonk*. "Yup. There's Allan's lead story for the next newsletter."

Manny shook his head and reset the pieces. "You got me again—this makes how many times?"

"One hundred and ten since I first taught you how to play, but who's counting? One day I might let you win—a teacher really isn't a teacher until his student surpasses him. Want another go?"

Manny rose from his lounge chair and grabbed his rifle. "I'll have to surpass you some other time—unlike some people I know, I don't have the luxury of goofing off today. I got CQ in an hour, and umpteen things to do before that."

Eric comfortably stretched in the gaudy red robe he had made sure to pack back in Wisconsin. "Look at you!" Manny said indignantly. "Twenty-four hours without LP/OP or CQ duty, and you look like Hef at his mansion!"

"Better yet, it's your mansion," Eric quipped as Manny left with a groan. Eric stepped to the glass to take in the wooded mountain view. Opportunities to goldbrick, he knew, would evaporate with the warmer weather; green had begun to poke through the snow, and spring planting would follow soon. A row of tables along the sunroom's glass walls held shoots of young tomatoes, peppers, broccoli, and other edible plants that Roger would transplant when the time was right—Manny and Carmen had wanted to build a greenhouse, but the Unraveling struck first. Eric's back ached with the very thought of having to dig up much of Manny's spacious backyard for gardening. If there was one mistake that many of the post-apocalyptic fiction books he had read had in common, it was laughably underestimating the amount of agriculture it took to feed even a small survival retreat; the work would make last fall's digging of defensive works feel like a YMCA pilates class by comparison.

Allan's newsletter brought back memories of a discussion Eric once had with his honors history class about the possibility of a hopelessly divided United States descending into a second civil war. "I wonder what the map'll look like in a few years," Julie said, ambling next to him as if sensing Eric's train of thought. "Can you imagine the US and Canada becoming a patchwork quilt of tiny countries like the Holy Roman Empire? Some, like Montana, being nuclear powers?"

Eric didn't respond. He drained the last of his coffee and offered yet another silent prayer for his students.

"Snow's starting to melt. About time," she added after a long pause.

"When it does, Manny wants me to take out a patrol and poke around," Eric said without looking at her. "You want in?"

"You bet your ass!" she blurted. "No offense to our hosts' hospitality, but I'm going bonkers in here."

"No shit. I thought life sucked during COVID-19—that was a walk in the park compared to this. Don't breathe a word of this yet—I don't wanna be pressured into any hasty decisions. I'm happy that spring's officially sprung, but the warmer weather's gonna come with a very big downside."

"Refugees," Julie said, shoving her hands in the pockets of her hooded sweatshirt. The group had had more than one heated debate about how to handle people who stumbled upon them and asked for a handout. Eric was torn over the issue—while he was confident he would have no problem telling some stereotypical big-city snob or spoiled twenty-something with a tremendous sense of entitlement to piss off, he had no idea what he would do when confronted by a desperate mother with starving children.

"You think anybody's gonna find us here in the middle of nowhere?" Julie asked.

She got her answer two days later.

CHAPTER 19

Travis cursed as his Marine Corps digital camouflage fatigue sleeve snagged on a thorn bush in the strip of trees lining the gravel road by the retreat.

"You kiss your mom with that mouth?" Susan teased while holding a tripwire taut so Travis could tie it to a tree-mounted flare—with the snow melting, she and Travis had been tasked with inspecting the early-warning devices the group had emplaced last fall. "Oh, God, I'm so sorry," she blurted apologetically. "That was so rude when we don't know whether our parents are all right."

Travis nonchalantly grabbed his Leatherman pliers. "No offense taken. One day in the Corps, true story, I made a crack about my friend's momma just after he got back from emergency leave to attend her funeral—I just did it without thinking—and he straight up punched me in the face. Nothing came of it—he was sorry, I was sorry, no one else saw, so it all worked out. I know Momma, whether she's alive somewhere, or dead in whatever's left of Nashville, would be happy to know I'm OK. And Doc, your parents would want the same thing."

"I really hate that nickname," Susan complained, eager to change the subject. "Does that have to be my call sign?"

"Absolutely! It's tradition," Travis said with a smile, snipping the excess tripwire from the knot on the flare's pin with a flourish.

Aside from "Base" for the CQ and "Eyes" for the LP/OP, regardless of who was staffing them, each member had a unique call sign for radio messages; coming up with them shortly after everyone first arrived was a memorable and fun exercise. Susan had laughed when Eric got the call sign "Einstein" after Manny let slip that it was his nickname in the Army on account of being a grade-A nerd. The veterans immediately chimed "Doc" in unison when Susan's turn came up; every Army medic and Marine corpsman was called "Doc" as a term of endearment, they explained. Susan complained that it made her sound like one of the Seven Dwarfs, and attempted to ask over their howls of laughter whether other members would be named Dopey, Bashful, or Sneezy in solidarity with her. When Eric informed her that line units had a cruder nickname for medics, and that they could call her "Chancre Mechanic" instead, she grudgingly accepted Doc.

"To hell with tradition!" Susan said. "Besides, you got a cool call sign with 'Shaft.'"

"It fits, just like yours," Travis said as they began to move to the trip flares by the front gate. "One, I was a cop, two, I'm black, and three, I'm a sex machine to all the chicks. You see, this cat Shaft is a bad mother—"

Travis's mouth snapped shut and his non-firing hand shot up at a right angle, fist clenched—the infantry hand signal to freeze. "Down!" he hissed, diving behind a tree and aiming his rifle down the road. Susan immediately followed his lead, gasping as the cold snowmelt soaked through her fatigues.

"We got company," Travis whispered. Susan saw them a second later—two people clad in blue hiking gear, about a hundred meters away, walking down the road toward them. "I got 'em covered. Call it in."

Susan grabbed the MURS radio from the shoulder of her tactical vest, silently regretting that she never had gotten around to buying a headset to talk hands-free. "Base, this is Doc, stand by for SALUTE report," she quietly intoned as she mentally compiled her report on their potential enemy's size, activity, location, uniform, time, and equipment.

"Doc, this is Base," Julie at the CQ desk responded after a brief delay. "Eyes spotted the bogeys a few seconds ago, right when the Dakota alert went off. You wanna call in the report or let Eyes do it, over?"

"I got it—have Eyes look around to make sure these two are alone."

Julie stabbed the button to the intercom that Pete had wired shortly after joining the group, her voice blaring throughout the house and barn ordering everyone to their battle stations. Group members bolted for their window firing positions, tactical vests and helmets on, and rifles in hand. Manny and Eric ran into the CQ, barely avoiding getting bowled over by Pete and Jay, who galloped out of Bachelor Country after their rude awakening following graveyard sentry shifts. Julie furiously scribbled as Susan succinctly sent her report.

"Sierra: One man, one woman, on foot.

Alpha: Walking down the road toward the retreat.

Lima: Fifty meters from the edge of the property line and closing.

Uniform: Civilian hiking clothes.

Tango: 1100 hours local time.

Echo: Large hiking backpacks. No visible weapons. How copy, over?"

"Refugees," Manny said as Julie acknowledged receipt and told Susan to stand by. After a moment's thought, he told Julie to order Travis and Susan to lie still and let them pass.

"Base, we have a problem," Susan said before Julie could relay the instructions.

***

"We know you're there. We saw you when we first rounded the bend," the bearded man yelled to the woods where Travis and Susan were lying prone. He and the woman raised their hands. "We don't want any trouble. We snuck out of Helena, and we're just passing through. Please don't hurt us. We have nothing of value." The motley pair continued to walk, much more slowly, as Susan relayed the man's words to the CQ.

"Whaddya think?" Manny asked Eric.

"We don't know much about the situation in Helena, but I bet they do. Let's offer them some hot chow and pick their brains."

Manny looked to Julie. "I'm glad Travis is out there—perfect job for him. Tell him to lock 'em down, and keep everyone at their posts in case this is a trick." He turned to Eric. "Throw on your boots and let's meet our guests."

***

"Don't move!" Travis bellowed in his disused police officer voice. The two travelers, now only about twenty meters away, jumped and froze, their hands still raised. "We're not gonna hurt you, if you are who you say you are! If this is some kind of ruse, you'll both be dead before you hit the ground!"

"Oh, God, no!" the woman screamed. "We're just trying to get to my parents in Kalispell! Honest! Please!"

"If we wanted to kill you, we would've done it already," Travis barked. "We're the good guys—we just wanna talk to you, because we're curious about what's goin' on in town. In exchange, we'll feed you and send you on your way with whatever charity we can spare. Does a hot meal sound good?"

The man and woman looked at each other, then looked forward and nodded.

"Do exactly as I say, and be truthful. Do you have any weapons on you? Guns, knives, anything?"

"Just a pocketknife," the man answered. Travis ordered him to slowly toss the knife in front of him, and commanded both of them, one at a time, to take off their backpacks and toss them forward. Both did as they were told.

"We're gonna search you and your belongings. This is for our safety and for yours. We're not gonna take anything from you, and ma'am, I'm not gonna lay a hand on you—I have a female here who'll search you, OK?" The woman nervously nodded. Travis ordered the couple to get on their knees, cross their ankles, and interlace their fingers on top of their heads. He threw on an N-95 mask that Susan handed to him and cautiously rose to search the man and his backpack while Susan covered him. When he returned to his position and had the duo covered, Susan donned her mask and searched the woman and her belongings.

The rustling of brush announced the arrival of Manny and Eric, who high-crawled up to Travis and Susan after skirting the iron fence at the edge of the property. Travis told the couple in a more relaxed tone that they could sit down, but stay still.

Susan glanced back at the refugees. "They seem healthy enough, by post-apocalyptic standards—looks like they took care of themselves before the world went to hell, but it's obvious they've lost a decent amount of weight and that their living conditions haven't been the best. I don't think anyone needs to wear masks, but I wouldn't touch them with bare hands or get too close."

Manny wiped his gloved hands on his fatigues and walked over to the seated couple as his friends covered him. "Good morning, sir, ma'am," he said, tugging the brim of his camouflage boonie hat to the woman. "My name is Manuel, but my friends call me Manny. This is my property. I apologize for our manners, but I hope you understand. What are your names?"

"Eli. Eli Sammons. This is my wife, Kayla," the young man answered. His unkempt beard, and the shaggy hair sticking out from the edges of his ratty knit cap, reminded Manny of old TV shows about unprepared hikers getting lost in the wild.

"Pleased to meet you both. Like my friends told you, we wanna learn about conditions in Helena, and we'd like to have you as our temporary guests. We'll fix you a nice lunch, and give you some supplies for your trip, in exchange for everything you've seen and heard, no matter how trivial. Sound like a deal?"

Kayla wanly smiled. "That's awfully nice of you—it's been a long time since we've seen nice."

"Table for two, then. My friend Eric and I will lead the way, and Travis and Susan, who you've already met, will bring up the rear. No sudden moves, please." Manny and Eric led them into the woodline and around the edge of the iron fence; Susan radioed Julie that they were returning with two guests in tow.

"Wow, you guys survivalists or something?" Eli asked as they passed by the drainage ditch bristling with sharpened wood spikes poking from the melting snow.

Eric turned to face the couple. "No comment," he said, walking backwards. "Nothing personal, but I think you'll understand our desire to keep our cards close to the vest."

"Got it," Eli said.

Eric looked at Susan, her rifle at the low ready, and smiled. She smiled back.

CHAPTER 20

"More, please, honey," Manny said, setting two empty bowls and plates on the kitchen island.

Carmen ladled their two ravenous guests their third helping of elk stew from the pot simmering on the wood-burning stove while Luisa piled the plates with hunks of fresh bread and fresh lentil sprouts from a Mason jar. "Those poor souls are shoveling it in like they haven't eaten in months! *Qué lástima,*" Carmen said, stepping away from the stove's heat to wipe her brow with her apron.

"Or maybe it's because you two make the best elk stew in Montana," Manny said with a wink and carried the food out to the backyard deck on the sunny and warming spring afternoon. Eli and Kayla had stripped off their windbreakers and hats to reveal thin frames and gnarled brown hair—it was obvious at a glance that Susan was right about their having had a rough go of things.

"We can't tell you enough how much we appreciate this," Kayla said as Manny set the steaming bowls in front of them on the wooden picnic table.

Manny grabbed a seat by Eric, Susan, Travis, and Pastor Kris. "It's all right. Please, eat all you'd like—but now that you've got some food in you, let's talk, starting with a bit about yourselves."

The young couple had met as students at the University of California, Irvine, Eli started with his mouth full—he majored in art and sculpture, while she studied agricultural science. He reached under his shirt and pulled out a gold necklace that held half of a heart with her initials engraved on it—he had proposed to Kayla by making a matching set for them.

"I was born and raised in Kalispell," Kayla continued, "so when I got a job offer from the Montana Department of Agriculture, we jumped at the chance and settled here. We both love hiking and camping, so it didn't take Eli long to fall in love with Big Sky Country. We didn't have much, but we were happy—I had a career and job security, and Eli worked odd jobs until he could find a gig as a jeweler or metalworker. I got pregnant last summer, and we were gonna be a family. And then . . ."

"Everything fell apart," Susan finished her sentence.

Kayla grabbed a tissue from the box that Pastor Kris had set out as she recounted their inability to contact their loved ones as the nation slid into anarchy, and their mad dash to grab whatever food they could and fill the bathtub and every container they had with water before it stopped flowing. "It was a nightmare," she continued as Eli rubbed her back. "We had to ration our food and water to make it last, but I was expecting, and I . . . we . . ."

"You lost the baby," Pastor Kris said.

Kayla sobbed into her hands. "We slipped out of Helena last night under cover of darkness," Eli said, his voice thick. "We're heading to her parents in Kalispell 'cause we heard things aren't as bad there. We had to wait out the winter—we woulda frozen to death if we had tried to leave any sooner."

Pastor Kris rose from her chair to offer comfort, but Susan grabbed her arm and whispered in her ear not to, in case they were sick or had lice or some other parasite. Kris dejectedly sat back down.

Eric discretely pulled out a pen and notepad. "Why'd you have to sneak out of town?"

"Because it's become a fucking gulag," Eli spat. "The military, the police, civilians working with the government, have it locked down like a fascist occupying army."

"Who's in charge?"

"Take this with more than a few grains of salt, because it's all straight from the rumor mill. We heard the governor's running everything. The mayor and city council are dead—word has it on the governor's orders because they didn't wanna play along."

Manny's eyes went wide. "*Madre de Dios.* Governor Kellerman did that?"

"No—word has it she's dead, too. Who takes over after her?"

"The lieutenant governor," Eric answered. "Jeremy Matthews—the guy who was caught up, just before the shit hit the fan, in a campaign finance scandal with some Silicon Valley tech CEO who lives out here. His name ring a bell?"

Eli shook his head. "No—sorry to say, we never followed current events or politics. The government, or whoever got the power and water back on, at least intermittently, has never mentioned the governor by name."

Travis leaned forward. "How bad are they cracking down?"

Eli nervously paused. "One day, the authorities pulled onto our block in several Humvees to go door to door searching for 'contraband.' No warrants, nothing. They took a few of our bags of beans and rice because we needed to 'do our part' for the recovery effort. A lot of people had guns confiscated. They took away our neighbor down the street for resisting, and they weren't gentle about it. Dudes were armed to the teeth—flak jackets, military rifles, you name it."

"They've set up places to distribute food," Kayla said. "Waiting in line is where we'd hear whispers about people having their stuff seized, or rumors of people disappearing. While the folks handing out the food seemed nice, the bastard rent-a-cops guarding them practically undressed me with their eyes, and made no attempt to hide it."

Eli pushed his empty bowl away. "Helena's under a dusk-to-dawn curfew, and they're not playing around with violators. We know hoofing it to Kalispell is a huge risk, but we couldn't take any more. We're experienced hikers, we got good equipment, and every day we waited was another day we became a little bit weaker and a little more tired. It was escape now or die slowly."

"Kalispell's almost two hundred miles through the mountains from here. You know that, right?" Travis asked.

"We've got nowhere else to go," Kayla shrugged. "I'm guessing that your, uh, survival retreat doesn't need an invasive species specialist and a jeweler."

"Sorry to be blunt, but no, we don't," Manny said. "But let's see what we can do about improving your odds of getting to Kalispell in one piece."

An hour later, Eli and Kayla were holding their packs open on the back deck so Benny could cram several MREs into each one. The couple glanced skyward as dark clouds to the west obscured the late afternoon sun. "An MRE has a little more than half the average daily caloric intake before America went down the tubes," he said. "Stick to one a day, and round out your calories with the peanut butter."

"I bet you guys have a million of these things squirreled away," Kayla said.

"Actually, no, ma'am. They're expensive, and their shelf life is largely hype—depends a lot on climate-controlled storage. The cost to buy a case of twelve before the collapse, provided you could even find 'em, woulda bought a month of beans and rice." Benny shoved a plastic jar of peanut butter into their packs. "Peanut butter's an awesome survival food—lotsa calories, fat, and protein. It's also a good source of fiber, which comes in handy 'cause MREs have almost none. And neither does this," he said, stuffing a large freezer bag of his homemade venison jerky in each pack.

Benny produced two small plastic bottles containing a milky white substance, which he explained was chlorine concentrate made from pool shock to disinfect drinking water. "At one part disinfectant to one hundred parts water, fill your twenty-four-ounce bottles with about a quarter ounce of this stuff—double if it's cloudy—and let it sit for an hour. Take this seriously—drinkin' bad water is the most likely way you two'll get sick."

Travis strode onto the deck with a chrome .38-caliber revolver and a box of ammunition taken from the Route 12 campground bandits. "This is the most firepower I'm comfortable trusting you with, seeing as how neither of you ever fired a gun before. We don't have time to give you two marksmanship lessons, but this is about as idiot-proof of a weapon as it gets." He gently pressed the gun, muzzle down, into Eli's hand. "Don't ever point it at anything you don't intend to kill, and don't put your finger on the trigger unless you're gonna shoot. But take my advice—stay discreet and stay hidden. If you two find yourselves in a situation in which you have to draw, you're pretty much dead, barring divine intervention."

Eli zipped the revolver in his jacket pocket as Manny, Carmen, and Luisa came through the sliding glass door. The wind began to stiffen.

"Care to stay for dinner?" Carmen asked.

Kayla smiled. "Sure, if you're offering—you're a very good cook, Mrs. Landeros."

Manny rubbed Luisa's head as she tried to squirm away. "Our official meteorologist here is forecasting rain all night, based on what the kitchen weather station's saying. So do those dark clouds rolling in—it wouldn't be right to send you two off in a storm." Manny pointed to the quarantine camper between the house and the woods. "You two can spend the night in The Cooler over there, and we'll see you off tomorrow morning after breakfast."

Luisa turned to her parents once they returned to the kitchen. "Mom, Dad, why can't we let them stay? They seem real nice!"

Carmen looked into Luisa's eyes—her daughter now stood at her height, and still had years of growing to do. "They do, honey. But our resources are limited—except for the garden and what we can hunt, what we have stored away is all we have."

"*Mijita*, we have to make tough choices," Manny said, putting his hand on Luisa's cheek. "If they had useful skills—like if Kayla was a doctor or something—we'd sit down as a group and talk about letting them stay. But they don't. We did what Jesus told us to do by giving them charity, but we can't take them in."

"I hope they get to her family," Luisa said dejectedly. "The whole world sucks right now."

"It'll get better, honey," Carmen said and hugged her daughter, not believing for a second the soothing lie she told her.

***

The rain finally let up an hour before daybreak. Pastor Kris offered a prayer for safe travels before Manny and Eric escorted their guests down the gravel driveway to the front gate as the warming rays of the rising sun peeked through clearing skies. A Steller's jay in the woods along the country road announced their approach with a high-pitched *whit-whit-whit-whit-whit*, which its black-crested brethren passed along.

"Guys, we can't thank you enough," Eli said, shaking hands to the steady dripping of water from the trees.

"I hope you look us up if your journeys ever take you to Kalispell," Kayla said. "We owe you a nice dinner at the very least. God bless you all."

"God bless everyone trapped in this lousy mess," Eric said. "Good luck. And remember—you were never here. We don't exist." Eli and Kayla nodded, then turned around and continued their trek.

Eric watched the duo disappear around the bend in the road. "You think they'll make it, compadre?"

"No," Manny admitted. "I don't."

CHAPTER 21

L uisa settled into her dad's leather office chair as he gave her a refresher course on how to use the landline connecting the CQ to the LP/OP.

"Respond if Pastor Kris calls in, but leave the other radios alone—don't use them under any circumstance," Manny said. "You have any questions, or hear something crazy, run and grab me, OK?"

Luisa nodded. "Thanks for trusting me, Dad. I won't let you down."

"I know, honey—that's why you got the job," Manny said with a grin and walked to the living room where the rest of the group had gathered.

Manny spent about five minutes summarizing the disturbing news that Eli and Kayla had relayed. "Well, folks, we've always worried that the government would take advantage of catastrophe to become tyrants, and apparently, that's what's happening."

Allan stepped forward. "Their accounts add credibility to similar stories we've heard on Redoubt Radio." He looked to Manny, who nodded his permission to continue. "We've long suspected that the bandits we killed at the campground last September weren't some random band of thugs exploiting the collapse—based on this new information, we're very confident that they were, in fact, working on behalf of this regime, whatever it is. Which means we may have royally pissed them off."

"Way too close for comfort," grumbled Matt, who held hands with Angel on the couch. "We've always talked about the federal government tearing what's left of the Constitution to shreds, but these despots are barely a stone's throw away!"

"What do we know about this lieutenant governor supposedly in charge?" Angel asked over her friends' nervous mutters.

"Jeremy Matthews?" Eric asked. "Not one hell of a lot, except that he and Governor Kellerman didn't get along—I understand it's a long-standing tradition in Montana politics for the governor and the lieutenant governor to hate each other's guts. Lieutenant governor is a do-nothing job—you're essentially a spare in the event the governor kicks the bucket."

Susan leaned forward on the side couch. "Eric, you said something yesterday about Matthews being tied up in some sort of scandal with some rich guy. Care to elaborate?"

"I can," Roger interjected. "Guy's name is Stuart Magnuson. He's been profiled in local news stories over the past few years—typical liberal media love letters to a fellow traveler. He was some Berkeley geek who struck gold with his software startup, and ended up at the helm of one of those Big Tech companies in Silicon Valley. Bought a mansion out here about five years ago—guy sounds like he's got more money than God."

Eric sipped his coffee. "Even though he kept a low profile, it looked like Mister Magnuson was keen on exporting his California politics to Big Sky Country. Just before the collapse, election authorities alleged that his contributions to Matthews violated campaign finance laws—I don't remember the particulars. Rumors were swirling in the political press that Matthews was gonna run against Kellerman in the primary, and maybe Magnuson was jockeying to be his bag man to fund the rematch. Dunno how this fits into the current situation, though."

"What about the Legislature?" Angel asked. "They're just letting this Matthews guy or whoever crown himself king?"

"I don't think there's much they *can* do," Eric answered with a shrug. "Heaven only knows how many of 'em are alive to begin with—and those survivors are scattered across a really big state with no mass communication. I don't see them in a position to demand any answers."

"It sounds like whoever's in charge is moving to consolidate power with the spring thaw," Julie said. "Besides uh, 'pacifying' the Helena area, for lack of a better word, they're sending aid and manpower to other towns along the Rocky Mountains. We have no idea how the larger cities are going along with this, but in the smaller towns, it sounds like these folks prefer the stick over the carrot."

Manny cleared his throat and raised his hands. "Regardless of who's pulling the strings, we need to have a plan if we come to their attention. Agreed?" Group members nodded. "We never got around to burying some of our supplies in caches in case we get overrun. Matt, I need you to pick us half a dozen cache sites—some of them close, some of them far. We're gonna fill the six plastic barrels in the barn with spare food, ammunition, clothing and other supplies." He pivoted to Allan and Julie. "Your top priority is to gather any information you can on this new enemy, particularly troop strengths and locations. Report everything you find to Eric. Benny, how much ammo we got?"

"A lot," he answered. "Everyone did a great job stocking up before the collapse, which was no small task, given all these years of crazy demand and prices. We got just under one hundred and fifty thousand rounds—about half of that is .22 rimfire, which is great for shootin' chipmunks but lousy for fighting a guerrilla war. We got enough raw materials to produce another ten thousand commonly used calibers with the reloadin' press in the barn if it comes to that."

"Let it come to that!" Pete proclaimed to grunts of approval. "We could fight 'em all the doo-dah day."

Manny grinned. "I'd like to think so, too, but we can't assume we'd be up against rabble like the campground bandits—if the bad guys come calling with a platoon of infantrymen and a Stryker, we're in real trouble. Let's all meet right here, this time tomorrow, to double-check our bug-out bags in case we have to evacuate *muy pronto*. I don't mean to scare you all spitless, but if professional bad guys decide to show their face here, I don't wanna be caught by surprise." He whistled and ran his fingers through his hair. "I don't know about all of you, but I can't wait for movie night tonight. Jay, I don't care if you crush your fingers in the reloading press—you're still on for making wood-stove popcorn, because you're the only person here who can do it without burning it. What's the movie tonight, Angel?"

"The Sisterhood of the Traveling Pants."

"Jay, I'm ordering you to crush Angel's fingers in the reloading press instead," Eric said to laughs from the men and dirty looks from the women.

As the group filtered out of the living room, Manny grabbed Allan's arm and pulled him aside. "I didn't wanna say this in front of everyone, but I got a feeling we're gonna need friends for what's coming," he muttered in Allan's ear. "Start, very discreetly, looking for other people like us. Report any possible leads directly to me."

Carmen hugged her husband in the archway connecting the living room and the dining room. "Remember all those late-night talks at Fort Irwin with Eric, Travis, and Matt about hypothetical scenarios? Now we're living one, and it still doesn't seem real."

Manny stared into Carmen's eyes. "What do we tell Luisa?"

"The truth. There are bad people out there, but when she sleeps at night, she's surrounded by men and women who would give their lives to keep her safe."

He kissed her on the forehead. "I feel very sorry for anyone who comes here looking to start something."

CHAPTER 22

Preparing for a potential fight added to an already full schedule of chores, first and foremost being spring planting.

The group had already planted onions, potatoes, peas, and other hardy plants, with carrots, radishes and more to follow when the threat of frost was more or less over. Roger decided not to plant to the garden's full potential—the group had years of food stored, and Roger humbly acknowledged that there could be a learning curve for him planting in the mountains outside of Helena, rather than what he was used to in Butte. The brutally cold winter and cooler spring also lent credence to Julie's concern that smoke from all the cities and towns that had burned during the collapse could have created a miniature nuclear winter that would throw the next couple of growing seasons out of whack.

Predictably, the large garden plot attracted woodland creatures wanting a more exciting diet than grass and wild berries. While it was advantageous in ensuring that the retreat had a steady supply of meat—large game would be shot from the LP/OP—it created extra duty in the form of a nightwatch on the deck, armed with a .22-rimfire rifle to dispatch smaller pests.

Roger and Pastor Kris insisted that everybody learn as much about organic gardening from them as possible, and there would be ample opportunity to practice—essentially, everyone's secondary full-time job would be farmhands. "One, if we die, and you folks don't know which end of the shovel goes into the ground, you die, too," Roger would say. "And two, you all insisted that we old farts learn how to play soldier, so all of you get to learn how to pull weeds and compost your table scraps."

The specter of a potential shooting war incentivized members to teach their skills to everyone else. Susan led a number of first-aid classes to at least get everyone the proficiency that the group's military veterans had. While everyone understood radio basics, Allan thought it prudent to start teaching the more complicated art of ham radio, and how to minimize the odds of their signals being triangulated. Susan and Jay, however, possessed highly technical skill sets not easily passed on to a group. For redundancy, Manny decided to give them both apprentices to absorb what they could. Angel began learning more advanced medical care under Susan, and Jay took Pete under his wing to teach him automotive repair, mechanics, and construction skills.

Eric and Travis taught classes on map reading and land navigation—finding one's way with a map and a compass had become a lost art in the pre-Unraveling world of GPS and smart phones. They devised an ingenious final exam; in four-person teams, group members had to find the six small colored flags marking where the caches would be buried in the woods, thus committing the locations to memory. The only casualty was a trip flare lost when Allan inadvertently set it off; members buried the caches the following week.

Luisa, who inherited her mother's talent for art, helped her father draw sketches for each window and the LP/OP that highlighted sectors of fire, mapped out dead space, and listed the distances to major objects in meters. Manny lacquered them onto sturdy wooden boards and nailed them to the walls.

To spice things up, Susan and Travis occasionally taught hand-to-hand combat. Travis had earned a first-degree black belt in the Marine Corps Martial Arts Program, nicknamed "semper fu" by Marines, while Susan held a brown belt in krav maga, an Israeli martial art known for its brutal application to real-world situations. Susan warned her students to rely on hand-to-hand as a last resort, given that many collapse survivors could be walking bags of infectious disease. Angel, who had taken karate as a child, asked Susan after one session why she chose krav maga; Susan advised her, if she ever decided to learn a martial art once the world returned to normal, to "choose one that teaches you how to kick someone's ass rather than break boards."

"Don't ever learn a fighting style that expects your opponent to play fair," Susan lectured her.

"There's only one rule in a fight," Travis added as he toweled off his face. "There are no rules."

***

News from the outside world continued to worsen.

A federal government radio broadcast tentatively, and many thought far too conservatively, estimated that almost one American in three had perished. Independent broadcasters painted an even darker picture. New England was almost completely depopulated, save for scattered upstate enclaves away from the coasts. Similar fates befell Arizona, New Mexico, and Nevada—people in the desert Southwest who survived the economic collapse and the flu didn't survive the loss of the water supply when the grid went down. Utah, full of Mormons with a philosophy of storing deep larders of food and water, was faring all right, but group members wondered what they would do when their supplies ran out, given the state had little arable land. Alaska was particularly hard hit, and ham operators relayed stories of a mass die-off over the long winter; in many places, only the hardiest outdoorsmen were left.

Eastern Oregon, which like eastern Washington had long chafed under the rule of Portland and the state capital of Salem, followed eastern Washington's example and split into a new state calling itself Pacifica. Idaho applauded the move and pledged its support, just as it had done with Cascadia and Jefferson. Redoubt Radio reported that Idaho was negotiating with these new states, as well as with Utah, Wyoming, and surviving portions of Colorado, about forming some sort of alliance. Montana was conspicuously absent, which made group members wonder what Idaho's leaders knew that they didn't.

The legislatures of Kansas, Nebraska, and North and South Dakota joined the growing list of seceding states, resulting again in angry threats from the ensconced federal government. While some reports claimed that military units were being massed to bring wayward states back into line, conflicting accounts alleged that the federal government was, for all practical intents and purposes, nonexistent.

Europe had fared little better. The flu devastated the United Kingdom, Germany, and the Benelux countries, and France was fighting raging domestic unrest—its police and military, under shoot-to-kill orders, turned the streets red with blood as they answered protesters' rocks with bullets. Winter had been particularly cruel to Scandinavia, and Russia, already economically and militarily pushed to its limits as a consequence of its invasion of Ukraine and the rapacious corruption of its ruling oligarchs, had disintegrated outright.

Middle Eastern nations collapsed along with the Western economies dependent on their oil, and the long-simmering proxy war between Sunni-dominated Saudi Arabia and Shia-dominated Iran had become a full-blown shooting war that ignited sectarian fighting throughout the Muslim world. What was left of Japan was starving with the end of oil and food shipments, and because runoff from shattered Chinese cities had fouled already overworked Japanese fishing waters.

Over the long winter, Allan had had no luck getting in touch with his older brother, or any other of the group's loved ones besides Angel's sister.

CHAPTER 23

The rising sun had barely begun to peek through the trees as Eric strolled to the barn, where the four friends he would be leading on the group's first patrol awaited him.

He took his time inspecting them. Eric had each person jump in the air to ensure their canteens weren't sloshing, and that no buckles or other metallic items were clacking together. "What does it mean if you hear three whistle blasts?" Eric quizzed Julie as he wrapped a noisy buckle on her tactical vest with a roll of black electrical tape—a good leader inspected soldiers' minds as well as their equipment.

"It means fall back to the last rally point," she answered without hesitation. Eric stepped over to Allan and gave his rifle the once-over. "How many legs are on our patrol this morning?"

"Four—we're visiting the three properties nearest to us, and then returning."

Eric stepped to Matt. "What . . . is the air-speed velocity of an unladen swallow?"

"African or European?" Matt shot back.

Everyone laughed but Benny. "I don't get it. Must be a gringo thing," he said before his jumping revealed the sloshing of a half-empty canteen.

"Head to the kitchen and top that off. Before you do, what's the challenge and password for this morning? And what's our running password in case we have to authenticate ourselves in a hurry?"

"'Espresso' and 'crayon,' and the running password is 'klaxon,'" Benny answered and jogged past Manny, who came out to see off the patrol.

Eric looked his people over one last time when Benny returned. They wore fatigues with camouflage boonie hats, and slathered their faces in green paint. Each carried six twenty-round magazines for their .308 Winchester rifles, on top of the one they had loaded. Their small field packs held rain ponchos, extra socks, two MREs, spare batteries, extra water, and a Katadyn water filter in case they ran out and had to drink from streams or other open sources.

"I know you're all looking forward to getting away from Manny Landeros's School for Gifted Youngsters, but this isn't a leisure stroll," Eric addressed the patrol. "Our job is to check the mile or so beyond our perimeter and report back what we find. Don't get us killed because someone sneaks up behind you and smashes your head in with a log while you're admiring the scenery."

Allan squirmed under the weight of his pack. "I don't understand why they call you Army guys 'light infantry.'"

"This is nothing, dude," Matt said. "A combat soldier's load averaged a hundred pounds—more if you had to hump the machine gun or other heavy weapon."

"In other words, suck it up, buttercup," Julie said, turning Allan's head toward her and smearing some of his face paint to cover up a bare spot on his cheek.

"I knew a snowflake somewhere had to survive the end of civilization. Freakin' figures that he'd end up in my patrol," Eric groused, pulling an elastic band from his pocket and handing it to Allan. "As the only person on this patrol who's ocularly challenged, you're gonna want to attach these to your eyeglasses— you don't want your specs flying off your face in a firefight."

"I should've gotten Lasik while I had the chance rather than spend my money on spares," Allan said as he attached the band.

"Woulda coulda shoulda, pal. There are a lot of things I would've liked to have done, but put off until it was too late," Eric said before turning to Manny. "I already gave you our five-point contingency plan yesterday, but I'll do it again for the benefit of the group. Quick, Matt, name all five parts."

"Where we're going, who all is going, how long we'll be gone, what to do if we don't return, and actions that we and the retreat will take if attacked," he recited.

Eric acknowledged the correct answer with a nod as he turned to Manny. "We're gonna recon the three nearest homes to us. I'm taking Allan, Julie, Benny, and Matt, and we'll be gone eight to twelve hours. If we're not back by then, try contacting us by radio every hour for another twelve hours. If we're attacked, we'll break contact and make our way home through an indirect route that doesn't lead straight back here. If the retreat is attacked, we'll return and attempt to outflank the attackers."

Matt saw Angel watching through the bedroom window. She blew him a kiss, which he caught, and sent back one of his own.

"Be safe, everyone," Manny said. *"Vayan con Dios."*

"Let's go—noise discipline from this point forward," Eric said and signaled the group to move out up the hill toward the LP/OP. His team fell in behind him, five meters between one another, to take their first baby steps into a changed and foreign world they knew only from radio broadcasts.

PART TWO

Fear of the state is in no sense subversive. It is, to the contrary, the healthiest political philosophy for a free people.

—Col. Jeff Cooper

CHAPTER 24

A majestic eight-point, white-tailed deer grazed in a small patch of spring grass between Eric's recon team and the first house they were tasked with visiting.

Two hours into their patrol, Eric had spread his team into a small perimeter about fifty meters from the backyard of the neighbors who had warned Manny about the Route 12 campground bandits before bugging out to Utah. The patrol removed their boonie hats to listen for any noises coming from what was supposed to be an empty house.

Eric drank in the tranquility of the woods and the light breeze rustling the pine trees and caressing his face. As thankful as he was for having safe harbor in a world that had become one giant Hieronymus Bosch painting of damnation, he had become thoroughly sick of Manny's property, and even sicker of winter.

The buck glanced in the patrol's direction before returning to his nibbling, somehow knowing they weren't there to hunt. Eric and Benny smiled at each other—while the hunting was good in Benny's native Texas, the outdoorsman thought he had died and gone to heaven when he moved to Montana. Even with the population die-off, Eric guessed there were probably more than enough hungry people left alive east of the Mississippi River to strip the forests of every last living creature. He once lamented during a cup of coffee with Susan about how many species would end up going extinct to fill empty bellies; as much as he had made peace with the ongoing breakup of the United States, he couldn't stomach the possibility of a North America without bald eagles.

Eric was about to pull his team in to review one last time how they would approach the house when a pleasant but out-of-place scent caught his nose. The buck's head shot up from his patch of grass and bounded away, snapping branches with his retreat.

Benny sniffed the air. "You smell that, boss?"

"Yeah. Wood smoke."

***

Manny stood at the CQ dry-erase board, black marker in hand, as Luisa flipped the *Merriam-Webster's Collegiate Dictionary* to a random page.

"Tomorrow's password, Dad, is 'charlatan,'" Luisa said, holding up the dictionary so he could spell it correctly—she had already selected "laconic" for the next day's verbal challenge.

"Hope you don't think I'm one," Manny said as he scribbled the password next to the frequency—MURS channel five—that the recon patrol was using.

Luisa lightly crossed out the word with a pencil. "Why do we pick the challenge and password this way?"

Jay, who was on CQ duty, set down a worn copy of *The Hunt for Red October* on the desk. "The short answer, kiddo, is so's that the words have no connection with each other. What's the first word you think of when I say, 'door'?"

"Knob."

"Well, if 'door' and 'knob' are our challenge and password, or 'snow' and 'ball,' it'd be easy for bad guys to guess their way into our perimeter. But no one's gonna guess 'charlatan' when presented with 'laconic'—hell, I got no idea what in the Sam Hill 'laconic' means."

Luisa turned back to her father, who was staring at the board listing every member's name, call sign, and activity; PATROL was scrawled next to Eric, Allan, Julie, Matt, and Cousin Benny.

"Worried, Dad?"

"No, honey, they're fine. Just jealous, that's all. I'm ready to get the heck outta here and go for a little stroll myself."

"I like your call sign. Culebra."

"That's what my buddies called me in the Army. They said I was like a snake—silent and deadly."

The leather office chair squeaked as Jay leaned back with a devilish grin. "You were silent an' deadly, all right, after last night's three-bean soup. You darn near fumigated the barn, with me in it!"

Manny stabbed his finger at Jay as Luisa broke out into laughter. "That's it, wise guy—you're on KP for the next month! And you, Luisa, are supposed to be with Roger and your mom on gardening detail—you've been talkin' me up to goldbrick. *¡Vamos!*" Luisa ran out of the room, still giggling.

Jay glanced at the wall clock and picked up the TA-1 field phone for his hourly radio check with Pastor Kris at the LP/OP.

"Any word from the patrol?" she asked.

"Not yet—they're not bound to regular check-ins. I'm sure they're OK, but any kind words you can say to the Almighty on their behalf would be welcome, I'm sure."

Pastor Kris set the TA-1 on the LP/OP's weathered and gouged wooden desk next to her battle rifle on its unfolded bipod, and prayed for the recon patrol; Eric and company had checked out with her, but it would most likely be Pete, who had the noon to 6 p.m. shift, who would welcome them back. She picked up her Steiner binoculars and scanned the woods on what was shaping up to be a beautiful spring day. *Except that I'm dressed like a commando and standing in a big hole in the ground, ready to blow someone's brains out*, she said to herself.

While Pastor Kris and Roger had grown up shooting hunting rifles and shotguns, they had had a hard time adjusting to handguns and semiautomatic military-style rifles. They each bought military-style rifles chambered in .308 Winchester and 5.56-millimeter NATO, as well as .45-caliber Ruger handguns, which Kris wore on the front of her tactical vest. Even though she was strong enough to wield the handgun, she hated its recoil; the women in the group preferred 9-millimeter handguns, but the veterans were adamant that they also own .45 automatics for their superior knockdown power. Pastor Kris glanced at her trusty Remington 700 bolt-action .308 rifle leaning against the LP/OP's reinforced wall; while she came to trust her military-style rifle, her Remington was her go-to weapon in the LP/OP if she needed to shoot something at distance.

She watched her husband through her binoculars as he prepared to plant seeds in the big backyard garden plot with Carmen and Luisa. Part of her was dying for a cup of coffee to go with the scenic mountain morning, but she had weaned herself off of it shortly after their arrival so she wouldn't suffer from withdrawal once it was gone. She hoped Eric, who had stocked up on freeze-dried coffee and green coffee beans from roasters who catered to preppers and survivalists, had the common sense to start cutting back as his supply dwindled—the caffeine monkey on his back would become a gorilla otherwise. She chased away the related thought of what it would mean for her husband when his supply of heart medication ran out.

Pastor Kris liked Eric a lot. He was a good man who wore his feelings for Susan on his sleeve, and she suspected that Susan was starting to reciprocate—a woman doesn't stay up past midnight to keep Christmas dinner warm for a man because she's concerned about his nutrition. She took a deep breath of pine-scented air and sighed as a red-tailed hawk screamed in the distance. *I hope those two figure things out sooner rather than later,* she thought. *In a world like this, later sometimes never comes.*

***

"Base, this is Recon, prepare to copy SALUTE report, over."

Jay slapped Tom Clancy closed, spilling cold water from his canteen onto his lap as he lunged for the MURS handset.

"This report's gonna be a bit unorthodox," Eric radioed in. "Is Culebra there, over?"

Manny snatched the mike from Jay's hand. "Right here—send your traffic."

"The first house is supposed to be empty, right?"

Manny answered in the affirmative as his thoughts drifted to former neighbor Tom Bannon, a retired businessman, and his wife, Drea. They had hunkered down when the collapse first started—as Mormons, they had stored a lot of food to see them through—but changed their minds when a friend over the mountain made it to them after being robbed and beaten by the Route 12 bandits. The Bannons crammed every nook and cranny of their truck and trailer with whatever they could, and bugged out for their daughter's house in Logan, Utah. "We're not ever coming back. The house and whatever's left inside is yours," Tom had told Manny and Carmen over the idling engine. "Won't be needing it, anyway—this is the end times and the Second Coming for sure." Manny quickly prayed that the Bannons had made it safe.

"We see three people in the backyard—two young men and one young woman, in military uniforms, hanging laundry and burning trash," Eric reported—as the recon team crawled through the forest to the edge of the property line, the toxic stench of burning plastic displaced the smell of wood fire. "They don't have their weapons with 'em, so it looks like amateur hour. An LMTV is parked at the side of the house, over."

Manny processed the information as Travis strode through the door, attracted by the commotion. "Only three?"

"Affirmative. I don't wanna make any potentially fatal assumptions, but my gut says they're deserters. I'd like to take 'em by surprise and find out what they're up to. If they're hostile, we don't want 'em building a nest right next to ours."

"Wait one," Manny said and turned to Travis. "Thoughts, Marine?"

"Sounds 'bout right—three kids decided they ain't gonna study war no more and found a hideout. If this was some kind of makeshift forward operating base, they wouldn't be washing their drawers and runnin' around without their weapons."

Manny keyed the mike. "Recon, proceed as discussed. Get to the bottom of this. If they're on the wrong side . . ." he paused, ". . . take care of it. If you find yourself in contact with a larger force, beat feet back here. Out."

While his recon team covered him, Eric slowly low-crawled as close as he could get without being spotted. His window of opportunity opened five minutes later when the two men turned away from the trash fire to talk to the woman.

"Don't move! We have you surrounded!" Eric hollered. The three young soldiers spun and looked into the woods, paralyzed into inaction and eyes wide as saucers. *Fight, flight, or freeze—they chose the worst option. Good start*, Eric thought. "Do what we say, and no one gets hurt! Are there any more of you? Don't lie." All three shook their heads no.

Eric ordered them to turn away from his voice, guided them into something of a line with five meters between each of them in the overgrown backyard, and ordered them to their knees, ankles crossed and hands on top of their heads. With a chop of Eric's hand forward, Matt and Julie popped up to frisk them before searching the truck and the house. After what seemed like an eternity, they walked out the back door and gave a thumbs-up that the house was clear. Eric told the prisoners they could sit down, as long as they didn't make any sudden moves or talk to one another; he lowered his harnessed rifle, grabbed a notepad and pen out of a ziplock bag, and motioned Julie over to help him interview them one at a time.

Julie thumbed at the LMTV behind her. "You'll wanna take a look inside the truck first."

Eric hoisted himself up onto the truck's tall ramp with a jump, and his jaw dropped the moment his tactical flashlight pierced the artificial darkness of the canvas cover. The LMTV was packed with wooden crates containing thousands of rounds of 5.56- and 7.62-millimeter ammunition, as well as a crate of hand grenades, and several crates of 40-millimeter high-explosive and tear gas shells—an adjacent box held several rail-mounted M203 launcher attachments for rifles like theirs to fire them. But one gem stood out in the truck like glittering treasure—an M240B heavy machine gun resting on its bipod legs.

"Well, fuck me running . . ."

CHAPTER 25

Their stories matched to the letter. The three deserters—ROTC Cadet Katie Gutowski, Specialist Liam Littlejohn, and Private First Class Tim McCormick—went AWOL from Fort Harrison on New Year's Eve rather than follow unlawful orders. They happened upon the vacant home by chance after a nerve-racking night of navigating a wintry maze of back roads to find a safe place to hunker down for the winter.

They had fled with five. One of their two sergeants, Andy Reese, decided to take his chances and hotwire the Bannons' old SUV to make it over the snow-covered mountains to his family in Deer Lodge—there had been rumors of a mass jailbreak at the nearby Montana State Prison. Several weeks later, their leader, Steve James, developed a terrible stomachache and a high fever that turned out to be appendicitis. The kids he had led to safety were powerless to do anything except watch him die. They were forced to leave him, frozen, in the truck—twice chasing off wolves—until the ground had thawed enough to bury him.

The deserters and the recon patrol ate MRE lunches together in the late morning sunshine to the chorus of spring songbirds. The young soldiers became at ease after learning that Eric and Matt had served in the Army.

"I gotta say, I admire your guts," Matt said with a mouthful of chicken and salsa, fresh from his MRE's water-powered meal heater. "You didn't just take off—you boosted a bunch of supplies to hurt your unit's ability to hurt others."

Eric tore open his MRE's tube of freeze-dried coffee and unceremoniously dumped it into his mouth before chasing it with cold water from the CamelBak water bladder on his back—he needed his fix. "I couldn't help but notice that your stash consists of old-school weapons and ammo—I thought the Army transitioned to the new M5 rifle and that wacky caliber it uses."

"The infantry and front-line troops did. We REMFs still get to use the old stuff," Tim said.

"REMFs?" Allan asked.

"Rear-echelon motherfuckers—people other than grunts," Eric explained with a smirk.

"It's too bad we couldn't make off with more," Tim continued. "But Sergeant James . . . um, didn't wanna push our luck."

Katie set down her canteen and pushed away a lock of brunette hair. "It's been awful, cooped up with no news of the outside world, not knowing if our families are OK. We're stuck here. Where do we go? To my parents in Boise? To Tim's, in Townsend? To Liam's parents and girlfriend, in what's left of Billings?" Liam, a man who obviously loved to hit the gym before the collapse, barely acknowledged the remark—he hadn't said a word since his interview at gunpoint.

Benny wiped his mouth on his sleeve. "So what're you gonna do?"

Tim shrugged. "We've only just started talking about it now that we're running out of food. The Army surely knows we deserted. We can't show our faces anywhere—we'd be dead the moment we stumbled upon a checkpoint or roadblock."

Eric closed his eyes and raised his head to feel the sun's warming rays on his face. *You couldn't do anything to save your students*, a powerful voice spoke from his heart. *But you can save these kids.* He laid his MRE in the matted weeds, stretched, and walked behind the truck to radio the CQ.

"Lemme get this straight—they have a truckload of 'goodies,' over?" Manny incredulously asked after Eric explained the deserters' predicament.

"I don't wanna elaborate on the air, but yeah. All three have strong backs, and heaven only knows what they've seen and heard while in the enemy's camp. They're in a tough spot, and we should think about taking them in."

Manny tapped the handset on his chin as he pondered the variables. "Don't bring 'em here. I'll suit up and bring a buddy with me to check out the 'goodie truck' and have a nice talk with them. Tell them they got a shot at joining us, but no promises—we don't know jack about 'em, and I don't want any degenerates living under the same roof as my wife and little girl—I already got you, and that's two degenerates too many. Got it?"

"Got it. Wilco and out," Eric signed off.

Manny examined their fifteen-soldier roster on the dry-erase board. "Whaddya think, Jay? We got room for more?"

"How many do you see?" an unfamiliar voice asked.

Jay sat upright. "Didja hear that? That came from one of the radios!"

"Which one?" Manny demanded.

The orange display screen of the cheap FRS radio at the edge of the CQ desk lit up. "Three in the garden. An older dude and two beaners—a woman and a girl."

"Hot damn, someone's got eyes on us!" Jay swore, bolting out of the CQ chair. The Dakota Alert blew the siren alarm for the vehicle probe under the road, and the detector monitoring the deer path in the woods. Three shots from a high-powered rifle rang out a second later.

****

"Kids, I may have a solution to your little conundrum of not wanting to assume room temperature," Eric told the seated deserters. "The honcho of our band of merry men and women is heading over, and if he thinks you have skills we can use and work ethics to match—and provided you're not batshit crazy, sex maniacs, dope fiends, or any combination thereof—we'll bring the three of you to a vote for membership. In exchange for putting a roof over your heads and food in your tummies, you give us 110 percent. And that," Eric stabbed his finger at the LMTV and its contents, "becomes community property. Sound like a good deal?"

"As opposed to dying alone of starvation? Sounds great to me!" Katie beamed. Tim enthusiastically nodded, and Liam cracked the slightest of grins.

Gunshots echoed from the direction of the retreat. Eric's radio blared to life.

"Recon, get your asses back here! We're under attack!"

CHAPTER 26

Pastor Kris scrambled behind her black military rifle the moment she spotted the two armed men creeping along the edge of the woods.

The scope's reticle bounced with her pounding heart, which she desperately commanded to slow as she thumbed off the safety and slid her finger onto the trigger. The men dropped to a knee behind two large trees and raised their AR-clone rifles to take aim at her husband, Carmen, and Luisa planting seeds in the black tilled soil.

"God forgive me," Pastor Kris whispered before shooting the nearest man three times. She shifted her aim with lightning speed as he crumpled to the ground and put another three rounds into his partner, whose chest exploded in puffs of red and pink.

"*Ruuuuuuuuuuuuuun!*" Roger screamed as the trio sprinted for the safety of the decorative rock wall at the edge of the rear deck, the woods behind them erupting with gunfire.

Group members thundered through the house to their battle stations and began returning fire, the roar of shooting indoors hammering their eardrums and the stink of cordite riding the spring breeze that had been wafting through the open windows.

"Get Kris on the horn and tell her something's comin' down the road!" Manny screamed at Jay before sprinting up the stairs and sliding behind the wall of sandbags below the master bedroom side window.

The white-hot intensity of a trip flare lit up the woods in Manny's sector of fire, along with the hapless invader who set it off.

"Gracias, cabrón," Manny growled and dispatched him with two shots, the deafening staccato followed by the tinkle of spent brass hitting the hardwood floor. *A handful of us against God knows how many of them! Get back here fast, Eric, or we're all dead,* Manny said to himself before his tactical assessment gave way to raw terror.

Carmen. Luisa. The garden!

***

"We're outta here in two minutes! Grab your shit and let's go!" Eric screamed at the wide-eyed recon team. He whirled on the three deserters as they leapt to their feet. "I'm altering the deal—fight with us, and you're in the club. What say?"

"Lock and load!" Katie yelled, pulling her M4 carbine close.

"Benny!" Eric barked. "Bring me the machine gun from the truck! Tim! Go with him and grab, hell, ten belts of 7.62-millimeter! Hey, uh, Meat Mountain—"

"Liam," the burly specialist corrected, stepping forward and towering a head and a half above Eric.

"Whatever—I need an assistant gunner, and you're hired. You got a rucksack?" He nodded. "Dump it and fill it with the ammo Tim brings you! Katie! Matt! Grab any colored bedsheet or fabric you can find in the house, and tear it into eight wide strips. Fast!"

"What the hell for?" Matt asked on the run.

"So we don't get our balls blown off by our own people!" Eric yelled as Benny galloped up and set the M240B at his feet. Eric spun his rifle onto his back, popped open the machine gun's feed tray cover, and pulled back the charging handle with a loud *clack*. "Where have you been all my life, baby?" Eric said, looping the large machine gun's padded sling over his head and shooting to his feet as Tim ran up, slouching under the weight of the olive drab bags of ammo belts slung over his shoulders. "Let's make some noise!"

Hang in there, Susan!

CHAPTER 27

Manny analyzed his lousy situation as he scanned for targets. He had six people shooting back—five in the house and one in the LP/OP. Jay was busy coordinating in the CQ, one-third of his total manpower was out on patrol, and the remaining three—which included his wife and daughter—were pinned down outside.

Susan, Angel, Travis, and Pete each covered a side of the house. When the shooting first started, however, they blindly ran to their assigned stations without taking the absent patrol members into account. Their enemy seized on the blunder, and several managed to advance past the woods to the quarantine camper; if they got much closer, they would be in range to hurl Molotov cocktails or other incendiary devices and burn them out. However, the group had a big advantage besides being entrenched—they could listen in on their enemy's radio communications. Manny prayed they would be able to exploit it as he fired two shots at the head of an invader peeking out from behind a tree.

"They caught us with our pants around our ankles, boss!" Travis screamed from Luisa's room.

"Zip it and watch your sector!" Manny screamed back, sick with panic. He was desperate to save his family, but couldn't leave his post with so few people on the line.

***

Two attackers sprinted toward the side of the barn to shield themselves from incoming fire from the house. It didn't shield them from Pastor Kris, who cut them down in rapid succession. The clacker on the TA-1 flashed as she stopped to slap a fresh twenty-round magazine into her rifle's well.

"I have bad guys all over the woodline!" Pastor Kris yelled into the field phone.

"No kiddin', Reverend!" Jay said from underneath the oaken CQ desk. "The Dakota Alert for the road went off—tell us what's comin'! Go to your MURS radio so you can talk with the rest of us! Channel five!"

Pastor Kris fumbled one-handed through her pocket for her bud earpiece and stabbed it into her radio. She pivoted to look down the road through her scope and caught a pickup truck idling at the far edge of the property, hidden by the woods. A bearded man standing behind the lead truck's cab alternated between watching the battle through binoculars and screaming into a handheld radio.

"That's the honcho!" Jay yelled excitedly. "We just heard him orderin' people not to shoot up our trucks or the solar panels! Kill the bastard!"

No sooner had Jay slammed down the TA-1 when Eric reported in; Jay listened in disbelief as Eric breathlessly summarized the situation while sprinting through the woods in the lead of the augmented recon patrol. Jay scrambled out from under the desk and punched the intercom button. "This is the CQ! Recon's headin' back, ETA five minutes! They're comin' in from the west! No time to explain, but there's eight of 'em, and they're wearin' red sashes, so don't shoot 'em! And if you hear a machine gun open up, that's Eric—repeat, the machine gun is a friendly!"

A sledgehammer blow pummeled Jay's right arm, knocking him against the wall. He fell to the floor to the cascade of glass from the shattered window.

***

"Everyone get that?!" Susan hollered from the bachelorette quarters across the hall as she knelt to reload. "Don't shoot the deranged maniac with the machine gun because he's *our* deranged maniac!"

She peeked over the sandbag wall and saw a face peeking back from behind an evergreen at the edge of the woods. She fired three shots as the man made a run for the ditch in the side yard—he dropped his rifle and clutched his wounded abdomen just before tumbling headlong into the spikes the group had hammered in last fall. A blood-curdling scream briefly rose over the withering gunfire before throttling to a halt. *I'm not looking forward to seeing that*, she thought before ducking back down with the sound of incoming fire peppering the side of the house. The upper window pane shattered into hundreds of glittering shards that rained down on her head.

"I'm runnin' low on ammo!" Travis bellowed from down the hall.

Manny cursed himself for his stupidity—Benny was in charge of ammo resupply in the event of an attack on the retreat, but he was out on patrol with no backup designated. "Jay! Run downstairs and grab some .308! Fast!" Manny hollered.

He got no answer back. "Jay! *Jay!*" he screamed, the veins in his neck bulging. "Where the hell *are* you?!"

***

Roger staunched the blood flowing from a gash in his forehead with a dirty rag as he cowered behind the deck's stone wall with Carmen and her daughter. Luisa sobbed on the ground while her mother laid on top of her to give her what little ballistic protection her own body could offer. The shattered glass door to the kitchen led to safety, but they didn't dare make a run for it.

He had never felt more helpless. His wife was alone in the LP/OP, and he couldn't even protect the two women he was with. The images that flashed through Roger's mind of what would happen to them if the attackers triumphed were not pleasant.

CHAPTER 28

Pastor Kris shoved her semiautomatic military rifle against the LP/OP's earthen wall and grabbed her bolt-action Remington 700. Consulting Luisa's sector sketch for the trucks at the far edge the property line, she adjusted her scope for a 550-meter shot—the furthest she had ever hit a target was an elk at four hundred meters.

She lined up her crosshairs on the invaders' leader, who flung his ball cap to the ground and hollered into his radio in desperation as the attack stalled. Her first round kicked up a puff of dirt just behind and to the right of the man, who ducked behind the truck for cover. Panicked, Kris chambered another round with a *click-clack* of the bolt lever before realizing she had a clear shot at the truck's driver; she adjusted her aim high and left and blew his head all over the cab. She chambered another round as the truck lurched forward, prompting the leader, in a momentary but fatal lapse of judgment, to spring up and reach through the driver's side window to stop it. Her next shot sliced through his abdomen and dropped him.

The victory in decapitating the enemy's chain of command was short-lived as another vehicle, a menacing black civilian model Hummer, wheeled around the truck and barreled toward the front gate, gruesomely finishing off the wounded man with its tires. Pastor Kris was about to ditch the Remington for her semiautomatic rifle when an ear-splitting roar erupted just outside the LP/OP, accompanied by what looked like red laser beams that punched down the Hummer's hood and shattered its windshield. The bullet-riddled Hummer hooked hard right off the road and crashed head-on into a large pine tree.

Pastor Kris spun toward the monstrous sound to come face-to-face with Matt sliding into the LP/OP on a wave of rocks and dirt. "Klaxon, klaxon, *klaxon*!" Matt screamed the running password to stop Kris from shooting him in the face. "Hold your fire! It's us!" She looked past Matt to see Eric pouring another long burst of fire into the Hummer with the largest gun she had ever seen.

Eric leaped to his feet. "Tim, Katie, stay here and cover the Reverend! Sorry, kids, but you don't know our people, and I don't want any friendly fire! Liam, stay on my ass! Recon, we bound forward as teams! Five-second rushes! Go!"

Julie and Allan sprinted behind a large tree and hit the dirt. "Got you covered!" they yelled. "Moving!" Benny, Matt, Eric, and Liam hollered before jumping up and hustling toward cover of their own under Julie and Allan's suppressing fire. As Eric cut down another attacker with a seven-round burst, Liam dutifully pulled a new ammunition belt from his rucksack to link with the last round dangling from the feed tray of the hungry automatic weapon. The woods became a target-rich environment as the remaining invaders, leaderless and severely outgunned, tucked tail and ran.

Pastor Kris sighed with relief when she saw her husband, bloodied but alive, briefly poke his head over the stone wall. She quickly resumed scanning for targets.

"Pleased to meet you, kids! My name's Kris. I'm the pastor here," she yelled to the new arrivals before drilling a fleeing attacker between the shoulder blades.

"I'll be sure never to skip church services!" Katie said to Tim.

***

The marauder in Manny's sights was stitched by machine-gun fire before he could pull the trigger. "I see you met my good friend, Eric!" he taunted the dying man. "*Run*, you sorry asses!"

Pete whooped in triumph from the living room as Eric and some musclehead laid down fire before dashing forward, both of them wearing red waist sashes like gaudy heroes from an old movie serial. "Crazy bastards! Wish you folks on the other side of the house could see this!"

"Do you see Matt?!" Angel hysterically screamed from her position.

"Yeah—he's fine!" Pete yelled. The crunch of broken glass and the thudding of boots from behind startled him; Pete whirled, weapon at the ready, to come face-to-face with Roger, Carmen, and Luisa running in from the kitchen.

"Don't shoot!" Roger shrieked, holding up his bloody hands as the ladies screamed and cowered. "We're OK! We're all OK!"

"Speak for yourselves," Jay croaked, staggering in on shaky legs, his face white as a sheet and his blood-soaked arm dangling at his side. "I don't feel so good."

CHAPTER 29

The prisoner lay on the floor of the barn cradling his bullet-shattered right foot, a rivulet of blood trickling toward the drain set in the epoxied concrete floor. His bruised and swollen face, and the cracked rib that stung with each breath, came courtesy of the rifle butts of the recon team that had found him whimpering in the woods.

Susan and Angel entered the barn to a loud yelp as Manny, flanked by Travis, Benny, and Matt, kicked the man's midsection with a steel-toed combat boot. Angel dashed to Matt and squeezed him hard.

"Jay's gonna be all right," Susan told Manny. "He lost a decent amount of blood, but the bullet went clear through and didn't hit bone—he'll be out of commission for a while, though. Angel stitched up the gash on Roger's forehead—she's a natural." Manny wordlessly pointed to the Band-Aid plastered to Susan's left cheek. "A scratch from the glass shower I got. I'm fine—can't say the same for my bedroom window, though."

Repairing the house, a task made much harder with Jay out of the picture, would have to wait. Manny decided the group would spend the next two nights at 50 percent security—half the group awake, half asleep, switching every two hours—in case any surviving invaders were stupid enough to regroup and come back for more. It would further aggravate already frayed nerves, but Manny didn't want to take any chances.

"Oh, I almost forgot—we found this on him," Benny said and tossed a green FRS radio to his cousin.

Manny knelt by the prisoner, face darkening. "I don't suppose you were the *gabacho* who called my wife and daughter 'beaners,' were you?"

"N-no," he stammered before Manny smashed the radio across his clammy face. Benny kicked the screaming man's side and drew his hunting knife. "Say the word, boss—quickly or one piece at a time."

The prisoner, bug-eyed with horror over the thought of being dissected, looked up at Susan, who glared back with contempt. "If you think I'm some frail flower who's gonna beg them to go easy on you, think again. I have no doubt what you and your pals would be doing to me right now if you'd won."

Travis seized a handful of the man's scraggly brown hair and violently yanked his head back. "We had to handle shitbags like you with kid gloves when I was on the force. Not today, motherfucker," he seethed, tightening his grip on the man's locks as he screamed in pain. "No body camera, no right to remain silent, no attorney. Let's talk, starting with how you found us!"

"Don't bother," Eric's angry voice boomed across the barn. He marched from the side door, the unloaded machine gun still draped across his torso and murder in his eyes. Travis let go of the man with disgust, almost knocking him off balance, before Eric squatted next to him and dangled two gold necklaces in front of his face—two halves of a heart, engraved with the initials of Eli and Kayla Sammons.

"No, oh no," Susan moaned as her fingertips flew to her mouth.

"We found these on one of your buddies. Unfortunately for you, we know the rightful owners. Talk, asshole. What did you do to them?"

The prisoner stared at the necklaces, saying nothing. Eric raised the bulky M240B over his head and brought the stock down on the man's wounded foot with a sickening crunch.

"Did that jog your memory?" Eric yelled over the man's wails of agony. "Answer the fucking question!"

"OK, OK!" the prisoner gasped, his words mushy from his swelling jaw. "They were walkin' down the road . . . we snatched 'em up . . . an' they told us about you . . . to get us to stop . . ."

"*Dios mío,*" Benny muttered and crossed himself.

"You killed them, didn't you? *Didn't you?!*" Eric screamed, his face the shade of the fresh blood oozing from the prisoner's foot. The man again sat silent, teeth clenched with pain, his eyes betraying the small part left in him that still knew right from wrong. "Fucking rapist murderer," Eric growled, angrily unholstering the .45-caliber handgun from his hip.

"No, mister, don't!" the man shrieked, cowering behind bloody hands. "I didn't rape her, I swear! The others did that—not me! Please!"

Manny stepped to Eric as the pathetic man broke into sobs. "A lot of this trash escaped from Deer Lodge when the collapse hit—Lord knows how many people they've killed. Cap'n Courageous here insists they're doin' their own thing and not takin' orders from the new government."

"So, what do we do with this piece of shit?" Eric said, gesturing at the man with his handgun. "It's not like we can call the sheriff to take him to the county lockup—"

The group dove to the floor as gunshots rang through the barn. The prisoner's last breaths gurgled and sputtered through the pink froth oozing from one of the holes in his chest. A wisp of vapor rose from the 9-millimeter handgun that Angel grasped, white-knuckled, in both hands.

"That was for that sweet girl," she said with no trace of emotion. Her friends slowly rose in shocked silence as Matt gingerly reached over to safe and clear the gun before walking his wife out of the barn.

Eric grabbed the dead man's arm, shaking his head to stop the ringing in his ears. "I'll add this creep to the pile."

"I'll help," Susan muttered and grabbed the other arm, her boot skittering a spent casing away as Travis and Benny moved as one to hold open the door.

"Next time, we leave one of these *putas de mierda* alive long enough to clean up their mess!" Manny roared, giving the dead marauder one final kick before Eric and Susan dragged the corpse away, smearing a trail of gore across the barn floor.

CHAPTER 30

"**S**on of a *bitch*!" Eric hollered as a needle of white-hot pain shot through his right foot, just steps away from the living room couch where he had planned to take it easy for the first time in the week since the attack on the retreat.

Susan, who had been reading Allan's latest newsletter tacked to the bulletin board, rushed over as Eric shooed away Luisa, Julie, and Pete, who were loafing around by the fireplace before turning in for the night. "I'm OK," he groaned, hopping on his good foot. "Don't need any help—just found another missing piece of the patio door, that's all!"

"It's gonna take us months to find all the shattered glass," Susan said, grabbing his arm and ducking under his shoulder. "Let's take a look at the damage."

"I said I'm OK—it's nothing!" Eric said before hissing with pain the moment she sat him on the couch.

Susan reached over and yanked Pete's first-aid kit from his tactical vest. "You wouldn't have screamed like that if it was nothing. You know better than to pull that macho bullshit with me—you're no good to us if you can't walk."

Eric grimaced apologetically as Susan wiped a pair of tweezers with an alcohol pad. "Sorry, Doc—we've spent the past week patching up the house while constantly looking over our shoulders, and here I go ruining your evening." After a few seconds of painful probing, she yanked out a bloody glass shard that sparkled in the candlelight illuminating the dim room.

"You didn't ruin my evening—the newsletter beat you to it," Susan said, dropping the shard into the wipe packet. Besides the usual litany of bad news, Alabama, Georgia, and South Carolina had seceded, and what was now called the Free State of Idaho had formally announced it was moving forward with negotiating some kind of pact with neighboring states.

Eric hissed again as Susan cleaned the wound with a Betadine wipe. "Don't be such a baby—you're doing a lot better than those twenty-five lost souls we dumped at the Route 12 campground," she admonished, shuddering at the memory of wandering the retreat in Tyvek coveralls and piling the mangled bodies of the invaders into the bed of their bullet-riddled pickup truck. Eric and Travis had drawn the short straws to drive, which required sitting in a cab sprayed with the previous owner's head, courtesy of Pastor Kris's marksmanship.

"One more wish scratched off my bucket list," Eric grunted. "As an added bonus, the vomiting and loss of appetite made for a great weight-loss plan."

Susan covered Eric's wound with a small bandage. "Let's not think about that anymore—or about you deciding it was a good idea to call out, 'Bring out your dead!'" Eric grinned, remembering how the gallows humor made everyone chuckle except Benny, who once again didn't get it; between that joke and the unladen swallow reference that had gone over Benny's head, Eric made a mental note to get Angel his digital copy of *Monty Python and the Holy Grail* for movie night.

Everyone was thoroughly exhausted after a week of nonstop repair work on top of the regular chores, but they counted their blessings that the damage wasn't worse and that the rooftop solar panels were undamaged—the sunroom was torn up, but the only total loss was the quarantine trailer, which burned to a charred hulk. With Jay unable to work, the group considered it divine providence that Liam had been a construction trades apprentice before the collapse—he crafted the wooden replacements for the shattered windows and the sliding glass door. Members also thanked their lucky stars that Manny had made sure to stockpile wood, Visqueen, and other building materials in the barn loft.

Susan tossed Pete his aid kit—which he intercepted with one hand without taking his eyes off his Bible—and slumped onto the couch next to Eric, rubbing the back of her neck with a groan. Eric wiggled his fingers. "May I? I owe you one—you saved me from the grim specter of getting to take it easy with a bad foot." She lifted up her hair, and moaned softly as Eric started working out the kinks in her muscles. He was in heaven.

Julie poked her head up from the game of checkers that she and Luisa were playing on the floor. "The new kids are fitting in like old hands. I really like Katie. She's sharp as a tack and has a great eye for detail—she remembers almost everything she overheard from her officers. And Tim, who flew that really cool drone of his to scout ahead to the campground? I've always been a sucker for high-tech toys. On top of it all, Katie's a good roommate, too." They had billeted Katie in the bachelorette room, while Tim and Liam made Bachelor Country's tight accommodations even tighter.

"Must be nice," Eric complained. "Liam and Travis sound like they're competing in the First Annual Post-Apocalyptic World Snoring Championship."

"You should hear Susan saw logs—she'd give them a run for their money," Julie said with a grin. Susan broke Eric's massage to lean forward, grab a book from the coffee table and slap Julie's backside with it.

Manny plodded in and plopped down on the side couch with a yawn. "Whatever's going on, I don't wanna know."

"Dad, this is the first time since . . . you know . . . that I've seen you sit down," Luisa said. She hadn't been dealing with the attack well, and group members had been going out of their way to show her as much love and attention as they could.

"Feels good—I just got done checking on Pastor Kris. She's still struggling with what happened to Eli and Kayla, and what she did in the LP/OP."

Pete closed his Bible with a loud snap. "What she did was save every last one of us."

"I told her as much. I also told her our respect for her has soared to astronomical heights—how can a preacher bless anything she isn't willing to do herself? I figured Eric would appreciate the quote."

Eric nodded to his old friend. "*Starship Troopers*. Everybody drops, everybody fights."

"That old movie with the giant bugs?" Susan asked.

Eric shook his head. "Blasphemy! The book it was based on. The movie was terrible—the book, on the other hand, is one of the greatest science fiction novels ever written. I have it on my Kindle if you'd like to read it—it'd make a nice break from Allan's newsletter."

"May as well. Milwaukee and southeastern Wisconsin are a write-off. I just need to accept that Mom and Dad, and everyone else I knew, are gone."

"I'm sure your parents are all right."

Susan turned to face him, the candlelight dancing in her eyes. "They're not. But thanks for saying so."

"I'm glad you made it through the fight in one piece, Susan."

She coyly smiled and pointed to the small nick that remained on her cheek. "Almost."

Eric stared into Susan's eyes and struggled with what to say next, only to be cut off by Manny's guttural snores. Julie and Luisa quietly packed up the checkerboard and crept out of the living room with Pete. Eric unfolded the white knit comforter from the edge of the couch and draped it over his friend. "Good night, buddy—if anyone's earned this, it's you," he said *sotto voce* as Susan blew out the candles. "But next time you ruin the moment, I'm shaving off your eyebrows."

"What did you say to him?" Susan whispered mischievously, sliding an arm around Eric to help him walk, which he happily reciprocated.

"I sang him, 'Rock a Bye Baby,' just like I had to do every night in the Army—he couldn't sleep otherwise."

"Are you ever serious about anything?"

"You mean, like that guy last week who rode to everyone's rescue with the big freakin' machine gun?" Eric shot back.

Allan intercepted Eric and Susan as they reached the dining room. "Either of you seen Manny?"

"Yes, and if you wake him up, you're gonna be my grappling dummy the next time I teach sparring," Susan said, poking him in the sternum. "Can it wait?"

"It can, I guess." Allan said, looking around and lowering his voice as he stepped closer to the duo. "A few weeks ago, Manny asked me to look for friends. I think I found some."

CHAPTER 31

Manny wound up and sidearmed the flat black skipping stone across the still waters of Park Lake. One, two, three, four, five, six, *seven*! he counted to himself, clenching his fist in triumph.

The morning sun danced on the lake's waters, bathing Red Mountain towering over its western shore in a deep crimson. Manny cautiously recalled memories of better times; the rocky shore of the lake was where he, a lifetime ago, taught Luisa how to skip stones on one of their many father-daughter camping trips. But this visit was business, and deadly serious business at that.

Liam hopped down from a large boulder as Manny eyed the rocky shore for another smooth stone. A herd of moose quenched their thirst in the shallows across the lake, always on the lookout for danger—just like them.

"Helluva view, isn't it?" Manny asked him, scooping up a viable candidate and brushing its dark gray surface clean of sand and grit with a gloved hand.

"You got that right, sir."

"Meat, if you don't stop calling me 'sir' or 'Mister Landeros,' I'm gonna skip this next stone right up your ass," Manny half-jokingly admonished. Liam and his fellow deserters needed radio call signs when they joined the group, and the impromptu sobriquet Eric had given him when the marauders attacked the retreat had stuck to him like glue.

"Got it," Liam nodded. "Manny, why'd you choose me to come with you to meet whoever it is we're meeting? You barely know me."

"Two reasons," Manny said, stepping to the water's edge. "One, you're the silent type—heck, this is the most I've ever heard you talk—so I don't gotta worry about you sayin' anything stupid. And two, you're a big mamma jamma, and first impressions are everything. Long story short, I trust you—take it as a compliment." He winged his stone, which skipped across Park Lake's pristine surface ten times before sinking, and a smile crossed a face that hadn't smiled nearly enough over the ten months since the collapse. "Eric may always whip me at chess, but that poindexter couldn't skip a rock if his life depended on it."

The Yaesu FT-60 handheld ham radio strapped to Manny's tactical vest crackled to life. "Culebra, this is Shaft—you got company. Olive drab pickup truck, two occupants, heading down the access road toward you, ETA two mikes, over."

Manny acknowledged the report and glanced at the nearby wooded hill where Travis, Susan, Pete, and Tim were covering them. The duo strode to Manny's beloved Chevy Silverado, which he hadn't driven since the collapse; he had parked it facing the gravel road with its doors open and keys in the ignition in case they had to get out of Dodge fast. Both men yanked off their boonie hats and pulled hunting balaclavas over their faces as the pickup truck, a large mounted antenna tied down over its cab, pulled into view from behind a copse of trees and skidded to a stop twenty feet away.

Two figures, also wearing camouflage and masks, stepped out. The passenger tugged at his balaclava with a pinch. "Great minds think alike," he said in a gruff, older voice with a Southern accent, and took several cautious steps toward Manny and Liam, hands to his sides and away from his chest-harnessed rifle. "One o' you guys the honcho?"

"Me," Manny answered. "You 'Animal'?"

"Roger that. You guys carryin' smart phones or anything traceable?"

Manny shook his head. "Wasn't born yesterday."

"Let's get down to brass tacks," Animal said. "You guys know what's goin' on?"

"Some kind of shadow tyrant government has taken control of our state, and it needs to be wiped out and a constitutional republic restored."

Animal's posture relaxed slightly. "So far, so good. We've been puttin' together a growing network of folks like you who didn't survive the end of the world just to end up with some despot's boot on our necks. We operate as separate cells that don't know jack about one another—gatherin' intel, hitting targets of opportunity, and bidin' our time for bigger things. My particular team consists of twelve people, all of 'em trained. Yours?"

"Seventeen, all but one combat ready."

"We knew ya had at least six—you two, and the four-man overwatch you got hidden on that hill over yonder," Animal said, nodding in their direction. "How much you know 'bout the folks in charge?"

"Not a lot. Whoever they are, they're backed up by police and soldiers who forgot their oaths, and hired muscle no better than petty thugs. I assume you guys know something about who's callin' the shots?"

"Ooooh, yeah. You got no idea—"

"Animal!" his driver interrupted, waving the truck radio's handset to get his attention. "Comms wants to talk to you—says it's urgent!"

Eric, the CQ, radioed Manny the second Animal jogged away. "Cule-bra, if you're near your truck, tune to 950 AM. You're not gonna believe this."

CHAPTER 32

"My fellow Montanans, words cannot describe how humbled I am to assume the state's highest office during this great tribulation," Governor Stuart Magnuson addressed the joint session of the State Legislature. "Thank you, state lawmakers, for choosing me to get Montana back on its feet—we're going to get through this together."

He raised his hands from the polished wooden lectern of the Montana House of Representatives to wave down the applause, scattered as it was. "Governor Claire Kellerman left me big shoes to fill—she shepherded us through the early days of this crisis with courage and conviction before a brain aneurysm took her from us. The mantle then passed to Lieutenant Governor Jeremy Matthews, who, sadly, became so despondent that he took his own life. Please join me in a moment of silence to honor their memories."

The handful of news cameras stayed fixed on the new governor—fewer than half of the members of the House and Senate were present. On both sides of the dais, outside of view of the cameras, stood a bevy of state troopers and private security decked out in military gear. Red Beard stood below the dais, also out of camera view, but in full view of the lawmakers and press as a subtle reminder of what awaited anyone who stepped out of line.

"We've made great strides. In Helena and elsewhere, power, water, and sewer service has been restored, and we get closer each day to getting utilities up and running statewide. Let me dispel one rumor right now—the federal government still exists, and is actively aiding in the recovery. With our federal partners and our friends in agriculture, we're getting food back on Montana's tables, and we're working with FEMA to acquire life-saving medicines from the federal Strategic National Stockpile.

"We're reestablishing order in cities and towns across this great state, winning victory after victory over the dregs of society who have exploited this crisis to rob, rape, and pillage. However, much more work lies ahead of us. In many places, bandits still operate freely, and are attacking and murdering innocent people and relief workers. Until we stop them once and for all, the martial law decree enacted by the president at the start of this crisis will stay in effect and will be enforced. We're working with our federal partners to bring in whatever assets they can spare to aid in humanitarian and law enforcement efforts. And while I deeply respect the Second Amendment and Montana's long tradition of gun ownership, I will exercise my emergency powers by signing an executive order requiring the surrender of privately owned assault-style and other semiautomatic firearms to maintain public safety. More details will be made available by your local authorities, on the radio, and on television where service has been restored.

"Let me say this plain—Montana is not going to secede from the Union. I believe the states that have chosen to abandon the United States are foolish, short-sighted, and guided by ignorance and intolerance. We're stronger together, and together we will stay as long as I am governor.

"I was born and raised in California, and The Golden State is where I made my riches as an innovator, but Big Sky Country is my home. I pledge to do everything I can to return us to prosperity. The economic collapse and the H7N9 flu knocked us down, but we're not out, and we'll rise again, better than ever. God bless you, God bless Montana, and God bless the United States of America!" Stu said to sustained applause.

***

"Hijo de puta," Manny grunted with disgust and stabbed the truck radio off.

"Well, now ya know," Animal said as Manny and Liam walked back to him. "Those 'friends in agriculture' are gonna have a bumper crop this year, courtesy of all the fertilizer ole' Stu just shoveled on us—his goons have been seizin' everything edible from local farmers and LDS wards. And of course, like any petty tyrant, Stu dropped the cherry of gun confiscation on top of his bullshit sundae—in the name of 'public safety' to protect us from the bandits he's secretly been turnin' loose on everybody to cow 'em into compliance. With friends like that, who needs enemies?"

Manny kicked away a baseball-sized stone at his feet. "This asshole's name came up shortly after we heard that some kinda government was bein' reestablished—dude sounds like a liberty-hating sociopath."

"You don't know the half of it," Animal replied. "Governor Kellerman died of high-velocity lead poisoning, not an aneurysm, and Lieutenant Governor Matthews pulled the trigger at Stu's behest—fella didn't take a dump without askin' Daddy Warbucks for permission. The senate president and the house speaker—the two other folks in line under the law for the top job—also ended up gettin' erased. But rather than spend his life as a puppet with Stu's hand shoved up his ass,

Matthews apparently grew somethin' resembling a guilty conscience and a pair of balls, and Stu had him snuffed, too."

"None of this makes any sense," Manny said, shaking his head. The thought of the evil that had taken root so close to his home ran a chill up his spine. "Why's this guy even doing any of this?"

"The same reason why rich assholes have screwed us over since time immemorial—because he can. Like all those oligarchs that used t' meet every year in Davos an' openly talk about turnin' all us regular people into bug-eating serfs—when you got all the money in the world, the only thing left that can get your rocks off is controllin' people," Animal said. "On the bright side, Stu finally goin' public with his coup makes my spiel easier. You folks look like you got your shit together. You're disciplined, observant, and you established your street cred when you zapped a bunch of Stu's goons at that campground—don't worry, your secret's safe with us. We need your help cancellin' Stu's birth certificate. You in?"

"I gotta put that to a vote—I can't volunteer my people against their will to fight a guerrilla war."

"Fair enough. Meet here, same time tomorrow?"

Manny nodded. "I'll bring my wife's tamales."

Animal paused. "My wife and daughters were visitin' her mother in Portland when the shit hit the fan. They never came back," he said matter-of-factly. "Been forever since I've had home cooking. Tomorrow, then." Animal's driver revved the engine. "One last thing," he yelled over the growling motor. "If it turns out you're a mole, I'll kill you myself."

"I was about to tell you the same thing," Manny shot back. The truck belched a cloud of noxious black smoke and sped out of sight around the bend.

Manny pulled off his balaclava and turned to Liam, who was staring at a raft of mallards dabbling for food on the lake as the growl of the truck engine receded into nothingness. "You all right? Animal's story must've hit home," Manny said—Liam's girlfriend and parents lived in Billings, which by all accounts was nothing but charred rubble.

Liam scratched his shorn straw-blonde hair. "I vote we fight," he said as if Manny hadn't brought up his family at all. "No one's gonna accuse me of being a coward."

"Lives, fortunes, and sacred honor," Manny said as they walked to their Chevy to pick up the overwatch team.

CHAPTER 33

The group, minus Liam at the LP/OP, sat in stunned silence in the barn after Manny laid it all out. A cool breeze freshened by a spring storm blew through the barn's open front door.

"Ho-lee *shit*," Matt uttered in disbelief. "Sorry, Reverend."

"That's quite all right," Pastor Kris said. "Frankly, you summed up my feelings quite nicely."

Pete fidgeted in his folding metal chair and ran his fingers through his hair. "Surviving the end of civilization just wasn't enough, huh? Now we gotta fight a war, too?"

"Looks that way," Susan said. "I read a magazine article a few years ago about wealthy people becoming survivalists—you know things are really going to hell when the rich start prepping. What rotten luck that the one who dug in nearest to us is a control freak who decided after he poked his head out of his hole that he wanted to boss everyone around."

"It looks like he means business, too," Allan chimed in. "His minions are conducting a lot more presence patrols statewide to make sure everyone knows the new governor isn't to be trifled with. But all their radio chatter keeps referring to some leader named Red—we have no idea who that is."

Katie shot up straight and snapped her fingers at Tim. "The bad-assed redheaded guy!" Tim's eyes went wide with recognition. "There was this dude in charge of the local riff-raff who came to Fort Harrison for resupply. Red hair, red beard. Scared the hell outta everyone."

"That's good to know, but let's get back to the big decision of whether to join this resistance movement to fight this dictator," Manny said. "We'll vote by secret ballot, but feel free to speak your minds."

The legs of Travis's chair screeched across the floor as he stood. "I took two oaths to defend the Constitution—one as a Marine, the other as a police officer—and they didn't come with an expiration date. I'm a 'yes.'"

Jay gingerly wiggled his right arm in its sling. "I ain't gonna vote, 'cause I'm too gimped up to fight—it wouldn't be fair to sign you guys up if I can't do it myself. But I'll do whatever for the cause, short of becomin' a suicide bomber. Count me in."

"Count me out!" Carmen snarled, her anger embellishing her accent. "Manny, I'm not gonna apologize for being selfish and wanting you to myself. I'm not raising Luisa alone because you get killed on some fool crusade!" A rumble of thunder underscored her ire.

"You sure this 'Animal' guy's legit, cousin?" Benny asked after an uncomfortable pause.

"As sure as anyone can be of anything these days. He figured out the Route 12 ambush was our doing, and spotted our overwatch—they could've killed all six of us in a heartbeat, but didn't. This guy has Green Beret written all over him, which makes sense, given that they specialize in training insurgents." Manny turned to Eric. "I've known you longer than everyone here except Carmen and Cousin Benny. What's on your mind, brother?"

Eric leaned forward, hands clasped on his chin. "What's on my mind is that I was wrong. I thought we could hunker down in our little Shangri-La and ride out the tempest. But barely a month after getting here, we were forced to dole out frontier justice to a band of marauders before they showed up at our doorstep. Two weeks ago, another band of marauders *did* show up at our doorstep. And now, a despot has crowned himself absolute ruler barely fifteen minutes hard ride from here. It's only a matter of time until Governor for Life Stu Magnuson discovers us sitting on a bunch of guns and food, right smack in his backyard. Anyone think he's gonna let us be?" He sighed and slowly gazed around the room. "I don't want to refresh the tree of liberty with my blood, or any of yours—I wanna die of old age, and any solider who says otherwise is a liar. But we have no choice. It's us or them. We wipe them out, or they wipe us out. I say we fight."

Another thunderclap echoed through the barn as Susan patted the adjustable plastic stock of her rifle. "I don't like guns very much—I know I just ruined my chances of being voted Most Popular in the retreat yearbook, but there it is." Eric and a handful of members smiled.

"When I first joined the group, I didn't have a position on guns one way or the other until I had to respond to a shooting. Five people dead at the hands of a maniac who never should've gotten his hands on a high-capacity rifle. Now I'm forced to carry one everywhere, and I've twice been forced to kill—if we vote to fight, I'll be doing more of it." She gripped her rifle with both hands. "I'll have to take lives in order to save more lives down the line. I'm OK with that. You're my family—probably the only family I have left."

Manny gazed down at the circular metal drain at his feet, its edges stained rust red from the blood of the wounded marauder Angel had put out of his misery. "I got a confession to make. I miss America—the old one, before COVID-19 and our garbage ruling class drove this nation off the rails. Luisa should be messing around on her iPad and trying to get away with wearing inappropriate clothing, not sitting on CQ duty so we can vote on fighting a war—or hidin' behind a stone wall while bandits shoot up our house. I should be planning for her *quinceañera,* not an insurgency." Out of the corner of his eye, Carmen's mask of anger started to melt as she pondered the childhood their daughter had been denied.

"America's gone now, but we can bring back civilization. We can bring back law and order and government—a good government limited by a strong Constitution so that it never again gets so bloated and so over-reaching, or is able to crash our economy." He pointed to Matt. "Will this simpler life be so great if you and Angel decide to have a family, and she dies in childbirth?" His finger moved two seats over to Jay. "What about you, if you cut yourself with one of my rusty tools and the infection gets so bad that Susan has to saw off your arm? And I don't know about all of you, but I'm sick and tired of standing in a hole in the ground for six hours a day watchin' the woods. It sucked when I was in the Army, and it sucks now."

Manny looked into his wife's eyes, appealing to her with his closing argument. "The world fell apart, but we can help pick up the pieces and build a better one—and I know for damned sure that I don't want the fascists who just seized power here, or whatever's left of the federal government whose policies ruined us, to have anything to do with it. For those reasons, and for my daughter, I'm voting to pick up my rifle."

Angel's crying broke the quiet that had fallen across the barn. "I miss my first graders. They were all sweethearts—even the troublemakers. I like to think they're still alive, but . . ." Matt put his arm around her as she sobbed. "I see them every time I close my eyes. They look back at me with gaunt faces, nothing but skin and bones. I see them lying dead, or orphaned and alone, sitting in the rubble. I wonder every day if I abandoned them by coming here."

Susan turned to Eric, whose lower lip quivered as Angel's struggles with survivor's guilt hit home, and squeezed his hand; he mouthed *thank you* as his eyes met hers.

Angel's tear-streaked face contorted in agony. "A few weeks ago in the LP/OP, after I shot that guy right here in the barn, I . . . I put that same gun in my mouth . . . I couldn't go through with it."

Shock flashed across the group's faces, except for Matt's. "I can't help my students anymore," Angel sniffled, her voice rising with growing conviction. "But there are children, right here, who I *can* help, and I'm not gonna ignore their suffering so I can organize Parcheesi tournaments and *Star Wars* movie marathons. These kids have the right to a happy childhood, and food and medicine, and the only way that's gonna happen is by getting things back to normal—and if that means we have to wipe this new governor and his lackeys off the face of the Earth, we're in."

"I guess I'm drafted," Matt said without taking his eyes off his wife.

Travis leaned forward and hugged them from behind with two large arms. "Damn straight—I wasn't gonna do this without you."

"My turn to bare my soul," Pastor Kris said as she wiped away tears. "There's an old saying that evil wins when enough good people do nothing. That was America, ladies and gentlemen. That was me. We allowed lawmakers to be bought off by special interests, and pass deficit budgets we knew would one day bankrupt us. We didn't speak out against the insanity overwhelming this nation, smothering common sense and basic human decency, because we were afraid of being cancelled by the woke mob. I stayed silent as apostate pastors filled our churches—pastors who loved government more than God, and feared losing their tax-exempt status more than they feared the Lord's righteousness."

She stared at the gray sky outside the barn door. "Well, I've paid for my folly. Two weeks ago, I sent at least half a dozen souls to face His judgment, and I'm sure He's gonna have some choice words for me when it's my turn. I'm not going to cheapen my freedom by sitting idle while other people fight and die to fix things for me." She squeezed Roger's hand and looked at Manny. "Praise the Lord and pass the ammunition."

Silence again descended across the barn as the spring rain turned into a deluge, falling in sheets outside the barn door and hammering the roof with a constant drumbeat. "In this case," Eric cautiously ventured, "I think we need to go all-out. I think that this situation absolutely requires a really futile, and stupid gesture, be done on somebody's part!"

"And we're just the guys to do it!" Benny exclaimed and stabbed his finger at Eric. "Now *that* movie reference I get!"

"Was it over when the Germans bombed Pearl Harbor?" Susan yelled. Eric's joke acted as the quick release on a pressure cooker, and raucous laughter echoed through the barn.

"Decision time," Manny said and handed Eric pencils and blank slips of paper. "'Yes' means you vote we fight, 'no' means we stay out of it. And Benny, be ready to find us ten thousand marbles."

CHAPTER 34

Manny, Liam, Animal, and his driver wolfed down Carmen's signature dish while they basked in the sunshine on the rocks at the Park Lake Day Area where they had met the day before. The vote to join the fight was unanimous.

"This beats the hell outta MREs," Animal mumbled with a mouthful of tamales.

"Everything beats the hell out of MREs," Manny said. "Meals, Rejected by Everyone."

The masks had come off with the handshake sealing the deal. Animal's appearance—gray hair shorn to a flattop crewcut, steely gray eyes, and a rough face—further stoked Manny's suspicion that he had been a special operator before the collapse.

"Please give my compliments to the chef, but it's time to get y'all set up and get the hell outta here," Animal said as he popped the last bite into his mouth and brushed the crumbs from his hands. "Your group's designation is 'Team Romeo.' My group—the one you'll be dealing with—is 'Team Zulu.' Never speak these names to outsiders, especially on the radio. How're you fixed on gas?"

"I got an underground storage tank of stabilized diesel. We can hold out for a few years, provided we drive only when necessary," Manny answered.

"Good, 'cause we prefer cloak-and-dagger stuff over broadcastin' our business on the air." Animal motioned Manny and Liam to a nondescript gray rock by a tall pine tree, and kicked it aside to reveal an ammo can buried in the dirt. "This is our post office for droppin' thumb drives for each other. We're always monitoring 3.7 megahertz in the eighty-meter band—we figure the bad guys, if they're doin' any eavesdropping at all, are stickin' to local UHF and VHF frequencies. If we leave a drop for you, we'll call for station WH8GSM; it spells out, 'We hate Governor Stu Magnuson' so you'll remember it. Never leave a written note unless it's an absolute emergency—if you gotta pass along paper, scan it into a PDF. You got a scanner and thumb drives?"

Manny nodded—Julie had collected a bunch of thumb drives before the collapse. Animal tossed him a ziplock bag containing half a dozen jet black crypto drives, which erase themselves after ten unsuccessful attempts at the password. "Use these instead, and be sure you spritz 'em with WD-40 to keep your fingerprints off 'em." He fished another thumb drive out of his pocket containing standard forms to write up enemy contact and intelligence reports and handed it to Manny.

Animal tapped with his boot a line of three red granite rocks that sparkled in the sunlight. "Always scout this drop from a distance before approaching. If these rocks are touchin' the ammo can rock at four, eight, and twelve o'clock, it means this site's been compromised. Haul ass and don't ever come back. We'll be in touch to figure out an alternate location."

The group strolled toward Animal's truck. "For now, we want you to engage in hit-and-run attacks—sabotage, eliminatin' enemy soldiers, and other targets of opportunity. Avoid collateral damage to civilians and their property at all costs. Once our enemy is weak and demoralized, we'll move in for the kill. Either of you guys know the story of the wolf on the

Capitol mural?" Manny and Liam shook their heads. "There's this huge mural on the wall behind the house speaker's dais of Lewis and Clark meetin' the Flathead Indians. Well, the painter, who legend has it hated the then-speaker, painted a snarling wolfhound in just the right place so it looked like it was tryin' to bite his head off whenever he addressed the House. Looked the same for Governor Stu—camera caught 'im just right."

Manny laughed. "Wouldn't be surprised if the cameraman did that on purpose."

Animal's face turned deadly serious. "That's us—ready to pounce at the time of our choosing, without mercy, without warning. Good huntin', son." Animal and his driver stepped into their olive drab truck.

"You were a snake eater, weren't ya?" Manny called after him.

"I can neither confirm nor deny whether Uncle Sam, God rest his soul, ever issued me one of them fancy green berets," he said, slipping on a pair of sunglasses. "Now y'all go kill people and break things."

The truck spun around, kicking up a wave of gravel before speeding down the access road, leaving a trail of white dust in its wake. Manny radioed Eric, who led their overwatch, to let him know they were leaving to pick them up.

"Esther 4:14," Liam said.

"Say again?" Manny asked as they turned for his Silverado.

"The passage is misquoted all the time, but the spirit behind it holds true. Maybe this moment—this fight—is why God put us here."

Manny eased himself into the driver's seat and turned the key. "Well, I hope He isn't in a big rush for me to meet Him. But I'm not gonna spend a few days sloshing around in a whale for telling Him no."

"That's from the Book of Jonah, actually," Liam corrected. "Esther was—"

"You've been hangin' around Eric too much—he likes to spout knowledge, too," Manny said, gunning the engine. "One of the main reasons why he couldn't get laid in a chicken coop."

Liam barely stifled a laugh. "Something funny, Meat Mountain?" Manny asked.

"He said the same thing about you."

"The knowledge part or the chicken coop part?" Manny asked. Liam broke, his laughter answering the question.

Manny grabbed his radio again. "Hope you brought your walkin' shoes, Einstein—we'll meet you back home," he said with a sly grin as he put the truck into gear.

CHAPTER 35

Governor Stu Magnuson stepped out the sliding glass door of his spacious bedroom to the equally spacious second-floor balcony of Gaia, his eco-mansion in the Lewis and Clark Mountains northwest of Helena—a gift to himself when his net worth reached half a billion dollars. He commanded the house computer to kill the lights before raising the blackout curtains; even out in the middle of nowhere, he couldn't risk a flash of electric light shining as a beacon to reveal his home.

Stu walked to the ledge and waited for his eyes to adjust to the dark of the unseasonably warm late April evening. Muted conversation below him revealed two of his security guards preparing to begin a roving patrol of the property. *Governor—that's going to take some getting used to*, he said to himself. *Ending up as a backwater state's chief executive wasn't the plan, but then again, the plan got fucked into a cocked hat the moment the world got fed into the shredder, didn't it?*

The cabal of wealthy executives and leaders to which he had belonged—a who's who of movers and shakers whose faces were well-known from Washington to Jackson Hole to Davos and every corridor of power in between—had long waited for the inevitable collapse of the United States after decades of political, economic, and cultural decline. Once the United States destroyed itself from within, and western capitalism fell with it, they would be in position to take the reins when the dust settled and save what was left of the planet, and civilization, from itself.

They cultivated the malaise from the shadows whenever they could, wreaking financial instability, influencing easily bought congressional leaders toward implementing disastrous policies to help the ailing environment but harm the economy, and sowing distrust to fan the flames of the USA's ever-growing political divide into nothing short of a cold civil war. They secretly welcomed the unexpected COVID-19 pandemic, reveling in the economic and cultural chaos left in its wake.

America's day of reckoning came just as the patrician conspiracy had anticipated, and the only thing that Congress and the Federal Reserve could do was sit back and watch as the economy crumbled. What the conspirators didn't anticipate was the simultaneous arrival of Pandemic 2.0; H7N9 devastated the world so fast that the talking heads on television didn't even have the time to come up with a clever name for it. Stu's decision to move from California to Montana, knowing that the economy was living on borrowed time, likely saved his life—he had no idea of how many of his fellow plotters had survived, if any.

The vodka martini Stu absentmindedly sipped brought back the memory of Jeremy Matthews stomping into his office and drunkenly resigning before Red Beard, Stu's personal bodyguard and right-hand man, killed him as dispassionately as a teenage fast-food worker cooking a batch of fries. It had been so easy, Stu mused, to buy the allegiance of Matthews, a typical politician cursed by insatiable ambition that far exceeded his limited intellect. Stu thought he had found the perfect marionette with which to rule from behind the scenes, until Matthews belatedly developed a soul and became a liability.

The inspiration to take charge himself had struck as Red Beard dragged Matthews' corpse out of his office. The collapse had truly turned him into a god among insects—an ability to lead what was left of humanity out of the abyss and remake society in the way he and his fellow elites had long envisioned. It presented a once-in-a-millennium opportunity Stu couldn't let pass, and if it turned out that some of his fellow alphas had managed to survive, he'd be in a prime position to be the leader of the pack.

Sometimes, if you want a job done right, you have to do it yourself, Governor Magnuson.

The buzz of the satellite phone in Stu's robe pocket snapped him from his self-adulation. The advanced phone was one of a handful he had—a token of appreciation for his company's help in writing the software to fulfill a Department of Defense contract for robust communications. *Either this idiot is going to have a really bad evening, or I am,* Stu silently groused—he had left explicit instructions that he was not to be bothered except for an emergency.

No number appeared on the caller ID. Stu set his drink on the nearby deck table and answered the call.

"Congratulations, Governor," a slightly reedy male voice responded. "That power play of yours took guts. Straight outta Machiavelli."

"Who the hell is this?"

"Forgive my manners. The name's Dave Glampers. We briefly met two years ago after your TED talk in Vancouver. Quite inspirational, by the way."

"You say your name like it should matter, or like it explains how the fuck you got this number."

"I'll get to the point. I was Secretary of Defense Ramirez's right-hand man before everything went to hell. You remember him, of course, seeing as how he was a fellow member of your little Take Over the World Club—for someone so high up, he couldn't keep secrets for shit."

Stu sipped his martini. "OK, you have my attention. Go on."

"When things started going sideways, the president, may he rest in peace, was smart enough to recognize my talents and ensconce me somewhere safe to take over for him in the event the flu killed him along with the vice and speaker; he trusted Ramirez as far as he could throw him, and given that he belonged to your cabal, the old geezer was onto something. Unfortunately, I have competition from the two surviving Cabinet members who didn't get the memo. I want the job, and you have something I need to help me get the job. I think we can help each other."

"Who says I need help?" Stu sniggered.

"Oh, you will, Mister Governor—all the help you can get. A whole bunch of your, uh, 'constituents' aren't gonna go along with the woke statist bullshit a fellow like you undoubtedly intends to cram down their throats. Or they're gonna discover the truth about your rise to power and rise up with torches and pitchforks—if Claire Kellerman died of a brain aneurysm, I'm Taylor Swift. I have assets under my control I can get to you right away, with a lot more to follow once I become president; reports of the demise of the United States are greatly exaggerated. So, you wanna hear me out, or should I find someone else to ride my coattails?"

Stu eased himself into a deck chair and casually stirred his drink with a toothpick impaling two garlic-stuffed olives. "I'm listening."

CHAPTER 36

Alexandra Chase snuck a last sip of honey tea as the clock in the Idaho Panhandle hunting cabin turned pirate radio station ticked down ten seconds until 8 p.m. Pacific Standard Time—the collapse had, once and for all, ended the unnecessary and annoying practice of springing forward and falling back.

Her husband, Paul, silently counted down with his fingers, pointing at her with a wink at the top of the hour. An opening riff of rock music played before Alexandra's mellow, reassuring voice sounded from shortwave and ham radios across a shattered nation.

"Good evening, survivors and patriots, and welcome to the Alexandra Chase Show on Redoubt Radio, the voice of the ongoing rebirth of American freedom! We're coming at you strong from somewhere in the Free State of Idaho, despite an attempt by the entity formerly known as the United States to shut us down, and tonight's episode is dedicated to the air defense artillery soldiers who joined the right side in this fight and graciously shot down the assault team that tried to fly in from Joint Base Lewis-McChord to, how shall we say, revoke our nonexistent broadcast license."

Alexandra grinned as Paul jokingly gave an exaggerated wipe of his brow. *"But enough about little ole' me. Our top story tonight is the full-blown uprising in Montana against the tyranny of their illegitimate governor. It took our eastern neighbors a while to wake up, but they're making up for lost time . . ."*

***

The rusty brown pickup truck crawled to a stop with a squeal of worn brakes in the early morning twilight at the checkpoint on northbound I-15, near the small bedroom town of Montana City.

A scraggly guard armed with a military-issue M4 carbine sauntered up to the pretty young driver, while his partner approached the passenger side and a third guard lazily watched from the solar-powered LED work lamps illuminating the scene. "Mornin', little lady—what'cha doin' out so early? Curfew ain't over yet," the first guard asked, his eyes riveted down the front of her red flannel shirt.

The driver nervously nodded at a shivering man in the passenger seat, hands under his armpits and chin tucked into his denim jacket. "My brother's really sick. We only got a little gas left—we need to get to St. Peter's and see what they can do for him."

"Pro'bly won't be much. I think they're still waitin' on that shipment of meds from the feds—just like ev'ryone else in town!" the guard guffawed, revealing a mouth that looked like it hadn't been visited by a toothbrush in decades. "Tell ya what, little lady—we gotta search you 'n your truck, so how's about you step out an' have, um, a li'l talk with me 'bout things so's you two can get on yer way. Come out slowly, hon."

The woman apprehensively unfastened her seat belt as the guard opened her door and his partner did the same for her ailing brother. Her cleavage had its intended effect, and kept the guard from noticing the 9-millimeter Glock wedged by her seat belt buckle. Susan darted out of her seat and shot the lecherous guard between the eyes, while Eric made a miraculous recovery and killed the passenger-side guard with the Sig Sauer .45-automatic handgun hidden under his jacket. The third guard was smacked to the ground before Susan could draw on him—the report of a large-caliber rifle echoed from the adjacent hill half a second later.

"Little lady, my ass," Susan said to what was left of the guard's face before joining Eric to hurriedly toss the guards' rifles and cheap gear into the bed of their truck.

"Aw, thanks, buddy—you shouldn't have!" Eric said as he yanked a notepad from a guard's pocket containing a list of radio frequencies and call signs. Susan gingerly lifted a Molotov cocktail from a padded toolbox in the truck bed and laid it across the engine of the battered white Ford Explorer the guards had parked across both northbound lanes.

Travis, wearing his Marine Corps ghillie suit and carrying the .308-caliber bolt-action sniper rifle he had used to cut down the last guard, vaulted over the guardrail and jumped into the truck bed as Susan revved the engine. "Hang on back there!" she hollered over her shoulder before hooking the truck hard left over the grassy median into the southbound lanes.

"You OK?" Eric asked once they stopped jostling in the cab, fighting back the urge to vomit as adrenaline gave way to nausea.

"Doing great!" Susan exclaimed as the truck in her cracked side-view mirror burst into flames with a *whump*. "Casanova back there's having a lousy day, though." Two miles from the now-defunct checkpoint, Susan crept off the highway onto a dry creek bed and followed it to a dirt road that headed back toward the retreat.

***

"Idaho met last week with delegations from Cascadia, Pacifica, Utah, Jefferson, Colorado, and Wyoming to discuss what Governor Jed Curtis called, 'a mutual path forward, united in liberty and sovereignty.' Joining them were several observers from communities in British Columbia, Saskatchewan, and Alberta that survived the collapse of their national and provincial governments. While talk on economic and defense matters was fruitful, the subject of political union got a cold reception—after all, everyone just left one union of states, so why rush into another?

"Tomorrow is the start of the convention to draft Idaho's new constitution, and word has it the first change to be discussed will be a mandate that our currency be backed by gold and silver. Never again will the government be able to crash the economy by creating trillions of dollars out of thin air. While barter is back in a big way, and everything from silver coins to ammunition have become unofficial exchange mediums, it's gonna be a while, I think, before we see Idaho dollars, or whatever our money ends up being called, in circulation."

***

"I give 'em five more minutes, then we're leavin'," Mayor Elijah Bridger fretted over the late-night chorus of insects and frogs just outside the small town of Boulder. "You know the risk we're takin' even bein' out here?"

"Yeah, I do, but I also know we don't got enough food," Police Chief Martin Tomlin replied, swatting a mosquito on his neck. The duo anxiously waited at a bend in a gravel road near the Jefferson County Fairgrounds—to the north, Boulder's homes and businesses sat dark as pitch.

The crunch of tires on gravel rose over nature's symphony as a pickup truck with its headlights off rolled to a halt thirty feet ahead. "Think that's them?" Bridger whispered.

"It'd be an amazin' coincidence if it wasn't, wouldn't it?" Tomlin sarcastically replied and flashed his Maglite flashlight three times at the new arrival. The truck's headlights flared back twice—the proper response to their prearranged signal. Tomlin ushered the mayor close. "Don't be takin' this the wrong way, but this ain't no city council meetin' or Rotary breakfast. I arranged this, so let me do the talkin' at first, 'kay?" With Bridger's nod, the duo crept toward the truck, the arches of Tomlin's feet aching from his worn-down, duct-taped shoes.

"That's close enough," a man's voice echoed from the darkness.

"You got what we talked 'bout?" Tomlin asked.

"In the truck. Come see."

"How do we know we can trust ya?"

A small package landed at the chief's feet. He bent over to pick it up, and in the starlight discovered two boxes of EpiPens taped together.

Tomlin blew out a breath of relief. "Mister, you're a lifesaver. My daughter's been walkin' on eggshells since ev'rything went t' hell—I dunno if I could go on livin' if my grandson died from a bee sting or touchin' a peanut . . . I'm in your debt." The stranger beckoned Bridger and Tomlin to the truck. Food, medicine, and other essentials were packed under a tarp secured to the anchor points. "Got any insulin in there?" Tomlin asked.

"No. Sorry to say all the diabetics are dead by now, anyway."

"I know—my wife was one of 'em. We lost 'bout a dozen people here. Sounds weird, but I'm glad you don't got any. It'd be too much if the cav'lry rode in too late t'do her any good."

"We're sorry for your loss, but these supplies can help save some people who might otherwise die," the driver's companion said in a pleasant female voice, her face hidden by the darkness. "It won't put a dent in your overall needs, but it could make the difference for nursing mothers, babies, and young children. You have a safe place to hide all this and a way to get it there?"

"We got a truck in the woods with the last of our gas, an' a secure place just outside of town," Bridger chimed in. "Do I wanna know where you got this stuff, ma'am?"

"From some very bad people who don't need it anymore."

Bridger stepped forward and shook the strangers' hands. "You folks got yourselves a deal. You need a hidin' place, a warm bed, anythin' we can spare, it's yours. I don't care for Gov'nor Stu, any-way—sounds like an officious lil' turd, and his gun laws are a bunch of hooey. We'll hafta publicly play along with him and his flyin' monkeys, but we're in your corner now."

"We'll see what we can do about getting you some gas," the male stranger said, further sealing the deal by handing Tomlin a pair of boots to replace his threadbare footwear. "What about the other thing we talked about?"

"Usin' our weekly newspaper to publish underground bulletins?" the chief said. "The editor an' I have known each other since kinder-garten—she's in. Stu's usin' the low-power FM stations in the small towns 'round here to pump out his horseshit when he manages to get the juice on. She can't wait to balance it out with some truth."

"Let's get this stuff off the truck and into the bellies of some hungry kids," the woman said. "Oh, hey, Mister Mayor, the chief here says your son really misses Pop-Tarts. Hope strawberry's OK," she said and tossed him a box.

Bridger smiled at the thought of the look on his son's face at breakfast. "Thank you, ma'am! You're an angel."

"One of many," Angel said as she and Matt unhooked the tarp.

***

"Finally tonight, I'd like to welcome our new friends at Radio Free Texas, coming in strong from the Lone Star State. Texas, Oklahoma, Arkansas, and Louisiana are talking about an alliance, just like we are, and just like our new friends banding together in northern Wisconsin, northern Michigan, and the Upper Peninsula."

Alexandra picked up a handwritten note that she and Paul had triple-checked before the broadcast. *"I have some messages to pass along. For our friends in Cascadia, there's a fire at the neighbor's house. I say again, there's a fire at the neighbor's house. For our friends in Montana, we have an oldie but goodie—John has a long mustache. I say again, John has a long mustache. And for our friends in Pacifica—I swear I don't come up with these, kids, I just relay them—Satan eats Cheez Whiz. I say again, Satan eats Cheez Whiz.*

"God bless you all, whether you're safe in free states or behind the wire. We're witnessing a rebirth of freedom from these horrible ashes, and wherever you are, I pray you do whatever you can to nurture it. Remember—you're not alone."

"We're off!" Paul yelled, yanking off his headphones. Three men piled through the door, boots stomping on the dirty wooden floor, to break down the radio equipment. "We're outta here and on the road to the next location in half an hour!" he ordered as their crew got to work bugging out—the foiled assassination attempt still had him rattled. "Alex, baby, I love you, but why can't we just prerecord our show and ferry the tapes around?"

His wife flashed him a radiant smile. "Where's the fun in that?"

CHAPTER 37

The six young guerrillas, three men and three women, sat in a half circle around Manny and Eric in a remote corner of Helena National Forest, trying to absorb everything being thrown at them in the limited time they had.

"Your top priority is surviving—you can't fight if you're dead," Manny said. "Hit fast, hit hard, and hide to fight another day. Don't get greedy. If you kill one bad guy, you've had a great day—if you stick around trying to kill ten more to impress your buddies, you'll get pinned down, you'll get flanked, and then you'll get killed."

"You may think disabling a Humvee or killing some lone sentry isn't enough, but it is," Eric said. "You win a guerrilla war through death by a thousand cuts—by wearing your opponent down and making him want to quit. Don't try to win a medal, because we don't have any to give out. Don't try to get a high school named after you, and whatever you do, don't dee-lab."

"I forgot all about that acronym!" Manny laughed, remembering their days playing OPFOR in the Army.

"What's 'dee-lab'?" two teenaged guerrillas asked simultaneously.

"Delta, lima, alpha, bravo. Die like a bitch," Eric answered to the group's amusement.

Animal approached the impromptu class and tapped his wristwatch. "Let's wrap this up, kids," Eric said. "If you remember one thing we told you today, it's that there's a thin line between brave and stupid. Don't try to be heroes—you're already heroes for joining the fight. Hit, run, hide, then repeat. It'll get easier once you have some scraps under your belts. Stay alert, stay alive, and we'll see you all at the victory parade."

Animal studied Eric for a second as the students stood and stretched. "You were a teacher, weren't ya?"

"About a million years ago," Eric sighed—it didn't even dawn on him that he was once again, albeit briefly, in front of a class.

The three men strolled to their trucks parked just inside the woods at the edge of a small clearing. "Thank you, gentlemen," Animal said. "Oh, and pass on my gratitude to whoever it was who arranged gettin' our paws on a printing press."

"Sure—wasn't a big deal," Manny said.

Animal wagged his finger. "It's a huge deal—words are just as important as rifles and ammunition. Weapons give us the ability to fight, but words imbue *the will* to fight, and you can't win without that. If Stu gets food on people's plates and their lights back on, y'all will be amazed at how willin' they'll be to wear his yoke. Americans spent more than half a century surrenderin' their liberty for security a piece at a time; they were indoctrinated by Hollywood, media, and the schools—no offense, Eric—to accept the idea that all good things come from the government. Some folks woke up briefly during COVID-19, when they learned the hard way that the Bill of Rights could be suspended with the stroke of a governor's pen, but it didn't take ev'ryone long to go right back to sleep once the masks came off and the restrictions lifted. The survivors out there are desperate for something resemblin' normalcy, even if it means becoming serfs—and if that happens, then *we* become the bad guys, and liberty becomes the aberrant philosophy. We gotta motivate our people to fight, convince the fence-sitters to throw in with us, and convince the enemy to lay down their arms. If we can't do that . . ."

Animal cocked his head skyward. "What's—" Eric said before Animal's hand shot up to demand silence.

"Quiet!"

A dull chopping sound echoed through the woods, growing louder with each passing second.

"Take cover!" Animal hollered. The guerrillas scrambled to conceal themselves as the chops grew to an ear-splitting roar they felt in their bones.

Twelve UH-60 Black Hawk helicopters tore overhead, their faded black front wheels mere feet above the treetops. Animal dashed fifty yards to a drop that offered a magnificent view of the valley in which Helena sat—dozens of dark olive-drab military helicopters were converging on the state capital. Most were Black Hawks, some with pallets of supplies dangling underneath, but several were large twin-rotor CH-47 Chinook cargo helicopters.

"This changes things. Shit!" Animal cursed the moment everyone caught up with him. "Our people on the inside told us the feds might be sendin' Stu some muscle, but nothin' like this."

"Reinforcements?" one of the new kids asked as she struggled to catch her breath.

"Looks that way," Manny said with binoculars to his eyes, watching the sticks of helicopters peel off—some heading for Fort Harrison, others for the airport.

"Get scarce!" Animal bellowed, waving his arms over his head. "Go back to your AOs an' lie low 'till we get an idea of what we're up against! And stay off the radio—we'll get word to you when we know somethin'!"

Julie's agitated voice leaped from Eric's radio the moment he dove into the passenger seat of Manny's Silverado. "Base, if you're calling about the flying circus coming to town, we saw it up close and personal!" he yelled over Manny gunning the engine. "Stay off the air! If anyone's outside, get 'em inside! We're heading back!" Manny tore onto an old logging road, kicking up rocks as the new kids sped past on a parallel trail that branched away.

"Hope they only brought foot soldiers," Manny said, nervously checking his rear-view mirror. "If they bring any armor or other high-tech toys to the party, life's gonna get interesting."

"Remember what our drill sergeants told us, compadre," Eric said, grasping the roof handle to steady himself. "We volunteered for this shit."

***

Jay slid a plate of grilled venison, rice, sprouts, and fresh greens in front of Susan the moment she plopped down at the kitchen table after a day of tending to the garden with Roger. She popped a forkful of seasoned meat in her mouth and moaned with delight.

"You're welcome," Jay said, retying his stained apron. "Gotta earn my keep 'round here 'til I get back up to fightin' trim." Jay's wound had made him a permanent fixture on KP, which the group didn't mind, because his cooking was second only to Carmen's. The rest of the group still rotated mess duty when Jay and Carmen weren't available, except for Matt, whose utter incompetence in the kitchen resulted in his permanent removal from the roster. Eric said after the first and last meal Matt prepared that he would rather eat the compost heap than another of his culinary nightmares.

Susan eagerly speared another slice of venison. "Take your time convalescing, Jay—this is delicious."

"Right before I got shot—true story—Manny put me on KP for a joke I made at his expense in front of Luisa. Funny how things work out." Eric and Katie sauntered into the kitchen decked out in full gear, and Jay slid late lunches to his new customers as they leaned their rifles against the wall. "Hey, Eric, I've been keepin' this warm—Matt made it special for ya," Jay said with a sly grin. Susan laughed with a mouthful of Gatorade and suddenly found herself struggling to keep from spewing it out of her nose.

"Not funny, man," Eric grimaced as Susan pounded the table. "Matt's a great guy, rock solid soldier, but that dude could screw up a bread sandwich. I still get nightmares about that meal he served us." He looked at Susan and smiled warmly as she fought to keep her beverage down. "You OK?"

"I'm good," she croaked with a laugh before giving Eric the once-over. "Got a shift coming up?"

"Six to midnight on the LP/OP, and those dark skies look ready to open up—then again, I could use the bath. Katie and I had to visit the drop site to pick up a memory stick containing what Team Zulu found out about those reinforcements that flew into Helena four days ago." The troops turned out to be a mix of active-duty and federalized National Guard troops flown in via Joint Base Lewis-McChord in Washington, but Animal suspected they most likely originated from elsewhere, because every unit in Washington was committed to putting down the rebellion in Cascadia. While some of the reinforcements stayed in Helena, many continued northeast, presumably toward Great Falls, and smaller reinforcements had landed in Missoula and Butte.

"There's some good news, though," Katie said with a mouthful of salad greens—after a winter holed up without them, she always attacked fresh fruits and vegetables with gusto. "None of the reinforcements included tanks or APCs, either because they were needed elsewhere or because the feds have no way of delivering or supporting them. But a lot of the helicopters stuck around, so they may be able to flush us out with FLIR."

"FLIR?" Susan asked.

"Forward-looking infrared radar," Katie said, shoveling rice into her mouth. "Detects body heat. I got to see it in action once on a Black Hawk ride in ROTC. People light up like neon signs. Cuts through dark, fog, rain, you name it—there's no hiding from it."

Susan slowly shook her head. "None of this adds up at all. With all that's going on, Montana simply isn't all that important. Why fly in reinforcements to prop up a wannabe governor?"

"Dunno," Eric and Katie said simultaneously. "Jinx! You owe me a beer," Katie chuckled.

Susan eyed them with a raised brow. "Eric, mind if I ask you a personal question?"

"Shoot."

"How will you feel about killing men and women wearing the same uniform you did?"

Eric faced her. "We've all been given a choice. I chose to honor my oath to defend the Constitution, and they didn't." Eric thumbed at Katie. "She, Tim, and Liam did the right thing, and at great personal risk. Hell, we can't even try to reach their loved ones on the radio just in case the Army's still looking for 'em. The soldiers who flew in still have time to make the right choice. If they don't, and they end up in my sights, well . . . to answer your question, the only thing I'm gonna feel is the recoil."

Their eyes locked for several seconds until Allan shambled into the kitchen and sat with a groan. "You all right?" Susan asked him as Eric went back to wolfing down his meal. "You look and sound like you wrestled a hodag."

"A what?" Allan tiredly asked, running his hands over his face.

"It's a Wisconsin thing—you wouldn't understand," Eric grunted. "What's going on?"

"Just wrapped up another failed attempt with Pastor Kris and Roger to get word of their sons out east. I always feel so bad for them, but I feel worse because I had to shoo them out when we started picking up some disturbing traffic."

Jay slid Allan a plate. "Like what?"

"Reports from Great Falls of gunfire coming from Malmstrom Air Force Base. We're not talking potshots, either—operators are saying it sounds like World War Three started. I just briefed Manny."

"Any idea what's going on?"

Allan mixed his meat and rice together. "Something bad would be my guess—pessimism hasn't let me down since the whole world went away. Oh, and what's left of Minnesota and Iowa officially seceded, for those of you keeping score."

Eric handed his plate and silverware to Jay. "Thanks for lunch. If you'll all excuse me, I have things to do before I get pissed on for the next six hours." Katie stood, stretched, and excused herself, telling Eric that she couldn't wait to get out of her fatigues.

Susan turned to Allan the moment the duo disappeared though the archway. "Did they go out, just the two of them, to the drop site?"

"Nope," Allan grunted, chewing like a cow with a cud. "Tim and Matt went, too. Jealous or something?"

"Shut up, Allan."

"Shutting up, ma'am."

CHAPTER 38

The governor's security detail surrounded him the moment he and Red Beard alit from their armored Humvee in the middle of an eight-vehicle convoy that had halted just outside Marysville. The mountain hamlet, twelve miles northwest of Helena and not that far from Stu's mansion, had merited little attention before the collapse, but it happened to be near the Drumlummon Mine and its gold, both of which Stu seized with the signing of an executive order—unlike the defunct Federal Reserve, he couldn't just conjure trillions of dollars in fiat currency with a few keystrokes. The mine had shuttered years prior, but the former owners in the months before the economic collapse had begun moving equipment back as the price of gold skyrocketed.

A soldier from the lead Humvee trotted up and handed Stu a note; a smile spread across his face the moment he opened it. "Looks like Glampers got control of what we need," Stu told Red Beard and tucked the note into his shirt pocket. He glanced up the hill at the motley group of townspeople waiting for him to speak. "We safe here?"

"We swept each house for guns, yesterday and again today. Found some stuff on the banned list, but didn't haul anyone off to jail—didn't wanna generate bad feelings with you coming. Boss, why are you even risking talking to these people? You came here to see the mine."

Stu squinted against the stiffening mountain breeze. "If I'm going to be governor, I have to talk to people, don't I? Taking a few minutes to tell the *hoi polloi* what they want to hear builds good will—and maybe they won't put two and two together and start yakking about the gold mine to the resistance that's becoming quite the annoyance. Lead the way, please."

The entourage followed Red Beard, a mercenary who had fought in the worst hellholes in the world as long as the pay was good. It was his idea early on to turn their hired help loose on the countryside to frighten people into wanting a heavy-handed ruler to set things right; now was not the time for half-hearted measures with humanity's future at stake. A member of Stu's private army had endowed Red Beard with his handle—Stu was almost certain he was the only person who knew his real name. Everyone was deathly afraid of him, which served Stu's goals quite well, and his ultimate goal had become a lofty one with the collapse of civilization.

The old America of unsustainable consumerism and arrogant exceptionalism was gone, just as Stu and his fellow elites predicted would happen; it had hobbled on like a lame horse until the economic collapse and H7N9 put it out of its misery. Those who had survived the tribulation, and the years of chaos, unrest, and political division that preceded it, would be ready, eager even, to accept whatever limits needed to be set in exchange for stability; the people who were left had had enough of the roller coaster that was the 21st Century, and they wanted off. It would be a stability that Stu was now singlehandedly poised to deliver. America had fallen victim to its own pride and folly, and Stu was now in an unprecedented position to rebuild a progressive and egalitarian society on the ashes of the old. The era of gross excess—overeating, overpopulating, and conspicuous consumption—was over forever.

An alarming number of states had chosen to leave the Union, but the faction of the federal government he had aligned himself with had a plan to stop them, with his help. Once they were brought back in line, the resistance groups that had sprung up around him would be swiftly hunted down—he would then be firmly entrenched in the halls of power, and making the big decisions behind the scenes in a frightened, compliant, and depopulated nation. The old world was dead, and it was up to visionaries like him to create a brave new one. *Never let a crisis go to waste*, he mused.

Stu's entourage stopped a safe distance from the crowd, parting so he could address the town's hundred or so remaining residents. He had just grabbed a bullhorn from one of his mercenaries when a blow hammered his left side like a car at full speed. The merc slammed into him, knocking him to the ground as a rifle report echoed from the wooded hills.

"Wha—wha' happened?" Stu moaned as Red Beard dragged both men behind a cinderblock building to the thundering of indiscriminate return fire. Red Beard ripped open Stu's button-down jacket and breathed a sigh of relief when he saw that his body armor had stopped the rifle round, which spent a good amount of its kinetic energy passing through the poor soul with the bullhorn.

"You're OK, boss!" he yelled and spun to the medic tending to the blood-soaked merc who had inadvertently taken the bullet meant for the governor. "How's Spinney?"

"Dead, sir!"

Stu struggled to sit up, his anger burning white hot. Townspeople were splayed on the ground, some lying still, others screaming in agony or trailing blood and entrails as they tried to crawl for cover. Two soldiers from his detail lay face down in the dirt.

"You're safe here!" Red Beard yelled in Stu's face. "I gotta get this under control!"

"Like hell! Wipe 'em out!" Stu screamed and waved an arm at the carnage, a jolt of searing pain from his ribs increasing his rage.

"Say again?"

Stu's face turned crimson. "I said, I want these people *gone*! They tried to kill me! I want this town leveled! We'll blame it on the resistance!"

Red Beard stared at Stu for a second before bolting across the street to grab two soldiers by their tactical vests and haul them back to guard Stu and the medic, who was taping an ice pack to the ugly bruise ripening on the governor's side. "Plan Lima! I say again, Plan Lima!" Red Beard barked into his headset.

The soldiers gaped in disbelief at one another over what they had just heard Red Beard order the hired guns to do to Marysville and its residents. "Watch the governor!" Red Beard commanded before dashing forward to supervise the horrible command he had just given.

CHAPTER 39

Sylvia Marchand cried as she sat on the edge of the cot in the decrepit and sweltering room in which she had been kept prisoner. *Is is still May, or is it June now? I've lost track*, the eighteen-year-old asked herself, wiping her nose on her filthy sleeve.

The dust specks dancing in the moonbeam that shone through the knothole in the board nailed to her window told her it was still night. She had drifted off to sleep, only to once again relive in her nightmares the last time she saw her family alive.

Sylvia, her parents, and her younger brother had gathered with the rest of Marysville to meet the new governor in the hope of getting some sort of aid. Then a shot rang out and the slaughter began.

"Dad! Brian! Omigod, where are they?!" Sylvia screamed at her mom the moment they reached their front porch after a mad dash for their lives.

"I don't know!" her winded mom yelled over the firefight. "Go! *Get out!*"

"Go *where*?!" Sylvia shrieked before they dove to the ground with an explosion that blew out the windows of their neighbor's house.

Mom yanked Sylvia to her feet and shoved her toward the woods. "Anywhere but here! *Run!* Don't look back!"

Sylvia crashed through the forest in a blind panic for what seemed like an eternity until she crumpled, physically and emotionally spent, behind a guardrail along the nearby state highway. She broke down as the reality of her situation grabbed her by the throat and squeezed. Did her family escape? Where could she go? And who would help her when it was the authorities themselves she was running from?

As if in answer to her prayers, a van slowly crept into view, weaving between the potholes the brutal winter had scooped out of the dilapidated road. Sylvia jumped the guardrail and ran toward the van head-on, wildly waving her arms and screaming for help—the van screeched to a halt and the driver and passenger flung open their doors and bolted out to meet her. A minute later, Sylvia found herself bound and gagged in the back, her captors gloating about their incredible luck in stumbling across such a young and pretty "bonus" before slamming the van's door shut.

Dying with her family, Sylvia realized as she looked around her squalid prison, would have been preferable to the fate that awaited her. Her captors hadn't laid a hand on her, or on the other women whose screams Sylvia sometimes heard through the walls—they took a perverse delight in telling her they didn't want to spoil merchandise that would fetch them a hefty price in gold.

Sylvia brushed matted black hair from her face and walked to the knothole to glimpse what little freedom she could when the loud *pop-pop-pop* of gunshots rang from outside. She screamed in terror and scrambled under her cot for whatever meager protection it could provide, pushing away dust and mouse droppings and covering her head with her hands.

The staccato of gunfire, accompanied by screams and shouts, grew louder and closer. Heavy boots thundered up to her door. Sylvia clenched rigid, her heart pounding against the warped and rotting wooden floor as she waited to die.

Please, God, let it be quick.

She shrieked and jammed her eyes shut as the door shattered, her hands shooting to her ears with the deafening roar of a three-round burst of rifle fire from the hallway.

"Room clear!" a man hollered.

"Hostage under the bed!" a woman bellowed, violently flipping the cot across the room to reveal four of the most dangerous-looking people Sylvia had ever seen—rifles at the low ready, their night-vision goggles giving them an almost alien appearance in the dimness. "Keep calm—this is a rescue!" the sinewy woman commanded before scooping Sylvia up with minimal effort and handing her off to a large, bearded man who carried her outside. She yelped and covered her ears again with the sound of a flashbang grenade exploding further down the dark and musty hall.

The man set Sylvia down in the overgrown front yard of the dilapidated house by six other disheveled young women and a young boy. Two bodies—the men from the van—lay nearby, tight shot groups planted in each of their blood-sodden chests. Another of Sylvia's captors—a gaunt man who loved taunting her when he brought her food about wanting "first crack" at her—was on his knees with his hands on his head, and one of her rescuers towering over him with a rifle. The waxing gibbous moon illuminated the scene with a ghostly bluish-white pallor.

"Am I unner 'rest? I ain't sayin' shit! I wanna lawyer! I got th' right to a lawyer, assholes!" the man loudly slurred—Sylvia could smell the liquor on his breath from across the yard.

The rescuers, in two teams of four, trotted out of the house. "All clear," the woman told the man guarding the lone survivor.

He nonchalantly nodded at their prisoner. "Wanna do the honors, Jacobs?"

"Absolutely," she seethed, her voice dripping contempt.

"Who're you, bitch?!" the man snarled, barely coherent. "Gemme my fuggin' lawyer!"

"We don't have one, but I can arrange for you to see the Judge right away," Karina Jacobs spat before raising her rifle past her head with two toned arms and bringing the butt down with a sickening *crunch* onto the base of the man's neck. He dropped face down onto the ratty lawn and convulsed for a few seconds until his executioner ended him with two more blows to the side of his head.

"We wasted enough perfectly good ammo on you animals tonight," she growled. "Human trafficking scumbag."

Minutes later, the rescued prisoners bounced in the back of a pickup truck, huddled together with military-surplus wool blankets to stave off the mountain chill. They eventually stopped along an old logging road, where a middle-aged woman hopped on and handed out bottled water. Most eagerly gulped it down, but the boy held his bottle in his lap and stared blankly ahead.

"Before daybreak, we'll get you to a safe house with food, medical care, and warm beds," the woman said. "We'll eventually move you to sanctuary where you can sit things out while we try to contact your loved ones . . ."

A nearby conversation among several of their rescuers grabbed Sylvia's attention from the woman's comforting words. "Eight rescued, six predators dispatched with extreme prejudice, no friendly casualties—Jacobs led a textbook op," the bearded warrior who had carried Sylvia from the house told a fearsome-looking older man.

"Good work as always by Team Zulu, Mister Branson," Animal said as a heavyset man wearing camouflage hunting overalls hustled up to them. "Team Kilo's here to take these ladies to their next stop . . ."

"We got a big problem," the man interrupted, his face a mask of fear. "Our safe house is compromised."

"What?! How?"

"We had a secluded location set up just outside of Marysville, but . . . Marysville's gone," the man sputtered. "Razed to the ground—dead bodies all over the place. Bad juju."

"Damn," Animal spat, yanking a map from his tactical vest and slamming it across the truck's hood in the moonlight. "We gotta find another hidey-hole before sunup. Just when I thought the bandits were thinnin' out! This is ballsy, even for them."

"They weren't bandits," Sylvia blurted.

All three men looked up at her.

"Say again?" Branson asked.

"I lived in Marysville. I saw it all. My family . . ."

"Who was it?"

"The . . . the governor," she stammered. "His men."

"Change of plans! Everyone saddle up!" Animal bellowed, snatching the map from the hood and poking Branson's chest armor plating. "Get the team back to the ranch—clean your weapons, grab some chow and get some sleep. I'll be back in twenty-four hours, after we get these ladies to safety." Animal turned to the Team Kilo member. "How're you on gas?"

"Three-quarters of a tank!"

"That'll do! Get on our ass and stay there!" Animal barked before ordering his driver to follow his directions.

CHAPTER 40

Animal watched from the corner of Manny's barn as Team Romeo tended to the unannounced guests he had brought to their door in the dead of night.

"This is unbelievable," Carmen said, shaking her head and watching the rescued women wolf down food. "Just when you think people can't sink any lower."

"Believe it, ma'am," Animal said. "Civilization's like the skin of an onion—it's a paper-thin wrapper coverin' layer upon layer of foul-smelling nastiness that makes people cry. Human trafficking was alive and well back when the country had something resemblin' law and order. Now these savages are operatin' freely, but then again, so are we—the bastards who did this won't be hurtin' anyone else. And believe me, the governor and his lackeys will be joining 'em in hell in short order."

Team Kilo would wait until the following evening to smuggle the refugees to a safe house in Lincoln, a resistance-friendly town forty miles north, nestled in the mountains and thick with woods. Its reputation for solitude was cemented long ago by the Unabomber, who had built his cabin nearby—pre-collapse tourists would occasionally stop to see it, only to learn that it had been shipped to the museum at FBI headquarters. The Lincoln cell would then ferry them further north to Kalispell, which was rebel country. The resistance firmly controlled Glacier National Park and the Flathead and Kootenai national forests; the governor's troops never dared follow guerrillas in, because they knew they would never be seen again.

Animal rested his hand on Manny's shoulder. "Thanks for your hospitality, but I got two more favors to ask, Cochise."

"Anything."

"Before she leaves, I want your history teacher to get his Ken Burns on and interview Miss Sylvia Marchand at length, on camera, about Marysville. Besides lettin' the world know what happened, we need to start buildin' cases for when we put these sad sacks on trial after we win. I also need to borrow your drone jockey, and one extra person for security, so we can shoot video of what's left of town. We'll have 'em back by sunset—I'd like to *didi* within the hour."

Manny motioned Tim over to tell him he had thirty minutes to grab his drone and get ready to move. His eyes had fixed on Pastor Kris, who was holding the catatonic boy, concerns about contagious disease be damned, when Animal got beckoned several steps away by his driver. The driver spoke in hushed tones, but loud enough for Manny to eavesdrop. "Comms told me to tell you that, 'Jimmy and Ruth send greetings from Sheffield.' Said you'd understand," he told Animal.

Animal swore under his breath. "Stu just turned the dial up to eleven. Let's get that drone footage and haul ass back to the ranch."

Manny excused himself from Carmen, his imagination flipping through all sorts of worst-case scenarios regarding whatever bad news Animal had just received, and walked across the barn to his daughter, who was helping Susan patch up a teenage girl hurt in the rescue.

"This is gonna sting a bit," Susan warned her patient before dousing an angry gash in her leg with peroxide. The girl hissed, her calf stiffening in Susan's grasp. "OK, Luisa, pop quiz—what are the seven steps for evaluating a casualty?"

"Responsiveness, breathing, bleeding, shock, fractures, burns, and head injury," Luisa recited, counting on fingers covered by nitrile gloves. "Is there a better way to remember all that?"

Susan mischievously grinned with Manny's approach. "As a matter of fact, Eric taught me the phrase he learned in the Army: Rub Big . . ."

"Don't you dare," Manny warned Susan—like everything the pre-woke Army had taught to help young men remember things, the mnemonic for how to care for a hurt buddy wasn't for virgin ears.

"Aw, Dad, you're no fun!" Luisa whined.

"Guilty as charged. *Chiquita*, could you grab Katie from the kitchen and tell her to gear up, grab two MREs each for her and Tim, and report to me? It's important."

Susan's brow furrowed. "What's going on?"

"I'll fill everyone in later." Manny wanted everyone to learn about Marysville at the same time, rather than let the rumor mill do what it does best and degrade morale. He watched with pride as his daughter dashed for the house; her maturity and compassion impressed him more with each passing day. *I should tell her that more often*, he said to himself, *in case I don't make it through this alive.*

***

After tearful goodbyes, Team Kilo and their charges departed for Lincoln at sunset. Animal and his driver dropped off Tim and Katie shortly thereafter, with orders to save their footage to a crypto drive and leave it at the Park Lake drop site.

"I don't wanna see anything like that ever again," Katie told Manny, voice shaking. "The bodies are still lying there. One was being . . . torn apart by a pack of wolves. Tim's with Julie downloading the drone's memory—I wish I could download those images from mine."

The footage, plus Eric's videotaped interview with the lone survivor of what came to be known as the Marysville Massacre, proved to be invaluable. Sure enough, the governor and the remnants of the media he now controlled accused the resistance of the atrocity, but Sylvia's tearful, heart-wrenching testimony proved effective in refuting their claims. Her story spread at first through underground and samizdat bulletins, and pirate ham and low-power FM broadcasts. It wasn't long, however, before Redoubt Radio picked it up and blasted it worldwide. The ranks of the resistance swelled; for every cell that was crushed, two more sprouted up.

The authorities became obsessed with finding Sylvia and forcing her to recant her account, and several partisan groups used this to their advantage. One tricked a squad of infantrymen into searching for her at a remote cabin booby-trapped with a stick of dynamite and a jerrycan of gasoline. Team Romeo utilized Allan's communications wizardry to lure a dozen enemy soldiers to a rest area, where they had set up an ambush. The spoils of victory included an armored Humvee, which the group stashed in the woods behind their home next to the LMTV that Liam, Tim, and Katie had stolen from Fort Harrison.

Pastor Kris worried that some of her flock was beginning to enjoy their work a little too much, despite the dangers involved. In a Sunday sermon after the ambush, she warned that while they were doing God's work by fighting tyranny and protecting the innocent, taking pleasure in killing is an affront to Him; she paraphrased Mark 8:36 and lectured that it wouldn't profit them to win liberty at the cost of their souls. The fact that she herself had taken lives gave her words weight, and it was clear her audience had gotten the message.

The following evening, the group received another message that changed everything.

CHAPTER 41

Luisa bolted upright from her bed with a scream.

She gasped for breath, covered in sweat, as the marauders who in her nightmares had pillaged her house and slaughtered her family retreated back into the dark corners of her memory. Reality returned in the darkness like the comforting embrace of a friend—she and her family were alive, and the invaders who had attacked their home were dead. It was hardly the first time the monsters had haunted her dreams, and she knew it wouldn't be the last.

Wide awake, Luisa grabbed her bedside water bottle to wet her parched throat, only to discover with disgust that she had forgotten to refill it. She groaned with a glance at the alarm clock telling her it was three in the morning, and rose out of bed to plod to the kitchen; she had always preferred the filtered taste of their countertop Berkey water purifier to the house's well water.

Thirst sated and bottle topped off, Luisa stopped at the sound of a woman's calm, almost robotic voice floating down the darkened first-floor hallway from the ajar CQ door.

"Seven, niner, three, seven, five."

Luisa's skin broke out into gooseflesh, and she fought the urge to run to her room—she had been spooked enough for one night.

"Seven, niner, three, seven, five."

The rational part of her brain overrode her fear—her friends, not the Bogeyman or *La Llorona*, would be behind the door. She poked her head into the office to find her father, and Travis and Julie, huddled by the ham radio.

"*Six, niner, eight, four, one,*" the woman intoned; Allan, sitting at the desk, scribbled the new alphanumeric sequence onto a notepad.

"Dad, what's going on?"

"Hush," Manny grunted without even turning his head.

"*Six, niner, eight, four, one,*" the voice repeated.

"Secret message," Julie, dressed in her pajamas like Luisa, explained in a whisper. "Allan's decoding it with something called a one-time pad. Unless the bad guys manage to get a copy of it, the code's unbreakable."

"Can't they trace the signal back to us?" Luisa nervously asked, a chill crawling up her spine at the thought of their home being discovered and attacked once again.

Julie shook her head. "We're only listening, not broadcasting. And our people are broadcasting in the VHF band, skipping frequencies and rotating among several transmitters. I don't think the governor's folks are good enough to pin any of them down."

"Pretty serious to risk broadcasting rather than leaving a message at the drop, right?"

"Very observant of you," Julie said. "We were thinking the same thing."

The transmission complete, the group watched as Allan decoded the message, constantly referring to the tiny, palm-sized pad. Ten minutes later, Manny read the deciphered message as the pad page Allan had used burned in an ashtray, its smell wafting across the room.

"Well?" Travis asked after a pregnant pause.

Manny handed him the paper. "Looks like I'm going on a road trip."

CHAPTER 42

Animal had chosen a site in the woods near the mining ghost town of Comet for the rendezvous. The bumpy, back-road journey through the Boulder Mountains, which for almost all the participating cells had begun before sunrise, was long and frustrating, but driving down I-15 or state highways was considered suicidal. Security was paramount—Stu could decapitate the resistance with one blow if he learned of the gathering.

Manny, Eric, and Susan piled out of their truck after being directed to park under a canopy of large trees augmented by camouflage netting. They spent about an hour chatting with other partisans about their exploits, careful not to reveal too much about themselves or their area of operations.

Animal ordered the seventy-odd guerrillas to gather around him in a school circle underneath another large camouflage net that Team Zulu had set up. They needed no persuasion to sit in the shade—the cloudy, breezeless day promised to be a hot one. Several broke out food or precious tobacco, the aromas of which mingled with the scents of insect repellent and body odor.

"Y'all are probably wonderin' what was so gee dee important to have you burn precious gas to come out here an' run the risk of gettin' a JDAM shoved up our collective asses."

"The thought had crossed our minds," one silver-haired partisan quipped.

"To put it in small words you primates can understand, a faction of the federal government wants to nuke seceding states into submission, our illustrious governor is in on the plot, and it's up to us to stop 'em." A chorus of exclamations, mostly obscene, burst from Animal's audience. "I don't got time to draw this out in crayon, so do your best to follow along. Anyone here know what the acronym 'COG' stands for?"

Eric raised his hand. "Continuity of government—the systems set up by government to ensure its survival in the event of catastrophe."

"That's affirmative—nice to see your call sign wasn't bestowed upon you in irony, Einstein." Susan chuckled and elbowed Eric in the ribs. "The feds maintained a network of not-so-secret facilities—Mount Weather, Raven Rock, Peters Mountain, just to name a few—where the elites and their families would get to hunker down and sip cordials while we regular jagoffs got eaten by zombies. Also, and this is important, they kept a list of successors in the event that the president ended up on the wrong side of the grass. Hollywood made the line of succession appear cut and dry—terrorists blow up the State of the Union Address, and the Secretary of Agriculture who's watching at the Motel 6 because he's the 'designated survivor' becomes the commander in chief, right? Well, Hollywood's full of shit. Uncle Sam's succession plan was a clusterfuck waitin' to happen, and boy, did it ever."

Murmurs rippled across Animal's audience. "Right when the economy started its tailspin, the H7N9 flu hit Washington and hit it hard. It killed the president, the vice president, and the speaker of the house—the sneeze heard 'round the world, I guess—and the senate president pro tempore disappeared when DC started burning. That left the Cabinet to fill the leadership vacuum—that is, the members who didn't get killed or tuck tail and run—and they've been squabblin' over who takes the reins ever since. The Secretary of State, who's next in line, and the Secretary of Homeland Security, who's dead last despite her skill set probably makin' her the most logical choice for the job, both wanna be president, and won't take no for an answer."

"But there's more." Animal's audience hanged on his every word. "The feds haven't always followed their own rules regardin' the line of succession. There've been times, such as presidential inaugurations and other major shindigs, when the person chosen to be the designated survivor is some nobody. This brings us to Principal Deputy Under Secretary of Defense for Policy David Glampers—yes, kids, that's actually his title. Anyway, this little Ivy-League turd insists that the president anointed *him*, and he wants the job, too. But unlike the other two contenders, he has very little of the survivin' deep state and the 'movers behind the movers' in his corner."

Animal paused for effect. "However, he's well on his way to acquirin' a game-changer—our nuclear arsenal. And once he acquires it, he plans to use it."

"Wait—you just can't pick up a phone and launch a nuke like you're orderin' a pizza," a middle-aged woman chimed in. "For starters, you need the launch codes, and the ability to contact the military to release the weapons. Who's even controllin' 'em now?"

Animal flipped the canvas cover from a nearby easel to reveal a map of the United States as it was before the collapse, with locations of strategic nuclear weapons sites marked with red circles. "What's left of the military has control of 'em for the most part, and they're preventing any of these presidential wannabes from playin' with 'em. Carrier and sub commanders have put their weapons in lockdown, as have the airmen and Marines entrusted to guard our repositories of nondeployed warheads. All our nuclear-capable bomber wings are located in seceded states, and their base commanders have grounded the planes. As for our land-based ICBMs, two of the three missile wings—Warren Air Force Base in Wyoming, and Minot Air Force Base in North Dakota—also are in seceded states, and their base commanders have taken measures to ensure those birds can't be launched. That leaves . . ."

"Malmstrom," Manny and several other guerrillas groaned in unison.

"Yup," Animal confirmed with a nod. "Malmstrom Air Force Base, Montana, Governor-For-Life Stu Magnuson, owner and proprietor. When the chain of command started breakin' down, Malmstrom's base commander pulled his missileers outta the launch capsules 'til the question of who the new high mucky-muck was got answered to his satisfaction. But Stu and Mister Glampers struck a deal. Those reinforcements that swarmed into Montana were courtesy of Stu's new best pal, and their main objective was to seize control of Malmstrom and kill its leaders—the soldiers were deceived into thinkin' the base commander went crazy and was plannin' a launch." Another ripple of obscenities fluttered across the group.

Animal flipped the map to reveal a one-page breakdown of the preemptive strike his deepest intel sources warned was coming. "Once Glampers gets the right tools and the right people in place, he'll target warheads on both his challengers for the presidency. Then he'll nuke the capital of the Republic of Texas—plus a handful of other renegade state capitals for good measure—and then lob another warhead over the seceded southern states to fry their power grid with a low-altitude EMP burst. In one stroke, he'll eliminate his competition for the presidency, and scare states back into the fold with nuclear blackmail."

"But wouldn't the free states retaliate with the nukes they control?" another partisan asked.

"Would they?" Susan interjected. "How many even have the ability to launch them? Would they even know where the attack came from? After all we've been through, they'd probably buckle like a belt under such a raw display of brute force."

Animal nodded at Susan. "Exactly—especially if Texas is brought to heel. Texas is the engine that'll power the rise of all these newly independent states; it's got its own power grid, billions of gallons of petroleum, the capability to refine it, and so on. If they decapitate Texas and throw the rest of the South back to the Stone Age with an EMP, they take the wind out of everyone's sails, and the Union gets 'saved' by two assholes who are a far cry from Abraham Lincoln."

"What's EMP?" asked one of the kids from the cell that Eric and Manny trained the day the federal reinforcements arrived.

"Electromagnetic pulse," Eric answered, the hairs on the back of his neck standing up as he remembered the haunting novel he had read so long ago. "I'll skip the science, but if you pop a nuke in outer space, it creates a bunch of surges that destroy power lines, computers, anything that relies on complex circuitry. It would make what everyone's gone through so far look like a day at the county fair by comparison." Silence fell across the audience.

"In conclusion, we gotta take these sons of bitches down before they can pull this off, and we gotta do it fast, hence our little invitation-only party today," Animal said. "I was hopin' we could win this war the way our forefathers beat the British, the Afghans beat the Soviets, and the Vietnamese an' the Afghans beat us—by grindin' our enemy down until they lose the will to fight. But time is no longer on our side. We gotta strike decisively to stop these bastards, and pray that God deals us some lucky hands. Because nobody—*nobody*—messes with Dixie. Not if I got anythin' to say about it."

Animal paced in front of his audience, his voice rising like a football coach in the locker room at the halftime of a losing game. "Very few people in the annals of history get the honor—*the honor*, ladies and gentlemen—of being asked to save the world! That's what I'm asking of y'all now. If we prevail—if we stop this atrocity and string Stu and his cronies up by the balls—we get the opportunity, even rarer in history, to be the architects of a fresh start! The Declaration of Independence explicitly states that it's our God-given right to abolish any government that becomes destructive, and if you ask me, our federal and state governments were on that path long before the collapse. They got too big, too invasive, too controlling, too bloated—and they lived only to serve themselves, not answer to the people like the Founding Fathers intended. Now, what's left of our corrupt federal government is plottin' to slaughter millions of innocents for the sole purpose of ensuring its continued existence. Unless, that is, brave men and women take up arms and put a stop to it!"

Animal was screaming, his gray eyes blazing. "Your children, and your children's children, will grow up free! I'm willin' to lay down my life for that! I'm ready to take my place among heroes who defied the odds with courage and grit and changed history's course! *Are you?*"

His audience leaped to its feet and roared, pumping fists and rifles into the air.

Animal grinned. "All right, then! Seein' as how the winners write the history books, we hafta win first, don't we? We gotta craft a broad plan that's gonna have a lot of movin' parts, and can still work if half a dozen things go completely to shit—if we can't do that, we're all dead. And we gotta craft it fast, as in right here, right now." He marched to the easel and flipped to a blank page. "Let's get to work!"

CHAPTER 43

Katie fidgeted in her squeaky folding metal chair as she waited for Susan in the Landeros's former laundry room turned medical clinic. Her nervous gaze shifted from a worn copy of *Where There Is No Doctor* on the stainless-steel table to the rust-colored bloodstains in the tile grout from the day Roger and Jay were wounded in the attack on the retreat.

"Could be worse," she muttered to herself. "No one ever died of embarrassment."

Katie jumped as if she had sat on a tack with Susan's entrance into the room, immediately grimacing with extreme discomfort for the effort. "Well, someone's having a bad day," Susan quipped. "What's the problem?"

"Do you, um, have anything for poison ivy?" Katie asked sheepishly.

Susan snapped on a pair of nitrile gloves from a nearby box. "Yes, depending on how bad you have it. What kind of damage are we talking?"

Katie stood and gingerly lifted her olive drab Under Armour t-shirt to reveal an oozing and weeping rash covering her back from neck to waist.

"Good God, kiddo!" Susan exclaimed. "What in blazes were you doing? Rolling around in it naked?"

Katie's face flushed redder than her rash.

"Oh," Susan said, taken aback. "Tim, huh?" Katie bit her lip and nodded. Susan flashed her a reassuring smile. "I won't tell anyone if you won't—Manny frowns upon premarital canoodling under his roof or in his woodline. But please tell me you two used protection—an unplanned pregnancy isn't something we need right now." Susan told Katie she would hook her up with a bottle of calamine lotion, and one of the six-day courses of prednisone that Mina Houston had managed to grab from her hospital—the group owed much of its diverse medical stocks to Mina's uncanny ability to anticipate the injuries that would arise after a collapse. "I have LP/OP duty coming up, so have Angel help you rub that calamine on your back. Don't have Tim do it—he's done enough damage," Susan admonished, wagging a finger in her face.

"I'm so embarrassed," Katie groaned, staring down at the floor like a puppy caught chewing a new pair of shoes. "We've liked each other for a while, and I'm not that kind of girl, but . . . we may not live through this."

Nothing like the threat of nuclear holocaust to spark young lust, Susan silently mused. "Relax—I'm not judging you. But I wasn't kidding about being careful. I was a paramedic, not an OB/GYN—my childbirth experience consists of one, count 'em, one delivery in the back of my ambulance, and that's one more than anyone else here has done."

Katie stood. "Thank you, Doc."

"Remember—leaves of three, let it be. I'll be sure to tell Lover Boy that when he comes in here scratching like a dog with fleas." Katie wanly smiled and left.

Susan chuckled and shook her head as she headed to the kitchen for a glass of water. She had to elbow her way to the large steel Berkey filter on the counter—half a dozen people were furiously scrubbing and wiping the kitchen with homemade vinegar that had been slowly replacing the retreat's dwindling supply of household cleaners. Keeping surfaces sanitary, especially with eighteen people under the same roof, was a top priority, but Susan had never seen so many people pitching in so enthusiastically.

They're nervous about the big mission, and everyone's doing their best not to think about it, Susan realized, remembering the looks on her friends' faces when Manny told them what Stu and the rogue Cabinet official were planning, and that the fate of millions rested on their shoulders. She sighed as she reached the basement stairs to get Katie's medication from the supply room. *I hope things get back to something approximating normal if we win. Otherwise, what's the point?*

***

Leisure time all but evaporated as the group was forced to add preparing for battle to the daily toil of ensuring they would have enough food to survive the next winter.

Roger and a parade of helpers tended the large garden nonstop, the wood stove that cooked the group's meals and canned the garden's bounty adding to the sticky summer heat. Angel did as much as she could for morale, but everyone had too much on their minds. Pastor Kris found the demands on her time constant as friends sought her counsel and prayers.

Members rotated through a makeshift backyard range run by Travis, a product of the Marine Corps's intense marksmanship training, to ensure that their rifle, shotgun, and handgun sights were zeroed. Benny, the outdoorsman, ensured that everyone's utility knives were honed to a fine edge, and Susan made sure everyone's first-aid kits were packed with everything they would need to treat battlefield injuries.

The mission, given its scope and the stakes, would be all hands on deck—only Luisa, Carmen, and Jay would be staying behind. Manny had discretely asked Roger if he wanted to sit out the fight on account of his heart; Roger, not so discretely, told Manny that it would be a cold day in hell before he stayed behind while his wife put herself in harm's way.

***

Manny zipped up Luisa's bug-out bag at the foot of her bed after inspecting its contents. "Good job—remember, this stays here, and don't take anything out of it." He looked his daughter in the eye. "Now, tell me the plan."

"If you don't come back, then me, Mom, and Jay throw our bags in the truck and drive to the safe house." Animal had set up a fallback for dependents in case the mission failed and his teams' homes became compromised; from there, they would convoy northwest to the rebel-held enclave in Kalispell.

"Tell me how to get there," Manny said, and had Luisa recite the route from memory.

"Dad?"

"Yes, Princess?"

Tears rolled down her cheeks. "You're coming back, right?"

"We all are," Manny croaked, hugging his daughter under wall posters of teen heartthrobs who had died along with her innocence and their country.

CHAPTER 44

"Come on, key your mike again! You assholes were a bunch of Chatty Cathys an hour ago," Julie groaned, shifting her weight on a bed of pine needles and making sure not to unduly jostle the radio direction finder she and Allan had built special for their mission.

They lay prone in the woods on the side of a small mountain in the Lewis and Clark Range northwest of Helena; two Team Zulu men, camouflaged almost to the point of invisibility, protected their flanks while a third guarded their olive drab four-by-four truck on the dirt path behind them. The cloudy morning had just cleared into a beautiful afternoon when Julie perked up with the loud tone blaring from the bud in her ear. Her mission complete, Allan rousted their security detail with a quiet whistle as he and Julie rose and walked at a crouch to the truck.

Julie tore off her sweat-soaked camouflage boonie hat as the imposing Team Zulu man who called himself Raider spread a military topographical map on the truck's hood and handed her a clear military-issue protractor. She plastered back a strand of red hair dangling in front of her eyes and laid the protractor on their position to match the bearing of the signal she had just caught, drawing a line with a mechanical pencil that intersected another signal they had caught four hours earlier and three miles west.

"That's it," she said, circling the intersection and stepping aside to let Raider examine her work. "That futuristic-looking mansion over yonder is definitely the source—that's gotta be the governor's house."

"That's what we were thinking—thanks for nailing it down," Raider said, pulling off his ball cap and scratching his scalp. "Let's chow before we get you kids home. Stu's boys never send patrols or drones out this far, so we can let our hair down." They grabbed their MREs from the truck and walked back into the woods to eat.

"Score! Jalapeño cheese spread!" a young soldier exclaimed as he dumped his MRE's contents on the forest floor. "You won't crap for three weeks, but it's worth it."

"Speaking of gut-wrenching constipation, I'll trade you for my First Strike chocolate energy bar," his buddy, a thirty-something black man, said. The young man spurned the offer by squirting the contents of the cheese pouch into his mouth with one hand and giving his friend the finger with the other.

"Blue falcon," the man retorted.

"Never heard of that bird," Allan asked as he ripped his MRE open. "They endangered?"

"No," the black man laughed. "They're everywhere. You'll know one when you see one. Trust me."

Raider tore open his main course pouch containing a "rib-shaped, barbecue pork patty" and impaled it on his Marine Ka-Bar knife. "Sometimes I wonder if Uncle Sam used us as guinea pigs to see what hungry people would be desperate enough to eat," he joked, studying the red gelatinous blob. "Some mad scientist cackling in front of a Tesla coil came up with this."

"I wanna know who invented the drink mix that won't dissolve," the black soldier said before ripping off the corner of the packet and pouring it into his mouth, turning his teeth and gums a neon, fruit-punch red. "It's impossible to get the proportions right—you always end up with colored water and fruity quicksand bullshit. Best to just eat it straight."

Raider ripped off a hunk of meat with his teeth. "Way back when I was a private at Two-Nine, MRE spoons were made of brown plastic. We used to joke it was camouflage to blend in with the shit we were eating."

"I got a question to take our minds off the chow," the man with the cheese spread ventured. "Why are these guys usin' ham radio? It ain't very secure, even when they use digital mode."

"My guess is they have interoperability issues, and this is the only way around 'em," Raider answered.

"Interopera-what?"

"Different groups being able to talk to each other," Allan explained as he pushed his glasses up on his sweaty face and pulled his main course out of the MRE's water-powered heater—while he and Julie took the time to warm their meals, their Team Zulu guardians ate theirs cold. "The governor's troops are cobbled together from all over—local boys, police, military—and they all use different radios. The feds learned a hard lesson about interoperability on September 11 when the NYPD couldn't talk to the fire department, who couldn't talk to the Port Authority, and so on; they threw billions at the problem, but fortunately for us, these bozos couldn't get their act together."

"There's the range issue, too," Raider added. "Montana's a big state, and the western third is covered in mountains and forest. A military SINCGARS radio has, on full power, a range of about thirty-five klicks, and it doesn't look like our enemy has very many of those vehicle-mounted signal amplifiers. So ham radio it is—two-meter band for the local stuff, using the repeaters these two helped us find earlier, and HF bands for longer distances."

Allan looked excitedly at Julie. "Remember that map from the campground ambush with those pencil marks northwest of town? They were right around here—this explains it!"

"We weren't supposed to talk about that, remember?" Julie taunted, rolling her eyes.

"Don't ride him too hard—we know that was your work," Raider said with a mouthful of pork, gelatin, and artificial coloring. "That was bad-ass, by the way, for a bunch of newbies."

"So, between us girls, what's gonna happen to La Casa de Stu?" Julie asked.

Raider shifted on the pine tree he sat against to scratch his back like a bear. "Extreme remodeling."

CHAPTER 45

Jeans, a t-shirt, and her favorite sneakers put a spring in Susan's step as she strolled into the backyard on the beautiful July evening. In an act of magnanimity, Manny decided that members on garden detail, or who just wanted to step outside for fresh air, could do so in civilian clothes. The comfort, however, was tempered by the rifle across her back and the .45-caliber handgun on her hip.

Susan walked up to Roger and Pastor Kris, who were pulling weeds from the garden's black fertile earth; she never ceased to be amazed by how bountiful nature could be in the right sets of hands. "You seen Eric?" she asked the duo, who wore matching straw hats and overalls, their rifles within arm's reach.

Roger pointed a dirty gloved thumb at the barn. "Headed that way about twenty minutes ago."

Susan eyed the gentle, graying man. "You've been out here all hours the past few days. Everything all right?"

"I'm always all right when I'm gardening. Truth be told, if I end up meeting my Maker, I'm gonna spend the time I have left doing what I love the most, with the woman I love." Pastor Kris blew him a kiss. "I've always felt guilty, though, that my job here is also my passion—I'm sure Benny's hobby before the collapse wasn't sitting in his basement counting canned tuna and bandages."

"Weed on, my good man," Susan laughed, setting out on the gravel path from the house. She found Eric, out of view of the LP/OP, sitting with his back to the barn and staring into the woods.

Eric, who like Susan had opted for a shirt and jeans, almost jumped out of his skin upon catching her out of the corner of his eye. "Geez! You move like a ninja—damned near gave me a heart attack!"

"Lost in your thoughts?"

"When I have time to think, I like to do it here. Especially at sunset—God does Montana sunsets right."

Susan coyly smiled. "You know, you're breaking the two-man, no-one-goes-out-alone rule that you and Manny set when we got here."

Eric patted the ground next to him. "Well, I'm back in compliance, thanks to you." Susan accepted the invitation and leaned her rifle next to his against the weathering rust-red siding.

"What'cha thinking about?"

"The mission," Eric said with a long yawn—he, Manny, Travis, and Katie had spent the previous night bouncing ideas off of one another after Allan and Julie returned from their recon of Stu's mansion with a thumb drive containing orders for Team Romeo's part in the final battle. While the document contained their objectives, it was up to them to craft the plan to accomplish them. "Keep this to yourself, Susan, but we'll get everyone together tomorrow to go over things. In a few minutes, I'm gonna build a model of our objectives on the floor of the barn, just like we did in the Army," Eric said, staring at the setting sun's transition from orange to crimson.

"I know you too well—there's more on your mind than getting to play with green Army men," Susan prodded.

Eric grunted. "I guess I'm still trying to wrap my mind around the fact that the United States that I enlisted to defend is kaput."

"So you heard about the Free States of America, then," Susan said and leaned to pluck a tall weed. The southeastern states, minus the ones that had cast their lot with Texas, had officially banded together into a new nation.

"It's probably for the better, given what the USA became at the end," Eric said forlornly. "But I wore the uniform, Susan. I took an oath to protect a nation that's dead and buried. So did all the heroes whose stories I loved sharing with my students. George Washington. George Patton. Josh Chamberlain. John Basilone. Hal Moore," Eric sighed raggedly. "And my students, sorry to say, are just as dead as they are."

Susan shifted to face him. "Eric, America might be gone, but those heroes' stories will live on. There's no more Ancient Greece, but everyone remembers King Leonidas and the three hundred Spartans at Thermopylae. The Romans erased Carthage, but not Hannibal's bravery. Charlemagne? Alexander? Their empires are dust, but their legacies survived. And who knows? Maybe our story will find a place alongside theirs in the history books. Maybe you'll help write them."

"Provided I survive the next few days," Eric said. "And provided anyone's left to read them."

Susan leaned close to Eric and peered behind him. "What are you doing?" he asked, bemused.

"Checking for poison ivy."

"Susan, why the heck would I sit in a patch of pois—" Eric managed to say before Susan swiftly tackled him and put her mouth to his.

"I finally found a way to shut you up," she whispered, her eyelids fluttering shut as they kissed with the passion and hunger of two people living on borrowed time. Eric's hands roamed Susan's body with minds of their own. She giggled when he reached the bare skin of her waist, and stopped his hand's downward slide long enough to gently unholster the .45 automatic on her hip and gingerly set it aside.

Susan peeled off her t-shirt and tossed it next to her sidearm. "Please, no jokes about negligent discharge," she said with a mischievous smile and lowered her mouth back down to his, her blonde hair falling around him, moaning softly as Eric's hands made their way to undo her belt buckle and pop the buttons of her jeans.

"I've wanted this for so long . . ." Eric whispered as she pulled his shirt over his head and tossed it with hers.

Susan's finger darted to Eric's lips. "Hush," she ordered before silencing him with another deep kiss. Her hands slid to Eric's belt as he unfastened her bra and tossed it into the growing pile of clothes.

"Wait . . ." Eric said, fighting the inner voice screaming for him to keep his big mouth shut as her naked body pressed against his. "I don't have—"

"We'll be OK—I think I've timed this right," she purred in his ear, smiling at the memory of warning Katie to be careful. "Do as I say, not as I do . . ."

"What was that?" Eric breathlessly muttered as he kissed her neck and told the voice of caution in his head to go pound sand.

"Nothing. Nothing at all, " she whispered as their lips met again.

***

The LMTV and the Humvee crept out of the woodline and into Manny's barn under cover of nightfall.

Benny hopped from the armored truck's cab as Pete closed the barn's garage door behind them. "Wash and wax her and give her one of them pine forest air fresheners," he joked to Jay.

"All I got's patchouli," Jay fired back, opening an access panel on the LMTV with his good arm to activate the hydraulic lift to raise up the cab and expose the engine. He glanced at the LMTV's oil-stained yellow "dash-ten" Army maintenance manual sitting on the workbench. "This is gonna be interesting, seein' as how I never worked on anything military before—hopefully this won't be like a veterinarian operatin' on a person," he yelled over the *thump thump thump* of the cab tilting forward. "We can't assume the jokers we stole these vehicles from were keeping 'em maintained, so we'll hafta give 'em the once over the best we can with what we got."

"We gotta make sure they're ready to go for the big dance," Pete enthusiastically said as Tim climbed out of the Humvee's driver seat. "Me and Benny will help any way we can."

"I'm countin' on it with my bad arm," Jay said. He looked over at Eric, who was in the corner building his model of the objectives of what hopefully would be their last mission as a guerrilla army. "Sorry in advance 'bout the noise, chief."

"No worries, friend!" Eric beamed back in a chipper tone that made Jay raise an eyebrow.

Tim slung his rifle over his shoulder. "I'd love to stay and help, but I gotta grab some chow before my CQ shift," he said, furiously scratching his forearm.

"Skeeters get 'cha, *ese*?" Benny asked.

"I wish. Freakin' poison ivy. Just my luck."

"You see Doc about that?"

"Uh, yeah . . . yeah, I did. Gotta go," Tim stammered and hustled out the side door.

Jay guffawed on the sight of Eric inexplicably breaking out into a huge grin upon mention of Susan and poison ivy. "You been sneakin' booze from Roger's still? We're about to drive into the mouth of hell, and you're standin' there happier'n a butcher's dog!"

"Just high on life, I guess," Eric said with an exaggerated shrug.

"Well, I hope you don't mind listenin' to some tunes while you play with your little plastic dollies—it's against the mechanic's code to work without Lynyrd Skynyrd. We'll crank it just loud enough to get us motivated without Manny goin' bonkers over OPSEC."

Pete glided his thumb around the dial of a scuffed and grimy iPod hooked up to a beat-up speaker. The opening riff to "Gimme Three Steps" was accompanied seconds later by the popping of the Humvee's hood and the clinking of tools in expert hands.

CHAPTER 46

Lincoln Airport's darkened runway simmered a pea-soup green through Will Branson's older-generation night-vision goggles. It was his tenth time scanning the small airstrip in as many minutes—even though the airport and its namesake town were in friendly hands, the Team Zulu man wasn't taking any chances.

"Honest Abe, this is Spud One and Spud Two," a tinny voice echoed in his ear bud. "Echo Tango Alpha five mikes—we clear to land, over?"

Branson, a former Army Ranger who had moved to Montana a year before the collapse, smirked at the absurdity of their mission call signs. He grabbed his handheld radio—which Team Zulu's communications chief had illegally modified to transmit on aviation frequencies—and let the two incoming aircraft know the coast was clear. He snuck a quick peek at his wristwatch—it was the last hour of the Fourth of July. *We missed it by a day,* he mused. *But this time around'll be a lot more exciting than a bunch of old dudes signing a sheet of paper.*

Lincoln had fared better than many towns after the collapse, thanks to its topography. Route 200, which ran east-west through town, was the only way in or out, save for two tiny roads over the mountains that hemmed in Lincoln to its north and south. City leaders had wisely set up roadblocks at the start of the collapse to keep strangers and disease out—at least two criminal gangs had learned the hard way that Lincoln was not to be messed with. City officials were forced to play nice with the regime in Helena, but rarely got hassled, which was what Branson and Team Zulu were counting on. The small security force the governor kept stationed at the airport had been captured several hours earlier without a shot fired; the locals were keeping them under house arrest, along with two suspected quislings, in an abandoned home on the edge of town.

Two Cessna 408 SkyCouriers, flying without running lights, approached from the northeast and landed without incident. Branson, hardly a stranger to putting himself in harm's way, shuddered at the thought of landing a plane in pitch black as he climbed into the lead truck of a three-vehicle convoy that sped to the tarmac. The planes' passengers—mortarmen and medics from the former Idaho Army National Guard—hastily unloaded their cargo.

A grizzled soldier walked up to Branson. "Sergeant First Class Aaron Davis, mortarman for hire. You runnin' this dog and pony show, hoss?"

"Negative—I'm just your chauffeur," Branson answered before spurring on the gaggle of soldiers to get loaded onto the trucks so they could move out. He radioed the two sentinels he had placed at both entrances to town to stand by for pickup as he jogged to the pilots stretching their legs by the first plane. "Gotta hand it to you guys—it takes brass balls to land in boogie dark," he said.

"No balls here, and none on my co-pilot, but thanks, anyway," the woman replied, smiling with Branson's subsequent apology. "No worries—what am I gonna do, run to my safe space and rant on social media about your microaggression? The social justice warriors who would've had you cancelled are all dead, anyway. But if you don't mind, get your stuff off our planes so we can get the flock outta here before sunrise, lest we cause an international incident now that Idaho's our own country.

There's just enough fuel here to get us to Ravalli County Airport, where we'll take another sip and fly back to Potatoland."

Branson offered his hand. "Godspeed, ma'am."

"To you, too," the pilot said as they shook. "Sorry we couldn't provide you with more, but Idaho's got its hands full helping Cascadia and Pacifica. You maniacs look like you're about to do something stupid and dangerous."

"Roger that, ma'am—you need stupid and dangerous, call a Ranger." Five minutes later, the loaded convoy crept onto Route 200 to pick up their roadside security before rolling out to prepare for the opening curtain.

CHAPTER 47

"You will not fear the terror of night, nor the arrow that flies by day," Pastor Kris prayed the Ninety-First Psalm as everyone held hands in the barn, heads bowed.

Team Romeo had gathered in the barn at 2 a.m., an hour before step-off time, so their gear could be inspected and deficiencies corrected. Animal had ordered all teams to wear drab civilian clothes so as not to be mistaken for enemy troops—group members before the collapse had bought sturdy shirts and pants from clothing companies that catered to law enforcement. Green sashes circled their waists to identify themselves as friendlies to other teams they had never fought alongside before.

Training had continued nonstop since Manny and Travis briefed Team Romeo on its piece of the operation. Given that the mission would take them into Helena, they focused heavily on urban warfare, using the barn and the house to practice making entry, maneuvering on streets, and clearing rooms. Travis, the Marine, and Manny and Eric, who spent years as OPFOR, were in their element. Everyone trained the way they would fight, in full combat gear with full loads, plus knee and elbow pads taken from dead enemy soldiers to prevent injuries from taking cover too enthusiastically on hard surfaces. Many of the pads were dark with bloodstains from their previous owners.

Team Romeo had grudgingly ditched their .308-caliber rifles for their less powerful 5.56-millimeter AR-15s in order to improve resupply by sharing a common caliber with their allies, as well as their fallen enemies; most of the soldiers they would be up against were not front-line infantry troops, and therefore had not transitioned to the Army's new Sig Spear M5 rifle, which fired a 6.8-millimeter hybrid case round.

Eric would carry the machine gun, and like the day he acquired it, Liam would serve as his assistant gunner—the big man's rucksack was stuffed with heavy ammunition belts. Katie and Matt had draped bandoliers of high explosive and tear gas shells over their shoulders like modern-day Pancho Villas for the M203 grenade launchers now affixed to the rails underneath their rifles. Besides her combat load, Susan carried a large medic bag, which she fervently hoped she wouldn't have to open. Allan, whose tactical vest bristled with communications gear, would serve as Manny's radio operator—Team Romeo would rely on marine radios for communications among themselves, and a handheld ham to speak with other teams and the retreat. Their tactical vests and backpacks were crammed with as much ammunition as they could carry, plus two grenades each from the crate stolen from Fort Harrison.

The prayer concluded, Carmen pulled a scorched wood dowel from her back pocket and asked the group to pass it around.

"Well, this is it," Manny said, looking his people in the eye one by one. "When we volunteered to join this fight, I thought we'd be picking off lone sentries and scurrying back into the woods. Who would've dreamed we'd be asked to save the world by stopping a plot straight out of a Hollywood blockbuster?" He held up the dowel that had just made its way to him. "This was left at our drop site. It came from a baby's crib in what was left of Marysville." Manny paused to let the gruesome image of the child's last moments of life sink in. "It's time to end this once and for all, so that shit like this never happens again!" he yelled, spiking the dowel to the concrete floor, its hollow *thunk* echoing through the barn.

"I served with a lot of outstanding soldiers in two outstanding units, but if I had a choice of anyone to do this with, I'd pick you, without hesitation. We're going in with other irregular units that have become just as professional and deadly as ours."

"Almost as deadly as ours!" Katie interjected to grunts of approval.

Manny nodded. "I think the bad guys have been looking for an excuse to give up, and we're about to give it to 'em. Let's kick ass and get home in one piece. Are you with me?"

The group cheered.

"I said, are you with me?!"

They hollered back at Manny with a volume that would do any combat unit proud.

"Mount up, and don't chamber a round 'til I say so!" He turned to Carmen and held her tight. "I'll come back to you—I promise." Surprise crossed his face as catcalls and applause burst forth behind him—Carmen laughed and spun Manny around to see Eric and Susan locked in a kiss.

Pastor Kris squealed and clapped her hands in front of her face. "About damned time!" Travis yelled.

Matt devilishly grinned as the applause died down. "So who won, boss?"

"I'm curious myself. Allan!" Manny barked, not taking his eyes off his best friend. "What's the kitty up to?"

Allan pulled a notepad from his side pocket and looked over his glasses. "Twenty dollars in silver coin, and vouchers good for twenty-four pints of Roger's next batch of beer."

Eric doubled over with laughter. Susan, mouth agape, stared at her friends in disbelief as they joined in. "Are you *kidding* me? You perverts had a *betting pool* going on us?!"

"Based on a July 5 first confirmed public display of affection, the winner is . . ." Allan said as he beat his hands on his chest for a drum roll, "Luisa!"

"Yes!" she shouted, thrusting her fists in the air.

"The silver's your college fund, and no, you don't get the beer!" Manny said and hoisted his daughter into a bear hug. "I'll be back before you know it," he whispered in her ear.

Smiles disappeared as Team Romeo slowly climbed aboard their vehicles. Travis clasped Matt's hand and pulled him and Angel into a hug before starting the Humvee; Manny would be riding shotgun, with Allan and Pete in the back. Matt kissed Angel and lifted her onto the back of the LMTV before climbing into its passenger seat as Benny fired up the engine and released the airbrakes with a *hiss*. Manny, and Jay with his good arm, helped the rest of the assault team climb onto the truck.

"Watch your six, pal," Eric told Manny as he handed his machine gun up to Liam. "It took me years to mold your sorry ass into something useful, so don't you go dying on me."

Manny grinned as they revived their old Army tradition of insulting one another before a mission. "You're the one with the machine gun everyone's gonna try to take out, *mano*. All because you're overcompensating for God givin' you only two inches below the belt."

Liam pulled Eric up onto the truck bed. "See you in hell, Manny."

"You first," Manny shot back. He helped Jay lock the LMTV's metal gate flap upright, then jumped into the passenger seat of the Humvee.

"*¡Vámonos!*" he whooped, reaching through the window to smack the roof.

The small convoy rolled into the night, carefully following the winding gravel driveway to the country road toward Helena, past the shot-up Humvee from the marauder raid that the group left as a grisly warning for anyone else who came looking for trouble.

Carmen, Jay, and Luisa stood in silence as the sounds of diesel engines faded into the chorus of insects and frogs. Jay killed the lights to the barn and the world turned to darkness and starlight. "Honey," Carmen said, "you should go back to bed."

"Are you kidding, Mom?"

PART THREE

The strength and power of despotism consist wholly in fear of resistance.

—Thomas Paine

CHAPTER 48

The agonizingly slow ride to Helena in the rear of the LMTV reminded Eric how much he had hated them in the Army. Each rut in the dirt road on which they crawled slammed rear ends into the uncomfortable folding bench seats, and spines and ribcages into the side armor. The rough ride negated the benefit of having elbow space and legroom with only nine passengers, unlike Eric's umpteen rides of yore in which he and his buddies were packed like sardines and bombarded with the stenches of diesel exhaust and cigarette smoke.

Eric held Susan as the night sky started giving way to daybreak, the contentment of the embrace oddly coexisting with the anxiety of going into combat. He had loved Susan for so long, and now she was his. He had spent more than one sleepless night before the collapse lamenting that she would end up with someone else, or worse yet, that he would be trapped in Manny's house watching her, day after day, in the arms of another man. But *she* chose *him*.

Matt killed the engine, its loud diesel rattle instantly swallowed by the still of predawn. The growing chorus of birds awaiting the rising sun was joined by Manny's footfalls as he jogged to the side of the truck. "We're at the jump-off point. Showtime starts in a few minutes, once we take care of the roadblock. Get your helmets on and ruck up. Don't get off for any reason—we'll be tearing ass into town at a moment's notice," he said and dashed back to the Humvee.

Liam unwrapped a hunk of Benny's homemade pemmican and eagerly tore into it; Julie took one look at the glob of meat, fat, and berries, and vomited over the side of the truck. "Oh God, I'm sorry!" Liam apologized, mortified, as Julie's breakfast hit the dirt below with a wet *splat*.

"No . . . s'OK," Julie heaved, waving Liam off. "Just nervous. I made fun of Allan for puking once. Only fair . . ."

Susan instantly clicked into medic mode and rose to check on her friend. *Please, Lord, don't let the rest of our time together be measured in hours,* Eric prayed, looking skyward as he asked for God's mercy. The stars had begun fading with the early dawn, but Mars—the god of war—defiantly shone back at him. The feeling that some of them wouldn't be coming back alive twisted Eric's stomach into a knot.

***

Manny crawled to the edge of the steep hill overlooking the roadblock that defended the back road to Mount Helena Park on the southwest side of town.

"Two guards, probably bored outta their skulls," Travis whispered, the head of the taller sentry square in his sights.

"We can fix that," Manny said, resting his rifle on its bipod legs.

"Say the word, boss."

"Soon—real soon." Manny glanced down at his wristwatch as the first rays of sunlight cracked over the mountains on the horizon ahead of them.

***

"Mornin', boys!" Branson said to the two sentries patrolling the grounds of the governor's eco-mansion as he spied on them through night-vision binoculars. He turned to the seven Idaho mortarmen who had set up their two 81-millimeter tubes in a small clearing, ammo cans open and rounds prepped with charges. "You guys ready to export some violence?"

Sergeant Davis gave him a thumbs-up. "We've been ready, Ranger—if you got a pair o' them crappy Army-issue earplugs that don't do shit to protect your hearing, I'd put 'em in now."

"Just a few more minutes 'til we sound reveille for these bastards," Branson said. He thought about the rest of Team Zulu and the important mission they were on, cursing his bad luck for having rolled his ankle a week prior—*in a friendly game of* touch *football, no less*! He felt fine, but Animal decided to play it safe and assigned Branson to babysit the mortar maggots. *On the bright side, no one at the VFW hall will be able to top blowing up the governor's house*, Branson reassured himself. *I can live with a lifetime of free drinks.*

***

Officer Tamika Jefferson's mind, and her pulse, raced as she drove the Great Falls Police Department's fourteen-ton Mine-Resistant Ambush Protected Vehicle down darkened streets toward Malmstrom Air Force Base, its headlights illuminating dilapidated homes and shuttered businesses.

I can't believe I'm doin' this, she thought, her eyes focused like a laser on the road ahead. *Momma, God rest her soul, woulda called me crazy, but it'll be worth it if today's the last day and we can start settin' things right.*

Great Falls was a different world from Tamika's native Philadelphia, but she loved it so. She realized early in life that education was the key to escaping the web of poverty, crime, and drugs that had ensnared her older brother, and the father she never knew. She joined the Air Force after graduating high school, and in a decision that appalled the few friends she had, chose to join its Security Forces in the hope it would fast-track her to becoming a police officer. After graduating advanced training, she was posted to Malmstrom, where she spent four wonderful years, and decided that Big Sky Country beat the hell out of Philly. She used the GI Bill to earn a criminal justice degree from Montana State University Billings, and shortly thereafter moved back to Great Falls as the newest officer on the force.

Then the world went to hell. Tamika helped hold the line against the chaos and lawlessness, surviving the collapse only to find herself living in a totalitarian state and devising every excuse she could to avoid following orders she knew were wrong. A fateful airing of her misgivings with a trusted friend got her hooked up with the resistance, where she stopped complaining and started fighting back.

The Lord works in mysterious ways, she said to herself, sneaking a glance at her extremely dangerous passengers packing the rear of the armored personnel carrier. The seven men and one woman, dressed in a confusing blend of military and civilian gear, called themselves "Team Zulu"—they looked like they dropped out of their mommas' chutes able to bench press three hundred pounds, and bristled with enough weapons to start a war. *Then again, that's exactly what we're about to do, ain't it?*

The man she knew only as Raider pointed to a vacant elementary school several blocks from Malmstrom's former main gate—a Team Zulu man had let slip before the mission that his nickname came from his years in the special operations Marine Raider Regiment. "Park here 'till the welcoming committee's in position," Raider curtly ordered. "Kill the headlights but keep the engine running."

The colors of the rising sun shone through the ballistic glass as Tamika wheeled the monster armored vehicle around and brought it to a halt. "I don't wanna think about the felonies I've committed over the past three hours," she said, removing her helmet and running her hand down cornrowed hair. "Grand theft auto for the squad cars we just boosted—wonder how many extra years grand theft MRAP's gonna get me—aggravated assault for the crooked cops we locked in the holdin' cells, felony theft for emptyin' out the armory . . ."

"Only if we lose," Raider said. "We're not gonna lose."

"We can't lose." Tamika nodded to the gutted school beyond the driver-side window's armored slats. "Every school in America probably looks like this one. Windows smashed, squatters livin' inside for all I know. Kids need to be in school. I don't care what happens to me—this has gotta end, and if I gotta die to make that happen, so be it."

Raider tilted his head and pressed the radio bud in his ear to better hear the incoming message. "Twenty minutes, we go!" he yelled back to Team Zulu. "You remember the mission, Tamika?"

"Yeah—plow our way through the entrance and get you crazy pipe hitters to the ops building before Doctor Strangelove or whoever can let any nukes fly."

Raider leaned forward and slapped the MRAP's black dashboard. "This little toy you helped us liberate oughta help. Consider yourself an honorary member of Team Zulu—your super-secret decoder ring will be in the mail, once mail becomes a thing again."

Tamika sat back. "Ya know, I never liked that the feds handed out MRAPs and other war surplus to police. Even before all the 'defund the police' bullshit, I think that's where our disconnect with the public started gettin' really bad—give us soldiers' guns and tanks, and we start actin' like soldiers rather than community protectors. But this ride my department never shoulda got in the first place is gonna help save a lot of lives today."

"The Lord works in mysterious ways," a Team Zulu member chimed in from the back.

"Amen, brother—I was just thinkin' that," Tamika said. "His will be done."

***

"This blows," Mitch Ruggiero whined in the morning twilight as he stood guard at the two-man checkpoint where West Main Street led southwest out of Helena.

"I know, 'cuz it's only the hundredth time you said so," his annoyed partner, Adrian Kuchar, responded. "It's six a.m.—we got two hours 'till we get relieved and can go home, so shut your hole." Adrian's home was a two-bedroom house abandoned by its owners, or so he was told by the authorities who had given it to him—there had been rumors of the new government making people disappear. But he didn't care. Before everything went to shit, he spent his nights picking fights with the cops and ending up in the drunk tank for his efforts. Now, for all purposes and intents, he *was* the cops. He could do almost anything he wanted—and if that meant having to stand guard at a stupid roadblock with an even stupider partner, so be it.

Adrian gazed at the mountain sunrise and took a deep breath of fresh air sweetened by the woods—a much more pleasant scent than Helena's ambient post-collapse stink of garbage, burning, and sewage.

"It's been forever since somethin' happened," Mitch said. "No one's tried to leave or violate curfew in weeks!"

"I know! For fuck's sake, shut *up!*" *It's gonna be a long two hours,* Adrian thought as he leaned against the pickup truck they had parked across both lanes.

"Didja see that?" Mitch exclaimed a minute later.

Adrian slammed his hand on the truck hood in exasperation. "What now, dickhead?"

Mitch excitedly pointed at the ridge above their checkpoint. "There was a flash! Right there!"

"Prob'ly a glass bottle. Now quit botherin' me!" he growled, contemplating how easy it would be in this post-collapse world to kill Mitch and make it look like a suicide.

CHAPTER 49

Stu and his guards strode through the glass entrance to the Governor's Office in the Montana Capitol Building after a pleasant weekend at his mansion. He got to spend less and less time there; his security detail of military troops and private contractors saw more of Gaia than he did. For now, the official Governor's Mansion several blocks east of the Capitol was home to David Glampers, who had flown in from out east with his staff. The pieces would soon be in place for them to set their plan into motion and change history.

Red Beard shut the door to the private office. "What's the word, boss?"

"We're almost ready," Stu said, hanging up his suit coat—he had decided to spurn the casual work clothes and sneakers that Steve Jobs had made the *de rigueur* outfit for tech CEOs in favor of formal attire to meet the guest who would soon become the next President of the United States. "Glampers managed to corral the Air Force techs and equipment needed to reprogram the missile guidance systems. After that, it's just a matter of our newly installed two-star general putting missileers into the launch capsules to turn the keys and let fly."

"I'm amazed they found officers who're amenable to this," Red Beard said.

Stu grabbed a bottle of water from a small refrigerator. "It was easy, actually. The missileers and their families are safe on secure military bases while the outside world has gone to the dogs. Threaten to throw them out to fend for themselves, and you'll be amazed how fast people abandon their principles." Stu devilishly smiled and cracked open the plastic cap. "Of course, that means you and your boys will have some mop-up work to do. General Gordon will get bought off with two more stars, but the airmen and officers who are gonna reprogram the warheads and launch them for us are, shall we say, loose ends."

"Good thing you pay in gold," Red Beard said. "And Glampers is sure the Russkies won't misinterpret the launch and mistakenly retaliate?"

Stu nodded with more certainty than he felt. The collapse and the flu had hit the Russian Federation just as hard as the United States, and both nuclear powers were strategically blind as a result—the Russian Space Forces early warning center outside of Moscow suffered the same fate as NORAD did when Peterson Space Force Base got smashed up along with everything else along I-25 in Colorado. Glampers claimed to have a line to the remnants of the Russian government, and would place a call prior to the launch; he had reassured Stu that even if he couldn't get through, the Russians almost certainly would stand down when they detected only four launches rolling away from the North Pole. Glampers, however, knew little to nothing about the situation in China. He was confident that they, too, would quickly deduce that they weren't the target, provided they were able to detect the launches at all; not only was China dealing with a civil war of its own, but it also was in much worse shape, given that it was ground zero for the bloody swath that H7N9 had slashed through the world.

The satellite phone in Red Beard's pocket buzzed. "Probably someone back at the ranch who can't find the can opener," he said and took the call.

"What's up . . . slow down! You're *what*?!"

***

"Hang it!" Davis barked.

The young soldiers to the right of each mortar tube held a round over the top, the two soldiers behind them standing ready with reloads.

"Fire!"

The rounds slid down their tubes with ascending metallic pitches that ended with ear-splitting *booms* as they hit the firing pins and got sent on their way, the force of the launches hammering the mortar baseplates into the earth and launching geysers of dirt and rock. Branson watched, giddy with excitement, as the two roving guards looked skyward with disbelief upon hearing incoming artillery.

"Good morning, Mister Governor, this is your morning wake-up call!" Branson taunted in a mocking nasal tone just before the woods behind the mansion erupted in walls of flame and shredded trees. The guards dove for cover as the explosions shattered the two geodesic greenhouses on the spacious property.

Branson extended his left hand toward the mansion to estimate the correction needed to hit it—four fingers separated the explosions from his target. "Right one two five, drop one hundred!" Branson hollered. The soldiers behind the eyepieces mounted to the tubes' bipods furiously spun the traversing and elevation handles to adjust the impact point of the next volley.

"Hang it!" Davis ordered again, and the young soldiers raised the next rounds into place a split second later. *"Fire!"*

The next two rounds landed on Stu's front lawn, demolishing the mansion's façade and obliterating the two guards, who had made the stupid and fatal decision to run to the house for shelter.

"Add five zero and fire for effect!" Branson bellowed over the thunderclaps of the explosions that had reached them at the speed of sound. Davis ran a tight unit—within seconds, the correction was made and the next rounds flew. Branson watched with barely restrained glee as four more volleys blew the mansion and everything around it to smithereens.

"You need a repeat?" Davis yelled to Branson, his ears ringing like a bell tree.

"Negative!" Branson whooped, surveying the devastation through his binoculars. "You dogs of war didn't leave one rock standing on another! I ain't letting you guys go back to Idaho 'til we raid the Team Zulu liquor cabinet and get you all hammered! Sound good?" The men barked their support.

Sporadic small arms fire began echoing through the valley. "I got no idea what them dumbasses are shootin' at, but Ranger, it's time for us to un-ass this AO," Davis yelled.

Branson ordered Davis and his men to pack up, then spun to face the smoldering remains of the mansion and flipped both middle fingers. "That was for Marysville, you bastards!" he screamed in honor of Sylvia, the town's sole survivor, who he and Team Zulu had rescued from human traffickers. Branson was no psychiatrist, but he figured that going Old Testament on the man who torched her town and killed her family—an eye for an eye, with the mortars providing the fire and brimstone—would help her heal.

He realized when Animal gave him the mission that his feelings for Sylvia had grown more than platonic. Branson promised himself that, if he lived through the day, he would ask her out to dinner, which would mean he would have to cook, given that there probably wasn't a restaurant open in the entire state. She was eighteen, and he was twenty-six, but he didn't care; he wanted to get on with life, a good life, and wanted her to be a part of it.

Branson ran to the Humvee that led their two-vehicle convoy, and grabbed the radio to let Animal know that Stu was homeless.

CHAPTER 50

"There's that flash again!" Mitch hollered, excitedly jabbing his finger up the ridge top. "You see it now?"

"Yeah," Adrian warily said. "Wait a—holy smokes, that ain't no bottle! Someone's up there!" He had barely begun to raise his rifle when the top of his head exploded.

"Shit!" Mitch screeched and dove for cover behind the truck as Adrian's body crumpled to the ground, his rifle clattering on the asphalt. Mitch covered his head and screamed as the unseen attackers methodically shattered the truck's rear windshield and punctured three of its tires to flush him out.

"Oh shit oh shit oh shit," Mitch whimpered as he crawled to Adrian's body and ripped the radio from his vest. He had barely managed to report that he was taking fire before searing hot pain ripped into his left buttock and through his thigh—Mitch's screaming agony lasted several seconds until another shot splashed his brains on the pavement next to Adrian's.

Travis safed his rifle. "Damn sunrise reflecting off our scopes—Murphy's Law strikes again!" he yelled as the four men leaped to their feet and dashed down the ridge toward their waiting Humvee.

Eric propped his machine gun's bipod on the armored roof of the LMTV's cab the moment Benny gunned the engine. "Weapons out to cover your sectors of fire, just like we practiced!" he ordered everyone else in the truck. "Don't get jumpy—only shoot if you know for sure it's a bad guy!"

"Hang on!" Matt hollered through the window as Benny lurched the truck forward to follow the Humvee onto Main Street and through the former checkpoint. While Travis deftly skirted the pick-up truck blocking the road, Benny clipped it and plowed it out of the way with a crash of steel and glass; one of its rims slid with a shower of sparks through the shattered head of the late Adrian Kuchar, leaving a smear of gore across the pavement.

"So much for Benny's safe driver insurance discount—his dad's gonna kill him!" Pete joked with mock despair from the Humvee's back seat.

"You're not that far off, *bromista*—Uncle Ernesto was was one strict hombre," Manny said. "Heads back in the game, boys. Not too fast, Travis—don't drive us into an ambush. We balance speed with security. Remember—stay alert . . ."

"Stay alive!" the three men answered back.

***

"T-minus one minute!" Raider warned the rest of Team Zulu in the back of the MRAP. "Hey, Beast, how's about you get some fresh air?"

Kiril Grishenko rose to a crouch, his joints popping with the effort of moving his huge frame. He reached up with a tree trunk of an arm to open the armored vehicle's top hatch and prop his M240B machine gun on the roof.

"What does that guy eat?" Tamika asked incredulously as she fastened her helmet back on her head.

"Whatever the hell he wants," a teammate quipped. Grishenko, whose family fled Ukraine at the start of the Russian invasion of 2022, had served in the Marine Corps Force Recon; he was fiercely loyal to his friends, but lived up to his nickname when it came to fighting the "legitimate authorities" that reminded him of his mother country's Russian invaders and the old Soviet commissars and apparatchiks his grandparents had told him about.

Raider thrust his hand like a hatchet straight ahead. "Time to roll, Tamika—show us what this monster can do!"

"Let's boogie!" she nervously whooped as she threw the MRAP into gear and flew onto Fifty-Seventh Street North toward the base.

Raider spun around and locked eyes with Team Zulu's lone female member. "Hey, Karina! Don't get dead!" he hollered over the accelerating engine.

"Love you, too!" Karina Jacobs yelled back; their friendship had blossomed into much more shortly after she led the raid on the human traffickers.

"Savin' for a ring, Raider?" a teammate ribbed as the MRAP shifted into higher gear.

"It's not getting near my finger 'til we sign a prenup!" Karina said before Raider could answer. "You're not getting my guns in the divorce!"

Tamika turned right onto Second Avenue North, about half a mile from Malmstrom's gate—a drive she had made a thousand times when she was stationed there. "Slow down until the doormen let us in," Raider said.

A man and a woman sprinted from an abandoned auto repair shop into the intersection in front of the gate, each of them carrying an M141 Bunker Defeat Munition, a one-shot rocket launcher designed to take out hardened structures too soft for anti-tank missiles. They each took a knee and sent their warheads screaming toward the gate's two guard shacks, which since the collapse had been hastily augmented with sandbags and spare vehicle armor; both rockets found their mark, sending the shacks and the hapless guards inside them flying apart with earth-shattering explosions. The couple fled back to the garage, a deluge of small-arms fire covering their retreat, as two oily black mushroom clouds roiled skyward to reveal that the rockets had not collapsed the gate's archway over the road—the strike team's first lucky break of the morning.

"Go!" Raider yelled, slapping Tamika on the shoulder.

The MRAP closed the distance in a matter of seconds. Tamika drove up the sidewalk, knocking down a speed limit sign and smashing the decorative brick sign welcoming visitors before pulling back onto the road past the metal bollards emplaced to force incoming vehicles to slow down and zigzag. She plowed through the smoldering remains of a guard shack before rifle fire started pinging off the MRAP's front armor from a sandbagged fighting position that had been laid in the grassy median behind the gate. Grishenko answered it with deadly accurate return fire from his machine gun.

"Mow through 'em!" Raider ordered. "We gotta clear this road!"

"Forgive me, Jesus!" Tamika screamed as she straddled the median and floored the accelerator. Two soldiers, ripped apart by Grishenko's machine gun, were slumped over the sandbags, while two more foolishly stood their ground and fired at the MRAP. Tamika ran them down, grimacing at the *thump* of sandbags and bodies vibrating through her feet.

"Jericho, Jericho, Jericho!" Raider called into his radio. "Door's open, path's clear! Go, go, go!"

The auto repair shop's garage doors, and the doors of several units at an adjacent self-storage business, flew open with loud, metallic screeches. A swarm of squad cars and trucks driven by Great Falls Police officers and two resistance cells tore onto the road and up Goddard Drive into the base.

CHAPTER 51

"What do you mean, 'explosions'?" Stu demanded.

"That's what Hutch said," Red Beard replied. "He said Gaia was under attack, there were explosions, and then we lost the call."

"Get him back!"

"I've tried twice. Nothing."

"Get someone to try ham radio or police band!"

As if on cue, a mercenary charged into Stu's office after a courtesy rap on the door. "Three of our checkpoints reported they were taking fire, and now we can't raise them!"

Red Beard's sat phone buzzed again. "Finally, some answers!" Stu said with growing exasperation.

"It's not Hutch—it's General Gordon at Malmstrom." Red Beard swiped the screen to take the call. "General, this is a real shitty time—" Red Beard stopped, eyes going wide.

"Let me guess—they're under attack!" Stu yelled, throwing up his hands.

"We're taking fire too!" Red Beard shouted at the general. "Defend yourself—that's why you got all those extra troops! We can't help you, so you're just gonna hafta hold!" Red Beard ended the call with a stab and grabbed Stu's arm. "We gotta get you somewhere safe."

"And where, pray tell, would that be? My fucking house?" Stu growled. "Get everyone up and out, and order them to shoot anyone who doesn't identify themselves! And get Glampers and his people to safety!"

***

Carmen and Luisa sat on the back deck as the sun rose, both of them nursing their third cup of Mexican hot chocolate. Jay, who fell in love with the drink even though it lost something in the translation with powdered milk, had already downed his and walked into the CQ to scan the radio frequencies.

Mother and daughter were five minutes into a conversation about their favorite reality TV shows and which ones they missed the most when Jay returned, worry etched on his face.

"It's started."

***

Animal thumbed through his small stack of handwritten reports from the unfolding battle and smiled.

He had set up his tactical operations center to oversee the attack in a corner of the sprawling, thirty-six-thousand-square-foot Exhibit Hall at the Lewis and Clark County Fairgrounds on Helena's northwest side. Half a dozen men and women worked radios atop folding desks, collecting reports and plotting them on acetate maps nailed to the walls. Bundles of black cables and colored extension cords, hastily duct-taped to the floor, snaked outdoors to antenna arrays and a line of generators loudly burning precious fuel. The exhibit hall had fallen into disrepair like many buildings still standing in the former United States; sunrise peeked in through shattered windows, exciting the blue and orange barn swallows that had taken residence in the rafters and had decorated two maps, and one radio operator, with droppings.

Animal marveled at how sloppy their enemy had become—he had snuck his headquarters staff and two resistance cells into the fairgrounds right under their noses. He kept one cell to guard his TOC, while the other headed off shortly after midnight for a vital job outside of nearby Fort Harrison.

A young woman cut in front of Animal to mark on the Helena map that both St. Peter's Hospital and Shodair Children's Hospital were secured, and that the medics on loan from the Idaho National Guard were setting up at the former. "The guards at both hospitals gave up without a firing a shot," she reported without taking her eyes from her work.

"I hope we see a lot of that today," Animal said.

"The medical staff agreed to our protection, but said they'll be treating the wounded from both sides, and that we can sit on it and spin if we don't like it."

"So be it—but *our* medics treat our people and injured civilians first, and the enemy last with whatever supplies are left. You call 'em right now and let 'em know," Animal grumbled before shifting his attention to the state map. The battle was going well elsewhere—partisans and defected soldiers were clearing out the federal buildings in Butte and Missoula, and had surrounded the National Guard armories in both towns. The troops and militias the governor controlled in the small towns and Indian reservations dotting the large flat expanse of eastern Montana—provided the locals hadn't already strung them up—were of little concern. Except for his wholesale theft of food from farmers and ranchers, Stu had mostly left that part of the state alone, probably figuring they could be brought into the fold once the higher-value assets in the Rockies were under his thumb.

But all would be for naught if they failed to take Helena and Malmstrom, Animal knew. Millions of lives, and a fledgling rebirth of liberty, were in the hands of people who for the most part were fat and happy civilians barely a year ago.

But some of these folks had their shit together from the start, Animal said to himself as he ran his finger along the blue arrow identifying the route of Manny Landeros and Team Romeo, and the objectives they were assigned to strike along the way. The arrow, one of many, converged on the heavily defended Montana Capitol Building.

CHAPTER 52

Steady cracks of distant gunfire accompanied the crunching of glass and debris underfoot as Manny and his team skulked through Helena's shattered Walking Mall toward the news radio station they were ordered to seize intact. Manny chased away thoughts of the many times he and his family strolled past the brick façades of quaint niche stores and eateries that now stood gutted and blackened.

Second Squad, consisting of Angel, Pete, Tim, and Matt as squad leader, led their formation. Manny and Allan trailed behind them, while First Squad, consisting of Susan, Benny, Julie, Katie, and Travis as squad leader, brought up the rear. The group moved slowly, weapons at the ready, in wedge formations—inverted Vs like migrating geese, which allowed each squad to unload maximum firepower in any compass direction.

Manny had posted his Weapons Squad atop Tower Hill, not far from where the group had stashed their vehicles in the butchered remains of the woods of Anchor Park—Helena's survivors had made short work of the city's trees to stay warm and cook food. Eric's machine gun, with Liam, Roger and Pastor Kris in support, had a clear shot at the four-man sandbag circle that guarded the intersection next to the small building where KLGK broadcasted, and controlled the route to their next objective—the courthouse and police station one block east.

They hadn't seen a soul since wheeling into town; the surviving townspeople—those who had the calories to spare to mill about outdoors—had undoubtedly taken shelter the moment the fighting started. While Manny was relieved that he wouldn't have to worry about innocent civilians getting caught in crossfires, the empty streets flat-out gave him the creeps.

Matt signaled the group to halt when they reached the dilapidated Department of Corrections building just west of the radio station. Gunfire erupted around the corner the moment Manny and Allan jogged up to meet him.

"Here's our chance!" Eric's voice screamed from Allan's marine radio. "The assault on the cop shop just started—the intersection guards are facing the other way!"

"Count to ten and light 'em up!" Manny ordered Eric. He looked back at his two teams, who had already taken their rehearsed positions. "Get ready to move!"

Eric sighted his M240B on the soldiers, silently counting down the seconds they had left to live before pulling the trigger. He mowed down three with consecutive seven-round bursts, and just missed the fourth, who cowered inside the safety of his sandbag fortress; Eric began peppering the top of the shelter, showering the lone survivor with earth and rock.

Follow me! Manny screamed, charging across East Broadway Street with First Squad and Allan. Matt and Angel rounded the corner and took cover behind a decorative wall to pin the sandbag position in a crossfire, while Pete and Tim peeled left to protect First Squad's rear. The squad dashed for the radio station's front entrance as Manny dropped to a knee and shot the remaining enemy soldier diving over the sandbags opposite from Eric's fire in a desperate attempt to flee.

Travis slung his rifle and grabbed the Remington 870 tactical 12-gauge shotgun on his back to breach the station's door the moment the rest of the squad, with Susan in the lead, stacked along the building's front face, staying clear of its boarded windows. A blast of solid slug made short work of the lock; Susan bolted into the small lobby the moment Travis ripped open the shattered door, and ran headlong into an armed guard paralyzed into inaction. Too close to bring her weapon up to shoot, she parried his rifle barrel away with one hand, stepped in and smashed his nose with the other, then grabbed the shoulder straps of his tactical vest and kneed him in the groin, driving him forward so as not to impede the movement of the rest of First Squad behind her. Susan unbuckled the guard's rifle harness and disarmed him as he fell to the ground.

"Do what we say and no one gets hurt!" Julie screamed, rifle raised. Several heads poked out from under their desks in the adjoining office. "Are there any other guards in the building? Tell us the truth—if someone comes out, guns blazing, you'll be caught in the middle!"

A stocky, gray-haired woman rose on shaky legs, hands raised. "No, he was it," she said, nodding toward Susan's victim. "And for the record, honey, you shoulda shot that sumbitch."

Benny flex-cuffed the guard while Katie covered him. "Move, *pendejo*, and I'll fuckin' split you down the middle!" he snarled, shoving the guard against the wall. Three blasts from Manny's whistle outside let Second Squad know to come up.

Travis glanced at the battered guard, wide-eyed with terror and his nose bleeding like a faucet. "Remind me to never piss you off," he told Susan on his way to the front desk. "Change of format, ladies and gentlemen!" Travis yelled to the station employees. "Governor Stu's been fired as news director."

"Suits us just fine," said a younger bespectacled woman who obviously had lost a lot of weight since the collapse. "Whaddya want us to do?"

Travis handed her a script from the inside flap of his tactical vest. "Read this on the air. As many times as you can." He fished around in his pocket and tossed the woman a thumb drive. "And take my friend's music request."

CHAPTER 53

Small-arms fire steadily pinged off the MRAPs armor as it tore down the streets of Malmstrom Air Force Base toward the 341st Missile Wing Operations Center.

"Pizdyets!" Grishenko cursed as he slammed the MRAP's hatch shut, moments before a sharp turn flung him and his hot machine gun into the laps of three of his Team Zulu comrades. Tamika screamed and flinched with a bullet that cracked the ballistic windshield.

"I thought the airmen on post were on our side!"

"They are!" Raider shouted. "This is the muscle that got flown in!"

The MRAP took a beating as Tamika swerved as fast as she could around sets of staggered concrete barriers emplaced to slow down vehicles ahead of the ops building up the road. As the concrete and glass edifice came into view, Tamika's jaw dropped at the sight of the five-foot-long machine gun being readied in the sandbagged fighting position between them and their objective.

"Holy shit, they got a ma deuce!" she yelled as the soldier behind the menacing M2 Browning put his back into yanking the charging handle to chamber the first .50-caliber round from the weapon's huge ammo belt—the MRAP's armor would be about as effective as brie cheese against its thumb-sized bullets.

"Beast!" Raider screamed, red-faced, at Grishenko. "Get your ass back up top and take out that fifty!"

"No time!" Tamika hollered, flooring the accelerator. "Anyone remember them old Kool-Aid commercials?"

Raider flashed her a deviant smile and grabbed for his seat belt. "Brace yourselves back there!" he hollered to Team Zulu over loud swearing in English, Spanish, and Ukrainian.

Dammit, I screwed the pooch and we're all dead! Tamika screamed in her head, her heart sinking as the gunner took aim at the MRAP—she had no chance to close the distance in time before he shredded them to ribbons.

Suddenly, the hapless gunner and his assistant glanced in stunned surprise at their nonfunctioning weapon, and back up in horror at the armored behemoth barreling toward them. Team Zulu had just been dealt its second lucky break of the morning.

"Next time, try learnin' how to set headspace and timing with yo' dumb asses!" Tamika shrieked in triumph—she hit the curb and plowed through the soldiers and their useless machine gun, the collision with concrete, sandbags, and steel tossing her angry passengers around like lottery balls in a prize drawing. Tamika barreled toward the front entrance, cackling like a maniac—she and her new friends were unstoppable.

"Hey, Kool-Aid!"

"Oh, yeeeeeaaaaaah!" Raider howled with glee over the cacophony of shattered glass.

***

Pastor Kris watched in stunned fascination from the top of Tower Hill as fighting ripped through what remained of post-collapse Helena. Tracer rounds streaked across a sky darkened by fresh smoke plumes that further thickened the city's pall of burning wood and trash, the constant thud of explosions pounding the air like a drum. She quietly thanked God for her salvation, knowing that the scene before her was the closest she ever wanted to get to hell.

Eric shifted his machine gun to take aim at a police cruiser that rounded the corner and stopped with a screech of its brakes near the newly liberated radio station. Two police officers in tactical gear leaped out of the cruiser; one hastily tied green sheets to its antennas, while the other came around with a can of spray paint to mark the hood and both side doors with green Xs before piling back in and tearing down the road. *They're with us,* Eric breathed a sigh of relief.

"Einstein, link up with us down here," Manny radioed in. "Time to move over to our next job."

***

Carmen, Luisa, and Jay cheered the moment regular programming on KLGK was replaced by the newsreader announcing the call to arms to unseat the governor. Jay thrust his fist in triumph, immediately regretting it as pain shot through his bad arm.

"This message will be repeated every few minutes. But first," the announcer said in a cheery voice that belied the gravity of the situation, *"this one goes out to Carmencita."*

Mariachi music blared from the AM radio. "He's OK!" mother and daughter screamed in unison.

Jay smiled. "Catchy song, even though I don't understand a word. What is it?"

Carmen laughed. "*'Si Nos Dejan'*—'If They Let Us.' It's our song."

"Luis Miguel—Mom had a huge crush on him," Luisa chuckled as Carmen gave her a playful shove. She laid her head on her mother's shoulder. "Come back to us, Dad. You promised."

CHAPTER 54

"What in the hell's this happy horseshit?" Joe Longstreet, Animal's aide, asked no one in particular as Luis Miguel's baritone voice echoed through the exhibit hall of the county fairgrounds.

Animal smirked at the panache with which Team Romeo announced the seizing of their first objective, just minutes after his teams in Butte had taken over the Montana Public Radio station. "Just a man showin' off for his wife and daughter—no harm done, Mister Longstreet. But if they keep playin' tunes, call down there and tell 'em to knock it off—we need to be broadcasting news and instructions, not Twisted Sister."

The thunderous *boom* of back-to-back explosions shook the exhibit hall, teetering radios on their folding tables and sending a loose window pane to the floor with a crash. A radio operator ripped off his headphones and dashed to the Helena map to mark red Xs on the two small roads connecting Fort Harrison to town.

"Right on schedule—so much for the cavalry!" Animal said over the chatter of agitated swallows as he grabbed the black phone plugged into a nearby military SINCGARS radio. "This message is for the reinforcements from Fort Harrison who are tryin' to figure out how to get around the holes we just blew in the road."

"Who the hell is this?" an officious voice responded.

"The Angel of Death, as far as you're concerned," Animal snapped. "We're the patriots fightin' to overthrow the tyrant whose unconstitutional orders you've been following. Well, some of y'all on the right side, like the soldier who slipped us the radio encryption key we're usin' to talk to you right now. You got two choices—stand down or die. Your call."

"Get the hell off our frequency!" the man shouted.

"Well, boss, if I can't reason with you, I'll take my case directly to your men," Animal said and cleared his throat. "To the enlisted soldiers and junior officers hearin' this on the net, it's over. We're gonna win, and when we do, the officers who've been committin' treason and orderin' war crimes are gonna hang. Whether you hang with 'em is up to you. Turn back to post, arrest your idiot brass, and sit this out. Even if y'all manage to get your convoy 'round the craters and back on the road, we'll smoke you before you even reach town. Or, if you'd like, we could start the killin' right now."

Animal nodded to Longstreet, who spoke a single word into his radio; the teams that had set the road charges loosed a brief but furious deluge of small-arms fire at the convoy. "If that didn't convince you we mean business, I got two Warthogs inbound from Mountain Home Air Force Base in the Free State of Idaho, and they're lookin' to scrap. So what do I tell 'em? Head back home, or blow y'all clear into next week?" The A-10 Thunderbolt II, affectionately called the "Warthog" by grunts, was a tough-as-nails close air support plane that carried an ungodly amount of air-to-ground ordnance and was built around a huge tank-busting Gatling gun designed to destroy armor and ground convoys.

Ten seconds elapsed. "No movement," Longstreet reported.

"This is your last goddamn chance!" Animal thundered into the handset, spittle flying from his mouth. *"You gonna turn your sorry asses around, or do I call the funeral home to see if they offer a group discount?"*

Longstreet grinned and turned to Animal, radio pressed to his ear. "They're pulling back in a disorganized, disheartened, and very relieved manner."

Animal blew a sigh of relief. "Smart move, boys. We'll be in touch. Don't try anything stupid—I'm not kiddin' about those A-10s. Out." He handed off the SINCGARS to an enthusiastic young radioman and wiped his brow on his sleeve. "Keep an ear out in case those boys grow a backbone and have second thoughts."

"Wow, we got Warthogs comin' in?" the radioman asked.

"Hell no, son!" Animal chuckled. "Idaho has 'em all tied up in Cascadia, and barely enough jet fuel for even that 'til Texas starts refinin' more. My wife always said I had the best poker face around."

A middle-aged woman monitoring a ham radio yanked out her headphone jack and cranked the volume. "Uh, Animal? Speaking of Texas, you'd better listen to this."

CHAPTER 55

M att and Katie galloped up the dark and musty staircase to the roof of the three-story office building across the street from the joint headquarters of the Helena Police Department and the Lewis and Clark County Sheriff's Office. Below them, their friends and allies poured suppressing fire from the windows into the law enforcement center, whose occupants were caught in a crossfire from the rebels who had seized the old stone courthouse around the corner.

Acrid black smoke billowed from two squad cars set ablaze by tracer rounds in the street below, screening Matt and Katie as they crawled on their elbows across the gravel roof to the building's ornate stone lip and loaded tear gas shells into their rifle-mounted grenade launchers. The duo rose with the next burst of covering fire from Eric's machine gun and fired into separate broken windows of the law enforcement center's top floor, then reloaded and lobbed a second volley into the floor below.

The rebels ceased fire, and a bullhorn's whine cut through the coughing and retching that punctuated the hissing of tear gas. "This is Deputy Chief Grafton, speaking to the officers resisting us. Surrender if you wanna live—we arrested the chief and the sheriff right before the fighting started. I don't wanna hurt fellow brothers in blue, but so help me God, we will if we have to. Those first shells were tear gas. The next ones'll be high explosive. You got thirty seconds!"

Matt and Katie prepared to load the lethal shells when a white sheet on the edge of a stick appeared through the gas billowing from a shattered window and frantically waved to the cheers of their fellow partisans. "Better living through chemistry," Matt quipped as they crawled back to the door.

Team Romeo assembled in the wrecked and musty front office lobby, where Grafton crowed to Manny that the captured police dispatch center would help the fighters' communications immensely, once they aired out the gas. The deputy chief had made a name for himself by skipping town with a handful of like-minded officers and deputies once the illegal orders started flowing; they holed up at his hunting cabin and slowly recruited more officers to their cause, many of whom converged on the police station on this final day to take it back.

Travis reported that Team Romeo was good on ammo, water, and equipment. Manny turned to his soldiers, silently counting his lucky stars that no one had gotten hurt—but their biggest challenge still lay ahead. "We just might make it to sunset, kids," Manny said to the distant sounds of battle and the chattering of Allan's radios. "Let's get to our appointment with the governor."

***

"Fighting has erupted across Montana in a coordinated effort to overthrow Governor Magnuson. Fighting is heaviest in the state capital of Helena, and in Great Falls and Malmstrom Air Force Base, where sources say patriot forces are racing to prevent the federal government from firing the base's nuclear missiles at Texas and seceded southern states. We'll update this story as news comes in to Redoubt Radio . . ."

Animal's calloused hands balled into fists. "I'm gonna find the big-mouthed asshole who thought it'd be a good idea to blab this."

"I don't get what the big deal is, boss," one of his radiomen said. "Don't we want people to know how depraved the governor and the feds have become? Doesn't this help us?"

"Riddle me this, hotshot," Longstreet said with an icy glare. "If you were president of the Texas Federation, and you heard Montana was planning to nuke you, what would you do?"

"Shoot first," the radioman answered as the unfolding disaster dawned on him. "Kill them before they could kill me."

"Yeah," Animal growled. "That's why we never shared this information with other states, so they wouldn't slag us just to play it safe."

The ham radio operator turned to Animal. "Are Texas or the southern states even nuclear capable?"

"They don't need to be—even if they can't get those nuclear-tipped cruises at Barksdale Air Force Base programmed and loaded onto a B-52, those bombers can carry enough conventional ordnance to blow us clear to Mars." Animal spun to face the rest of the ops center. "New orders! Everyone get on the horn with every unit in or near Helena and tell 'em to converge on the Capitol Building as fast as they can!" Animal slapped a hand on the ham radio operator's shoulder. "I need you to get a hold of somebody, anybody, in the Texas government—president, secretary of state, the damned chicken inspector, I don't care!"

"Where you goin'?" Longstreet called out behind Animal as he dashed for the door.

"To the front lines to bag that paper hangin' son of a bitch before we end up glowin' in the dark!" Animal grabbed his sat phone on the run and called Team Zulu for an update from Malmstrom. He cursed when no one picked up, then dialed another number from memory as he, his radio operator, and a two-man security detail piled into his armored Humvee.

"Branson! Y'all in Helena yet? Out-fucking-standing—some good news for a change! Got a map handy? I got another job for ya."

CHAPTER 56

There was nothing Karina could do for Raider except complete their mission and avenge his death.

She looked up from his body and glared at the terrified Air Force colonel cradling the forearm that Grishenko had shattered when the hulking Ukrainian knocked his service pistol from his hand. "Beast, if that piece of shit moves a muscle, beat him like a piñata. Don't kill him—just make him wish he was dead."

"*Iz zadovolyennam,*" Grishenko said, grabbing a fistful of the colonel's dress uniform and lifting him two feet off the ground before forcefully slamming him into a corner chair of the plush top-floor office of the 341st Missile Wing Operations Building that Team Zulu had just secured. "Please give me an excuse to snap your bones like pretzels, *khuylo,*" he threatened in his accented basso tremolo over the colonel's screams of agony. "You will wish you had the balls to end your life like your general."

General Gordon, who had been installed by Glampers and Stu to implement their scheme to bring down America's fledgling independent states with Malmstrom's nuclear arsenal, was arched back in an office chair behind the wooden desk, his 9-millimeter handgun on the floor and the back of his head and much of his gray matter splattered on the broken window behind him. Sprawled in front of the desk was the body of the soldier who had stitched Raider with rifle fire as Team Zulu made entry; Raider's heavy body armor had stopped all but the last round, which caught him between the eyes. Karina, one step behind Raider, had emptied her magazine into his executioner.

"Friendlies comin' in!" Karina heard Bill Rising Sun yell as he ran in with Tamika and another Team Zulu member. The sight of Raider's body stopped them cold. "Aw, God, no . . ." the Lakota Sioux soldier moaned.

"We can mourn later—status report," Karina snapped.

"Base is locked down, officer housing areas are secured with the help of our Air Force friends," Rising Sun, a former Army Ranger, said. The base's Security Forces had decided shortly after General Gordon arrived that he was a traitor, as well as ten pounds of shit stuffed into a five-pound bag; they had provided the resistance with an almost complete order of battle of the occupying troops and boot lickers loyal to him. Once the shooting started, Malmstrom's airmen switched sides *en masse* to help Team Zulu and the ragtag group of audacious invaders they led.

Karina ordered Rising Sun to find Raider's sat phone—the only one Team Zulu possessed besides Animal's—and report that the base was secured and that they were in the process of accounting for every missileer. As Rising Sun frisked their fallen comrade, Karina drew her Ka-Bar knife from its shoulder-mounted sheath and walked menacingly toward the injured colonel; an operating room nurse before the collapse, Karina was powerless to save the man she loved, but Karina the former Marine Corps drill instructor could ensure that Raider didn't die in vain.

"I bet this asshole will help us if properly motivated," she growled, her eyes slits of pure hatred.

"Uh, Doc?"

Karina stopped and turned to see Rising Sun holding up Raider's bullet-shattered phone.

"I think we got us a situation."

CHAPTER 57

"*Shit!*" Travis barked as he swerved his Humvee around a derelict SUV with inches to spare in Team Romeo's mad dash for the Capitol Building. He shot a glance at the large side mirror with the *crash* of Benny's trailing LMTV clipping the dead vehicle and spinning it into an overgrown lawn.

"Dam*nation*!" Allan screamed, his helmeted head bouncing off the Humvee's armored shell with a *thunk*. "You trying to get us killed before we even get there, jarhead?"

"Not everyone—just you," Travis yelled, pulling into a stomach-churning turn. "If I was you, I'd be more worried about having a front-row seat to a nuclear explosion than my driving!"

Word of victory after victory had rolled in as Team Romeo headed back to the vehicles they had stashed at Anchor Park—partisans had seized Helena's airport, Stu's reinforcements were bottled up at Fort Harrison, and enemy forces in Butte and Missoula had surrendered. They had just topped off their magazines when the call came to converge on the Capitol Building with all possible haste.

Manny lunged from the front passenger seat and ripped the ham radio from Allan's chest, frantically stabbing the preset for the frequency his family and Jay were monitoring back at the retreat. Carmen got in a second to gush her relief before Manny cut her off to rattle off a to-do list in rapid-fire Spanish, starting with lowering the curtains and filling buckets to extinguish fires in the event that a bright searing flash to the east heralded the instantaneous deaths of the team and everyone else in Helena. He switched back to English and ordered Jay to kill the solar power to the house and run the ham rig on the backup battery chain.

"This is just in case, honey," Manny reassured his hysterical wife as the sounds of battle grew louder. "If the worst happens, all three of you get in the basement and stay there for at least two weeks. Two weeks, understand? Don't come out for anything!" Manny tossed the radio to Allan without waiting for a reply.

Debris in the streets and shrieking residents fleeing the rapidly intensifying firefight around the Capitol Building slowed their convoy to a crawl. Travis peeled off the road onto a ratty, trash-filled vacant lot and killed the engine. "Looks like we're going in the rest of the way on LPCs."

"Huh?" Allan asked.

"Leather personnel carriers!" Manny exclaimed and threw open his door, almost hitting a father carrying a hysterical toddler away from the fighting. "Stay on my ass, soldier!"

***

Rising Sun shoved General Gordon's corpse to the floor and ripped open his rucksack on the desk to find a radio that might reach Animal.

"I'll get back to the MRAP and see if police dispatch can relay your message!" Tamika yelled and dashed out the door, not wanting to watch Karina extract information from the colonel with her knife.

"Beast, the colonel's good hand, please," Karina ordered.

Grishenko yanked the colonel's left hand away from his broken arm and slapped it palm down on the desktop just in time for Karina to plunge her jet black Ka-Bar through it with a meaty, bone-snapping *thud*.

"I have some questions, now that I have your undivided attention!" she roared over the colonel's scream. "You tell the truth, the knife comes out, and we splint your broken wing and patch the hole in your hand. Lie to me, and this room becomes high school biology class and you become the frog. We trackin', buddy?" The colonel nodded furiously as Karina hovered inches from his pale, sweat-beaded face. "I have zero sympathy for a little shit who's willing to vaporize millions of people to advance his career. And I was talking marriage with that man lying dead over there. Don't you dare fuck with me," she growled.

"Do you have missile combat crews on station in any launch capsules?"

CHAPTER 58

Benny flinched with each bullet chipping into the decorative stone wall protecting him from the soldiers defending the west wing of the Capitol Building across the street.

"What the hell do we do now?!" he screamed to Julie, who laid flat next to him.

"Not get shot!" Julie screamed back as half a dozen rifle rounds punched into the Swiss-cheesed mustard yellow siding of the house behind them.

Team Romeo had made their way toward the Capitol Building against the current of adults and children fleeing the fighting—and over the bodies of the unlucky ones. They had cut across to a side alley a block away when they immediately drew fire from the building's defenders—some on the roof, some from the windows, and others dug into the grounds.

Eric and Liam low-crawled behind a large tree that had somehow been spared the axes and chainsaws of Helena's cold and desperate survivors. "We're gonna be drawing a lot of unwanted attention with The Pig here! You might wanna move!" Liam screamed to Katie, who was returning fire from behind the edge of the stone wall.

"Move *where*?!" Katie screamed back just as Eric ripped a seven-round burst at a soldier peeking out of his foxhole on the grounds.

"We don't got endless ammo!" Manny hollered from behind a detached garage, desperately looking around to locate all his people. "Don't piss it away trying to keep their heads down! Shoot only at clear targets! Let *them* spray and pray!"

An angry buzz behind Manny cut through the sounds of battle as Tim's drone rocketed into the sky. "We're in business, boss!" he yelled, panning the drone's camera left to right, giving Manny the locations of his scattered friends in a matter of seconds; Team Romeo was strung along a front line stretching across two homes, with Manny in the approximate center. Tim then gained more altitude to to get an idea of the size and locations of the enemy.

An eruption of gunfire down the block to their left signaled the arrival of another partisan cell to the fight. Manny barely had time to cheer the reinforcements before Tim tore away and sprinted toward Eric, Liam, and Katie on the right side of the line.

"Grenadiers on the roof, coming right for us!" Tim warned the moment he slid to a hard stop against the stone wall. The first grenadier had just popped up to lob a shell from his M203 when Eric cut him down. Katie followed up a second later with a high-explosive shell of her own that flew true, blasting parts of the stone building, and the other two enemy grenadiers, in multiple directions simultaneously. Tim screamed for covering fire and zigzagged back to Manny, breathlessly checking his video screen and almost crying with relief when he confirmed his drone hadn't been shot down.

Manny grabbed Tim's tactical vest and yanked his ear close. "You'll have to tell me later what the hell that was all about! Now land that thing and get back into the war!"

***

"Well, ain't this a shit show!" Animal said from the gravel parking strip behind the offices across the street from the Capitol Building's main entrance. *Name one firefight that wasn't*, he thought as he ran down a mental checklist of who he had and where.

Team Charlie was just ahead of him pouring suppressing fire into the windows of the stone edifice. To his right, Team Echo was engaging on the building's northwest corner, and Team Romeo was in the thick of it with soldiers defending the building's west wing. Three handgun shots followed by a deluge of automatic weapon fire echoed to his left, where rebels were clearing out the nondescript office building that housed the state motor vehicles, agriculture, and livestock departments. Black smoke began to waft from a shattered window.

"There's still a lot of people missin' from the party," Animal yelled at his radioman. "Where they at?"

"We got four more teams enroute, but ev'ryone else's still committed elsewhere!"

"Everyone got our message about Texas possibly endin' this with a couple of 350-kiloton crowd pleasers, right? Tell 'em all to get their goat smellin' asses over here!" Animal snarled. He stared daggers at his sat phone, as if trying to coax two important calls from it through sheer will; one would hopefully tell him that Team Zulu had secured Malmstrom's nuclear arsenal, while the other could make or break the battle raging in front of him. Serendipitously, the phone buzzed in his hand with the latter, and Animal almost hung up on Branson by mistake in his haste to answer.

"Wait three minutes and let fly! Danger close! This is a tough shot—don't screw it up!" He hastily pocketed the phone and grabbed his radioman. "Tell everyone at the Capitol to pull back! *Now!*"

CHAPTER 59

Pastor Kris sighted her rifle on a top-floor window of the Capitol Building and waited for her target to pop up again—he had gotten predictable, and would pay a horrible price. The soldier's head rose, the pastor's rifle bucked, and the young man fell.

It's them or my flock, Father. Forgive me.

A young girl bolted from the neighboring house into her side yard, her screams slicing through the cacophony like a knife. "Help! My daddy's been shot!" she shrieked, stomping her feet and grabbing her matted hair, oblivious to the battle raging around her. A piece of shrapnel that loudly whizzed through the air inches from her head didn't faze the hysterical girl, who screamed again for help before being drowned out by a burst from Eric's machine gun.

Angel scrambled for the girl, bullets peppering the ground around her as she dove on top of her like an offensive lineman trying to save a fumble. "Shit! *Covering fire!*" Manny desperately ordered to give Angel and the child a fighting chance to live.

Susan dropped to a knee behind the corner of a house and frantically fumbled for a fresh magazine when Pastor Kris walked past her up the middle of the alley toward the Capitol Building, completely exposed and methodically shooting into the building's shattered windows.

"Kris, *take cover*!" Susan screamed so hard that she became light-headed. "What the hell are you doing?!"

"Look at me! Not the little girl—over here!" Pastor Kris hollered at the top of her lungs, dropping her rifle on its harness and waving her arms over her head. "Big fat target out in the open! *Right here!*" She grabbed her rifle again and managed to crack off two more shots before return fire from a dozen defenders cut her down. Susan threw herself to the ground as the fusillade kicked up gravel and dirt and shredded the house's siding.

Matt sprinted to his wife with their attackers' unexpected shifting of fire to pull her and the child to cover, frantically patting Angel down for wounds while she clutched the young girl like a mother reunited with a lost child. "You gotta help my daddy! Please—you gotta help!" the girl bawled, eyes bloodshot and nose running down her filthy cheeks.

A new scream—Roger's—cut through the fighting. Almost as one, the group's rifles fell silent as they turned and saw Pastor Kris's bullet-ridden body.

"If you assholes don't start puttin' some goddamn rounds downrange, we'll all be joinin' her!" Manny raged at his friends, red-faced and frothing like a man possessed. "Eric!" he screamed, viciously stabbing his hand at the Capitol Building, "Get back on the Pig or I'll shoot you myself and find someone who will! Angel! Matt! Tell the kid to stay down and *get the fuck back in this fight*!"

Eric snapped out of it like Manny had slapped him in the face. He laid down a long stream of copper-jacketed death along the roof as his friends joined in. Susan and Roger darted to Pastor Kris and dragged her behind the small garage under Manny and Allan's suppressing fire. Susan ripped off her glove and put two fingers to her friend's neck as a formality before bolting back across the alley.

"No . . . no, no, no, no, no," Roger bawled, hugging his wife's body and rocking back and forth.

Allan hollered Manny's name several times over the roar of the firefight before smacking his helmet to get his attention. "Animal's ordering everyone to pull back at least two hundred meters right now!" Allan screamed in his face, waving the radio in his free hand. "They said, 'danger close!' I got no idea what that means, but it doesn't sound good!"

Cold fear immediately displaced Manny's homicidal rage over Pastor Kris's death. He pulled the pin on his one smoke grenade and side-stepped from the garage to throw it into the street ahead, fumbling the whistle tied to his tactical vest into his mouth and blowing three long blasts as the billowing white smoke created a screen he prayed would conceal them.

"*Fall back!* Two blocks! No time to break contact by teams! Haul ass! *Move!*"

Angel, with a strength she never knew she had, scooped up the girl with one arm and ran at a gallop with her husband. Eric and Liam, their lungs gulping in the sickly sweet chemical smokescreen billowing around them, put an entire hundred-round belt through the machine gun to cover their friends' withdrawal before bringing up the rear, hacking and retching as they ran. Susan tore Pastor Kris's body from Roger's grasp and flung her over her shoulder as Manny and Travis yanked Roger to his feet, pulling him along by his blood-soaked tactical vest and ignoring his wails to be left behind to die with his wife.

CHAPTER 60

"The colonel's story checks out, Doc," Rising Sun told Karina, radio to his ear. "All of Malmstrom's missileers are accounted for."

Thank God—it would've been game, set, and match otherwise, Karina said to herself. Malmstrom's missile fields were larger than Massachusetts, Connecticut, and Rhode Island combined; if the conspiracy had any launch facilities manned and ready to fire, there would have been no way for Team Zulu to get to them in time, to say nothing of the futility of trying to force their way into an underground capsule designed to survive a close hit by a nuclear warhead. But they still had the problem of letting Animal know.

"You just bought yourself some time, Colonel Klink," she said, yanking her Ka-Bar out of the colonel's hand and wiping it on his dress uniform; the trembling, clammy officer recoiled as if Karina had struck him. "You already have so much innocent blood on you—a little of your own won't matter much," she sneered before sheathing her knife.

Team Zulu raised their rifles at the sound of footfalls headed their way, and stood down the moment Tamika breathlessly charged through the door. "Emergency dispatch is tryin' to get a hold of your people in Helena, but they couldn't promise anything!"

A pregnant pause, lightly accented by the distant pops of withering gunfire, filled the room. It was the first real quiet they had experienced since barreling through Malmstrom's gate.

Buzz.

"Is that a cell phone?!" Tamika asked incredulously—she hadn't heard one since the collapse.

Buzz.

Karina looked around. "Is that coming from the general?"

"I searched him," Rising Sun said.

"Search him again!"

Buzz.

"Under the desk! He must've dropped it!" Rising Sun yelled and momentarily disappeared underneath. "Situation resolved!" he exclaimed a second later, leaping up with the late general's black sat phone. He glanced at the caller ID and smiled as it vibrated again in his hand. "Hey, Beast, you need to take this—do the Bullwinkle thing for us!" he said and tossed it to Grishenko, who swiped the screen and put the call on speaker.

"*Da?*" he asked in an almost comical embellishment of his already thick accent.

"General Gordon?" a perplexed male voice inquired.

"*Nyet*—Dzheneral Gordon is not available at moment."

The caller paused. "This is urgent—we need air exfil out of Helena. Who's this?"

"My name is Boris Badenov, and I am on *sekretny* mission from Kremlin to catch moose and squirrel," Grishenko taunted over the laughs of his brothers and sisters in arms. "Comrade General Gordon shot his brains all over wall. Your missiles will not be launched, *suka blyat'*. See you real soon." Grishenko hung up without waiting for a response and handed the phone to Karina, who silently gave thanks for their third lucky break of the morning—a sat phone in a building rigged with an antenna to allow for inside calls—as she furiously punched in Animal's number.

He picked up before the first ring finished. "Who the fuck is this?!" Animal panted on the run.

"It's Doc! Full quiver, I say again, full quiver! Objective secure, birds locked down!"

"About damn time! Where's Raider?"

Karina's silence answered the question.

"Damn. I'm so sorry," Animal said, catching his breath. "Things are still hot and heavy here. Hold the objective and wait for instructions. Good job," he said and ended the call.

"Fighting's over," Rising Sun reported matter-of-factly, holding up his radio. "Last remaining holdouts in Great Falls just surrendered."

Karina turned to Grishenko, fatigue rushing in as the adrenaline began draining from her body. "Beast, patch up the colonel. We'll be taking him with us."

She tiredly knelt by Raider and stroked his blood-streaked face. "We did it," she whispered with a lover's softness.

CHAPTER 61

Animal tore the walkie-talkie from his radioman's hands to call the TOC the moment he and his men and women halted their retreat from the Capitol Building.

"Full quiver—nukes are grounded! You gotten a hold of anyone in the Texas government yet?" Animal asked Longstreet as his winded and wheezing troops scrambled into a hasty perimeter behind homes, garages, and sheds.

"Still working on it!" Longstreet answered.

"Change of plans!" Animal barked, his fear rising that they would be bombed off the map by their fellow good guys with victory in their grasp. "Contact those freakin' blabbermouths at Redoubt Radio instead and let 'em know we got control of the nukes. In fact, have every operator and every AM broadcaster we got broadcast it in the clear, over and over. Time's runnin' out—our own! Move it!"

Animal's scowl turned to an evil grin with the start of a faint descending whistle overhead. "Hang on to your knickers, kids!" he yelled. "And get ready to run back so we can finish this!"

***

Stu anxiously peeked through the windows of the wooden doors of the Capitol Building's south entrance at the soldiers crouched behind the line of armored Humvees parked along the looped driveway. While battle raged on the building's north and west sides, the south side remained unmolested; blocks of parking lots empty since the collapse, except for one repurposed by locals as a garbage burn pile, offered no cover for an advancing enemy.

Red Beard dropped his sat phone to the ornate tile floor and smashed it with the heel of his boot, startling Stu and the equally nervous private guarding the entrance.

"I take it General Gordon can't pick us up?" Stu asked resignedly.

"He's dead."

"Who were you talking to?"

"The people who killed him."

"We should've left the moment the shooting started!"

"We wouldn't have made it half a mile when all these guerrillas started comin' out of the woodwork," Red Beard calmly retorted, snapping the phone's SIM card between the finger and thumb of his gloved hand. "We can slip away, now that they're concentrated here." He peered out the window. "Copter ride's out, but the first part of the plan still works—grab one of those Humvees, get the hell outta Dodge, and lie low at the safe house. The center isn't gonna hold much longer."

"Any word from Glampers?"

"Fuck him—he became worthless the moment we lost Malmstrom."

"What about the rest of us? What do we do?" the door guard managed to stammer before Red Beard nonchalantly raised his rifle and shot the young man in the face. Stu's hands flew to his ears with the loud report.

Red Beard looked at his horrified boss. "Can't leave a trail of bread crumbs."

A thunderous explosion shook the building, knocking the duo to the tile floor. Red Beard hauled Stu to his feet, his iron grip preventing him from falling as his foot slid on the pool of blood spurting in pumps from both holes in the door guard's head. White plaster dust rained from the ceiling like snow.

"What the hell was that?!" Stu screamed, wide-eyed.

"Let's not stick around and find out!" Red Beard barked, pulling his boss toward the exit.

The thick wooden doors flew off their hinges with a deafening roar, hurling both men backward on a wall of flame.

***

Branson whooped as the Idaho mortar squad's second shell found its mark and smashed the line of Humvees parked at the Capitol Building like toys swatted by a petulant child.

Animal had ordered them to the top of Meatloaf Hill, a part of Helena's hiking trail system that offered a commanding view of the Capitol grounds half a mile to the northeast; unlike their fire mission to smash the governor's home, softening up the enemy's defenses without demolishing the Capitol Building or neighboring homes required finesse.

Branson ordered the mortarmen to drop their next round on the enemy defenders dug in on the west side of the building grounds; Sergeant

Davis lowered his binoculars and shouted the correction back to his men.

"Sure you don't want the laser range finder, sergeant?" a specialist idling by the dormant tube asked.

"You'll be walkin' awful funny after I cram it up your ass," Davis replied. "I'll trust my Mark One Eyeball and its three combat tours over your high-tech doodad, thank you!"

"Ready!" the leader of the first tube barked.

"Hang it . . . *fire!*"

The round landed true, cutting a bloody swath through the entrenched defenders. As the smoke cleared, Branson saw that the explosion had knocked a ten-foot hole in the bottom floor of the sandstone and granite building.

"Oopsie—sorry 'bout that, Ranger!" Davis said with a grin that belied the fact that he wasn't sorry at all. "I'd say to take it outta my paycheck if I wasn't doin' this pro bono!"

"Don't be sorry—you guys just changed everything! Cease fire!" Branson excitedly ordered as he grabbed his phone to call Animal.

Davis looked back at his men. "I think we just blew those crazy bastards down there a new front door to end this once and for all. Come on up and watch the show, but be ready to haul ass back to the tubes if they end up needin' more fire support." The sound of steady gunfire pouring into the breach echoed up the hill like an old-fashioned teletype while the remaining outdoor defenders broke off and fled south and east. Flames fully engulfed an office complex behind the Capitol Building, its plume of black smoke joining others hanging over the city. The hilltop breeze whisked away the smell of mortar propellant that had temporarily displaced the stench of refuse from the subdivision behind them—none of the occupants had dared venture outside.

"Hey, Branson, what kinda name is Meatloaf Hill, anyway?" one of the privates asked, unable to take his eyes off the fight. "*The Battle of Meatloaf Hill* ain't a particularly catchy name for the movie they're gonna make about us."

"Hellfino," Branson said. "I'm from Ohio—I only moved here just before the shit hit the fan. You ever hear of *Pork Chop Hill*, though? Gregory Peck? Damned good film!"

One of the private's buddies punched his arm. "Nobody ain't playin' you in no movie. You too ugly. That, an' there ain't no more Hollywood."

Tracer rounds and rifle grenades flew into the breach, adding to the chorus of crackles, pops, and bangs. "I watched shit like this on the evening news growin' up," Davis said, lost in thought. "Witnessed it firsthand in the 'Stan, Iraq, Syria, Horn o' Africa. Never dreamed I'd see it here in America—even as bad as shit got near the end."

"I think this is gonna turn out different," Branson said. "We got sent to those other hellholes either to prop up some scumbag who was sittin' on a gazillion barrels of oil, or to depose one scumbag and replace him with another. This fight is just."

Davis slapped Branson on the back. "Well, Ranger, Idaho and Texas got their act together, so's I guess you can, too. I think I speak for my boys when I say we were happy to help."

Branson watched, transfixed, at the fighting through his binoculars. "We did our part—let's pray those grunts down there can seal the deal."

CHAPTER 62

Eric and Liam flung themselves back into their original position behind the stone wall and poured fire into the breach that had been ripped through the Capitol Building's west wall, joining scores of rifles down the length of the block in an effort to shred whatever slapdash defenses their disoriented and dispirited enemy could muster. The roar of high-velocity lead was soon joined by the hollow *thunks* of grenade launchers and the hammer blows of indoor explosions as the high-explosive shells found their marks.

Matt had just slapped a fresh magazine into his rifle when several long whistles blew along the line. He leaped to his feet and charged headlong for the breach, screaming as he sprinted across the buckled blacktop of Montana Avenue onto the Capitol Building's lawn under Eric's suppressing fire. A hundred other green-sashed resistance fighters followed Matt, exploiting their sudden change in fortune with speed and extreme violence of action. Fueled by rage over the death of Pastor Kris and almost losing Angel, he shot two wounded soldiers sprawled on the lawn before indiscriminately firing into the breach and climbing inside over the rubble.

Eric ceased fire as the flow of attackers into the building slowed to stragglers. He winced as Liam's rifle barked to his right to drop two defenders trying to make a run for it.

"That was for Pastor Kris!" Liam yelled. A helmetless soldier threw down her rifle and took off at a full sprint. "Oh, you think you're getting away?" Liam taunted as he fired at the woman before drilling her in the back on the fourth shot. He shifted back to the Capitol grounds and fired into the dead bodies. "Die! All of you just fucking *die*!"

"*Liam!*" Eric hollered, smacking the big man's helmet so hard that pain shot through the palm of his hand. "Get it together! How're we on ammo?"

"Low!" Liam reported as if he had never lost his cool. "Three belts left after this one! You need to start conserving!"

The duo ran for the breach and threw themselves over loose stone into the charred and pockmarked remnants of what had once been some bureaucrat's office. "Fighting's on the main floor! They're gonna want you 'n your pig up front!" one of the two rebels guarding the breach hollered over the din as Eric and Liam struggled to catch their breath over the stink of burnt wood and plastic. The rebel furiously pointed at a decapitated enemy soldier slumped in the outside hallway, the charred wall behind him sprayed with gore. "Take the stairs to the right of the Headless Horseman! It's a shootin' gallery up there! God be with you!"

Eric and Liam charged up the dark staircase to the next floor. The sounds of combat, amplified by the tight quarters, roared from around the corner, where another hallway opened up to the long Gallery of Outstanding Montanans leading to the central Rotunda. "Culebra! We're in!" Eric screamed into his radio. "Where you at?"

Liam and Eric ducked to a crouch as bullet holes punctured the wall at the end of the hallway. Two sets of booted footfalls pounded toward them. "Comin' to you! Don't shoot us!" Manny yelled seconds before rounding the corner. Allan tripped and slid hard into the wall before scrambling on all fours to safety.

Manny grabbed Eric by the shoulder straps of his tactical vest. "We're pinned down at the Rotunda!" he hollered over the crackle of gunfire. "Everyone was charging for the Governor's Office at the far end of the east wing, but we started taking heavy fire! We got good cover behind two sandbag walls they kindly left for us, but we're the only ones holdin' the line—Animal took everyone else up the side stairs to clear the rest of the building an' try to flank 'em! We need fire superiority, right now!"

"Fire superiority's my middle name!" Eric nervously yelled, shifting on the balls of his feet. "We go on three! One . . ."

"Covering fire!" Manny hollered to the rest of Team Romeo and took off around the corner, his boots grinding the shattered remnants of the display case that had held Montana's current and former constitutions. Eric, Liam, and Allan swore simultaneously and ran for the sandbags as their friends covered their advance. Manny and Allan slid behind the sandbag wall on the left side of the gallery; Eric and Liam leaped over the bodies of two fallen resistance fighters and slid into the opposite sandbag position next to Travis, Susan, Benny, and Julie.

Eric's eyes locked with Susan's the moment she dropped back behind cover. "I wanted dinner and a movie for our first date, but hey—we got outta the house!" he yelled.

Susan, pale with fear, dumped her empty magazine and ripped open the Velcro pouch over her left breast to grab a reload. "You as good with that machine gun as you are with smart-ass remarks?"

"You bet!" Eric boasted, hoisting his M240B on top of the sandbags and thumbing off the safety. The thundering of the machine gun and Team Romeo's return fire reverberated through the demolished Rotunda, further punishing tortured ears. Eric methodically fired long bursts into each enemy sandbag position, making his way down the wide hallway. Much of the Rotunda's ornate decor lay in ruins, its wall art and marble columns peppered by stray bullets.

Travis ripped a hand grenade from its pouch and popped up just long enough to hurl it across the Rotunda into the east wing, where it banked off a bullet-riddled wall and behind the first row of enemy defenses. *"Fire in the hole!"* he bellowed as he and Team Romeo ducked behind their sandbags—a handful of screams were silenced a second later by a violent explosion.

"Cease fire!" Travis ordered after realizing that the enemy had stopped shooting back; tinkling glass and falling timber and plaster accompanied the cries and moans of the wounded as the *pop-pop-pop* of gunshots from their fellow rebels echoed from the upper floors. "You're *done!*" Travis screamed down the hall as dust and smoke from the explosion billowed over Team Romeo's heads. "You got ten seconds to show us some hands—the pastor you motherfuckers killed today would've wanted us to give you a chance to live. Take us up on our generous offer before we change our fucking minds."

Their enemy remained silent. The walls shook with the explosion of another grenade elsewhere in the building. Travis angrily yanked open the pouch holding his second grenade. "Have it your way! Here comes another party popper, kids!"

"Holy Jesus, don't shoot! We surrender!" a shrill voice shrieked from down the hall.

"Finally! Someone with a brain!" Travis yelled, cautiously rising to his feet and stepping out from the sandbag wall, rifle at the low ready, as his teammates took aim down the hall. "I want everyone to drop your weapons and, one at a time, stand with your hands on top of your heads and walk toward the sound of my voice into the Rotunda. Any sudden moves, the deal's off and you all die. Would the first contestant please step forward?"

"Why not?" a gurgling voice croaked from the wide staircase to Travis's left. He barely had time to turn before rifle fire tore into him and flung him back onto Susan and Eric. Julie and Benny ducked behind the sandbag wall with no clear shot, while Liam fell onto his back and pushed away with his feet across the debris-strewn floor to escape their unseen assailant's line of fire.

Katie leaped from behind the other sandbag position on the left side of the gallery, saw Travis's attacker a split second before he saw her, and shot him five times before her magazine ran dry. She dropped her rifle on its harness and quickly drew her Ruger .45-caliber handgun from her hip, sidestepping the pockmarked bronze bust of a former senator to cautiously approach what was left of the man sprawled at the base of the stairs. It was obvious that Travis's assailant had had a very bad day before Katie worsened his problems by several orders of magnitude. Burns covered the man's face, which had been peppered by glass and wood splinters that had put out his left eye, and bone jutted through charred clothes from a compound fracture of his left arm. The man stared vacantly at Katie with his good eye as blood ran from the corner of his mouth and past his singed, red goatee.

A flash of recognition replaced Katie's scowl. "Hi, Red, or whatever you call yourself. Remember me? The naïve little cadet from Fort Harrison who went AWOL with a truckload of your stuff? You should've looked harder for us," Katie growled before putting Red Beard out of his misery with a *coup de grâce* to the forehead.

Manny scrambled to his feet to reassert control and fight the terror swelling inside him as Susan and Eric squirmed out from under Travis's mangled body. He screamed for Katie to lead Benny, Pete, and Tim to clear out the downstairs stairwell from where Travis's assailant had come; she holstered her handgun and slapped a fresh magazine in her rifle as the three men stacked behind her. "Follow me!" she commanded and led the way around the corner.

A stampede of boots thundered down the marble staircase above them. "Friendlies comin' down!" Animal cried out from the lead.

"Hold up!" Manny shouted to prevent Animal and his troops from running headlong into a kill zone should the surrendering enemy soldiers change their minds. He stepped, exposed, into the middle of the Rotunda to the grunts of Susan and Matt ripping off Travis's gear. "We're still here, and we got reinforcements!" Manny screamed down the east wing. "You *cabrónes* still wanna give up, or do we finish this right now?" Two dozen men slowly rose from behind shelters of sandbags and desks with their hands raised. "Animal, you got this? We got a man down!"

With a nod, Animal sent his men and women down the stairs where they quickly and roughly subdued the prisoners and began sweeping the east wing room by room. "If Stu's cowerin' in his office, I want him alive!" Animal yelled after his soldiers.

Pete ran from behind the stairs to Manny and Animal. "Ask and ye shall receive!" he triumphantly boasted and beckoned them to follow.

Manny, Animal, and Allan chased after Pete behind the grand staircase, through a screen of oily black smoke wafting through a shattered window from the Humvees obliterated by the Idaho mortarmen. They stepped over the toppled statue of the first woman ever elected to the US House of Representatives, and trotted down a smaller flight of stairs to the first floor, where Benny, Katie, and Tim stepped aside to reveal their prize. Curled up in a bloody ball beside one of the thick wooden doors blown loose by the mortar round was none other than Governor Stu Magnuson.

Animal kneeled next to Stu, who groaned in pain. "Stuart Magnuson, you're under arrest for treason and crimes against humanity. We'd place a man of your stature under house arrest, but seein' as how we blew up your house, we'll take you to the county calaboose instead 'til we can figure out what to do with you. It smells like smoke an' piss, but it's a roof over your head and three squares a day, which is more than what a lot of people have had, thanks to you." Stu covered his head with a whimper as Animal's shadow blocked the sun peeking in through the gaping hole that had been the south entrance. "Knock it off—I'm not gonna tan your hide, as much as you deserve it, and we'll fix you up good as new. You're gonna be in top physical condition the day you're hanged." Animal turned to Katie's squad. "Drag this piece of shit to the Rotunda. Get him away from this exit."

"Manny?!" Eric's quivering voice echoed from up the stairwell. "We need you! You'd, uh . . . better move fast!"

Manny and Allan broke and flew up the debris-strewn stairs to the sight of Travis lying in a pool of blood, his head resting in Susan's lap, surrounded by his teammates. Susan met Manny's forlorn stare with a shake of her head.

"Shoulda seen . . . shoulda seen 'im . . ." Travis gasped. "Got cocky . . ."

"You were kinda busy," Matt stammered as his hometown friend's life slipped away. Travis convulsed and spewed bright red blood onto his chest. "Don't die, buddy," Matt cried. "We have a pitcher to split back in Tennessee, remember? We'll road trip back to Barstow and hit all those dive bars you used to drag me to. Drinks are on me. Forever. Just hang on . . ."

Travis's labored breathing slowed. "Momma? Big Sis? Missed you . . ." Angel patted his right hand. "Not fair, Momma . . . not done yet. Scared . . . Kris? . . . hi . . . go together? Oh . . . OK . . . OK . . ."

His chest didn't rise. Susan checked his neck for a pulse, then gently closed his eyes.

Animal respectfully approached the group after ensuring that the prisoner who had cost them so much to capture was receiving medical attention. "If Manny didn't tell y'all, you folks just bagged the ex-governor in mostly one piece. Your friend died a hero."

Susan's bloodshot eyes drilled into Animal. "So it's over."

Animal shook his head. "The shootin' is, but we still got a lotta work to do—we can't win the war but lose the peace." He knelt in front of Susan. "Doc, there's nothing you coulda done for your friend, but you could make the difference today for a lotta hurt people."

A feeble, effeminate yelp echoed through the Rotunda. "Knock it off, you big baby, or I'll give you something to cry about, and to hell with my orders!" a woman sternly admonished.

"I gotta stop my medic from killin' Stu instead of stabilizin' him," Animal said. "We still need your help, Team Romeo. Believe it or not, all this shit was the easy part." The click of his boots on the mauled tile melted into the chorus of footfalls and barked orders echoing through the battered Capitol Building.

Manny tiredly plucked the Yaesu ham radio from Allan's chest. "The hard part for me officially starts now," he sighed before walking over to tell the foursome guarding Stu that Travis didn't make it. As they huddled together, Manny did an about-face for the shattered front entrance to call his wife and daughter and tell them that Travis and Pastor Kris wouldn't be coming home.

CHAPTER 63

"Nothing except a battle lost can be half so melancholy as a battle won."

Eric, Manny, Allan, and Liam stood at the top of the first flight of concrete steps leading to the Capitol Building's demolished front entrance. Exhausted, dirty, and reeking victors milled about on the overgrown grass in front of the blackened edifice as they ate, tended to their wounded, and mourned their dead. A growing number of desperate civilians weaved among them, trying to wheedle food or medical attention for themselves or loved ones.

"Say again, brother?" Manny asked Eric.

"Arthur Wellesley, First Duke of Wellington. Defeated Napoleon at Waterloo, but lost a lot of friends and comrades doing it. I didn't appreciate the quote until today."

Fighting in Helena had petered out as remaining holdouts surrendered or fled. Wisps of smoke still wafted from some of the Capitol Building's windows after Eric had led the effort to extinguish small fires before they got out of control—with so much history around the world in ruins following the Unraveling, he wasn't about to sit idly by and watch more of it burn. The department of motor vehicles building across the street was engulfed in flames, and pleas had gone out over the liberated radio stations and first responder frequencies for firefighters.

Animal marched down the Capitol Building's steps, yelling into a handset connected to his trailing radioman. "We need to get civic leaders up here pronto to form interim city and state governments with us. Find us community volunteers, faith leaders, local business owners, whoever—but I want constitutionalists, and absolutely no one with any connection to either Stu or the old pre-collapse government. We're not gonna replace one shitty regime with another, or with a military junta that doesn't know dick about feedin' hungry people and keepin' the lights and water on . . . ya think I got time to debate this? Just do it! Out!"

He stopped in front of Team Romeo's gaggle. "I'll say it again—great work, gentlemen. We couldn't have won without you. I mean that."

"I hope all this was worth it," Manny said, waving his hand around the battered city. "We lost two good friends."

"I know about Travis. Who was the other?"

"Pastor Kris Reynolds."

Animal took off his hat. "Your padre. May flights of angels carry her to her rest. I lost one of my own today, too."

"What was his name?" Eric asked.

"We called him Raider."

Allan bowed his head. "He kept Julie and me safe while we triangulated Stu's mansion and his radio repeaters. He was a good guy."

"We lost a lot of good people, but we saved, Lord, millions more—ourselves included," Animal said. "We found out shortly after y'all snagged Governor Douchebag that Texas and the southern states were preparin' to launch some kind of strike, which they kindly called off when they heard Big Sky Country's under new management."

"Any word on what happened to Deputy Under Secretary Douchebag?" Eric tiredly asked, scratching his head.

"Glampers, ya mean?" Animal sneered. "You can see what's left of him in front of what's left of the Governor's Mansion. Not as many locals rose up to fight as I woulda liked, but Glampers and his lackeys had the misfortune of runnin' headlong into an angry mob that did. Looks like a roadkill possum—barely enough of a corpse left to piss on." He paused, suddenly looking like a consoling father rather than a military leader. "I promise, on my oath as a soldier, that your friends' sacrifices will be remembered for the next thousand years. Now, if you'll excuse me, gentlemen, my day's just gettin' started. There's no more FEMA, and no Marshall Plan to help us pick up the pieces. We gotta do it ourselves, and that process starts today."

Animal continued his stride down the steps toward the burning office building. "Where're the goddamn firefighters?" he bellowed to his radioman trotting behind him. "We didn't liberate Helena just to watch it burn down! Get Team Yankee on the horn right now!"

The four men watched the larger-than-life guerrilla leader fade into the distance. "Anyone given any thought as to what the hell we do with ourselves now?" Allan asked, breaking the silence.

"We live free and do our part to rebuild," Manny said with conviction. "Make sure this new government returns to the principles the Founding Fathers envisioned so we don't hafta do this all over again one day. We go back to the retreat and homestead. Survive. No, survive isn't the right word—we thrive."

"Not me."

"Liam?" Eric said.

"Been thinking about this for a while," Liam said, not taking his eyes off the inferno across the street. "I'm going back to Billings. Find out what happened to my parents and my girl. Madison and I . . . I was saving for a ring. I need to know."

That's the first time he's ever spoken her name, Eric realized. "Buddy, that's hundreds of miles from here."

"I better start walking, then. After we pay our final respects to Pastor Kris and Travis."

Manny swallowed hard and put his hand on the big man's shoulder. "You're not walking anywhere. You're getting a truck, and all the supplies we can spare for you and your family. You'll always be welcome in my home, Liam. If you don't find what you're looking for, please come back to us."

Liam looked down at Manny. "It was an honor fighting at your side. Sir," he added with a smirk and walked away.

"That sucks," Allan said.

"What happened to his family, or his leaving us?" Eric asked.

"Both."

"Katie!" a young man's voice cried out behind them. The three men turned as Tim and Katie ran to each other on the concrete steps, throwing themselves into one another's arms when they met halfway.

"What the hell has been going on under my roof?" Manny growled in annoyance as the young lovers kissed passionately and Eric and Allan doubled over laughing. "First you and Susan, doing God knows what, God knows where in my house, and now this?!"

"'God knows where' for Julie and me was the quarantine trailer until those marauders blew it up," Allan said. Manny shot him an angry glare. "I'm kidding!" he chuckled with hands raised.

"You oughta open your home as a couples retreat—get a nice side hustle going," Eric said, wiping his eyes. "'Life gettin' you down? Kids drivin' you nuts? Well, leave the little a-holes with Grandma for the weekend and drive up to Manny's Casa de Amor!'"

Manny shoved his friend. "I'll have a room with a blow-up doll and a bike pump and call it the Eric Jaeger Suite."

Allan's laughter trailed off with a sigh. "Is this normal? Two of our friends are dead and we're cracking jokes."

Manny sadly nodded. "It is. You're happy we won, and elated that you and Julie lived through it. That, and you're too tired right now to feel the pain. That'll come later. Trust me."

Eric stared for a long moment at Tim and Katie. "Excuse me, guys, but I gotta go see about a girl. Speaking of living our lives, I'm starting right now," he said and headed back toward the Capitol Building to find Susan, who was helping care for the wounded.

"Eric?"

"Yeah, buddy?"

"Glad you made it."

"Right back at you."

Manny looked skyward and welcomed the summer sun on his face as he mentally accounted for his people. Most of them had commandeered a patch of the grounds where, before the Unraveling, workers would plant floral designs to commemorate the state's history. Angel held Annalisa, the little girl she had rescued, as she devoured one of Angel's MREs; they had yet to tell her that her father had bled to death before help got to him. Pete and Benny were ferrying wounded to St. Peter's, and prisoners to the county jail. *Thank God we didn't lose Cousin Benny,* Manny thought before chastising himself for his selfishness.

Roger kept vigil over the poncho-wrapped body of his wife, who had sacrificed her life for Angel and the child. Travis's body laid next to hers; Matt sat beside his friend, hugging his knees and gazing blankly forward with the thousand-yard stare of a soldier who had seen enough war for one lifetime. Manny shook his head to chase away the memory of Carmen's wails when he broke the news of their deaths over the radio, but he knew it would return like an unannounced and unwanted guest, again and again, for the rest of his days. *We're hurting bad, and the person who was supposed to help us through it is lying under one of those ponchos. God help us.*

He turned to Allan, desperate to think about something else. "Hey, pal, seeing as how Eric's looking for Susan, why don't you go find Julie? I'll track you down if I need you."

"I'm not going anywhere," Allan said, pushing up his glasses. "I'm your radio operator—you told me to stick to you like glue, and dammit, that's what I'm gonna do. I learned on day one of all this bullshit that the safest place on Earth is next to you. We all did."

The past year—its triumphs and tragedies, the good and the awful—came back to Manny in a deluge. He had always forced his feelings to take a back seat to the constant demands of the retreat, but he couldn't hold them back any longer, and he cried like a lost soul. "It's OK," Allan said and hugged Manny, doing his best not to get his skinny frame crushed by a sobbing man hardened by a lifetime of backbreaking labor and exercise. "We owe you and Carmen our lives—we'd all be bleached bones if it weren't for you two. Everything's gonna be OK . . ."

"Thank you," Manny sniffed and wiped his nose on his sleeve. "Say one word of this to Eric . . ."

"And you'll fix it so I won't be able to sire any children to help repopulate the planet—mum's the word."

"Well, soldier," Manny said, dabbing his eyes, "seeing as how you won't leave my side, how about we find Julie together?"

"As Eric likes to say, follow you anywhere, scumbag," Allan said as they stepped off.

***

The seriously wounded were being stabilized on the Capitol Building's southwest lawn and moved to whatever added level of care St. Peter's Hospital and the Idaho National Guard medics could provide. The Humvees demolished by the mortar attack, and the remains of the soldiers who guarded them, still smoldered nearby.

Eric found Susan draping a wool blanket over the mangled leg of a woman who had been caught in the fighting. Susan's medic pack sat on the ground at her side, ripped open like a purse stolen by a mugger and its edges stained crimson with blood; the ground all around them was littered with bloody bandages and medical wrappers.

"Don't look at it—you're gonna be OK. We're gonna get you to the hospital," Susan said as she scribbled a "T" and a "P" on the woman's forehead in black marker to let other caregivers know that Susan had tied a tourniquet on her leg, and that the patient was a priority case who could be saved with immediate care. Susan jumped up to flag down a resistance fighter Eric remembered from Animal's briefing at the abandoned mining town. "This patient goes on the next truck! No ifs, ands, or buts!"

A moan drew Eric's attention to a wounded resistance fighter with an "E" from Susan's marker scrawled on his forehead. Expectant—as in expected to die, and a waste of scarce medical resources. Eric shuddered.

"You just gonna stand there?" Susan asked, startling him; her clothes and gear were caked with the blood of Travis and Pastor Kris. "I lost two friends today, and sent a bunch of enemies to the next world. Help me save some lives and balance the books."

Eric ducked as a stray bullet pinged off of the side of the building. Susan didn't flinch—there were people who needed her.

"Yes, ma'am. What are your orders?"

"Do what I say, when I say it." Susan handed Eric a pair of nitrile gloves and flashed him the briefest of smiles. "And get used to it."

***

Allan and Manny found Julie sitting on a bench, consoling a large, middle-aged man with his face buried in his hands.

Julie sighed raggedly, her eyes redder than her hair. "He joined up for the big fight and rode all the way in from Kalispell to find his daughter and son-in-law. Their names were Kayla and Eli Sammons."

Manny stopped his jaw from dropping to the ground. The man lifted his head, his face twisted with agony. "Are you Mister Landeros?"

"Yes, sir."

"Your friend tells me you people helped my little girl and son-in-law."

"All they could think about was getting back to you."

"And that you killed the sons of bitches who took 'em from us."

"They came looking for a fight. They got one."

The man rose to his feet, towering a full head and a half over Manny, and offered a meaty, calloused hand. "Thank you," he sputtered. Manny tried his best not to cry again. It was a gentle handshake for such a big man.

"We still have the lockets Eli made for them," Julie said softly. "If you're not heading back to Kalispell right away, we'd be happy to return them to you."

"Tomorrow at noon? Right here?" the man cried. Manny bit his lip and nodded. "This is gonna kill her mother. Her world revolved around her little Kayla," he said dejectedly as he grabbed his woodland-patterned hunting rifle from the bench and lumbered away to find his comrades.

Allan kissed Julie's forehead as they hugged. "God damn everyone who led our country to this," she said flatly—she had run out of tears. "Wherever you are, God damn each and every one of you."

Manny jerked his head back the way they came. "Let's get back to the rest of our family."

CHAPTER 64

It's amazing how far we've come in the past year, but there's so much more to do.

Eric set down his journal and pen to sip the coffee he hoped would join forces with the ibuprofen to stop his throbbing head, courtesy of the retreat's celebration of Montana Independence Day the prior afternoon. Roger had brewed a special batch of beer to celebrate in style, and distilled some of the garden's bumper crop of potatoes into a vodka that likely could have doubled as paint thinner. He gazed out from the deck at the breathtaking scenery of Montana, which after growing up in Illinois would never get old. A soft hand on his shoulder brought him around to equally breathtaking scenery of a beautiful blonde in jeans and a t-shirt.

"I'm heading off to CQ," Susan Jaeger said—the retreat's rules had been relaxed to no longer mandate wearing fatigues for desk duty. "Just checking if you need any medical attention after yesterday's excess."

Eric rose from the folding lounge chair. "I wasn't that bad, honey. But 'medical' isn't the attention you're making me want," he said, slipping his hands past her rifle to the small of her back and bringing his lips to hers.

"Eric! I'll be late!" she protested with mock anger.

"You can't call in sick?" he joked. "You're beautiful. I can't help myself."

Susan glanced down at her stomach. "Enjoy the view while it lasts, honey—I'll still expect regular flattery when I look like a beached whale. The good news is that, as group medic, I'm officially writing myself a 'no guns' profile once I hit the second trimester, just like I did for Katie." She peeled herself away from her husband. "Anyway, I can't be late relieving Pete because a certain someone can't keep his hands to himself. I love you."

"Love you, too. I'll bring you a cup of apple cider later," Eric said and returned to his journal.

An interim Montana Congress, which included one Senator Manuel Landeros, was convened a week after Stu's overthrow. The Capitol Building was still a shattered mess, but it radiated with an aura of freedom being rekindled like a phoenix rising from the ashes—there was just something right about it.

The first order of business for the Congress was secession from what little was left of the United States. The Republic of Montana was declared on the First of August, hence the four-alarm hangover I'm nursing right now. Lawmakers overwhelmingly voted to join the Union of Free States, which now stretches from the Dakotas in the east, to Utah and Free Colorado in the south, and to the new Pacific coast states of Pacifica, Jefferson, and Cascadia, which won its independence from old Washington State with an audacious and decisive military victory.

With the federal government now consisting of two idiots fighting over who gets to rule what's left of the Northeast, the Rust Belt, and southern California, six of Montana's seven Indian reservations threw in with us, realizing the odds of survival on their own weren't good. The sole holdout was the Fort Peck Assiniboine and Sioux Tribes in the northeast corner—the welcome mat is out for them if they change their minds.

Lawmakers called a convention to draft a new Constitution reflecting Montana's sovereignty, and to ensure that the mistakes that doomed the former United States don't get repeated. Each legislator got to nominate two delegates, who could serve only if they actively aided the rebellion, and had no ties to the old federal or state government. Susan and I were honored that Manny chose us. I had a front-row seat to the rot that had set into Illinois—the corruption, the excessive taxation, the nanny state run amok—and Susan and I wanted to make damned sure it wouldn't set in here. Montanans ratified the new Constitution in a landslide, and elected poor Manny to a full four-year term in the Senate.

In the end, the key to reforming government was taking the profit out of it. We returned to a gold- and silver-based redeemable currency like the rest of the Union of Free States, which will curb inflation by preventing future lawmakers from printing all the money they want. We strictly capped the amount this new government, as well as all local governments, can collect in taxes, and mandated that Montana's budget be balanced except in times of declared war. We improved on Montana's already exceptional term limits by forbidding lawmakers from ever becoming lobbyists once they leave. Not that lobbying is really lucrative or influential anymore—we capped campaign contributions at a very low annual maximum. The era of corporations buying our elected officials and forcing taxpayers to bail them out to rescue them from their own greed and ineptitude is done.

As for stopping government from again encroaching on liberty, we beefed up the Declaration of Rights and ditched any ambiguous language—for example, gun ownership is now just as inviolable a right as freedom of speech and assembly, and if Big Tech ever comes back (God forbid!), government can't conspire with it like little weasels to impose censorship by proxy. Voters have the right to recall any lawmaker or judge at any level. Among the changes made to our new and much simpler criminal code is that convictions for political corruption now carry a mandatory life sentence without parole—I'm proud to say that one was my idea after growing up in Illinois.

It was after we had a legitimate constitutional government in place that Stu Magnuson and his senior lackeys went on trial. They were found incredibly guilty and hanged. Some of his military leaders asked for a firing squad, but were denied—war criminals who desecrate their oaths don't get the honor of a bullet. A handful got life imprisonment or lengthy sentences, and they're put to hard but humane reconstruction work. It's only fair they help fix what they broke.

The Union of Free States is about as benign a polity as one can imagine. It's essentially a free trade and travel zone and mutual defense pact; it has a bicameral legislature, and judicial and executive branches with extremely limited powers. It's similar to the Heartland Confederation (Kansas, Nebraska, Iowa, Missouri, Minnesota, northern Wisconsin, northern Michigan, and the UP), and the Free States of America (Mississippi, Alabama, Kentucky, Tennessee, the Carolinas, Georgia, and the Florida Panhandle—the rest of the Sunshine State, sorry to say, is nothing but a pile of rotting corpses). The Texas Federation (Texas and its surrounding states, plus they claim largely depopulated Arizona and New Mexico), is more centralized, but that's not by design—the Lone Star State just tends to be the dominant personality in the marriage.

All four fledgling nations are still figuring out how to integrate what's left of the United States military. They agreed to maintain a unified strategic nuclear capability, rather than four separate ones. It looks like each nation will maintain their own conventional forces, but with most of the manpower coming from state and local militias, just like the old days—which also means that the days of squandering the public treasury to fight a bunch of stupid Mideast wars is over. There's talk of maintaining standardized training so everyone can work together if, or more likely when, the next Hitler or Putin crawls out from under some rock to pick a fight.

We're still dealing with the humanitarian catastrophe of the Unraveling. Montana was lucky—it had only about a million people when the shit hit the fan, and we really didn't have to deal with the H7N9 flu. But Montanans are scattered across a huge state that could fit Germany inside it and have room left over. Last winter was brutal, and many of the young, old, and sick who made it through the first winter weren't so lucky the second time around. I thank God every day for bringing our survival group—our family—together, and for the deep larder we squirreled away through good planning and hard work. Walking past the wall in Helena's Performance Square, still plastered with photos of the dead and missing, is a sobering reminder of just how blessed we've been.

Sadly, our family is slowly flying the coop. We haven't heard from Liam since he left to find his parents and girlfriend, and Allan and Julie returned to Cascadia shortly after the Battle of Helena to help their fight for independence. Happily, it sounds like everyone else wants to stay local; the consensus seems to be that we'll stay at the retreat one more winter and see what spring brings.

Susan and I have been talking about what we're going to do with the rest of our lives—that is, once Montana gets a steadier supply of gasoline, tires, and auto parts. Governor—darn it, President—Karina Jacobs, courtesy of one Senator Landeros, asked me to put together and curate a museum dedicated to the Unraveling and the creation of our new nation. I wasn't about to say no to the Hero of Malmstrom, especially since she could kill me without breaking a sweat. I need to do something, and I don't know if I ever want to step foot in front of a classroom again; I wonder if that Eric Jaeger is dead and buried.

Manny and Carmen insist, once we all go our separate ways, that they'll still be the little pigs who built their house out of brick, and that we'll fall back here if another Big Bad Wolf shows up, no questions asked. And Carmen has demanded that Susan and I show up for dinner every night, just like the old days in their tiny on-post house at Fort Irwin with Matt and Travis.

I miss Travis and Pastor Kris so much. Susan and I would have loved for her to have married us—Roger did the honors instead. It sounds like Roger has no plans except to tend our garden and be near his wife, who we buried next to it. He moved in with the bachelors when Susan and I got hitched so we could have their bed. I hope he finds peace—I think the garden will help.

The tough lesson the Unraveling retaught its survivors is that tomorrow isn't guaranteed to anyone. Even as things return to "normal," Susan predicts that lifespans will decrease to early twentieth-century levels for the foreseeable future—it's going to be years before medical science catches up to pre-Unraveling levels and the more advanced treatments become available again. In short, I could live to a hundred, or I could die next week from an infected cut; it's up to all of us to make the most of every moment of our second chance. The past two years have taken a lot out of us; hell, Manny and I are starting to go gray and we're not even forty yet.

I've heard more optimistic people talk about the beginning of a new golden age. I don't know about that. However, a decent silver age will suit me just fine.

CHAPTER 65

"What'cha drinking, Daddy?" Travis Jaeger asked his father by the rows of white tables in the Landeros's backyard.

Eric smiled down at his four-year-old food and drink moocher; scant seconds after Senator Manny Landeros handed Eric a bottle of the strawberry blonde ale they brewed special for their annual Montana Independence Day bash, his son sensed it like a dog senses bacon.

"Beer, little man. And no, you can't have any. It's yucky."

"If it's yucky, why are *you* drinking it?"

Eric bent down and tickled his son with his free hand. "Wiseguy, eh? Now run along to Mommy and your little sister."

"I wanna stay with you," Travis said and started to climb into one of the eight empty folding chairs at a table set apart from the rest.

"You can't sit there, buddy."

"Oh. These are for the people up in heaven."

"Yes."

"Will the Other Travis come down and eat with us?"

"I hope so."

"OK. I'm gonna play with Mommy," Travis said and ran to Susan, who was holding his fourteen-month-old little sister, Kristine, while chatting with Carmen and Luisa, who had just started her sophomore year of college. Carroll College had reopened two years after the war ended, and hosted the Republic of Montana Museum that Eric curated. Luisa was studying to become a doctor, which Eric proudly attributed to the example his wife set.

Luisa had blossomed into a stunner. Her boyfriend, Jonathan, stood next to her, not even daring to hold her hand while surrounded by a half dozen overprotective surrogate fathers. *Poor bastard*, Eric chuckled to himself, wiping his brow with the cold beer to ward off the humidity as a cicada in the nearby woods set off a chain reaction of high-pitched screeching. This year's party was going to be a hot one.

Eric felt a pang of loss as he ran his hand across the chairs set out to honor absent friends. Three were set for Ed and Mina Houston, and their unborn child, who never got out of Colorado when the Unraveling first started six years prior. Two were set for Pastor Kris and her husband, Roger.

Pastor Kris could have been buried in Helena at Patriots Memorial Cemetery next to Travis, but Roger insisted she be laid to rest near their beloved garden. While group members slowly moved out as things returned to something resembling normal, Roger stayed, with Manny's and Carmen's blessing; he spent his days tending the garden that had helped keep the retreat fed, and his nights scouring the amateur radio bands for information on the fates of his two sons. Three years to the day he became a widower, Carmen found him dead of a heart attack, lying among the hop trellises he planted so his extended family could enjoy the occasional pint of beer. They buried him by his wife; a local monument maker donated a headstone, free of charge, for two heroes of the Republic of Montana.

Montana and neighboring Idaho had become the economic power-houses of the Union of Free States, courtesy of their abundant natural resources. While bartering still continued, Montana's currency, backed by gold and silver and redeemable on demand, had quickly become the coin of the realm. But while Montana's new Constitution provided for a minimalist government, lawmakers had enacted strict environmental protection measures to ensure that mining the state's bounty of precious metals didn't mean a return to the days of laissez-faire capitalism that had poisoned so much air, land, and water. Montana's vast forests, a diligently managed renewable resource, provided wood for rebuilding efforts all over the Union. Montana and Idaho did very brisk business with the Texas Federation; petroleum products shipped north, and wood and minerals shipped south. The Federation had a voracious appetite for building materials, not only to fuel its rise as North America's economic superpower, but also to deal with its unfortunate location in Tornado Alley.

Trade had made Cousin Benny rich beyond the dreams of avarice. Benny had scraped together enough venture capital to acquire a beat-up semi truck and some spare parts and tires to haul goods. He now owned a fleet of trucks and employed an army of drivers and mechanics; much of what shoppers found on Montana's shelves came courtesy of Rodriguez Trucking, Inc. He owned two homes—one outside of Helena, not too far from the charred remains of the late Stu Magnuson's mansion, and another in the Texas Hill Country of his and Manny's youth.

"¿Qué pasa?" Benny exclaimed as he bear-hugged Eric—despite his busy schedule, Benny never missed the annual party and reunion. His new wife, Esmeralda, gave Eric a less rib-crushing embrace.

"It's going great—I have a cold beer, and Susan's handling our two little maniacs, so I can't complain."

Benny pulled a bottle of Jack Daniel's from his bag. "One of my truckers picked up a load from Tennessee. Brought it for our friend from the Volunteer State," he said, setting it at Travis's place at the table of honor. Esmeralda pulled a small pair of maracas from her purse and gave them a playful rattle. "We also brought something from *Tejas* for Travis's namesake," Benny said with a grin. "Have fun sleeping tonight, buddy!"

"I should've fragged you at the Route 12 campground when I had the chance," Eric said with feigned anger.

"Me and Travis were overwatchin' *you*, remember?" Benny shot back with a laugh as he and Esmeralda left to say hello to Carmen and Luisa.

Eric reverently draped the whiskey bottle with the gold medal on a deep blue and gold lanyard that was laid across Travis's place setting. The Montana Congress had created a Medal of Liberty to bestow upon those who had acted with gallantry during the Unraveling and the war, and Travis was among its first recipients; lawmakers were expected to bestow one upon Pastor Kris as well at their upcoming session. The state had entrusted Manny with Travis's medal because he had no known family left; many years later, Manny would tell a Union News Network reporter interviewing him after his election to a second term as Montana president that keeping watch over his friends' medals was the most important job he ever had.

Not a day went by when Eric didn't think about Travis's last words before his mother and Pastor Kris escorted him to his eternal reward; he longed for the day that his children were old enough to learn about the heroes they were named after. Eric had just started homeschooling his son, and taught history once a week at Carroll; he thanked God every day for helping him make peace with the souls of his former students and returning to teaching—he would make sure the sacrifices of everyone who won his students their freedom would be remembered.

"Hey, slacker, you doin' anything right now besides taking up space?" Manny called from the sliding glass kitchen door; through silver and barter, he had eventually managed to get the damage from the marauders' raid on his home properly repaired. Eric helped Manny carry trays of meat and vegetables to the grill, where Jay was waiting to cook the food, as he did every year. Beef quickly reappeared on dinner tables once Montana's rich ranching heritage recovered—the state before the Unraveling had boasted twice as many head of cattle as people.

"Thought you two were killin' the cow yourselves," Jay quipped as he laid the meat down with satisfying sizzles with his good arm—his wounded right arm had never recovered its full strength or range of motion. Jay's girlfriend, Andrea, whose husband had died fighting with the resistance, greeted Manny and Eric with a wave.

Benny had hired Jay as head mechanic when his trucking business began to flourish. The pay—sometimes silver, sometimes commodities—was good, and Jay loved having a brother-in-arms as his boss, but he quit after a year, partly because his arm couldn't handle the work, but mostly because he yearned to spend his remaining days doing something spiritually fulfilling. He found his purpose when Matt and Angel brought him on as handyman and watchman of their school and home for displaced and orphaned children. They named it "Colin's House," after a precocious young boy from Angel's first-grade class that she dearly missed—she learned after the war ended that Colin, along with Angel's parents and much of her hometown, had died from a cholera outbreak several months after the collapse.

Matt and Angel rode herd on sixty children while raising their own. They adopted Annalisa, the girl Angel saved in the Battle of Helena, and had twin boys shortly thereafter. Manny and Eric waved to the couple as they drank beer and chatted with the ambassador from the Free State of Idaho while Annalisa, now a very responsible twelve, watched her brothers play in the side yard.

Besides the orphanage, Matt and Angel headed a relief agency that worked with Montana and other Union states to reunite refugees with their families, and fight human trafficking. Matt shared Jay's mind-set—his engineering background would have made him fabulously wealthy in a world with so much to rebuild, but the war, and his wife's passion, changed him. Among their employees was Sylvia Branson, *née* Marchand, the lone survivor of the Marysville Massacre who was saved from traffickers by Team Zulu and her future husband. Sylvia, now twenty-three, arrived at the party with Will and their newborn daughter. Sylvia's face was well-known in state government—she had successfully fought for the ruins of her hometown to be preserved as a memorial so that history, maybe for once, would not be forgotten and repeated.

Eric and Manny polished off their beers and stepped into the garage to drop the empties in one of the many recycling bins lining the wall before helping themselves to another round from Manny's man-fridge. The brief blast of chilly air was a welcome respite from the summer heat. "Let's have a cold one with our friends," Manny said, formally starting their annual tradition of drinking their second beer of the party in honor of the fallen.

Manny and Eric, just like their days as young Army privates, saw each other almost daily. Eric and Susan had moved into the abandoned house next door where they had found Tim, Katie, and Liam; the previous owners, who gave the house to Manny when they fled after the Unraveling started, had never returned. Eric, and Susan when she could, helped tend the large garden that sustained both their families. Summer meant fresh produce, and winter meant eating what they canned and preserved; they donated the surplus to Matt and Angel's orphanage.

The duo strolled into the side yard, where a drone buzzed inches over their heads and almost made them drop their beers. Tim, holding the controls with his son, Steven James, in his lap, flashed an embarrassed grin. "Sorry, guys!" he yelled.

"How's your poison ivy?" Manny yelled back—the story of Tim's and Katie's roll in the hay had slipped out at the reunion three years ago. Tim, still smiling, covered his son's eyes with the drone controls and flipped Manny the middle finger with his free hand. Tim and Katie got married shortly after the war ended, and Stevie was born almost nine months to the day. They lived in Townsend and owned a repair shop with Tim's parents, who like Katie's parents in Boise, had survived—in a post-apocalyptic economy, the ability to make things last as long as possible was in very great demand. Business was wonderful, courtesy of a picture snapped after the Battle of Helena of Katie and Tim leading a flex-cuffed Stu Magnuson out of the Capitol Building; the couple always downplayed their roles in the fight, and chafed at being called heroes, but didn't mind the boost the now-iconic photo had given their livelihood.

"You keep that piece of history intact, you hear me?" Eric said as he and Manny continued toward the garden—Tim had promised that the drone would be donated to the museum once its operational life had ended. There was an obsession with preserving history among the survivors who had lived it and made it; there was even talk of making the Landeros home a historical landmark to show how people lived during the Unraveling. Manny and Eric had removed the spikes and the barbed wire from the lawn years ago so the children wouldn't get hurt, the CQ had been converted back into an office, and the LP/OP hadn't been used in years, but all could be restored, if Manny ever agreed to it.

The duo strolled past Benny and Esmeralda, who regaled one of Manny's fellow senators with stories of the Highway of the Damned—the fifty-mile stretch of I-25 that cut through the ruins of the Denver metro corridor. The Free State of Colorado, via local militias, provided armed escort for Benny's drivers in exchange for a toll, payable in silver, fuel, or a cut of the cargo. Benny usually paid silver; because the currencies of all ten Union states were on a bimetallic standard, there was no hassle over exchange rates.

Eric and Manny reached the table of honor by the garden, which over the years had been augmented by the self-sufficiency hacks Manny had wanted to add before the Unraveling. Members, with the help of a dog-eared copy of *The Encyclopedia of Country Living*, had built a chicken coop, a root cellar, and a small greenhouse. Manny had wanted to add an apiary, but Carmen, who was deathly afraid of bees, had put her foot down.

Manny lifted Travis's medal from the whiskey bottle, running his finger and thumb around its engraving. "Travis probably would've been happy being rewarded for his heroism with just the fifth of Jack."

"Here's to you, jarhead," Eric said as they took a pull from their bottles.

Manny pulled a silver flask out of his pocket. "Travis ain't the only person Cousin Benny hooked up, *jefe*." Eric raised it to his nose and instantly recognized the aroma of tequila. He greedily knocked back a gulp that hit his throat like a hammer.

"Wow! Been a while," Eric barely managed to reply.

"Benny said supply's improving as things get better in Mexico," Manny said and took a drink from the flask. "He promised to bring us a few bottles for next year's party, and a case of lemons and limes so we can have margaritas like civilized human beings."

"I'd much rather have Central America get its act together when it comes to coffee," Eric groused. Supply in Montana could still be hit or miss—he practically kissed Benny when he first managed to procure some. "I'd gladly trade Jose Cuervo for Juan Valdez."

"Don't forget his trusty mule, Pedro," Manny said and raised his beer. "To Ed, Mina, and the baby." The beer went down smooth after the bite of the tequila.

"To Pastor Kris and Roger," Eric said. Another drink.

"To Pete," Manny said, and clinked his bottle with Eric's before taking another pull. Pete, like Jay and Matt, sought purpose after the war. He returned to his hometown of Butte and found work as an electrician before the Lord told him to follow Pastor Kris into the ministry. Pete enrolled in a one-year Bible college in the mountains, and soon became the pastor of his own flock. Two years later, lightning sparked a forest fire that threatened a number of neighboring towns. Pete and his congregation were part of the massive effort to stop the blaze, but at the cost of his life and the lives of fifty-three other brave volunteers.

"This one hurts the most," Eric said. "To survive the Unraveling and the war without a scratch, and then to die like that. So young, too."

"So much lost potential," Manny said and raised his bottle. "To Liam—wherever you are."

Liam left for Billings the day after Pastor Kris's funeral. The group tuned up the truck liberated from the Route 12 bandits and packed it with supplies, wrote a letter vouching for him in case any reemerging law and order mistook him for a looter or thief, and saw him off for Billings. He hadn't been heard from since.

While picturesque Bozeman to its west was rising from the ashes, Billings, like many other large cities in the former United States, remained a mostly burned-out shell. On top of the fact that rebuilding metropolitan areas still presented an almost insurmountable challenge, the survivors of the Unraveling—who had lived through two pandemics on top of years of urban decay and civil unrest—were in no rush to go back to cramming themselves on top of one another.

Eric offered a silent prayer for his trusted assistant gunner. "Ole' Meat Mountain's alive somewhere. I feel it. I think he did what a lot of guys who returned from past wars did—left it all behind, settled down to raise a family, and tried to forget everything. Maybe, one day, he'll let us know he's all right."

"I hope so. He was—is—a good man."

"I'll drink to that. And as long as we're honoring MIAs, let's belt one back for Animal."

The Republic of Montana owed no small debt to Animal, who had organized a bunch of separate partisan groups into a guerrilla army that stopped a megalomaniac and saved countless lives. Animal disappeared shortly after the war ended, leaving his home and possessions to his surviving Team Zulu comrades in a handwritten note with no explanation why he was leaving, and no clue as to where he was going.

"You suppose he's still alive?" Eric asked.

Manny polished off his beer. "An hombre like him is too bad-ass to die—he's not in Valhalla yet. I'm betting he would've settled down had he not lost his wife and daughters. A man like that spends the rest of his days trying to do right in their eyes. He's fighting the good fight somewhere else."

"We never even caught his real name," Eric said. "Guys like him fade into legend, then myth—I bet historians two centuries from now will be arguing over whether Animal actually existed."

"I bet he'd like that," Manny said. "Still waters run deep for those crazy SF guys."

Eric absentmindedly waved off a swarm of gnats from his face as he pictured more and more empty chairs replacing their extended survival family until they all passed into history. He hoped his children, and their descendants, wouldn't foolishly trade their freedoms for security and entitlements, and end up having to shed their blood once again to water the tree of liberty. He cleared the lump that had risen in his throat with the last of his beer. "I just hope that Animal and Liam, wherever they are, have found peace."

"Amen, brother." Manny held up his empty bottle. "This, old friend, is a crisis we need to resolve right now. Let's go back and reload."

They stopped to greet the Wyoming ambassador, members of several other militia groups that had fought in the war, and several of Manny's fellow legislators. It would have looked like any backyard gathering before the collapse, had it not been for most everyone's attire. Almost everyone was armed, and people were dressed in a peculiar mix of pre-collapse clothes and items made since—"a blend of Little House on the Prairie and The Gap," Eric observed to Susan after one reunion. Eric and Susan, who had prudently stocked up on simple clothes before the Unraveling, found them baggy and in need of hemming, courtesy of their simpler diets and constant physical exertion.

Katie walked out of the kitchen into the backyard, her yellow summer dress draped over a belly swollen with her second child. "Hey, everyone! Allan and Julie are calling on the radio! Any takers?" A cheer rose from group members—Allan and Julie rarely made the trip from Cascadia to the reunion, preferring to radio in instead. Cascadia was doing almost as well as Montana and Idaho, for the same reasons: smart people and abundant resources. Allan and Julie had a four-year-old daughter, Cheyenne, and one-year-old twin sons, Raider and Jed.

"It's amazing he got through in daylight," Susan said as she strolled up to Manny and Eric. "Sunspots have been awful."

"I always told you he was the best," Eric said. "Saved our posteriors more than once."

Susan handed Eric his giggling daughter. "Speaking of posteriors, Kristine filled her diaper. Your turn, honey."

"Aw, man," Eric said with a grimace. "I can't wait until some enterprising soul starts manufacturing disposable diapers again. There's nothing in the world worse than cleaning the cloth ones." An enterprising soul in Helena had in fact opened a diaper laundry service, but their neck of the woods was farther than she was willing to drive.

Manny laughed. "Sucks to be you, dude. Remember what our drill sergeants told us . . ."

"I volunteered for this shit, yeah, I know." Eric wrinkled his nose with a whiff of his impending chore. "In this case, literally."

"Have one on the house to ease your pain," Manny said and offered Eric his flask. Susan intercepted the handoff and took a long pull as if it was filled with water.

"Not too shabby—I'll put a paramedic's liver up against a grunt's any day of the week," she said, wiping the corner of her mouth with the back of her wrist. "By the way, the looks on your faces are priceless."

"You're priceless," Eric said and kissed Susan, smiling as he tasted the tequila on her lips.

"Get a room," Manny groaned.

"We prefer behind your barn," Susan mumbled, causing Eric to laugh and break their liplock.

"What?"

"Nothing." Eric carefully shifted Kristine to his other arm.

Travis stumbled up to them, munching on a cheeseburger on a freshly baked bun, his hands, face, and shirt smeared with homemade barbecue sauce.

"Travis, honey, you can't stay clean for one minute, can you?" his mother said.

"Burgers are good," he mumbled with his mouth full.

"Soup's on, everyone! Get it while it's hot!" Jay said, wiping his brow. "And could one of you apes please get me a glass of water?"

CHAPTER 66

The Jaegers got home late after helping Manny, Carmen, Luisa, and Jonathan clean up. They laid Travis in his bed, and Kristine in the crib Eric had built after he first learned he was going to be a father. Woodworking had become a hobby for him, and he was slowly replacing the furniture that came with the house with his own hand-crafted creations.

Eric lit the large candle on the living room coffee table—while their power supply was reliable, the same still couldn't be said for the availability of light bulbs, and their homemade food dehydrator got top priority when they managed to find extras. He carefully opened his old laptop computer so he could work on his book about the Unraveling and the rebellion against Stu Magnuson. Computer manufacturing had just restarted in the successor nations to the former United States, given that the collapse and and civil wars had turned China, Vietnam, and other nations where the components had once been built into charnel houses; people had to make their electronics last as long as they could. Eric hoped future generations didn't repeat the stupid mistake of shipping manufacturing overseas to exploit cheap labor.

Susan sat at the kitchen table in her pajamas, scrolling through articles on her iPad from the website of Alabama-based Free State News. The internet was slowly coming back wherever entrepreneurs could get servers and infrastructure back into place; Helena's access was spotty, and its speed reminiscent of the ancient days of dial-up, but the small business charged a reasonable fee. Access was better at St. Peter's Hospital, where Susan worked part-time.

"Holy cow!" Susan exclaimed, shooting out of her seat and almost spilling her glass of water. "Eric, look!"

Eric quickly padded to his wife, a finger over his lips reminding her that they had two sleeping children, but she was too excited to quiet down. "Free State News has a webpage for people searching for their loved ones. I was looking for Mom and Dad, but on a goof, I looked for . . ."

"Roger and Kris's sons!" Eric finished her sentence. He realized as he pulled up a seat that his voice had risen as well, but he heard no stirring from upstairs—they had two good little sleepers.

"Searching for Roger and Kris Reynolds, of Butte, Montana, and Micah Reynolds, of Miami, Florida," the title read. It was posted three days prior by Jonah, the older son.

"Dear family: I pray every day you're all OK," Susan read aloud. "I really worry about you, Little Brother—I heard most everyone in Florida died. I hope you got out all right. I've searched for you all in vain the few times I had access to ham radio, and it was just last month that our small town got something resembling internet access. As for me, I'm lucky to be alive."

Susan and Eric read Jonah's harrowing tale of Atlanta's rapid descent into anarchy with the economic crash and rioters raging unchecked, spreading chaos and the H7N9 flu. Jonah escaped with little more than the clothes on his back, losing count of the bodies as he fled on foot from the burning city lighting up the sky behind him. He ended up in a FEMA camp set up on the Tennessee border to handle refugees from

Chattanooga, and the conditions were abominable; one of the camp's many gangs beat him and stole his meager possessions, including his shoes. Refugees weren't allowed to leave, but things reached a boiling point several weeks later and they staged a mass breakout in a driving thunderstorm.

Soaked to the bone, barefoot, and weak from malnutrition, Jonah headed east to the small town of Chatsworth, but the townspeople had erected manned roadblocks and weren't letting anyone in—several corpses were left to rot on the roadside as mute testament to the fact that the locals meant business. Jonah was burning a high fever and knocking on death's door by the end of the day, when he collapsed on the steps of a church in the tiny town of Oakman.

He woke up three days later in the guest bedroom of the pastor and his wife. A retired country doctor who lived down the road diagnosed him with pneumonia, but with no antibiotics available, it took him a month to recover. While the pastor's family was generous, there wasn't enough food to go around, and Jonah lost even more weight.

After a month of doing odd jobs, and digging more graves than he cared to for people who succumbed to disease and preexisting health conditions, the opportunity arose to hitch a ride with a family heading to Murphy, North Carolina, a town nestled in the Appalachian Mountains and Nantahala National Forest. They journeyed without incident, and the introductory letter the pastor wrote for Jonah, along with the fact he was a pastor's son, convinced city leaders to let him stay.

"Two years ago, I married a woman named Kelly, who lost her husband in a car accident before the collapse," Susan read. "Oh, by the way, you're grandparents, and Micah, you're an uncle. Jonah Reynolds Jr. was born July 25th, weighing a respectable seven pounds even—expectant and nursing mothers around here get first crack at the food. I hope you get to meet them one day."

Susan's voice broke as she struggled to keep reading. "Mom and Dad, there's something I want to tell you—you were right. All my life, you warned that a day of reckoning was coming, but I didn't listen; I thought you two were just doing the right-wing nut job thing from too much talk radio. I wanted to live in the big city with other young people, and point and laugh at folks like you while we bought cryptocurrency and ate our twenty-dollar avocado toast. King Solomon was right—this fool blindly went forward and was punished.

"Once a week, I'm able to check out what little of the Web there is at the local internet café. (I remember you both telling me about those places before everyone had the web in their pockets—Lord help me, but I miss my iPhone!) I'll be checking here every other Saturday. Please let me know you're all right. And if anyone stumbles across this who knows my family's whereabouts, please reach out to me! God bless all of you. I'll be waiting. Love, Jonah."

Eric and Susan stared at the screen for a long time, the iPad and the candles casting lonely shadows across the kitchen. "Honey, what do we tell him?" Eric asked, breaking the silence.

Susan wiped her eyes and slipped her hand into Eric's. "How his parents lived. How his mom kept us sane, and how she gave her life to save a child and a friend. How his dad's garden kept us alive. How they never stopped searching for their boys."

Eric drew Susan's face to his and kissed her. "I think this calls for raiding our precious coffee supply—I don't think either of us are gonna sleep much tonight."

He stood, stretched, and opened the creaky wooden cabinet with the grounds as his wife's fingers started a sad dance on the glass of her tablet.

Acknowledgements

I've got so many people to thank, but I'd like to start by thanking you for reading my debut novel! If you liked it, it would mean the world to me if you would take a short minute to leave a heartfelt review on Amazon. Your kind feedback is very appreciated, and very important to me.

The novel you're holding in your hands is the end result of a wonderful, awful, and bizarre six-year journey.

It took me almost two years to write it, and another year collecting rejection letters from snarky New York City literary agents until I beat the one-in-a-thousand odds and found an agent willing to represent it. Two months after we sealed the deal—in a case of rotten luck for the history books—COVID-19 struck. This left my agent with the unenviable task of shopping around a manuscript about a pandemic in the midst of an actual freaking pandemic; it went exactly as well as one would expect.

So here we are, via the self-publishing route. If I thanked everyone who inspired me, or helped me along the way, I'd easily be able to fill a second book, so this significantly expurgated list will have to do.

Thank you to my lovely wife, Kristin, who was always there for me.

This first book is dedicated to my dad, and his red correction pen that put the fear of God into so many of his students—I really wish he could have seen me do this. I also owe thanks to my mom for not having me institutionalized after a childhood of constantly checking out survival books from the library.

Thank you to my son, Logan, and to my firstborn Grace, who can grasp the Chandrasekhar limit that determines whether a neutron star will collapse to form a black hole, but still has a hard time understanding why she can't eat candy for breakfast.

Thank you to the men of Charlie Company, my brothers now and always. And while I hated your ever-loving guts when we first met, I owe a great deal to Drill Sergeants Tijerina, Whitson, Haney, Aponte, and Fitzpatrick for helping turn a naïve boy who could barely do five push-ups into a grunt.

Thank you to Kurt, Dan, Aracely, and The Donkey Boy, who created the most fun news bureau in the history of American journalism until the main office squashed it like a bug because fun was *verboten*.

The Survival Group Handbook is a definitive guide to the people and talents you would want to have in a mutual assistance group if the manure ever hits the oscillating air circulator. The thought experiment I conducted after reading it—if I could build a prepper "dream team," who would be on it?—planted the seeds that became this novel. Thank you to its author, survival consultant Charley Hogwood, to whom I owe no small debt.

Ironically, the old saying that you can't judge a book by its cover is patently false when it comes to actual books! If you're a fan of post-apocalyptic prepper fiction, I think it's a safe bet that one of the main reasons you're reading this book is because you were drawn in by its awesome cover. Thank you so much to the legendary Christian Bentulan for his beautiful work and his clairvoyance in knowing exactly what I would want. Be sure to visit his website, www.coversbychristian.com, and follow him on Facebook and Instagram, to marvel in his raw talent.

Thank you to Nicholas Meyer, Lynne Littman, and Barry Hines, whose movies that laid bare the unthinkable horror of nuclear war—*The Day After*, *Testament*, and *Threads*—set me on this course as an impressionable child by scaring the living hell out of me. (Congratulations to you, dear reader, if you're a child of the 1980s who caught the *Threads* reference I dropped in Chapter 40.)

Thank you to the late Frank V. Bibb, of Topeka, Kansas, You-nited States of 'Murica, who didn't know squat about political correctness and tact, but knew everything about motivating people to give it their all. As long as I'm thanking the dearly departed, thank you to the late Tom Haag, who once told me that every good book needs to have a little sex in it.

Last but certainly not least, thank you to David Wright, Ph.D, former co-director of the Global Security Program of the Union of Concerned Scientists, for taking some of his precious time to share his expertise on the range and capabilities of the Minuteman III ICBM—and for not forwarding my email to the FBI in which I asked if it was possible to launch a missile from Montana to nuke Texas.

Kevin Craver
November 2023

About the Author

Kevin Craver had a comfortable childhood devoid of zombies, post-atomic mutants, or cyborgs trying to kill him before he could grow up to lead the human resistance to victory. He turned a side hustle of drawing a nihilistic comic strip for his college newspaper into a living as a token conservative in the world of newspaper journalism, earning eighty state and national writing awards over his twenty-year career. Somewhere along the line, he realized that his life didn't suck enough, and spent fourteen years and two deployments as an infantryman in the Army National Guard.

When he's not writing about the end of civilization or hoarding cans of bacon in his basement—because the living will envy the dead in a world without bacon—he caters to the whims of his wife, daughter, son, and Ragdoll cat. He enjoys Mexican food, German beer, and frequent trips to the gym to work off both.

Visit Kevin's website at www.kevincraver.com for updates, and to sign up for e-mail updates on his upcoming books.